The Pope's Son

Rick Friend

PEACH PUBLISHING

Published by

PEACH PUBLISHING

For my own son,
Saul

Prologue

Bouhay, Liège, Belgium. 1939

"Do you think the Nazis will invade Belgium?" asked the novice as he walked alongside the elderly priest.

They moved through the shadows of the cloisters. The old man stopped and leaned on his stick, but did not answer. He gazed up at the weather vane on the tower of the Priory church and listened as fragments of plainsong filtered through its grey stonework. A swallow returned to its nest, oblivious of the fact that twenty-four hours earlier the Second World War had begun.

"There are many Jews in Belgium," the young man said as he took the priest's arm.

They followed the stone path that led into the open fields, the afternoon sun lighting up their faces: the novice's rugged and handsome; the old priest's troubled, moulded by the passage of time into a mask of sadness.

Father Pius Maria Mortara was silent.

"If only we could help them," said the novice, the low timbre of his voice resonant with the headstrong idealism of a determined nineteen-year-old.

"The Jews – yes, if only…" replied Father Mortara with his gentle Italian lilt. He watched the sunlight dancing on the corn and into the boy's eyes. Those eyes had seen so little of the world – just a few hills and valleys around the village of Bouhay on the outskirts of Liège in Belgium.

"Do you know any Jews?" asked the novice.

Father Mortara stopped in his tracks and studied him. He wondered what this boy knew of Jews, this simple, honest country boy with whom he now shared his days.

They had got up at the crack of dawn and read psalms together at Matins; they had sat in the cloisters in meditation before the bell rang for Lauds. He had studied the novice and

1

his solemn expressions and sensed that he was struggling with his feelings and thoughts. They had celebrated Mass together with the canons and the lay brothers, along with some local farm labourers and villagers who came into the church on their way to work, and they had broken the long quiet of the Magnum Silencium after a breakfast of bread and quark. They had spent the morning together in prayer, chanting at Terce and praising the Lord for his everlasting mercy, by way of Psalm 118 at Sext; they had eaten a lunch of boiled ham, boiled potatoes and boiled cabbage together, and drank beer (nowhere else in the world, except in Belgium, had he ever had beer in Holy Orders with monks who sometimes got drunk). He had asked the boy about his family and friends. Raoul had mentioned a girl, Delphine, and Father Mortara sensed immediately that she had played a part in the young man's sadness – maybe she had been the catalyst that had made Raoul decide to take his vows as an Augustine monk and join the Priory of Notre Dame de Lourdes just two days previously, on the day the Nazis invaded Poland.

He turned to the novice. "Do I know any Jews?"

Father Mortara looked out across the fields, the sunlight half-blinding him. In the distance Farmer Delacroix was cutting the wheat with a two-horse harvester. Some of the labourers were helping with scythes. It was a good crop. The summer of 1939 had been wonderfully sunny.

"I have known many Jews. My mother was Jewish. My father was Jewish. And for the first year of my life I was indeed a Jew myself."

Chapter 1

It wasn't a knock at the door, but the gut-wrenching clang of metal on wood. The knocking was followed by voices and the sound of horses neighing and snorting and of hard leather boot soles hitting the ground.

"Open up! Police! By order of the Inquisition! By order of Pope Pius the Ninth! Open up!"

The order was repeated over and over again.

Anna Morisi got up from the chair by Edgardo's bed and peered through the shutters of the tiny bedroom window. She could just make out the shadows of a number of uniformed men down below in the Via Lame. Gendarmes! Some were on horseback; others standing on the narrow cobbled street, their gun barrels pointing towards the house.

"Open up! Police! By order of the Inquisition! By order of the Pope!"

Someone ran down the stairs and through the vestibule. There was a loud metallic crash as the bolt of the hatchway in the front door opened.

She heard her mistress screaming. "What do you want?"

"We want the child," growled a low voice, "the Christian child!"

Her mistress's cries grew louder. "We are not Christians!"

"We know you have a Christian child in there: Edgardo Mortara! Open the door before we break it down!"

Anna withdrew into the room and lowered her eyes. She looked over to the bed where Edgardo was sleeping soundly. She lit a candle and watched him for a moment. His face, normally endowed with fiery animation and laughter, was now softened by sleep and dreams. His long black locks streamed over the lace-trimmed pillow and his arm was hanging delicately over the side of the bed. He had the air of a fresco angel, cloud-borne at the gates of heaven. She caught the rhythm of his breathing and the rise and fall of the linen sheets. She leaned over and kissed him on his brow. He stirred. Anna heard the screams of her mistress and the sudden crashing as the bolts of the front door opened. She fell on to her knees in a wild panic, bursting into tears as she begged the Mother Mary to answer her prayers, just as she had done six years earlier on the feast day of the Blessed Virgin when she was fourteen and Edgardo had been a tiny baby, not yet a year old…

***

How many times had her mind raced back to that day?

Edgardo had been ill for over a week, and after countless visits by the leading physicians of Bologna was showing no sign of recovery.

His father, Signor Mortara a lace merchant, would not go to work. He stayed at home and buried his head in a book of Jewish prayers. His mother, Marianna, wept over his crib. The five brothers and sisters sat quietly in the little courtyard at the back of the house, annoyed at being told to keep quiet all the time, to read and not to play. When they entered the house they crept around with miserable faces, peering through doorways and over the banisters of the stairwell, trying to hear what visitors were saying about their baby brother. The doctors were all so serious – the friends and relations filing in at regular intervals for updates on Edgardo, behaving in a more formal manner than usual. Even the Padovanis, their mother's wealthy relations, addressed their normally playful father not by his customary nickname Momolo, but by the formal sounding Salomone.

Between them, Anna and Madame Mortara nursed Edgardo through the long days and nights. Signor Mortara prayed to the God of Abraham and Moses that he would spare Edgardo while Anna prayed to Jesus and the Virgin Mother, although deep in her heart she believed that his death was inevitable.

"Today is a Saint's Day for the Madonna – may I go and pray for Edgardo?" she asked her mistress.

"Pray for him and go to the druggist again, Anna. We need to keep stocking up on the tinctures." Madame Mortara wiped away her tears with her sleeve and handed her a prescription note.

"The medicines are not working," Anna replied.

"The medicines will work. They must work! Go!"

From the stillness, the darkness, the coldness of that gloomy house, Anna ran out into the street, into the sunshine, breathing in the warm air, catching the fragrance of newly baked bread from one house, of oregano and onions from another, and kidneys roasting with garlic as she crossed the via San Gervasio – and, as always, just a hint of sewage in the narrow streets that led to the centre of Bologna.

Crowds were already gathering in the Piazza Maggiore to celebrate the birth of the Blessed Virgin. She followed them as they made their way from the Cathedral of San Pietro towards the Saragozza Gate and then on to the Portico of San Luca. She had never seen so many people in the covered arcade that ran up the hillside for two miles to the Sanctuary of the Madonna.

The worshippers moved in a snake-like procession, following the icon of the Madonna of San Luca, with some thrusting their arms forward in their attempts to commune with its reputed miraculous powers. Anna weaved her way through the procession, her long black hair flowing behind her. Occasionally she stopped to catch her breath under the arches of the arcade – over six hundred of them in all, each housing a holy figure or a tiny chapel erected by a patron Bolognese family. She struggled to overtake women with parasols, husbands, admirers, children, maidservants, lecherous old men, policemen, musicians and Austrian soldiers. The Austrian 'Whitecoats' had been present in the city for decades to suppress uprisings against Papal rule and curb nationalistic tendencies towards a unified Italy. Anna ran through a group of them, their young faces animated with bold laughter. Her heart sank. She immediately recognised one of the soldiers by the blond curls falling below his tall black military cap. He turned round; he was handsome in his white tunic and blue trousers braided with gold. He smiled as he grabbed hold of her and pulled her towards him.

"Are you coming out tonight?" he asked, taking off his cap.

She stopped in her tracks as he continued. "We can meet behind the tobacco factory."

"I can't," she replied, "The baby's still ill."

"You shouldn't be looking after a Jew-boy," he told her, "It's against the law." He tried to kiss her. His friends all laughed. She freed herself and spat on the ground.

"Austrian… *Cazzo… Cazzo Porco…* Pig Penis!" she cried at him before continuing on her way.

"Jew-lover!" he shouted back.

She tossed her hair behind her as she turned round to look at him.

He laughed at her, because he knew how close he was to conquering her heart.

She reached the basilica, the Sanctuary of the Madonna, nestled above Bologna in the forested foothills of the Apennines. The air was sweet and dense with the scent of pine. She caught her breath before pushing her way into the church.

An elderly woman swore at her and elbowed her in the ribs, but she managed to jostle her way through till she could clearly see the icon of the Madonna. While Mass was sung she knelt and put her hands together to pray.

"Please, Virgin Mother, save Edgardo," she whispered, and repeated herself about fifty times.

She lit a candle for him, once again repeating the plea, before she ran out into the sunshine and hurried back to the centre of Bologna, retracing her steps through the crowded narrow streets. She made her way to the druggist's.

"How is the boy?" asked Lepori, the elderly apothecary.

"He's not getting any better," said Anna as she handed him the prescription. "We need some stronger medicine."

"There is nothing stronger, not for a baby." The apothecary put two tincture bottles on the counter for her.

"There must be something else?" She cast her eye over the decorated porcelain jars that lined the wooden shelves. She saw labels of powders and herbs and medicinal plants – malva silvestris, fennel, basil, laudanum, lavender, bezoar stone, juniper… "There must be something… there must be!"

"Wait a minute," said Lepori, as he went into his back room. He returned with a small phial of clear liquid and put it down on the counter.

"What is it?" she inquired with a hopeful smile.

"Holy Water!" he said.

"But what's the use of that?"

Lepori spoke carefully. "If the boy is going to die, you must baptise him. Then, at least, he will not die an infidel. You can save his soul and guide him to heaven… Come."

Lepori said this as a matter of fact. His words shocked Anna as she realised that Edgardo's destiny now lay with her. She followed the apothecary into a back room where he showed her how to perform the sacrament of baptism.

***

Anna ran home through the narrow streets, the tinctures and the phial of Holy Water safely contained in the cloth bag that she carried over her shoulder.

She spied the Austrian soldier in a doorway. Everywhere in Bologna she seemed to see him. If Edgardo hadn't been so ill she might have lingered. She might have let him chase her through the dark porticoes; might have let him block her path before he took off his plumed cap and loosened his gold-trimmed tunic. She might have stayed with him till the last rays of the sun disappeared over the rooftops, turning the city a deep crimson. But now she had to get home to Edgardo. She thought she loved the Austrian, but she loved Edgardo even more – as if he were her own baby. Edgardo's parents were always busy with the other children. She was fourteen. Edgardo might as well have been her own child. She ran home.

When Anna entered the house in Via Lame, Madame Mortara was at the large wooden table, lighting the Friday night candles as she made a blessing. The table was spread for dinner, the children gathered round.

"Tell the Signor to come and eat," Madame Mortara said to Anna. "He must take a break. And ask Doctor Saragoni to join us for dinner. Did you get the medicine?"

Anna nodded and ran up the stairs into the front bedroom where Signor Mortara was talking quietly with Doctor Saragoni. He held Edgardo in his arms. She put the medicines down on the dresser, which was stacked with tincture bottles. The doctor picked up two of the little brown bottles with their pipettes and trickled amber liquid from one and green liquid from another into the baby's mouth.

Signor Mortara hugged Edgardo. He sang a lullaby to him. Anna recognised it as a folk song about women spinning yarns in the mountains, which she had learnt as a child in her Piemonte village outside Bologna. Then he switched to Hebrew and prayed for the baby's recovery.

"*Baruch atah Adonai, rophay cholim...*" He translated the words for Anna and the doctor. "Blessed are you O Lord, the faithful and merciful healer." He closed his eyes silently before continuing with the blessing.

Edgardo started to cry.

"Madame says to take a break and eat – and the doctor

too."

Signor Mortara finished his prayer. He handed Edgardo to Anna. She kissed him and felt his brow; he was clammy and burning up.

"His fate is in the Lord's hands," Signor Mortara said as he went downstairs with Doctor Saragoni.

Anna was alone with Edgardo. His eyes were closed. She kissed him as she rocked him in her arms and quietly hummed the lullaby that Signor Mortara had been singing. When he stopped crying she began to whisper to him. "You are going to be saved, Edgardo! I am going to secure a place for you in Paradise. That I promise!"

Clutching him to her breast, she ran down the stairs into the vestibule and opened the front door.

She heard Madame Mortara in the dining room. "Augusto, put your puppets away. Behave yourself at the Friday night table; show Doctor Saragoni what a good boy you are!"

Anna ran down the steps and into the Via Lame. She hurried to the end of the street, crossing the main road and quickly reached the Salvator Church, just as a priest and a small group of worshippers were leaving.

She entered the silent building, carrying Edgardo down the nave and over to the font. The moonlight streamed through the stained glass windows and lit up his face.

"You need not fear death, for you will go to heaven, Edgardo," she whispered to him as she got out the Holy Water. She held him over the font.

"I baptise you…" She continued to utter the Latin words of benediction, which she had learned little more than an hour before.

"…*in nomine Patris, et Filii, et Spiritus Sancti…*" She sprinkled the Holy Water over his head, made the sign of the cross, and kissed him.

"Now, you are a Christian, Edgardo, and now you have a Christian soul…"

Chapter 2

Bouhay, Liège, Belgium. 1939

Outside the window a wooden shutter crashed against the wall.

Raoul's hand moved up to his temple; baptismal waters were trickling down the side of his face. Above him, the images of statues, stained glass and the ornate gold ceiling of a church were suddenly interrupted by the ghostlike face of a girl of fourteen, smiling as she bent over him to kiss him, her black hair enfolding him. She rocked him from side to side and then ran out of the church carrying him in her arms, through the streets and endless alleyways and porticoes. People started to chase after them. The girl screamed and dropped him...

Raoul woke with a start, half expecting to see Anna Morisi sitting by his bedside. The room was pitch dark. He heard the wind howling outside and tried to remember where he was. He spread his hands over the rough sheets around him, which were knotted and filled with holes. He picked up the musty scent of the bedding and a strong smell of linseed from newly varnished furniture. He slowly realised he was in his cell at the Priory of Notre Dame de Lourdes, his new home.

He lifted his arms out of the bed, feeling a hard pillow under his head and behind that a rough wooden headboard. There was another huge bang as the shutter crashed against the window frame. He lay there listening to the storm, his breathing shallow. The sheets were damp; he felt drops of sweat creeping down his temples.

He got up. The stone floor tiles were cold against the soles of his feet. He could just make out where the window was; a glimmer of light penetrated the parchment-like cloth of the window-hanging. He pulled it to one side and opened the window. A storm was raging: a couple of elm trees swayed violently against a new moon, which quickly disappeared behind dark clouds. The rain lashed his arms as he managed to secure the shutter with its hook. He closed the window, made his way across the room and sat on the edge of his bed in the darkness.

He felt drained and empty. His decision to become a priest had been rapid. It was only two days ago that he had been living at home with his parents. One month before that he had walked into Notre Dame de Lourdes and asked to see the Prior. It had been an impetuous decision to become a novice in the Church; an alternative to running away or ending his life.

He had known the Prior since he was a toddler. His family were part of the parish community, even though his parents had always felt that the Prior was unfriendly: a cold man.

He recalled the Prior joking about how the word 'novice' in Roman times meant a newly acquired slave. The Prior had laughed – a manic high-pitched laugh – and then completely out of the blue had asked Raoul if he knew how to make nettle beer. Most of the villagers did make nettle beer, but what a question! Raoul had stared out of the window. He could see some of the local farm workers in the cornfields and wondered if he might not be happier becoming a labourer. The Prior had asked him why he would not rather go to college or university as his academic results were good, and he found himself saying unconvincingly that he felt his future now lay with the Church. He half expected the Prior to tell him to go away and think about his decision, but instead he had said if he had his parents' blessing he could join the Priory immediately.

I am nineteen; I do not need their blessing, Raoul had thought. He also knew that he did not have their blessing; not really. He knew that his parents were as unhappy as he had been when his relationship with Delphine ended. Religious as they were, they could not understand why he would rather join the

11

Church than go to university and make something of himself, or why he would not rather settle down with another nice girl and have a family. They had been told he would have no problem getting into the University of Liège to study applied sciences or engineering.

He thought back to the moment when he told them he wanted to become a priest. There was a long silence, no words; just an incessant staring from sad eyes framed by rough faces that harked back to generations of Belgian farm labourers.

"I thought you wanted to be an engineer, not a priest," his mother had said eventually in bewilderment.

His father had stopped eating, a sure sign that he was upset. He pushed away his tin plate, shook his head, and abruptly got up from the table, leaving his apple tart untouched. He moved over to the fireplace and lit his pipe, muttering repeatedly that it was a shame things had not worked out with Delphine. In the end Raoul had got up from the table shouting that "Yes! It *was* a shame, a fucking shame!" His father had asked him how he could think about becoming a priest when he used language like that.

Raoul had gone to his tiny bedroom next to the outhouse, thrown himself on the bed, and for hours had lain there in tears, hating his life, hating himself, and hating the fact that in some way, with or without taking his life, it had indeed ended.

So, yes, he would join the Priory and become a slave! And he would pray! He would pray for rebirth, for hope, for redemption. He resolved to spend his life in prayer, pleading with God for help, for answers, for a future. He would pray for this terrible world and an end to the Nazi threat hanging over Europe. As he wept, all the muscles in his body shook, and he had raised his voice and started shouting, "Why?"

His mother had knocked on the door and shouted, "Raoul, are you all right?" before entering his room. He quickly wiped away his tears with his shirt sleeve and tried to force a smile through his red eyes. She had put her arm around him and squeezed his shoulder as if to reassure him, though they both knew his pain was almost unbearable.

He half imagined he would be peeling potatoes all day at the Priory, or cleaning bathrooms and toilets, perhaps on better days tending the beehives or raking the gardens. But the Prior had called him into his study and said he wanted to assign a very special task to him.

"There is an old priest, Father Pius Maria Mortara. He is Italian – you may have seen him at services in the Priory church. He has lived here in Bouhay for as long as you have; he may even have helped at your baptism, I can't remember. He was certainly younger then – as we all were." The Prior had laughed again, with the annoying, high-pitched laugh. He looked at Raoul expecting to see a smile on his face, but was met with a blank, silent stare that masked the boy's pity and despair.

"I want you to look after Father Mortara, or Brother Pius as we call him. He is now old and infirm, and has had a number of stomach problems, but is very stubborn when it comes to seeing doctors. How long he has to live is in the Lord's hands – well, to a degree it will be in your hands as well!" The Prior laughed again, his top lip curling towards his nose. The laugh was certainly going to test Raoul's patience. "Brother Pius is not doing too badly at the moment, but his health fluctuates, along with his moods." Another laugh. Raoul replied quickly in an attempt to curb it. "I will help and care for Father Mortara in any way I can; I am at your service."

"Well this, the start of your noviciate, is a test of whether you are at the Lord's service, not mine," the Prior replied in a somewhat irritated and smug manner.

He is angry with me because I did not laugh with him, Raoul thought to himself, half closing his eyes. *The Prior is cold; my parents were right.*

"As you are aware, Raoul, you begin your noviciate for a trial period, several months as a postulant, and looking after

Brother Pius is certainly a good way for you to embark on your life as a monk. You are to be there for him night and day. You are to help him wash and get dressed and see him safely to Mass; more than anything, you are to be there for him as a companion, as a friend..."

A friend! What did that mean? Raoul thought about his own friends, Guy and Mathieu, so close for so many years, how as kids they had dressed up as musketeers and how they would most probably now drift apart. Guy was starting his history degree at the University of Liège, while Mathieu, who lived across the street, had gone to work on his grandfather's farm in the Bois de Beyne. He then thought about Delphine; she had been a friend and a musketeer, too, and could beat any one of them at marbles. She had gathered together an enviable marble collection, including a Lutz with its green and gold ribbon swirls made of copper flakes. Yes, Delphine had also been a good friend, before she had been his girlfriend and before she had left him for Jean-Louis.

The Prior's words had become amorphous: something about studying Latin and learning about prayer and the liturgy in addition to looking after Brother Pius; about the main purpose of the noviciate being to continue to search for God and to decide if the monastic life was his true vocation. He heard something about temporary vows, of stability and obedience, and then about solemn vows.

Raoul recalled running around Liège with Guy and ending up at one of the bars in the Féronstrée, the looming excitement of university heralding a new era of their lives. He remembered their raucous laughter, the beer and tobacco-infused fog, and Delphine walking in to join them. Only Delphine could light up a dark room with her omnipresent smile. Their eyes had met in unison.

"You have commandeered Bouhay's one and only dream girl," Guy had whispered to him with a hint of envy. It was true: no one in Bouhay came close. Who had the zest for life, the looks, the intelligence, the style of Delphine? She had broken the village mould. She wore elegant, slim-line skirts and tops when the women of Bouhay still harked back to the previous century, wearing pinafores over their billowing peasant smocks, blanket shawls and sometimes even lace bonnets. Only she knew how to wear a sprig of dried flowers or a cheap brooch and give it the life of a Fabergé creation. She was more Brussels than Bouhay, but she was not shallow, and could hold her own with any intelligent man. She loved to discuss all and everything – science, politics, art – and she had a fire and a passion for life, yet was equally modest and generous. Delphine had time for everyone and all the children of Bouhay adored her, as did Raoul. The thought of her caused his heart to race; the vision of her enlightened his whole being, his whole life...

He closed his eyes and quickly opened them. He did not want to dwell on what might have been, nor did he want to be self-indulgent.

"I can see you are taking this very seriously," the Prior said. "You will have a lot to learn from Father Mortara. You will not find him dull: he knew Pope Pius the Ninth personally! I am sure he will tell you all about that himself."

The Prior then told Raoul to come into the Priory church and asked him when his last confession had been and whether there were any sins for which he wished to be reconciled with God. Raoul said there were and the Prior had asked him to go into the confessional booth and confess. Raoul had knelt at the screen.

"In the name of the Father, and of the Son, and of the Holy Spirit... I have sworn..." He stopped. Did he have to go into every detail of the profanities he had shouted at his parents since his last confession a month ago?

"I could have been a better son; I could have argued with my parents less," he offered, "because I know this is a difficult time for them. I know they feel they are losing a son."

The Prior sighed. "They are not losing you."

"I wonder what sort of priest I will be." Raoul was almost whispering.

"You really wish to become a priest?"

Raoul did not reply. He almost wanted to hear the high-pitched laugh again.

It was a strange confessional. The Prior gave him very little. What he did give him left him feeling desolate.

The Prior broke the silence. "Are you truly sorry for your sins and for all the sins of your past life?" he had asked him sternly. "Are you resolved not to commit these sins again, out of the love you have for God?"

"Yes," Raoul replied.

"Anything else?" asked the Prior.

"For not being the best of sons, I am sorry… and I hope and pray that my motives for joining the Church are real and true enough, that I am joining the Church for the right reasons." Raoul was about to tell the Prior that he had had a girlfriend, but stopped himself because he could not bear to say she had found someone else.

He thought the Prior might question him more about his motivation, but all he said was, "Well, there we have it."

'*Well, there we have it!*' That was it.

The Prior had brought him out of the confessional and tapped him on the shoulder.

"Having doubts about dedicating one's life to the Church is not unusual, and certainly it is not a sin. It is not an easy path you have chosen. With God's grace I will do all I can to help you in your predicament. You will report to me and keep me informed. Remember you are a novice, and that this is a period for you to test your commitment before you become ordained. If this life is not for you, it is better we all know as soon as possible."

Raoul wondered if the Prior was trying to get rid of him before he started, but he was a difficult man to read. And he was cold.

The Prior had taken Raoul to the refectory and pointed out Father Mortara.

"There is Brother Pius," said the Prior. The old man was sitting at one of the long tables drinking coffee and staring blankly into his cup.

"You will be spending a lot of time with Brother Pius. Do you have any questions?"

Raoul felt drained and numb; all he could muster was a feeble "No."

The Prior had then introduced Raoul to the old priest.

"Raoul is joining us here at Notre Dame de Lourdes and I am assigning him to look after you," the Prior explained.

Father Mortara offered Raoul his hand and said he was pleased to meet him. He then turned to the Prior, saying, "But I don't need looking after!"

The Prior laughed. "We all need looking after. Think of Raoul as a companion, as I am sure he will brighten up your days."

Father Mortara did not look pleased.

***

The storm was not abating, and Raoul wondered if he would ever be able to commit himself to the Church. He was nervous; he always felt more desperate in the middle of the night. The rain lashed against the window and triggered his insecurities about joining the Priory. He tried to still his mind, but could not stop analysing and questioning his motives.

Yes, he was religious – to a point; yes, he was suited to a monastic lifestyle – to a point; and yes... he was running away from Delphine.

He went over every detail of the day it had all gone wrong. He had arranged to meet her at their tree – a solitary apple tree in the wheat fields. He'd promised to be there: that day was going to be for them alone, to talk, to have a picnic and drink a bottle of wine, and then, and then...

His father had had an accident; he'd cut his hand quite badly. Raoul had bandaged his hand and offered to help him; to do his labouring work for him, but at various hours of the day he had managed to leave notes at the tree for Delphine. He left one in the morning on a piece of paper under a stone. 'Can't make noon. I'll be here at 2.30. R.' When he returned, she wasn't there. He kept returning throughout the day and left more notes. 'Where are you?' 'Why aren't you here?' 'I've waited an hour; I'll come back later,' 'I've come back and waited; I'm not waiting any more.'

That evening in the village as the sun was setting, casting long shadows that seemed to both threaten and mock him, he had seen her walking home. He grabbed her shoulder. She turned round, her eyes widening with anger.

"Where were you!? I waited, but you didn't come!" he'd said.

"How dare you! You reneged on your promise!"

He had tried to explain about his father's accident but she didn't hear him.

"You promised!" Anger and grief had taken hold of her and she'd wept bitterly. She had thrown her basket down on the ground and the bottle of wine in it fell out and smashed on the street. Delphine had continued to storm at him, saying: "All you can think about is your fucking self! You don't care about me at all. It's always you, or your family, or the fucking Church. Never me!"

What she'd said, particularly in relation to the Church, had stung Raoul into a rage. He slapped Delphine hard across the face as he said, "You bitch! How fucking selfish can you get! It's you that always thinks about yourself. You never think about me; you always expect me to do whatever you want. Christ! I've had enough." Then, shaking, he had walked away.

For weeks afterwards he would walk to their tree in the wheat field and sit aimlessly, hoping that Delphine would join him, but she never came. Two months later she met Jean-Louis who was clearly very attracted to her.

Raoul lay in the dark. He tried to fathom what made her find love with Jean-Louis. He went over all the possibilities, feeling ever more worthless with each one. At twenty-six Jean-Louis was older, perhaps cleverer. She basked in the attention he gave her. He was a schoolteacher, suave with his moustache and black hair slicked back like Clark Gable's in 'It Happened One Night'. Surely Delphine could not be that shallow?

He got up again; his eyes were getting used to the darkness. He could make out a candle in its tarnished holder on the rough wooden dresser and beside it a matchbox. He lit the candle and looked into a small oval mirror hanging above the dresser. His young face seemed haunted and eerie, under-lit as it was by the flame. His unkempt fair hair gave him a rough edge. He spent several minutes staring into the mirror. He looked at his jaw: the bone structure was strong. He tried to convince himself that it was a handsome face. It was, but he could not quite believe it. Anyway, as a monk he did not have to worry about what he looked like. He knew he had some way to go to shed his vanity; as a monk he would not need that.

Why Jean-Louis? Jean-Louis was handsome: he had black hair and deep blue eyes. Was that why she had chosen Jean-Louis over him? Were Jean-Louis' eyes bluer than his? Did Delphine not understand that they were meant to have a future together? Was Jean-Louis really more suited to her? Did she love him more? In the mirror Raoul's eyebrow was raised. Jean-Louis! They would have beautiful children together. Raoul closed his eyes. He would never be able to escape from them. They would haunt him for the rest of his life: Jean-Louis and Delphine and their beautiful children, having their baptisms at the Priory church. Would he be allowed to refuse to officiate at their baptisms? He imagined himself looking on from the shadows at the back of the nave, and imagined the beautiful children growing up, running through the cornfields and bathing in the streams around Bouhay with their beautiful parents, laughing and shrieking.

He opened his eyes again. There was a haunted, sad look in them, an intelligence to a degree: the look of an intelligent country boy. He frowned as he stared into the mirror, and the furrows of his brow creased up – more than they should in a boy of nineteen. Did he see the face of a priest? Or was it the face of a boy who was running away? He tried to imagine himself as an old priest. Would he still be in this same room? Would he find happiness here?

Raoul blew out the candle and got back into bed. He told himself he must sleep. He turned over, his beating heart pounding, his head feverish. Outside the window the shutter had loosened itself again and was banging relentlessly against the wall. Raoul buried his head in the pillow and prayed he would find peace. He wrestled with his prayers till the morning.

When the storm had calmed he prayed for strength to take on the day's challenges: strength in his new life as a monk and strength to face a new day without Delphine.

Chapter 3

Bouhay, Liège, Belgium. 1939

"Following my secret baptism, and contrary to all expectations, I made a miraculous recovery. For almost six years I had no idea that I was a Christian."

Father Mortara spoke slowly. He put his hands down on the table and looked up at the sky through the stained glass of the library windows.

"Bologna, in the days before the unification of Italy, was an occupied city, overrun with Austrian soldiers. As I ran through the narrow cobbled streets around my home in the Via Lame, through the maze of terracotta archways and porticoes, piazzas paved with river-stones, watched over by the crooked medieval towers, I had no idea that I was a Christian. My father, of course, whose eyes bulged as he blew smoke rings through puffed out cheeks, and sparkled as he went round the house singing Giordani's 'O caro mio ben' – he had no idea either. Neither did my mother as she made her vermicelli puddings bursting with dried fruits, nor my brothers and sisters shrieking and laughing as they ran alongside the canal by the tobacco factory. Only Anna knew: Anna, our beloved servant girl, mischievous, beautiful Anna, laughing and singing songs about wagon drivers as we made paper boats with stick masts and brightly coloured cloth sails, glove puppets and spinning tops."

It had been two months since the Prior of Notre Dame de Lourdes had asked Raoul to watch over Father Mortara. After lunch, they would either go for short walks in the fields around the Priory or sit in the common room listening to radio broadcasts about the European war. Mostly they would spend the autumn afternoons in the library, a coal fire burning in the hearth, old tomes spread out in front of them on a large table.

It had taken time for Raoul to warm to Father Mortara. At first he had found him rather cold and detached: a sad old man who rarely smiled and said little, unlike some of the other monks: cheerful Walloons, who, once the Long Silence was over, could be found at various corners of the Priory, peppering their lay activities with convivial chit-chat or, like the Prior, chuckling and grinning inanely in the most trivial of circumstances. Father Mortara had only slowly opened up, progressing from discussing general matters such as the illustrations in the books, much as a teacher might with a student. He liked to talk about art and sculpture. He would ask Raoul to open an illustrated book of psalms or a very heavy Book of Hours. A drawing of the Annunciation would yield revelations like, "I once saw Donatello's relief of the Annunciation in the Basilica of Santa Croce in Florence: it was magnificent."

Raoul was not familiar with Donatello, nor had he heard of the Basilica of Santa Croce, but he knew that if he was patient Father Mortara would return to telling his story – how he had been secretly baptised as a baby but how he still had no idea of this as a six-year-old Jewish boy in the back streets of Bologna; at that time part of the Papal States – the Pope's territory.

Once Father Mortara got going, very little could silence him – only the frequent naps. His eyes would start to close. As he nodded off his mouth would open to show a collection of gold- and silver-filled teeth supporting a loose denture, and his head would fall down on to the back of his wooden chair.

Raoul waited patiently. He thought about Delphine; his thoughts would always return to Delphine. He walked over to the window and looked out across the cornfields hoping she might be there, even though he knew she was studying at her teacher training school in Liège.

He sat down again, wondering if Father Mortara might

wake up quickly, for he wanted to hear more of his story. It was the only thing that took his mind off Delphine.

Eventually the old man opened his eyes. Raoul took his hand and held it for several minutes. Then he began to speak again.

"On Friday nights, the Mortara house in Via Lame was an open house, crammed with aunts and uncles and a gaggle of family friends who crowded round the dining table. My mother, Marianna, made the weekly blessing and lit the Sabbath candles, and then Anna would serve dinner: a banquet that had been cooked over a period of two days by the local Jewish womenfolk. Vegetable soup with dumplings and stuffed pasta, fava beans and lentils was followed by kosher meatballs, goose salami and special Sabbath risotto, brightly coloured with saffron. Then came the dessert: *pizzarelle con miele*..." Although Father Mortara relished the double 'z' and rolled his 'r's, Raoul had no idea what he was talking about, and when the old priest explained they were fried matzos with pine nuts and honey he screwed his eyes up because he still did not understand what they might be. Father Mortara tried to explain, "Matzos are crispy, unleavened breads, you know..." but Raoul did not know and he strained to be patient while Father Mortara attempted to explain what pine nuts were.

"My favourite dessert was *bollo* or sweet bread flavoured with anise, the crust stuffed with dried fruits. And if the family went for Friday nights to Mama's wealthy relations, the Padovanis, we had lemon sorbet, which stayed cold even in Italy and tasted tart and sweet at the same time and was creamy and packed with chunks of citrus fruit." Father Mortara closed his eyes and licked his lips at the same time.

"On Saturdays and High Holy Days, we attended the little Hebrew Oratory with all the other children from the congregation of twenty Jewish families who resided in Bologna. I wore a long prayer shawl and skull cap, and sat downstairs with Papa and all the men, while up in the gallery my mother and sisters, dressed in their finest lace blouses and chemisettes and velvet skirts, would smile down, their hair parted in long sausage curls.

"On the Day of Atonement, when Jews repent for their sins, all the adults fasted. Everyone looked so serious and hungry, but my eldest brother Augusto always had something sweet to eat up his sleeve, not to mention the odd toy mouse, spider or his collection of little glove puppets. To my delight he would animate these behind an unsuspecting child's back and my laughter would raise more than a few eyebrows before being drowned out by the sound of the Rabbi blowing the ram's horn.

"At the festival of Purim we would all dress up in masks and fancy costumes – even Mama and Papa – decorate spinning tops with coloured chalks and bang on drums and cymbals, before re-enacting the story of Queen Esther. My father would pose the same question every year. 'So tell me, why do we celebrate Purim?'

"I remember the last Purim I spent at home. I was the first to reply with great enthusiasm: 'Because Queen Esther saved the Jews. She was married to the King of Persia. No one knew she was a Jew!' I laughed. Little did I know then that Queen Esther and I shared the same predicament. I was precocious, perhaps in an annoying way, but I was such an enthusiastic and good-natured child that my brothers and sisters adored me almost as much as my doting parents did. Everyone clapped at my words of wisdom – except Anna, who lowered her eyes and left the room.

"'Queen Esther slept with gentiles like Anna Morisi does,' Augusto blurted out.

"'Keep your tongue still, Augusto!' Mama snapped at him.

"'It's true. I've seen Anna doing naughty things with Austrian soldiers – not just one, either. Does that mean she's a *puttana?*'

"My father put his fingers to his lips. 'Ssh!' He lifted me up

24

and gave me a cuddle. 'You are a clever little boy, Edgardo, and a very good Jew to boot. Papa will buy you a lovely present.'

"'Will you buy me a rocking horse, Papa?'

"'We can't afford anything like that, Edgardo. Be happy with what you have.'

"'I am Papa. I am!' I smiled and hugged him back."

At this point in telling his story, Father Mortara grinned.

"Be happy with what you have! I was happy. I knew we lived in an agreeable house near the centre of Bologna. I knew I was lucky to have lots of people to play with: chess and board games with my brothers and sisters; *scopa* and card games with Papa; and hide-and-seek with the maidservants out in the Via Lame, who all made such a fuss of me. I knew I was good at mathematics, history and Italian; I knew more than most boys of my age."

Father Mortara stopped.

"But I did not know I had been baptised."

Raoul squeezed his hand. They sat in silence.

"Only Anna Morisi knew. In Italy, unlike some places in Europe, you cannot tell a Jew or Christian apart. Many Jews have been there for nearly two thousand years. We are dark... we look the same. We share the same way of life. Only religion divides us, but the greatest sin in that noble Catholic country is not to worship Jesus Christ as the Saviour of the world. I had no idea that I was a Christian, but I soon became painfully aware I was a Jew."

Chapter 4

Bologna, The Papal States. 1858

Anna laughed and chattered as she held Edgardo's hand, only pausing to sing snippets of songs. They made their way into the centre of Bologna, running down the narrow streets past bakers' and butchers' shops, cheesemongers, fishmongers, confectionery shops with mouth-watering macaroons, biscotti and amaretti biscuits, the coffee shop and the beautiful toy shop in the alleyway, where they always stopped to look at the rocking horse framed in the window as if it were in a sacred grotto.

Edgardo pulled Anna through a long portico into the Piazza Maggiore. They bought pasta from one of the *maccaronaros* in the street and watched him as he cooked it over his charcoal fire and then sprinkled it with grated sheep's cheese. They ate it with their bare hands and laughed while they listened to storytellers and watched acrobats on stilts. Anna started to chase Edgardo around the Fountain of Neptune and through the market stalls, where farmers sold their fruit and vegetables from dawn till dusk. She chased him through long strands of pasta drying in the sun and into the cavernous alleyway of the Palazzo del Podesta, used by countless generations of Bolognese lovers for their secret trysts. She pretended to whisper sweet nothings to him, her voice transformed into a loud echo when it reached him at the opposite side of the alleyway.

She chased him out of the square, all the way to the steps of the Cathedral of San Pietro and he giggled with delight before running into the arms of a stranger who was casting his eye over a group of pretty flower girls. It was an Austrian soldier.

Anna ran up the steps. The soldier left Edgardo and followed her. He put his arms around her. She pulled away, making the sign of the cross as she did so, her mood quickly changing. Edgardo watched them. Over the years he had seen her like this with many Austrian soldiers, talking in half-whispered tones.

"I'm leaving Italy; I've been called back to Austria," the soldier told her.

Anna put her hands to her face. "No!" she cried.

She lowered her voice. "But I think I'm pregnant."

She opened the door of the cathedral and told Edgardo to go inside.

He wandered down the nave, overwhelmed by its size; mesmerised by frescoes and paintings of saints and angels; by monks and priests and incense and a myriad of candles; by worshippers kneeling and praying; and by statues of the Virgin and Child. He stopped at a statue of Jesus on the Cross. Suddenly he felt hands being placed around his eyes.

"Jew!"

It was a boy's voice.

"Don't you dare to look at our Lord, you dirty little Jew-boy," came a second voice.

"You killed him, didn't you?" the first one repeated.

"Say it; say it: 'I killed Jesus!'"

Edgardo stared at them, but said nothing. He recognised two of them from the Via Lame. The boys dragged him out of a side door of the cathedral.

"Say it: 'I'm a dirty little Jew-boy. I killed Jesus.' Say it!"

The boy hit Edgardo across his face. Another boy threw him on to the ground and then ripped open his breeches. "You can only go in there if you've got a foreskin," he shouted.

The first one kicked him. Others started to kick him as well. One of them spat in his face. "Circumcised Jewish pig! Don't you ever go into our cathedral again! It's not for you!"

The boys ran away.

Shaken, Edgardo picked himself up off the ground, his clothes torn, his nose bleeding, his face and hair dishevelled. But he shed no tears. Clutching his breeches, he made his way back to the front of the Cathedral, where he saw Anna embracing and kissing the Austrian soldier on the steps. Edgardo stood and watched them. The soldier noticed him and Anna quickly turned around. She ran over to him, shaking her head. "What's happened to you?" she cried.

Edgardo said nothing.

"You'd better take your little Jew-boy home," the Austrian said to her, resentfully.

"He's not a Jew!" Anna quickly bit her tongue. She glared at the Austrian, took off the bracelet he had given her, and threw it into the gutter.

"*Dio Cazzo!*"

Anna took hold of Edgardo and walked away. She turned round, but the soldier had gone.

That evening at dinner Edgardo said little. Mama did not notice. She was too busy nursing the new-born baby Aristides. All his elder brothers and sisters were being entertained by Augusto and his puppets. Anna brought in a hot plate of roasted artichokes, lentil broth and warm bread.

"Augusto, put your puppets away," Madame Mortara said as she handed Aristides to Anna.

Augusto ignored her.

"Augusto, not now, not when we are eating! I will tell Papa when he gets home."

"Where is Papa?" Augusto asked her.

"He is meeting clients; he has a big lace order to deal with. Behave!" And she began the grace before meals. They all joined in, all except Edgardo.

"*Baruch ata Adonai...* Blessed are You, Lord our God, King of the universe, who feeds the whole world through His goodness, with grace, kindness and mercy."

Anna cleared the dishes away before serving Madame

Mortara her coffee. It was only she who noticed the change in Edgardo. She moved over to him, smiled at him and gently took his hand.

"I think I'd like to go to bed now," he told her.

"Good boy, Edgardo," said Mama.

Chapter 5

Bologna, The Papal States. 1858

Edgardo woke up. The room was dark except for the light of one candle. Anna was sitting on his bed, stroking his brow. Edgardo threw his arms around her.

Anna heard Madame Mortara wailing at the main door; she heard the gendarmes piling into the house; she heard the neighbours shouting and asking what was going on. Soon she heard a familiar voice in the street: Signor Mortara returning home.

"What in Heaven's name is this?" he demanded.

He did not wait for a reply. He ran through the crowds, past several armed gendarmes, up the steps and into his house.

He found a sergeant, a number of police officers and a man in black civilian clothes in possession of his home. In the middle of all these people stood his wife Marianna, pale and distraught. The sergeant introduced himself, and then introduced the man in black as an agent of the Holy Office, sent by the Inquisition in Rome.

"You are Signor Salomone Mortara?" the sergeant inquired.

Signor Mortara nodded.

"You have been the subject of an act of betrayal. I have to inform you that one of your children has been baptised."

The sergeant's words took a while to register with Signor Mortara. "There must be a mistake," he replied. "This can't be true."

"I'm afraid it is. I must see your children." The sergeant looked through his notebook. "All eight of them."

"It is late. Please do not disturb them."

"I have my orders," repeated the sergeant.

"Orders? Whose orders?"

"The orders of the Inquisitor-in-Chief of Bologna: Padre Feletti."

The sergeant produced a warrant. "Feletti's orders come from a higher place – from the Holy Office in Rome. Please gather your children." He gestured to a number of gendarmes to start searching the house.

Signor Mortara rushed up the stairs where three of his younger children: Augusto, Arnoldo and Ercole, all half asleep, had come out on to the landing. He embraced them. The other children: Riccardo, Ernesta and Erminia followed and with them Edgardo, holding Anna Morisi's hand.

"Sergeant – do not ask us to herd the children among armed men like animals."

Edgardo looked over the stairwell. His mother ran over to the sergeant and begged him to reconsider his position. "This is a sad household," she said. "We have recently lost our baby son, Aristides. He died less than a month ago." She began to weep.

The sergeant looked away with an air of discomfort. He knew his humanity was being tested. For a moment his eyes revealed a glimmer of compassion. He looked at Signor Mortara and turned to the desperate man's wife. *Could all this be a mistake?* Then he took possession of himself. "Which is your second youngest son, the one named Edgardo?"

Signor Mortara pleaded with him. "Officer, Edgardo is not a Christian."

"According to the authorities, he has been baptised. You are illegally harbouring a Christian." The sergeant's voice was now faintly trembling with emotion. "He can no longer continue to live here; I have orders to take him away. He is to be sent to Rome."

Anna's eyes clouded over.

Signor Mortara struggled to find his voice. "Edgardo has not been baptised; we are Jews!"

"I'm afraid you must hand him over," said the sergeant.

Madame Mortara ran up the stairs and clung on to her young son. Edgardo stood silently and fixed the sergeant with his stare.

Signor Mortara tried to reason with the sergeant. "Officer, my wife's relations are the Padovanis – well known here in Bologna. Let me speak to Feletti. We have to make an appeal."

The sergeant stopped. He knew that the Padovanis were wealthy bankers.

Edgardo ran over to his father. "What is happening, Papa?"

Signor Mortara kissed him on his forehead. The sergeant looked around at the family. The Padovanis, although Jews, were respected in Bologna. They could make trouble. He nodded.

"I will give you leave to call upon Padre Feletti tonight," he said.

**

It was past midnight when Signor Mortara reached the Convent of the Dominicans with his wife's uncle and nephew, the Padovanis. The Inquisitor, Padre Gaetano Feletti, was about to retire to bed.

"I can do nothing for you," Feletti said, almost relishing their predicament as he sat at a large wooden table in his grand apartment. "A baptism has been administered."

The men bombarded Feletti with questions: "Who baptised Edgardo?" "When?" "How?"

Feletti looked at them, trying to make them out in the candlelight. The boy's father was quite tall for a Jew, he thought; quite handsome with his black curls, green eyes and pleasant face. The elder Padovani, a serious man with a fixed expression, seemed well-educated. The younger Padovani talked too much.

There was little compassion in Feletti's face. A lifetime of religious idealism transmuted into bureaucracy had made it hard, and he evaded their questions with a veiled concern. "I am not at liberty to say," he kept repeating. "My orders come from the Archbishop of Bologna."

"Can't these orders be annulled?" the younger Padovani chimed in.

"We have not got the power. Once news of the baptism became known to the ecclesiastical authorities in Bologna, and indeed to the Archbishop of Bologna, the case was deemed to be too serious to be dealt with here and the matter was referred directly to the Roman Curia."

"Who reported this case?" the younger Padovani chipped in.

Padovani tapped the table with his quill. "I am not at liberty to say."

"You mean you won't say! You must be able to do something for us. We are a desperate family asking for your compassion; in the name of human decency; in the name of God!" The younger Padovani desperately juggled his words in an attempt to get through to Padre Feletti.

"I am merely the Inquisitor-in-chief of Bologna," Padre Feletti said, his inflated air of self-importance at odds with his words.

"I cannot help. The Archbishop and I are directed from Rome," the Inquisitor added. "But I can tell you a hearing was given."

"Yet my uncle was told nothing of this hearing, and nothing of this baptism…"

"If indeed there was a baptism," Signor Mortara added.

Feletti ignored this comment. "Your arguments would have been represented."

"By whom? Are these the proceedings of the Holy Office made in the absence of the accused? A man hears nothing until he is condemned?" Signor Mortara became agitated. "Is this how you operate in this enlightened age – in the nineteenth century?"

Feletti was becoming irritated. "The only means of recovering your son is to be baptised yourself," he told Signor Mortara.

His wife's uncle tried to restore reason. "We must ask for a little time to appeal to the Archbishop of Bologna and to the Governor of the city."

"More time? I was instructed to expect the boy this evening. He is due to be sent off to Rome tonight," Feletti replied. I cannot see how an appeal, either to the Archbishop or the Governor, could possibly help. You must understand my directives come from Rome and ultimately from the Holy Father himself. I am a mere pawn in a long chain."

The younger Padovani was incensed. "Then we must break this chain! The Padovani family is well known to the Governor of Bologna. We are bankers."

"Sadly you are not known to the Holy Father," Feletti replied. He looked hard at them. He knew they were bankers, but first and foremost they were canny and persistent Jews. His instinct told him that he should at least appear to be reasonably flexible. He agreed to a delay of twenty-four hours.

**

When Signor Mortara returned to Via Lame, he found the sergeant and the gendarmes were keeping watch on all the rooms in his house. In the main bedroom, where Edgardo lay sleeping, they mounted a guard, by turns for the whole night, two at a time, changing shifts at intervals of every four hours. Signor and Madame Mortara didn't go to bed that night. Anna heard them whispering and crying on the landing, as she sat on her bed, paralysed with guilt.

For five years she had remained silent: she had kept her secret when Edgardo had been baited by bullies for being a Jew; she had kept it when Lepori the apothecary had blurted out that she had once baptised a child; and she had ridiculed him for talking nonsense. She had also kept it when a local priest had started asking her questions about "Things he had heard."

But when Edgardo's baby brother Aristides had fallen ill and been given up by the doctors, she could keep her secret no more. She had confided in Regina Bussolari, the ageing maidservant who lived next door. "When Edgardo was ill, six years ago, when he was a baby, in the same state near the point of death, I baptised him," she had told her and then launched into the whole story. Regina could hardly contain herself. Her eyes bulged as she adjusted the apron strings over the rolls of her midriff. "You should baptise Aristides then, like you did with Edgardo – the poor little blighter, him being on the point of death and all," she had said to her.

"No! I won't do it again," Anna told her. "Edgardo lived on after the baptism; it wouldn't be right."

"It wouldn't be right not to," Regina had said, and for the next few days she had goaded Anna constantly.

Anna knew she shouldn't have told Regina. "You baptise Aristides if you care so much about him!" she had shouted at her.

"Me? I wouldn't know where to start," Regina had said to her laughing. "I don't know a font from a pulpit," she said, trying to make a joke of the situation.

This annoyed Anna. "You don't even like Jews, Regina; what do you care? You're always saying that if you had your way you'd chop all the Jews into little pieces." Regina would often say this, usually when she was chopping onions or raw meat. Anna had seen her take her knife and make speedy cutting actions while she said it, screwing up her little nose between her big cheeks as if to demonstrate how distasteful it all was.

"Well, if they were baptised they wouldn't be Jews, would they? The trouble with you is that you're a Jew-lover."

Anna felt terrible. Day after day she'd relived Edgardo's baptism and wondered if she should indeed baptise Aristides.

Then all of a sudden Aristides had died, before she'd had an opportunity to repeat her pious deed.

The next day she sobbed her heart out to Regina as she was engulfed in her fleshy arms. "I could have saved his soul," she kept repeating. "I should have baptised him, like I did with Edgardo."

It had not taken long for a gossip such as Regina to tell the local priest. The priest approached Anna and she confessed everything to him, never imagining that news of the baptism would be brought to the attention of the Archbishop of Bologna and his Inquisitor-in-Chief, Padre Gaetano Feletti, or, indeed, that it would eventually reach the Eternal City and the Supreme Pontiff himself.

Anna heard the children crying in the next bedroom. She heard the police guard changing and Signor Mortara entreating them. "It is needless to say that we will not be going to bed tonight, but please, for decency's sake, will you not move away from the bedroom to the passage or to the staircase?"

"We have orders to keep the prisoner in sight at all times," a young gendarme replied.

Anna got out of bed and began to pray to the Virgin Mother. She prayed until silence prevailed in the house again and continued to pray until the dawn began to light the red rooftops of the Via Lame.

***

The following day a fruitless appeal was made to the Archbishop of Bologna and to the Cardinal Governor of the city. Neither was in Bologna. A vicar, standing in for the Archbishop, said he would be able to inform Signor Mortara of the decision that evening.

"But that will be too late!" pleaded Signor Mortara, because the removal of the boy to Rome was to take place at sunset.

That afternoon Signor Mortara took his children by carriage to the Padovanis, who lived in a distant quarter of the city. In the evening, back at home, with the gendarmes still in attendance, he walked up and down the rooms and passageways of the house with Edgardo in his arms, dishevelled in his shirtsleeves and worn down with lack of sleep. Madame Mortara sat motionless, her head in her hands and never moving from the chair by the front door.

Signor Mortara looked out into the street where more gendarmes were guarding the house. He saw a couple of neighbouring maidservants gossiping as they looked over from across the street. He put Edgardo down by his wife's chair and ran down the front steps and over to the servants. "What do you know about this?" he shouted.

The maidservants shook their heads. A couple of his neighbours entered an alleyway. Signor Mortara ran after them and grabbed them. "What do you know about Edgardo?"

"We don't know anything," one of them replied.

As they entered their homes, Signor Mortara ran back into the street. The ageing maidservant Regina came out of her house and walked past him. She moved over to the other maidservants and immediately started gossiping with them. He grabbed hold of her. "Who baptised my son? Tell me what you know." He started to shake her.

"Leave me alone!" she cried.

"Tell me who did this to us!" he shouted.

"Get your hands off me, you filthy Jew!" she shrieked.

Anna looked out on to the street from the front bedroom window. A gendarme rushed over to them and prised Signor Mortara away from Regina. He dragged him back to the house as the neighbours and maidservants looked on, pushing him up the front steps and throwing him onto the floor at Edgardo's feet.

Signor Mortara slowly got up and took Edgardo's hand. He closed the front door.

Anna came running down the stairs into the vestibule. "Signor, I must speak to you. Alone," she said.

Signor Mortara let go of Edgardo's hand and walked down one of the passageways with Anna. "What is it?" he asked her.

Anna stopped and turned to him. "Please forgive me, Signor." She paused. "It was I who baptised Edgardo."

"What do you mean you 'baptised' him?" said Signor Mortara in total disbelief.

Anna stood looking at him. "I baptised him."

She saw the lines of his eyes and forehead gather into a frown and thought he was going to lash out at her. She wished he had; it would have made things easier for her. But all he said was one word: "When?" in a soft voice that made her feel ashamed and worthless, instantly drawing tears to her eyes.

"When he was a baby; when he was ill and we thought he was going to die."

Signor Mortara could not understand her words. "We never thought he was going to die!" He believed his words were true. In six years he had forgotten and rewritten the family history.

Sobbing, Anna continued. "But Signor, you kept sending me out for medicines, and every day when he was ill Madame Mortara kept crying and shouting that she thought Edgardo was going to die! I only wanted to help! I, too, thought he would die – and that if he was baptised he would go to Heaven." Anna wiped her eyes. "I admit I was surprised at how quickly Edgardo recovered; I would have baptised Aristides when he fell ill, but then he died…."

Signor Mortara could hardly bear to listen. She had been no more than a child when she had joined his household; how could she have baptised his son? He tried to make sense of Holy Water given to her by the druggist, Lepori, and of her sprinkling it over his baby's head when she was alone with him in the Salvator Church, but he couldn't.

"How can you call that a baptism?" he pleaded. "You thought you could change a Jew into a Christian just like that?"

"Padre Feletti said it was a baptism…"

Signor Mortara despaired as he heard the name. Padre Feletti had given the girl a hearing but had denied one to his family. It would be on her evidence that his son would be sent to Rome that night. His confusion quickly turned to anger. "Did you hate us so much?" he asked her.

"No, Signor, I have never hated you."

"Did we not treat you like a daughter?"

"You did, Signor. You did."

Signor Mortara grabbed her to him. Something had broken in him. "We took you in off the streets, fed you, clothed you, even loved you, and this is how you have thanked us. You have betrayed us and you have deceived us for all these years."

"I thought he was going to die! Please, please forgive me, Signor. Please."

A gendarme came down the corridor to see what all the noise was about. Signor Mortara let go of her.

"When you stole money from your previous employers, we forgave you for that. When you were whoring with Austrian officers we forgave you for that, too, but for baptising my son, Edgardo, I can never forgive you!"

Anna ran up the staircase.

"How could you do this to us?" he shouted after her. "You have destroyed our lives!"

"I did it because I love Edgardo!" she cried. "I thought he was going to die!"

Signor Mortara was sickened all the more because he knew she was telling the truth. She was an ignorant Catholic girl, but she had loved, and still loved, Edgardo.

As she packed her bags, his anger turned to sorrow. She appeared half an hour later. Edgardo ran over to hug her. She stepped forward, her eyes red from crying and kissed him. Signor Mortara watched them, and when she left he sank down on to the floor and he also wept.

***

For endless hours Signor Mortara sat hugging Edgardo. Night fell and once again there was a loud, relentless knocking on the large wooden door. Madame Mortara got up from the chair, her face frozen with grief. A detachment of Papal officers entered the house. Signor Mortara was ordered to hand over the prisoner. He carried Edgardo outside into the street where a large crowd had gathered. A carriage accompanied by an escort of mounted police arrived to take him away. The agent of the Holy Office sent from Rome jumped out on to the cobblestones. A gendarme tore the child from his father's arms; another pinioned him to prevent his resistance. Edgardo was carried down the steps and handed over to the agent.

"Do not harm him," begged Signor Mortara.

"Shame on you!" cried a neighbour as he vented his anger on the officers.

As the carriage pulled away Edgardo saw his neighbours and the maidservants with whom he had played hide and seek; he saw the boys who had taunted him in the Cathedral; he saw Lepori the druggist, and, standing on her own at the end of the road, he could see Anna Morisi.

Madame Mortara pushed through the crowds and followed the carriage, crying for her son and begging the God of Israel for his mercy. Along the Via Lame, through the centre of Bologna, and through the streets beyond she ran. For two miles she ran until, falling from exhaustion, she could run no more. She lay in the road helpless as the carriage with its prisoner and escort drove off for Rome.

Chapter 6

Bouhay, Liège, Belgium. 1939

The monks ate breakfast huddled together in clusters at long dining tables. They chewed on thick slices of buttered bread and sipped their coffee in silence. The light of an autumn sun streamed in through large arched windows, bouncing off dust particles and enamelled tin plates. Martin, Raoul's fellow novice, scrubbed the floor by the ash-wood serving table. Carbolic fumes started to mask the smell of lavender-tinged beeswax. Father Mortara pushed his omelette away. He watched Martin as he moved backwards, his spindly legs and big rear squeezed into tight trousers; he had the air of an overgrown beetle. He worked vigorously, well equipped with scrubbing brush in one hand and large red bar of soap in the other. Although his arms stretched in large arcs he still managed to miss most of the parquet tiles.

Raoul got up and went over to the serving table. He helped himself to a spoonful of pear jam, then leaned over to Martin and rested a hand on his shoulder. "Maybe now is not the best time to do this while the monks are eating. I'll help you move the tables later, when I get back from Liège; we can do a good job together."

Martin quickly stopped in his tracks, his chubby face clouding with disappointment and a hint of indignation. "You don't think I'm doing a good job, do you?" he shouted. Brother André put his finger to his lips; breakfast was part of the Long Silence.

Raoul said nothing. He was weary because he was still getting used to the night-time hours in the Priory, but he managed to smile at Martin. He returned to his place by Father Mortara's side. The old man watched him intensely.

41

"You move with grace and determination," he whispered to Raoul. He would embarrass the boy with compliments in this way all the time and say things that most people do not say. What he said was intimate, more so than he was used to; strange, a little Mediterranean perhaps. His parents had never spoken to him like that. He flattered Raoul, telling him he was 'able, intelligent, no doubt about it'. When Raoul read him sacred texts or newspapers, it was always with 'clarity and understanding'. He looked forward to the boy reading to him in his Liégeoise accent. When he argued about doctrine, he told him he was 'passionate' or 'persuasive'. When he sang in the Priory, he said it was with 'enthusiasm and gusto'. When he whistled in the gardens he told him it was with 'melodious charm' – not like the majority of northern Europeans who have an annoying habit of whistling loudly to show how hard they are working or how happy they are. Everything Raoul did he did well, and details were observed and acknowledged. Father Mortara would watch him making a fire in the library, setting old rags or birch bark as tinder, and the compliments kept coming. "How do you know just where to place the twigs and pine cones as kindling?" Raoul would smile back at the old man. Sometimes he would laugh, his laughter deep, guttural and infectious. He found Father Mortara amusing; he helped him to escape from his sadness.

"A boy like you would be better off in Rome," Father Mortara said, "not stuck out here in Bouhay, looking after an old man like me." Brother André put his finger to his lips again.

Raoul reached for the coffee jug and filled Father Mortara's cup. He rested his hand on his shoulder and then sat down at his side, taking his hands between his own. He looked up, noticing how deep set the old man's green eyes were. They looked like topaz jewels. He did not look like a Jew or even overtly Italian, but he did look different to most of the other monks in the refectory because he was imposing and

42

distinguished-looking – handsome in a mildly Mediterranean sort of way – and still had a full head of white hair. The skin behind the pallor still had a hint of olive; his lips were full and refined; and his posture still excellent for a man of nearly ninety. Raoul stared at Father Mortara, not with awkwardness but more with a reassurance that he was there for him. The monks were sensitive to the growing connection between the two of them, even Brother Eugène who did the accounts and was the Priory chatterbox. They couldn't fail to notice that since Raoul, or Brother Luc as the Prior had named him, had been looking after Father Mortara, he seemed a little happier – less distant and more content. Brother Eugène was about to sit down next to them, but noted that Brother Luc and the old man were having one of their moments together. "I won't disturb you; I can see you are communing," he said as he headed for the other side of the table and whispered something about their deep and meaningful relationship to Brother André who laughed loudly.

"So much for the Magnum Silencium," said Father Mortara, putting his finger to his lips with a big smile on his face.

Raoul spoke to himself. "I would love to go to Rome one day and see all the places you talk about: the Vatican, the Forum, the Church of Saint Peter in Chains, the Quirinal Palace, the Tiber…" he said in a voice too low for Father Mortara to hear, "but for now I am content to be here in Bouhay with you." Raoul was intrigued by Father Mortara and his story and was keen that his curiosity should be satisfied; he was also aware that hearing about his past might be a catalyst for him and Father Mortara to share something indefinable, something deep and beyond words that served to help both of them at this time in their lives. *I will care for you and look after you and I am content to serve you*, he thought.

Raoul was learning how to serve: how to be a servant. He was not servile and he did not feel in any way demeaned. He thought that he liked to serve: it satisfied him. It took him away from the troubles in the world. He would serve God and he would serve man, and his life would be a lot simpler.

Still holding Father Mortara's hands he smiled. Father Mortara was touched. The boy's expression reminded him of his father's when he did well at school as a child; even more so it reminded him of his spiritual father Pope Pius. It was the kind of smile that lit up the eyes and the whole face with a radiant warmth. *The Priory needs smiles like that*, he thought. Notre Dame de Lourdes was cold, even in summer, but on a November morning it was especially chilly. The stone slabs that covered most of the Priory floors kept the air cold, so different to the warmth of the cobbled streets in Italy. It was a relentless coldness, conducted up the body to faces that were already serious through study, prayer, or religious subjugation.

"At least here in the refectory there are wooden tiles on the floor; it is not quite so cold in here," Father Mortara whispered.

Raoul had no idea where that remark had sprung from. He rubbed the old man's hands as if he were trying to warm him up, which made him laugh.

For a moment he forgot about the Magnum Silencium. "Would you like to come into Liège with me, Father Mortara?"

The Prior overheard them as he entered the refectory. "I'm not sure Brother Pius is well enough to make the journey into Liège. He is eighty-eight, you know, and hasn't been very well." The Prior turned to Father Mortara. "You've left half your omelette, Brother Pius," he said, as though he were talking to a toddler, he himself completely ignoring the Long Silence as if by divine right. Then he sat down on the long wooden bench at the breakfast table.

Father Mortara turned to the Prior and spoke in a loud voice. "It's undercooked and slimy!" he said with such strength that droplets of spittle shot through an opening in his dentures and regrouped themselves on the Prior's spectacles.

The Prior turned towards the elderly monk sitting across

the table. "Brother André is eating his omelette," he said as he wiped his spectacles with his handkerchief.

"Brother André will eat anything," Father Mortara replied, directing his words to Raoul for greater sarcastic effect.

"Brother André is not fussy," the Prior added, "he knows that this is a monastery, not a restaurant on the Spanish Steps in Rome."

"You clearly haven't been there. There are no restaurants on the Spanish Steps in Rome!" Father Mortara shouted as if he wanted the whole refectory to hear.

"Let us not forget the rule of silence," the Prior said as he cleared Brother Pius's chipped tin plate to one side.

"Yes, let's not!" Brother Pius said glaring at him.

Raoul was taken aback by the Prior's hostility in speaking to Father Mortara. He tried to work out if the Prior's raised eyebrow indicated distastefulness for menial chores or a disdain for the old priest himself.

The Prior took a notepad and pencil out of his pocket and scribbled some words in large letters. Raoul peered over to see what he was writing. The Prior handed the notepad to Brother Pius. Father Mortara screwed up his eyes as he read the words; 'You are ill stay here!' He threw the pad down, defiantly grabbed back his tin plate and took a bite of his bread roll. He stood, reaching for his long yew walking stick, which was gnarled and bony down one side like the back of his hands, and started to wave it above his head. "See, I'm ready to go." He got up and shouted a loud "*Andiamo*".

"I suppose Father Mortara knows his own mind," the Prior whispered. "Make sure he doesn't fall, Brother Luc. We've had more than one elderly monk break their limbs here over the years."

***

Clutching his old school satchel, Raoul ran to the bus stop

and flagged down the bus as it came down the hill from Bressoux. He asked the driver to wait for Father Mortara who was slowly descending the steps leading from the Priory.

The farm workers started muttering impatiently; one of them took out a tin pocket watch that he kept staring at repeatedly. The women looked impatient too, but when they saw the old priest hobbling through the monastery gates and on to the bus they smiled, and two elderly ladies crossed themselves.

A young farm labourer got up to give his seat to Father Mortara. Raoul thanked him.

How many times had he taken this bus into Liège? He sat down opposite Father Mortara, only to stand again almost immediately to offer a stern-faced old lady his seat. She stared at him: a look of irritation and recognition in her eye. It was Madame Joiret, whose yard backed diagonally on to his parents' yard. Raoul smiled at her, but she wasn't going to acknowledge him. She just stared. It was a cold, lifeless stare; the same stare she had given him five years earlier when his ball had landed in her rosemary pot. He had screamed at her to give it back to him and when she wouldn't he jumped over her wall and literally grabbed it out of her hands, almost pushing her over. The rosemary pot had fallen off the wall and smashed into a hundred pieces on the ground. She knew exactly who he was, but she wasn't going to acknowledge him. The villagers were like that. They often pretended, even with a population of less than two hundred, that they didn't know you. He purposefully smiled at her again, which seemed to irritate her even more. She clutched her shopping bag tightly as if she thought he was going to grab it, turned to the woman next to her and began to talk in a loud voice, which miraculously changed in an instant to an almost inaudible whisper. She occasionally turned back to Raoul, for no other reason it seemed than to show him her continuing disdain. She was clearly talking about him. He heard the words 'rosemary pot'. His mother had always said the Joirets were 'rubbish'. He caught himself saying "Rubbish". He repeated the word, and then started to feel guilty. Would he ever be capable of forgiveness? Maybe he should start practising contriteness. He wondered if Madame Joiret had heard that he had joined the monastery; that he was to become a priest. He was wearing his day clothes: old, grey trousers and a much worn tweed jacket that was crying out for leather patches on the elbows. Raoul turned away, his half-mast smile still hanging on his face. The bus was full and alive with chatter as the village folk travelled into Liège for market day. There was talk of where the best tomatoes could be bought, which seamstress could run up a pair of school trousers cheaply, whether the fish from de Clercq's was as fresh as it used to be and whether the jeweller Becker was too expensive for watch repairs – and whether he was in fact a Jew. Madame Joiret said something about how it was the Jews' fault that Belgium was in such decline, her tones now those of a bellowing cow. Raoul looked over at Father Mortara, who was staring out of the bus with the innocence of a child, his face reflected in the window between a line of poplar trees racing by. No one would ever have imagined that this old man with his long black priest's cassock was a Jew. Thankfully he couldn't hear what they were talking about.

The trees, the woods, the fields, the hill on which stood the Fort de la Chartreuse and the parklands turned into urban streets. The bus crossed the Pont des Arches where down below them on the north bank of the River Meuse, market stalls, snaking along the quays, were piled high with fruit and vegetables, blocks of Herve cheese and cheap clothing. They pulled up outside the Palais de Justice.

Raoul helped Father Mortara off the bus. "The Prior has given me a list of things we must shop for," he told him as he got out a small notebook. "First, fuse wire and secateurs." They walked slowly through the streets of Liège and headed for the hardware store; then on to the Post Office for stamps. They called in to the optician's to drop off Brother Paul's broken reading glasses and were told that they would be mended in half an hour.

"Let me treat you to a *matoufèt* while we wait," said Father Mortara as they reached a little *crêperie* opposite the optician's. Raoul wanted to decline; he didn't much care for them. To him they were neither *crêpes* nor omelettes: he found the salty ones too bitter and the sweet ones, drenched in white powdered icing sugar, too cloying. He wondered if he was too fussy to be a monk, but nevertheless accepted Father Mortara's invitation out of politeness. He watched the elderly priest tucking in, scooping all the crispy bacon bits on to his spoon. There were no more errands to run. They didn't need to do any food shopping as all the meat and vegetables were delivered to the Priory by truck, together with the milk and the beer, but Father Mortara wanted to buy a large tub of Sirop Liègeois. He liked the thick apple and pear spread on his bread. "It takes the taste of the Priory cooking away," he said.

After they had collected Brother Paul's spectacles, Father Mortara announced that it had been a while since he had visited Liège Cathedral. "Can we go there and say a prayer?" he asked. "Maybe we can both confess."

"Of course," Raoul replied, even though he had made his confession the day before at the Priory. They made their way to the Cathedral, a few streets away. On entering the building they crossed the black and white marbled floor overlooked by the large gothic arches straddling the main nave. They sat down on one of the pews.

A young lady with a pillbox hat and black lace hanging down over her face waited to go into the confessional. Raoul watched her, thinking he could detect tears and mascara running down her face. He wanted to ask her if she was all right, but stopped himself. He thought she was beautiful, but decided he would have to programme himself to start thinking like a priest.

48

"Let's pray for our parents: mine and yours," said Father Mortara. "It's not easy for parents to lose their sons to the Church. I'm sure your parents did not want you to live a life as a monk." He looked at Raoul to see if he was right and noticed that the young man was still watching the young lady. He closed his eyes to pray.

When the lady went in to the confessional Raoul fancied that he heard her saying something about being pregnant. Twenty minutes later she came out looking no happier than when she went in, but she managed a smile for Raoul before she ran out of the church. He helped Father Mortara into the confessional.

Raoul went back to the pew and wondered what the worst of his sins were. He was suddenly overwhelmed by the ridiculousness of his life, and immediately felt guilty that he should have had such a thought. The sheer size of the cathedral made him feel lost and isolated. In truth he was confused; he wanted to be a monk, but he knew that in part he was running away. He saw no future for himself anywhere, and yet he had taken refuge in the Church. His throat began to tighten and he broke into a hot sweat. He remembered a time when he had been full of hope, energy and wonder. Now it was as if he was losing his spark. In joining the Church, part of him felt that he was losing his identity. He was dying; he felt he should say a prayer of mourning for the part of himself that was dead. He began to pray and begged God for mercy and a way out.

Father Mortara came out of the confessional and slowly walked towards him.

"Go in if you like, Brother Luc," he said.

"I'm all right," Raoul replied, immediately aware of how banal his response sounded. He knew Father Mortara was constantly testing him. He really didn't want to go into the confessional box while Father Mortara was sitting outside. It would feel as if he was sitting behind him, watching him taking a pee. Father Mortara kept repeating that he would wait for him while he went in. Raoul entered the confessional. He made the sign of the cross while saying, "In the name of the Father, and of the Son, and of the Holy Spirit..."

A voice on the other side of the wooden lattice said, "I invite you to have trust in God."

It was a warm, rich voice, with a middle-class Walloon French accent.

Raoul said 'Amen'. He knew the ritual. Then he listened as the priest read the 'Parable of the Prodigal Son', Luke 15: 11–32. "He was dead but now is alive again..." Raoul wished he would stop. When he finished, he explained the teaching of Jesus made it clear that the love of Our Lord is greater than sin. "The father's deep affection for the sinful child leads to the sinner leaving his miserable state and coming home, and results in a great celebration. The father is so elated by his son's return that he calls for all to celebrate with him." The voice continued and then added, "There is great joy in heaven and in God himself." The voice was very well-meaning, jovial almost. "Now for your confession. Greetings!" the voice said.

"Greetings, Father," Raoul said through the wooden lattice.

"When was your last confession, my son?" asked the priest through the screen.

"Yesterday," Raoul replied.

"Yesterday?" the priest answered with some amusement, "Where was that? Here, in St Paul's?"

Raoul didn't want to answer and was silent for a moment.

"You don't have to tell me, but I can assure you I cannot break the confessional seal." The voice stopped for a moment before it continued, "Under penalty of excommunication!" There was a little chuckle.

"It was at the Priory of Notre Dame de Lourdes," Raoul answered quickly. He had no idea what he wanted to confess, but did not want the priest to think he was a hard-nosed criminal.

"And you feel the need to confess again so soon? Have you

50

examined your actions since your last confession yesterday?"

Raoul did not answer.

"Have you transgressed since then?"

"I am sure a day does not go by when I do not transgress, Father," Raoul replied.

"Well then, let's start your confessional," said the voice.

"Bless me Father for I have sinned. It's been one day since my last confession..."

Once Raoul started he couldn't stop. "I wasn't planning to confess again today but I find myself here and I am continually questioning the wisdom of my joining the Church as a novice... My actions in joining the Church continue to hurt the people I hold most dearly in life, namely my family, who I believe would have been much happier seeing me marry a local girl and raising a family with her. Your sermon about the Prodigal Son is almost unbearable for me to hear. At least the Prodigal Son came home, but I will not be coming home. I have deprived my parents of the pleasure of a family, of continuing their line... and not a day goes by when I do not feel guilty of the deprivations I have afforded them..."

Raoul became aware that he was babbling on. He found himself telling the faceless priest that at school he had excelled in most subjects and had been planning to go to university.

"Funnily enough, I was not that hot on religious instruction. In my worst moments I feel that the Church is my only refuge... and then again maybe I am not cut out for the Church..." Raoul's thoughts turned to Delphine. He would tell the priest about her, but the priest stopped him.

"The act of penance is a vehicle for those who desire to live a more holy life, to be closer to our Lord Jesus Christ, and to show to others the love and compassion that he himself showed. The sacrament of penance is a healing sacrament for sin, which injures and weakens man..." The joviality had disappeared from the priest's voice. "If I may give you counsel, I would say you need to trust yourself more. Have faith in

God. And I am not really hearing here any real sin for which I need to impart you absolution. However I hear your sorrow for what you think is sin and for that I will give you absolution." And with that the priest asked God to give Raoul pardon and peace and absolved him from his sins, in the name of the Father, and of the Son, and of the Holy Spirit.

"Do you not get any counsel from the Prior of Notre Dame de Lourdes?" the priest asked him.

"I have not told the Prior of my doubts," said Raoul.

"You need faith, my son, and you need to pray and someone to talk to. In confidence I can tell you that I am more than happy for you to talk to me if you need to." He laughed, and then said; "I don't think confessing every day is the answer for you. Would you be happy to speak to me outside the confessional?"

Raoul said that he would and the priest asked him to step outside.

A man who looked as though he was a youthful sixty-year-old stepped out of the confessional. "Let me see you my son."

Raoul walked forward.

"What is your name?" the priest asked him.

"Raoul. Raoul Dubois – but as a novice at the Priory I am known as Brother Luc."

"I am Monsignor Kerkhofs. I am the Bishop of Liège. Have you got time to talk now?" He looked around the cathedral. "I don't think I have any more sinners."

Raoul was a little taken aback. The bishop of Liège was offering to help him in his confusion.

Awkwardly he looked over at Brother Pius, who was sitting in the pew in front of them. "I should not stay and talk now, for I have to look after Father Mortara. He is nearly ninety. I ought to take him back to the Priory."

"Father Mortara, from Notre Dame de Lourdes in Bouhay? Is that Father Mortara?"

"Yes," Raoul said, not knowing whether or not he should

have told him. "I am looking after him, or perhaps I should say he is taking me under his wing."

"You are very privileged; I am sure you know how renowned he is in the Catholic Church."

"Yes, I have heard, and I'm hearing the same thing all the time," Raoul replied.

"His story is remarkable; I'm sure he has told you about it himself. He was a protégée of Pope Pius you know." Monsignor Kerkhofs sighed as if acknowledging some kind of miracle.

"He has told me about parts of his life, but... he is quite a private person. I would love to know more about him."

"I'm sure you will," the Monsignor replied, and started to head over to Father Mortara. "I must say hello to Brother Pius."

His voice, much louder than it had been in the confessional, boomed around the cathedral. "Brother Pius, we met a couple of years ago..." he sat down, "...at a dinner organised by the Prior of Notre Dame. Do you remember?"

Father Mortara looked at him. "Of course I remember! It's Monsignor Kerkhofs, isn't it? How are you?" He stood up and they both embarked on a radiant bear hug.

Raoul left them to chat for a while. He wandered around the vast Gothic cathedral with its three naves and ornate pulpit, and found himself staring at the fleur-de-lis at the bottom of the crucifix hanging from the ceiling. He couldn't stop thinking about Father Mortara's baptism.

Monsignor Kerkhofs returned, beaming. "Do you often come into Liège, Brother Luc?"

"I'm sure I shall be coming into town to do a few errands and some of the shopping for the Priory."

The Bishop looked at his watch. "Brother Luc, forgive me, but I have to officiate at a funeral. Why don't we meet next week? Come and visit me at my house." He took a calling card out of his pocket and handed it to Raoul. "You can telephone me if you like. You won't often find me here doing confessionals."

And with that the Bishop of Liège was gone.

Raoul went over to Father Mortara and sat with him for a while. They admired the stained glass windows, but Raoul's mind was elsewhere. He suddenly spoke out. "Was it a valid sacrament of baptism, Father? Your maidservant was so young, only fourteen, little more than a child. She did not have your parents' consent." Raoul found himself becoming more and more perplexed. His face reddened.

"She thought I was at the point of death. Her one desire was to send a soul to heaven. By canon law she was justified," Father Mortara replied.

He asked Raoul to pray for Anna Morisi. "That maidservant was my spiritual mother. I never expressed my gratitude to her, but trust I shall meet her in Heaven."

Raoul could not believe that a maidservant was justified in overriding the parents' rights over their child, but he reluctantly nodded, put his hands together, closed his eyes and joined Father Mortara in a prayer for her. The old priest started to sway uncertainly. He began to speak in broken sentences.

"Eighty years ago, the whole world knew my story... You must know that I was truly singled out... for the special love of God."

Raoul helped him to his feet and took him outside for some air. They slowly retraced their steps to the Palais de Justice. As they travelled back to Bouhay on the bus, Father Mortara began to speak again.

"The journey to Rome was long..."

Chapter 7

The Papal States. 1858

For three days the carriage and its escort sped through the Romagnan countryside and the Apennine Mountains.

Edgardo spent much of the journey crying for his parents. "Take me back to my mother!" he kept on shouting as he glared at the agent of the Holy Office who was dressed from top to toe in black.

"You have no mother now but the Church," the agent told him as he tried to put an ornate chaplet and cross around the little boy's neck.

Edgardo did all he could to resist. "No!" He opened his shirt to reveal a silver amulet tied around his neck. He took it in his small fingers and showed it to the agent.

"My *mezuzah*, see!"

"What is it?" the agent asked him.

"It's a Jewish charm," Edgardo informed him. "It's got a little scroll inside the case with passages from the Bible in Hebrew. It has God's name written on it. All Jewish children have them!"

The agent tore it from his neck. He looked at the little silver tube with its bronze- coloured Star of David on the front and then handed it back to him. "You won't be needing that now."

Edgardo started to cry again. "I will be needing it! I will!" he shouted. "I shall pray to God that my mama and papa will come and rescue me and take me home – away from you."

The agent laughed.

They drove through a Tuscan village where a group of small children formed a procession and were following a priest to the local church. The children waved at Edgardo as the carriage drove by. He pressed his sad face to the glass window of the carriage.

"Wave back," the agent said to him, but Edgardo shook his head.

The agent shouted to the coachman to stop the carriage.

"Let's get out and stretch our legs. You must be hungry. We can have a bite to eat," said the agent. He jumped out of the carriage and lifted Edgardo down to the cobbled street.

They crossed the main piazza where there were market stalls selling fruit and vegetables, meat and cheeses. Edgardo went over to a drinking fountain and cupped his hands to catch the cold mountain water. He then sat down on a bench in front of the fountain while the agent bought various foods for them to eat. He came back with bread, prosciutto, tomatoes and two pieces of artichoke flan, and sat down next to Edgardo on the bench.

"Is the meat ham, signor?" Edgardo asked. "I don't eat pig meat."

"No! It's prosciutto," he answered, his face erupting into a beaming smile, "it's made from wild boar I think. In any case, now you are a Christian, you can eat anything you like." The agent handed him a few slices with a big piece of bread and a tomato.

"It's good, eh?" the agent said as he watched Edgardo wolfing it down. "Have some flan as well."

The agent noticed that Edgardo was now swinging his legs to and fro.

"You do know that Jesus started life as a Jew like you, don't you? And then he was baptised by John the Baptist in the Jordan River: baptised, like you were!"

Edgardo laughed. "I wasn't baptised in the Jordan River by John the Baptist."

"No, you were baptised by your maidservant, Anna Morisi, in the Salvator Church, when you were a baby," said the agent with a big smile.

"How did Anna Morisi baptise me?" Edgardo asked,

looking confused.

"She sprinkled Holy Water over your head," explained the agent.

"Can a maidservant baptise people just like that?" Edgardo stopped swinging his legs. "Shouldn't a priest have baptised me?"

"Baptism is usually done by a priest, but Anna Morisi said she baptised you properly and the Pope said that was all right," replied the agent, raising an eyebrow, as if he were trying to make sense of his own words.

"The Pope?"

"Yes the Pope of Rome, himself. He said that Anna Morisi had turned you into a Christian. See how special you are? You and Jesus are both very special: Jewish boys who became Christians. That is indeed a blessing. And in honour of that, look what I have here." The agent took two plums out of his pocket and gave one to Edgardo, which he started to eat.

"It's quite bitter," he said, pulling a face.

"In that case…" the agent pulled a paper package out of his pocket, "you'd better have something sweet."

He handed it to Edgardo. "Open it."

Edgardo peeled back the paper. Inside there was a white marzipan mouse with a little red nose.

Edgardo's eyes lit up. "Thank you," he said as they walked back to the carriage.

Back on the road to Rome, the agent of the Holy Office tried to put the chaplet and cross around Edgardo's neck again, but still Edgardo resisted. "I've got my *mezuzah*," he kept on repeating.

"You're not a Jew any more," the agent told him. He showed him the silver cross with the figure of Jesus hanging on a chain of polished stones. "Isn't it beautiful?"

Edgardo stared at it. Finally the agent managed to place it around Edgardo's neck.

"You really are a Catholic boy now, Edgardo. Kiss it; it will bring you good luck."

The agent grinned at him.

By the time they arrived at the Convent of San Pietro in Vincoli in Rome, twelve hours later, Edgardo had leaned back and kissed the cross.

"Here they will make a good Christian out of you, Edgardo," the agent said as he helped the boy out of the carriage.

The Rector Canon Sarra and several priests emerged from the building. They stood for a moment staring at him.

Edgardo noticed a statue of the Madonna over the gate. "Why does she weep?" he asked.

"Our Lady of Tears? She weeps because the Jews do not become converted and are not willing to acknowledge her Divine Son!" the Rector proclaimed.

"Then she must be weeping for my father and mother," Edgardo replied.

The Rector and priests exchanged smiles as they took Edgardo into the building.

Chapter 8

Rome, The Papal States. 1858

Edgardo sat with the Rector Canon Sarra in the dining room of the Convent as the boys left for their morning lessons. He looked out of the window across the square of San Pietro.

Brother Claudio, a surly young monk in his twenties, came striding over to them. "I have to take Edgardo for his lesson in catechism now, Canon."

"No. Edgardo will not be having lessons this morning. He is to finish his breakfast and then his baptismal ceremonies are to be completed in the Church..."

"But..."

"This has been decreed by the Holy Inquisition, by Cardinal Antonelli no less. He will return to class after the sacrament has been completed..."

Brother Claudio left with a surly smile glued to his upper lip. It did not sit well with him that Edgardo received so much attention and was given special treatment. It undermined his power over the boys.

"I hear you are doing well at your catechism, Edgardo," the Rector said to him. Edgardo said nothing. "Do you like it here at San Pietro in Chains?"

"Yes," Edgardo replied as he stared out of the window.

"Have you made lots of new friends here?"

"I don't know if I have any real friends yet."

"There are one or two other Jewish boys here at the convent who have converted to Christianity. Giuseppe and Samuele were both Jewish too."

"Yes, but their families wanted to convert to Christianity as well," Edgardo said sadly.

"Well, perhaps when your parents see what a good Catholic

59

you have become, they will convert too. I am very happy with your progress as a Christian scholar," said Canon Sarra as he poured himself a cup of coffee and filled up Edgardo's glass of milk. "As you know, today you are going to be given an extra baptism here in the Church of San Pietro." He held up a letter. "I have a message here from the Holy Father himself. You are to be baptised by Cardinal Ferretti who will be here shortly."

"But I have already been baptised!" Edgardo said as he ate his bowl of semolina with honey.

"You have indeed," the Rector said with a big smile. "But the baptism was carried out by your maid-servant; what was her name?"

"Anna Morisi."

"Yes Anna Morisi. I'm sure she did it very well, but these things have to be done properly. Do you remember your baptism?"

"No. It was six years ago; I was a baby!" Edgardo laughed. "I am sure she baptised me very well. She was very good at all sorts of things, especially card games like *scopa*. She always swept the board at *scopa*!

"In that case Cardinal Ferretti's job will be very easy indeed," said Canon Sarra.

"Who is Cardinal Ferretti?

"Well, he's a cardinal for a start..."

"What exactly is a cardinal?"

Canon Sarra took his time to answer. "He is a prince among the Holy men of the Roman Catholic Church, which is why he wears magnificent red robes and a red skull cap."

"When I was Jewish I also had a skullcap," said Edgardo.

"A Jewish skull cap is not the same as a cardinal's skull cap," Canon Sarra replied curtly, wanting to wipe out any kind of comparison. "And furthermore, this cardinal, Cardinal Ferretti, is the Pope's nephew, a very important man. He will complete your baptism and make sure that there is no question with regards to your being a Christian."

60

"And not a Jewboy?" Edgardo put his spoon down and looked up at Canon Sarra who raised his thick black eyebrows that joined over the top of his broad nose.

Canon Sarra wondered how many of the boys in the convent had been calling Edgardo a Jewboy. He himself had referred to Jewish boys as Jewboys, but nevertheless found himself asking Edgardo, "Who calls you a Jewboy?"

"People who are not Jewish have always called me a Jewboy," Edgardo said. "Brother Claudio calls me a Jewboy nearly every day. If I didn't know that my name was Edgardo, I might even think I was called Jewboy! Even Giuseppe, who used to be Jewish, has called me a Jewboy."

"I see," said Canon Sarra as he tapped the table.

"But when I am fully baptised, there will be no doubt that I'm a good Catholic boy, will there? People won't call me Jewboy any more, will they? And if my parents convert too I can go back home to live with them, can't I?"

"Would you like that?"

"Yes. I would rather live in Rome than in Bologna, but if my parents converted – maybe they would come and live in Rome too, and they could be near the Pope as well."

"And if they won't convert?" Canon Sarra poured Edgardo a glass of milk.

"Then damn them! They can go to Hell, and I won't ever want to see them again!" Edgardo screwed his face up as if it was a ball of anger.

The Rector again raised his monobrow. He reached into his pocket and took out a shiny red apple and a piece of *pan forte* wrapped in rice paper and placed it on Edgardo's plate. He was extremely pleased that for the most part Edgardo was settling well into his new life as a Roman Catholic and into his new life at the House of the Catechumens. "Then we can only hope that your parents have your wisdom and foresight," he said.

When Edgardo had finished his breakfast, Canon Sarra

took his hand and led him out of the dining room. "Let's find my maidservant – she is also called Anna; she can help you get dressed in your baptismal robes."

Later that morning a black and gold carriage pulled by four plumed horses arrived at the Church of Saint Peter in Chains. Cardinal Ferretti, the Pope's nephew, a jovial, middle-aged man, entered the church with an entourage of three priests. He was dressed all in red but was not wearing a skullcap; instead he wore a wide-brimmed red hat. He immediately sought out Edgardo, who was standing in a white robe by the font. The cardinal took an ornate metal box out of his pocket and gave it to the boy. There was little formality as he told Edgardo to open it. Inside was a medal.

"Edgardo, this is a gift from Pope Pius. It's a silver medal of the Blessed Virgin," the Pope's nephew told him. "He chose it for you himself; he can't wait to meet you!"

Edgardo smiled.

The baptism ceremony, performed with Canon Sarra and a couple of priests present, was over in minutes. Cardinal Ferretti and his entourage departed as quickly as they had arrived.

"Now your religious status can no longer be in doubt," Canon Sarra said to Edgardo as he took him back to the Convent.

Chapter 9

Two young Swiss Guards with scarlet-plumed silver helmets and blue and gold pantaloons escorted Edgardo through the Sistine Chapel, where the Great Choir was in rehearsal. He was intoxicated by the swelling tones of the organ; the sublime notes of the trained singers – eunuchs and young boys; by images of Jesus on the Cross; statues, sculptures and paintings; carved wooden angels and the gold embroidered robes of the priests.

They proceeded through the magnificently proportioned hallways of the Vatican, encountering cardinals and priests and councillors with their bright red hats.

They entered the Vatican Gardens, walking under tall palm trees and fine citron and orange trees growing under a canopy. They walked through formally laid out Italianate gardens with magnificent fountains; through oak groves where wild flowers grew; along rural pathways strewn with ancient fragments of marble; around rose-beds with fragrant blooms of red, orange and pink roses; and finally along a sunlit pathway to an imposing terrace situated in front of one of the huge towers of the Leonine Wall. There on an ornate garden seat, which afforded a wide view across the Valle dell' Inferno, was a distinguished and splendid-looking man. He had white hair and was around seventy years old. Pope Pius the Ninth, the Supreme Pontiff, sat in his white and gold regalia. He turned to greet his young guest.

Edgardo stopped a distance away from him and stood silently, all the while looking at him. One of the Swiss Guards, who had a big smile on his face, tried to gesture him to bow down to the Pope, but the Pontiff waved his hands, not wishing for any formalities.

The young guards retreated to the entrance of a small summer house.

Pius called out to them. "Thomas, Laurent, go and fetch Moretta." The Swiss Guards immediately ran across the lawn.

"Come, my child. Tell me your name," said the Pope.

"Edgardo... Edgardo Mortara," replied the boy.

"Do you know who I am?" asked the Pope.

"You are Pio Nono the Vicar of Christ!" declared Edgardo.

The Supreme Pontiff looked at him, angling his head as if to get a better sense of the boy, and then smiled. "Do you understand what has happened to you?"

"Yes, I have been baptised," answered Edgardo.

"By whom?" asked the Pope as if he was hearing the story for the first time.

"By Anna Morisi, our maid-servant," the boy replied. "And also by your nephew, Cardinal Ferretti. He gave me this present from you. Thank you, Sir." Edgardo showed him the silver medal of the Blessed Virgin round his neck.

"My pleasure," said the Pope.

A large droning bee circled Edgardo's head, which made him put his hands over his face.

"Don't worry, it's far more concerned with the flowers in these gardens than with either you or I," the Pope reassured him.

Edgardo lowered his hands and they both studied the bee as it dived into a bed of yellow roses.

Pope Pius continued with his questioning. "Are you angry with Anna Morisi?" he asked.

Edgardo smiled. "Angry? Why no. I bless her name."

"You bless her name? Why do you do that?"

"Because she has given me to Jesus."

"Jesus?" asked the Pope, as though he had never heard of him.

"Yes. Jesus Christ," Edgardo replied.

Pope Pius was enchanted. "And tell me, who is Jesus Christ?"

"Jesus Christ is the Saviour of men whom the Jews crucified," said Edgardo with great seriousness.

Pope Pius was a little taken aback. "How did you come to learn this?"

"At my new school. Canon Sarra and Brother Claudio have been teaching me about my new religion."

"Are not your family Jews?" Pius asked.

"Yes," replied Edgardo.

"Do you not want to turn Jew again?" asked Pius.

"No! The Jews have no altar, no Holy Virgin and no Pope! Now that I am baptised, the Holy Trinity is mine forever."

Pope Pius nodded. "Yes, these are sublime truths which even a child knows," he said. "You have already learned, Edgardo, that which our free-thinkers ignore."

The Supreme Pontiff got up, took Edgardo's hand, and started to walk around the garden with him.

"But what about the fourth commandment? Should you not honour thy father and thy mother?"

"Yes, but my father and mother will not become Christians!" Edgardo replied with frustration.

Pius persisted. "But the Lord thy God has commanded thee to honour them… 'Honour thy father and thy mother…'"

Edgardo interrupted him. "…that thy days may be long upon the land which the Lord thy God giveth thee!"

The Pope was impressed. Edgardo remained pensive for a moment and then spoke out. "You are the Pope. You know the commandments better than my father and my mother… better than me. I shall do whatever you say."

"Perhaps you should go back to Bologna," said the Pope.

"No, that is not possible, not until my parents become Christians," Edgardo insisted.

"And if they won't, you will have to stay here in Rome," the Pope told him.

Edgardo suddenly looked very sad. Pius studied him. He was a handsome child, aware and intelligent beyond his years, a Jewish child of six who now had a Christian soul. Wasn't it his responsibility to look after him and guide him back to his true Father in Heaven?

"So if your parents will not convert, you would be happy to stay here in Rome?" The Pope spoke delicately. "What would you do here?" he asked him.

"I would become a priest," Edgardo replied without hesitation.

"A priest?"

"Yes, then I could indeed convert my parents. They would have to convert. And after that I would devote myself to the conversion of all the Jews!"

Pope Pius pressed Edgardo to his heart and with his hand marked the sign of the cross on his forehead.

"I am a little concerned and worried that you will feel lonely here in Rome without your parents."

Edgardo did not reply.

"It might be a difficult time for you," said Pius taking his hands, "but I will help you all I can."

Edgardo looked up into Pius's deep blue eyes. "How will you help me?"

"I will be your adoptive father," Pius declared.

"You will be my new father?" asked Edgardo, and then smiled.

"Yes. You must not worry about anything. I will take care of you and make sure you have a good life. I will pay for your education myself, and will do all I can to secure a happy future for you, Edgardo."

Pio Nono returned to his seat, just as Thomas and Laurent came striding back over the lawn. They knelt down in front of the Pontiff and handed him something. Edgardo strained to see what it was. The Pope placed it in his lap and started stroking it. "This is Moretta," he said.

"It's a kitten!" cried Edgardo, watching her with wide eyes as she curled up and wrapped her tail around her body. "How old is she?"

She's four months old," said Pio Nono. "And she loves to be cuddled."

Edgardo knelt down in front of the Pope and stroked her gently. Moretta was purring ever so quietly.

"Why do you call her Moretta?" asked Edgardo.

"What does her face look like?" said the Pope.

"It's like a mask."

"Exactly – it's all black like a Moretta mask that a reveller wears at a carnival," said Pio Nono. "But look, her whiskers are white…"

"And her eyes are green; and her paws and legs look like she's wearing little white socks," said Edgardo as he laughed.

The Pope's Major-Domo entered the garden. He bowed before addressing the Pope. "Sovereign Pontiff, the carriage is ready to take you and Cardinal Antonelli to the afternoon fête for King Dom Pedro of Portugal," he announced, before placing a tiara on his head.

Pius handed Moretta to Laurent. "When you next come to visit me you can play with Moretta. You must help us to look after her."

That afternoon Edgardo rode home with Pius the Ninth and his Secretary of State, Cardinal Antonelli, in a golden coach drawn by purple-plumed black horses. The two Swiss Guards, Thomas and Laurent, helped him out of the carriage, just as a long line of young boys, chaperoned by a group of priests, arrived at the Convent gates on foot. They looked on in amazement as the Papal carriage set off again, with the Supreme Pontiff inside waving goodbye to their classmate Edgardo.

***

As Edgardo entered the Convent, he was unaware that news of his story was already spreading into a violent storm. It spread through Sardinia, a single corner of Italy where, under the liberalism of Charles Albert and his son Victor Emmanuel II, religious tolerance was clearly proclaimed. It spread to Turin where the official government paper printed in full a European appeal and called on every civilised country to join in demanding the boy's release from the Roman Convent. Then it spread throughout Europe and America.

News of the 'Mortara Affair' was agitating the minds of Jews and Christians alike.

Chapter 10

Signor Mortara and his wife's brother, Signor Padovani, were shown to the apartments of Cardinal Antonelli by a supercilious young chamberlain who couldn't wipe the grin off his face. He led them through the magnificent halls and corridors of the Vatican, passing a group of brightly costumed Swiss Guards, before they ascended a splendid marble staircase with a deep-pile floral carpet acting as a runner. A sea of tapestries, paintings and gilt-framed mirrors covered every metre of the vast walls; crystal chandeliers hung down from fresco-laden ceilings, throwing light and shadow on to statues of Greek and Roman gods and goddesses who wore hardly a stitch of clothing.

As they passed the first landing, the youth, who was dressed in black breeches and wore a hat with a feather on it, stated that this was the floor on which the Pope resided when he was not at his other official residence – the Palazzo del Quirinale, across the river. "But he is well and truly in residence here at the moment. He prefers the Vatican," he added, in such a smug tone that one might have believed this was for the Holy Father to be near the youth himself.

"If we had known that, we might have pressed harder for an audience with the Pope rather than with the Secretary of State," Padovani said to his brother-in-law.

"It is very difficult to be granted an audience with the Pope," the youth said as they climbed the stairs to the second floor. He checked their faces to see how they would react, but they barely acknowledged his remarks. He didn't appear to be much older than Signor Mortara's fourteen-year-old son Riccardo.

69

At the second level he took them down another long corridor strewn with Persian rugs and lined with endless alcoves and tall, leaded windows, each draped with red velvet curtains trimmed with gold braid and tassels. The chamberlain stopped at a large wooden door where two adolescent Swiss Guards stood, legs apart, in their red, blue and gold jackets and pantaloons, striped all the way down from their stiff white collars to their black leather shoes. Metal helmets topped with garlands of scarlet feathers obscured their boyish smiles, and Signor Mortara thought he saw one of them offer a playful wink to the youth as he knocked on the door. They lowered their steel-tipped wooden halberds; *the only signifiers that they were soldiers rather than Commedia dell'arte performers at a carnival*, Signor Mortara thought to himself.

"We are now at the apartment of the Secretary of State, the Prime Minister of the Papal States – the Prime Minister of His Holiness Pope Pius the Ninth," the youth announced to his Jewish visitors.

"Cardinal Antonelli lives above the Pope; clearly he is not the underdog around here," Signor Padovani whispered to his brother-in-law.

The door opened and another pair of Swiss Guards admitted them. The young chamberlain took them down yet more corridors before entering a palatial salon and announcing their names.

Cardinal Antonelli was sitting on a large sofa. He was in conversation with a striking woman in her thirties, who immediately got up. She was clutching a shawl, which did little to hide the revealing nature of the thin chemise gown she wore.

Cardinal Antonelli took her hands and gave her a lingering look and a long, almost whispered, conversation of goodbye. She took her leave.

Antonelli, a man in his early fifties, was extremely courteous: well-spoken, albeit in an affected manner. His accent still revealed vowel sounds and diphthongs that had their origins in the mountains around Sonnino in the Lazio region, more renowned for bandits and highwaymen than men of the Church. He was handsome and rugged; the mountain air had rendered him robust, with a wide forehead, heavy jaw, thick lips and a swarthy complexion, which appeared to make his long teeth whiter than they really were.

He stood up and greeted Signor Mortara and his brother-in-law cordially and shook their hands energetically, before leading them to an enormous table.

As he took his seat, the attendant and the youth sat his two guests opposite him, before retreating to the opposite side of the room where they stayed in attendance. After some expertly delivered small talk about the small Jewish community in Bologna, a subject with which he seemed to be familiar, Antonelli sensed that his visitors were very anxious to place some papers in front of him.

"What is it you wish to show me, Signor Mortara?" the Cardinal asked.

"The first document is a certificate, proving upon oath, that the servant woman, Anna Morisi, who said she had baptised my child, is... let us say, an extremely questionable character," Signor Mortara explained as his brother-in-law laid out the pile of papers. "After a period in our employment, she went to live in the service of one Madame Helena Bignati, who very shortly dismissed her having discovered that she was a thief and that her conduct was... how shall we say... shameless?"

Antonelli repeated the word: "Shameless?"

"I think it's fair to say that Anna Morisi slept with half the 'Whitecoats' who were stationed in Bologna. Even at the age of fourteen!"

"And yet, Signor Mortara, you were happy to take the girl back into your service for many years," Antonelli replied as he smiled at him.

"Indeed we were forgiving; we treated her like a daughter,"

Signor Mortara pointed out.

Antonelli brushed aside Signor Mortara's words, making light of them, and speaking softly asked, "Do you have daughters?"

Signor Mortara nodded.

"I'm sure you would not let your daughters sleep with Austrian officers," said Antonelli. He did not wait for a reply; he was shrewd. He knew when to pounce and when to listen attentively – a true diplomat. He also knew how to quash all his emotional responses. "It is, I accept, unfortunate for you that Roman civil law adheres to the regulations laid down by the Catholic faith and by our Holy Fathers. Pope Gregory the Thirteenth, as I'm sure you know, long since issued an edict forbidding Hebrews to employ Christian domestics."

Signor Padovani was irritated by Antonelli's moralising tone. Everyone in the Italian Peninsula knew that he had been involved in a string of amorous intrigues, and some even said he kept a mistress. He intervened in support of his brother-in-law. "With due respect, Cardinal, Pope Gregory issued his edicts nearly four hundred years ago. This is 1858!"

"But however old his edict is, his edict still stands! Alas, if Signor Mortara had upheld this law, baptism would not have taken place." For Antonelli, Pope Gregory's edict was a fine example of the need to safeguard Christians from the non-believing influence of the Jews; even so, he nodded with concern.

Signor Padovani produced another document as he made a further appeal. "This second document is a medical affidavit, proving that the child had not been seriously ill at the time when the woman claimed she had baptised him. Professor Daveri and Dr Saragoni, two of the leading doctors in Bologna, have signed it."

Signor Mortara could hardly contain himself. "This was an illicit baptism; Edgardo should not have been taken away from us!"

Cardinal Antonelli again nodded with concern, but he left the document on the table. "I do not wish to encumber you with the ordinances of the Catholic Church, Signor Mortara," he said, "but Pope Benedict the Fourteenth a century ago laid down that even in cases where baptism has been illicitly administered to a Hebrew infant, the infant is to be separated from its relations and educated in the Christian faith."

Again Padovani jumped in. "With due respect your Eminence, Pope Benedict the Fourteenth expressly forbids the baptising of Jews against their will, except when they are in imminent danger of death. And he says that when a baptism is secretly administered, the bishop must be informed of the fact. This was not done at the time. In view of this I must ask you to allow us a fair trial and to confront Anna Morisi. Let us hear her testimony."

Antonelli studied the man with some suspicion. "I see you have been doing your homework, Signor Padovani. Are you a lawyer?"

"I am a banker," Padovani replied.

"A banker! I believe you have missed your true vocation in life."

Padovani ignored the remark. He had no wish to hear Antonelli talking about vocation. Antonelli's vocation, it seemed, was to live in wealth and abundance, enjoying every worldly pleasure that came his way. He had done well, he thought, entering the seminary as a young man and almost immediately giving up on the idea of becoming a priest. He had escaped the sacrament of ordination; having to say Mass; having to confess penitents. He had, however, gained something much more valuable: the friendship of Pope Gregory XVI, which had led to his meteoric rise in becoming a prelate, a magistrate, a prefect, and ultimately the Secretary of State under Pius IX, with unlimited power, an enormous fortune, assets to rival Prince Torlonia's, the pick of Rome's most handsome women and, in addition, a red cardinal's hat.

A world away from the mountain bandits of Sonnino, Signor Padovani thought to himself before repeating his request. "Anna Morisi should present her evidence in a fair trial."

"I am very sorry; that is not within my jurisdiction," Antonelli answered, before turning to Signor Mortara. "I can, however, confirm that it was indeed the opinion of the maidservant, Signorina Morisi, that the boy was on the point of death."

Padovani interrupted him. "Cardinal, I can assure you that that was not the case. His condition was a slight worm fever, very common among children."

"You yourself say Professor Daveri and Dr Saragoni, two of Bologna's most prominent doctors, signed a medical affidavit to say that the child had not been seriously ill at the time. I ask you, would you normally have the top physicians in a city like Bologna attend a child with a slight illness, day after day, night after night?"

Signor Mortara's cheeks were reddening. "He was only a baby, about a year old. I admit we were worried, yes. But it turned out he was not as ill as we first thought and as we all know, in the end he made a rapid recovery."

"I'm wondering," said Antonelli, as he handed the documents back to Padovani, "how much of this is fact and how much mythology. The mind can play tricks over five or six years. Clearly you feared for the boy's life. Signorina Morisi, too, is quite clear that the child had a serious condition – neuritis I believe – and as I have said, it was her opinion that the boy was on the point of death when she baptised him into the Catholic fold."

"And clearly you accept her actions?" Padovani challenged him.

"Her actions, Signor Padovani, suggest that she was a devout and pious young Christian girl, who only had the child's best interests in mind."

"But you must accept that her actions cannot be considered

legally binding,"

"I accept nothing of the kind." Antonelli looked at his stopwatch. "I have to tell you that the Pope accepts the baptism of your son Edgardo as valid. I'm afraid it's a hopeless case for you to change his view at this stage. I think you would agree, Signor Padovani, that it would be unorthodox for a man of your religion to presume to try and teach the Church, and indeed the Pope, how the dogma of baptism is to be understood. You must accept that the baptism is valid in the eyes of canon law." The Cardinal paused and began to fondle a gold signet ring on his little finger before continuing. "Consequently the child must be educated in Christianity, the indelible and precious character of which it already bears in its soul."

Signor Padovani became incensed. "The child has a name! Edgardo! How can the Holy Office take the word of a servant girl of low morals over that of the leading physicians of Bologna, let alone that of the parents? Where is her evidence? There is none! It would seem the Holy Office is above the Law! There has been no legal examination, nor has any witness been called or confronted! So immoral was this girl that in any other country the removal of a coin would not have been judged on her evidence, let alone the abduction of a child! Yet the Holy Office hangs on her every word!" Padovani continued with unabated passion. "She has spoken on the subject after five years of absolute silence! She was fourteen at the time of the baptism! She was young and ignorant! How can you even be certain that her recollection of fulfilling with zealous precision all the requirements of something as sacred as baptism to be accurate? How *can* you?"

The Cardinal remained silent.

"And for all this my child has been abducted," Signor Mortara groaned.

The Cardinal corrected him. "Not abducted, Signor Mortara, merely separated from you," he said as he got up from his seat.

"Separated! Separated for how long?" Padovani also got up. Doesn't your Church see that there is nothing on earth that belongs more legitimately to a father and mother than their child? I cannot tell you how much injury this is doing to my sister, Edgardo's mother."

"I assure you the injury is not as great as that which would have been done to a dying child if the sacrament which opens Heaven were withheld," Antonelli said, turning his back on Padovani. He took Signor Mortara's hand. "It has been my pleasure."

"Cardinal, will you at least allow us to see our child?" begged Signor Mortara.

"I'm sure that will be possible," replied Antonelli after a long silence.

He would not say any more on the subject. The young chamberlain stepped forward and, with a haughty smile, showed the two men out.

Chapter 11

The Bishop of Liège smiled at Raoul as he led him into his oak-panelled salon that looked out on to a walled garden with manicured hedges and lavender bushes and a small fountain at its centre. He offered Raoul a seat in a plush settee. The Bishop sat down on a wooden, throne-like chair that had biblical scenes painted on its back. It seemed rather incongruous with the soft, powder-blue furnishings in the rest of the room.

A maid came in with a tray on which was a coffee pot and various items of Delft crockery and two slices of apple cake on an ornate cake plate. She set the tray down on a marquetry coffee table.

"Marguerite makes very good apple cake. The apples are home grown from the orchard at the back of the house," said Monsignor Kerkhofs as the maid handed Raoul a slice of the cake.

Raoul immediately picked it up with his fingers, ignoring the cake fork and took a big bite. "Delicious," he said as he smiled at Marguerite.

"How is Father Mortara?" asked the Bishop.

"He is fragile, but still going strong for his age. As stubborn as ever!"

The maid poured them both a cup of coffee. She was young, with long red hair. Raoul smiled at her again and thanked her.

"He's been through so much," said the Bishop. "We can only imagine what he must have experienced as a child." He couldn't help noticing that Raoul was still gazing at his maid.

"You know, of course, that he was born Jewish?"

"Yes," said Raoul as the maid left the room.

"And you know that he was separated from his family as a

youngster?"

Raoul nodded as he spoke, some pureed apple hanging off the edge of his lower lip. "Yes, I know. His nursemaid sprinkled some water over his head when he was a baby and made a Christian out of him, and he was taken kicking and screaming off to Rome." He completely changed the mood in the room with his sarcasm.

Monsignor Kerkhofs laughed at the boy's irreverence; he sensed disillusionment and a rebellious streak in him, and he liked the boy for that. "I suppose it does seem a little ridiculous to us now. However it was a fateful act that led him to the Church, led him to Rome and the Vatican. They used to call him the Pope's Son, you know."

Raoul leaned forward in his armchair. "Forcing a Jewish child to be a Christian doesn't seem right to me. Why would the Church inflict that on him?"

"You don't agree with conversion to Christianity?"

"Of course I agree, as long as both parties have a free hand in their decision, but otherwise... I don't agree, no. Actually, I can't help feeling it was all tied up with anti-Semitism."

"Really?" The Bishop suddenly became serious.

Raoul's words to the Bishop were brave. Being parted from Delphine had made him angry. In the past he would have sparred and argued with her about anything: whether the Belgians should have held on to the Belgian Congo after stripping Leopold II of his power, the shortest route to walk into Liège from Bouhay, how much icing sugar should be sprinkled on waffles, or whether waffles were better in Brussels or Liège. "I think so... to take a child away from its family with no regard for its religion... At the very least it is incredibly disrespectful, but I can't help feeling there must have been veiled anti-Semitism in the Vatican, don't you think?" Raoul didn't wait for an answer. "I don't understand why there is so much hatred of the Jews – in Germany and here in Belgium. Why does everyone hate the Jews? Why does Hitler want to exterminate them? Why does the Rexist party in this country incite such hatred against these people?"

Monsignor Kerkhofs clutched the gold cross around his neck as he studied Raoul. He was impressed by the boy's passion, his honesty, and fiery spirit. After a while he spoke quietly. "For centuries the Jews have proved to be a suitable scapegoat – vilified since the Middle Ages." The Bishop reflected. "Why? They were seen as Christ-killers, and were associated with money and lending. The truth is, of course, that in the Middle Ages Christians were banned by the Church from handling money or lending it, and the Jews were roped in to do their dirty work for them. It is unfortunate that the association of Jews and money has stuck. As for the Vatican: was this anti-Semitism at work or was it business as usual? Father Mortara as a child had been baptised and the Pope thought it was his duty to send him to heaven."

Monsignor Kerkhofs paused and looked out of the window. The maid came back and topped up their cups.

"The sad thing is that we are all children of God. Isn't that so, Marguerite?" He smiled at the maid and her face lit up with a large beam.

When she left the room the Bishop spoke again. "Take that girl."

"Marguerite?"

"Yes, Marguerite. What is your impression of her?"

"She seems to be a very nice girl; she has a warm smile… and lovely, long red locks. I cannot say more about her."

"Do you think she is a Christian or a Jew?"

"I imagine she is a Christian as she works here for you."

Marguerite entered the room again. She smiled at Raoul as she took away the dirty plates. Raoul watched her. "But on the other hand she could well be Jewish," he said when she had left the room.

The Bishop was intrigued. "Why do you say that? Are you familiar with any Jewish people?"

"No," said Raoul. "But I did notice the way she looked down when you said Father Mortara was born a Jew."

"Goodness, you did study her well!" said the Bishop. "In confidence, I will tell you then that Marguerite is Jewish. I have known her since she was a little girl and I fear that if the Nazis invade Belgium, or if the Rexists take over, terrible things will happen to her and her family. I am confident that if she works for me no one will suspect she is a Jew. As for the rest of her family, if things become more sinister I will help them to hide. I know people who will help to conceal them and other Jewish families, should this become necessary. We have to stand up to the evil that is in the world. As a Christian and, dare I say it, a devout Christian, I believe it is my duty to do all I can to help people of other faiths."

"Monsignor Kerkhofs, should it come to that, I would be more than happy to assist you."

"I am sure you will be busy with your novitiate, but, yes, any help would be warmly received. We must not let a load of evil megalomaniacs have the Belgian people living in fear and taking us back to the Middle Ages."

Marguerite entered the room and took the cake stand away. As she left she gave Raoul another smile.

Monsignor Kerkhofs stood up and Raoul stood with him. The Bishop took his hand. "I have been thinking about what you said at the confessional when we first met. You told me that you felt you had deprived your parents of the pleasure of a family. Just remember: the Church and being a monk is not for everybody. If you feel that your calling is to be a family man rather than a monk, you must follow your heart in taking the right path. I will help you in any way I can."

The Bishop saw Raoul to the door. "Please come and visit me again soon. Perhaps after Christmas… By the way if you want to know more about Father Mortara, to get a sense of how remarkable his story was you should pop in to the Librairie Pax in Place Cockerill. There was a book in the

English section at the back. I sat and read it there one rainy afternoon – the diaries of an English philanthropist who went to Rome in 1859 to try and rescue the boy, Edgardo as he was called then - after he had been taken to Rome." The Bishop stopped to think. "Sir Moses Montefiore was the gentleman's name. I believe he was a relation of Georges Montefiore-Levi who founded the Institut Montefiore here in Liège. I'm sure the book must still be there. Can you read English?"

Raoul nodded. "A little."

"See if you can find it. I'm sure it will be of interest to you."

Chapter 12

Rome, The Papal States. 1858

"It's nearly a month now, and not a single word from the Vatican!" Signor Mortara was angry as they trudged up the steep hill that led from the Coliseum to the Piazza of San Pietro. He cursed the hot sun that was making him sweat.

Madame Mortara handed him a lace handkerchief to wipe his forehead.

He began to shout. "Your relations can get an audience with the Austrian ambassador at the court of Rome, and with the French ambassador who told them that under instructions from Paris he had protested to the Cardinal Prime Minister Antonelli. But all in vain! We have heard nothing back and they won't let us see Edgardo. How are we supposed to function? We have hardly slept for a month now!"

They reached the Church of San Pietro in Vincoli and took the lane from the main square that led to the convent. Signor Mortara knocked loudly on a large wooden door with a brass door knocker. A young monk opened the door.

"We are Edgardo's parents," said Madame Mortara. "We must see him."

"It is not possible," the monk replied.

Madame Mortara grabbed hold of his arm. "Please, please, we beg of you."

"The truth is he is not here."

"We know he is living here." Signor Mortara said.

"Yes... but he has gone with the Rector, Canon Sarra, and some of the brothers to the country for *villegiatura*."

"What is that?" Signor Mortara asked.

"It is the passing of a few weeks in the country; some of the boys, including Edgardo, have gone with them." The young monk smiled. "He will enjoy it there. As well as prayer and religious study, the boys will get to play and see something of the flora and fauna outside Rome. I went when I was a boy; it was the best few weeks of my life."

Signor Mortara was not interested. "Whereabouts in the country have they gone?"

The monk clearly did not want to answer.

"Where?"

"I can't say...."

Signor Mortara grabbed him by the collar.

"You mean you won't say?"

"You are hurting me," the young monk said.

Signor Mortara threw him back against the door.

"I can't help you," said the young monk as he slipped back in to the convent and closed the door.

Signor Mortara and his wife went to sit on the stone wall opposite the convent. His wife looked down at the ground. A scorching sun made the air dry and the yellow dust beneath her feet, hot. She could feel the heat though the leather of her boots.

She was dazed; there was no fight left in her.

Signor Mortara took her hand.

"Death would be better than this," she whispered.

After about half an hour, a rotund laundry woman with a bright red face came out of the convent, carrying a basket of laundry. She smiled at them.

Signor Mortara seized his opportunity.

"Do you need help with that?" he asked.

"I'm fine; it only weighs half what it normally does. Most of the priests and the boys are away in the country."

"It must be quiet for you. Whereabouts do they go?"

"Alatri, up in the hills outside Rome. There's a villa there that belongs to the convent. It's a good day's journey they tell me."

Signor Mortara helped his wife up from the wall. Two

hours later they were on the road to Alatri, in a broken-down carriage they'd hired from a dubious stable owner they managed to find in the Via di San Giovanni in Laterano. It was all they could afford to hire. The journey was slow and exhausting. The horses looked as though they were on their last legs, and had to be fed and watered at every village they passed through. After a day and night they reached the town of Alatri. They dismounted at the inn and immediately discovered the location of the villa belonging to the Roman convent.

An old peasant woman let them into the villa, telling them that the Rector and his party were at Vespers. She pointed down the road to a church. Signor Mortara asked the woman to look after his wife for a while. "You look exhausted, dear," said the peasant as she took Madame Mortara next door to the priest's house for some food. Signor Mortara went on to the church. The large wooden door was closed. Inside he could hear singing. He pushed it half open.

Edgardo was in the midst of several priests and a small congregation. Signor Mortara stood for a while looking at him. The boy was dressed in a little black cassock, a square cap and shoes with buckles. He was singing. Signor Mortara had hoped to see despair and unhappiness on his son's face, but he saw none, and was dismayed to see a happy child. He was a good singer: a boy soprano with a high treble voice. He was singing with enthusiasm, with gusto and charm. It saddened Signor Mortara to see him like that, embracing his new life with no regard for the past. He desperately wanted to call out to Edgardo, but restrained himself for fear of causing a scene and offending the worshippers. He waited outside the church. Presently the congregation, consisting mainly of women, dispersed and Signor Mortara approached the vestry. The door was open. Edgardo was standing in the middle of a group of priests. Their eyes met and Signor Mortara stepped forward.

"Papa!" his son cried out.

The door was slammed in his face.

Signor Mortara banged on the door with his fists.

"Edgardo! Edgardo! Bring me Edgardo!" He tried to open the door, but it was locked. He could hear the priests inside talking in low tones.

For half an hour he waited, but they remained inside. He continued to bang on the door, shouting and pleading but there was no response.

He walked away from the church. There was a stone seat opposite. For another half an hour he sat there with his head in his hands.

The church door suddenly opened. The Rector and a young priest emerged from the Vestry, with Edgardo between them.

Seeing Signor Mortara they charged off in the opposite direction, awkward in their robes, dragging Edgardo along between them as they made for the open fields. Signor Mortara ran after them. The Rector looked back angrily before they made a bolt for a nearby pine forest. Signor Mortara tried to keep pace with them. He ran and ran, stumbling over the roots of oak and juniper trees, and as the forest paths gave way to overgrown tangled trails he ripped his trousers and scratched his legs on the thorns. He stopped in a glade. Night was approaching and he knew he had lost them. He threw himself on the ground under a mulberry tree, his white shirt stained red like blood from the squashed berries on the forest floor.

Suddenly the young priest appeared and helped Signor Mortara to his feet.

"I am Brother Giovanni. Canon Sarra, the Rector, asks that you to go back to the villa where he will follow with Edgardo," he said.

Signor Mortara grabbed him by the arm. "I want to see him now. Tell him to come out of his hidey hole in the woods right now..."

"Please, Sir, I cannot do any more. I am sure they are no longer in the forest; they are most probably heading back to the village."

Signor Mortara closed his eyes as he pushed the young priest away. He thrust himself against the mulberry tree and began to bang his head against the trunk repeatedly, begging for God's mercy before looking up at the forest canopy and crying out loudly in Hebrew.

"Signor Mortara, please let me take you back," shouted the young priest, not knowing if the man was cursing or praying. "They say there are brown bears and wolves in the forests here."

"And do you think I care if I am mauled by a wolf or a bear?" Signor Mortara shouted. "Do you think I care if I die in this forest?" He looked at the young man. "You have chosen to be a priest. That is your choice. You will never know what it is to be a parent and have a child torn away from you." The priest looked genuinely sad for him. Signor Mortara knew that what had happened was not the priest's fault, and for that he started sobbing.

Brother Giovanni led him back to the village and to the priest's house, where Madame Mortara was waiting. No Rector came. No Edgardo. Looking out of the window, they could make out military uniforms – they saw Carabinieri walking up and down in the darkness. They appeared to be on guard. Signor and Madame Mortara were alarmed. They decided to walk back to the inn. The Carabinieri followed them.

"What is it you want?" Signor Mortara asked them, but they failed to reply. They continued to follow the couple.

Arriving at their inn, Signor and Madame Mortara went upstairs to their room. No sooner had they sat down on the bed than there was a loud knock on the door. They opened it to find a Police Inspector and a gendarme standing there. The Inspector addressed them. "Signor Mortara, Madame Mortara, I am the Chief of Police in this town. Your arrival here is a matter of grave concern."

"And is the kidnapping of my son also of grave concern?"

"I have no knowledge of your son being kidnapped."

"But you *know* my son's been kidnapped!"

"I don't know that, no."

"Can you imagine what this is doing to my poor wife?"

The Police Chief looked across at Madame Mortara who was sobbing on the bed.

"The Governor of Alatri wishes to see you. I must ask you to follow us," the Chief of Police said in a matter-of-fact voice.

Signor Mortara's heart sank. He took his wife's hand, which felt lifeless. They followed the police, now joined by several Carabinieri, across the main piazza of Alatri. To their surprise the whole square was filled with a mob of people, who were clearly agitated and excited. A number of priests were among them. They entered the Governor's palace on the far side of the piazza and climbed the stairs to his apartment.

"What brings you to Alatri?" demanded the Governor.

"I think you know, Sir, as well as I do," Signor Mortara replied.

"Well, I know you have come to see your son," said the Governor, "and I also know that you have had no leave from the Holy Father to do so."

"Sir, that is not true," replied Signor Mortara. "I have the permission of the Holy Father's Cardinal Secretary of State to see my child."

"According to the Rector of the Convent, that is not the truth," replied the Governor.

"Then the Rector lies," shouted Signor Mortara. "Allow me to speak to him."

"Signor Mortara, I'm afraid that no more meetings in Alatri will be possible." The Governor was solemn. "The Bishop of Alatri is adamant that you must leave the town immediately." The Governor walked over to the large window looking out on to the square. "Look out there. Look! There is already civil unrest in Alatri because of your arrival here. You will have to comply with the Bishop of Alatri's request."

"We want to see our son. Surely on the grounds of human

decency and compassion you will be able to help us?"

The Governor shook his head. "I cannot do any more. It is best for your son that you leave the town." He nodded to an assistant who showed them out of the apartment and down into the square, which was now packed with a disorderly mob. People stared at them, muttering and whispering among themselves. Signor and Madame Mortara heard the word "Jew" several times. They pushed through the crowd; people were now jostling them and throwing insults at them. They heard: "Go piss in your bed!" "Fuck off Jews and let the palsy get you!" The insults became more threatening and profanities started invoking the body of the Lord. One crazed and toothless hag put her face up to Madame Mortara's and started shouting "Christ's cunt!" over and over again at her, until a laughing Carabiniere told her to get her facts right and understand that they were "filthy Jews."

Terrified, the Mortaras ran back to the inn. A well-dressed young man sidled up to them and spoke softly but urgently. "Leave this place as soon as you can," he said. "The priests have told the people that you have come to murder your son because he is a Christian, which is why they are so wild and excited. Your lives are in danger."

Signor and Madame Mortara thanked him and ran up to their room to collect their bags. Signor Mortara handed the innkeeper all the spare coinage he had while asking him to help them harness their poor tired horses to the hired carriage. Within minutes they were back on the road to Rome.

Chapter 13

The Vatican, The Papal States. 1858

"Our laws do not allow for a Jewish family to raise a Catholic child," Cardinal Antonelli explained to Signor and Madame Mortara as he sat down at his large table. The supercilious youth was once again in attendance. Cardinal Antonelli continued, "I also understand that, as a Catholic, Edgardo feels he can no longer remain in your household. He has a strong wish to receive a Catholic education."

Signor Mortara was incensed. "The boy is six years old!"

"He is by all accounts an intelligent child who understands his predicament very well. If you could only see things through his eyes." The Cardinal sneaked a look at his jewelled pocket watch.

"If we could only see him, perhaps we might try. When last we met, I asked to see our child. You said you were sure that would be possible, but we have been obstructed from doing so at every turn."

Madame Mortara intervened. "Cardinal, I beg you, by all that is good in the Catholic faith, please allow a desperate mother to see her young child and to embrace him. Please!" Antonelli looked at her gravely. She knelt down on the ground before him and grasped his hand. She was weeping uncontrollably. "Please. Please, Father. I beg you…"

Cardinal Antonelli recoiled from her. At the far end of the room there was a knock at the door and an elegant lady walked in. It was the same lady who had been present a month earlier when Signor Mortara had first visited the Cardinal with his brother-in-law.

"Giacomo…"

Antonelli looked over to her and slowly shook his head.

She retreated, and the young chamberlain closed the door behind her.

Antonelli again looked at his watch. "As it happens, I have already yielded to your request in so far as to order Canon Sarra, the Rector, to return to the city with the child," he said. "I grant you permission to see him. I must, however, add that this is on condition that you do not hold any conversation with him that might interfere with his conversion."

It was enough. Madame Mortara grasped his hand and kissed it.

"Thank you your Eminence; thank you!"

***

Signor and Madame Mortara counted the hours and the days, and made sure they were at Saint Peter in Chains from dawn till dusk. They sat on the stone wall opposite the main door, watching for every cart or carriage that stopped outside the convent. Some delivered fruit and vegetables, others chairs or brooms, but none contained the cargo they were waiting for: Edgardo.

Finally, after three days, the Rector's carriage arrived home. Signor and Madame Mortara leapt up off the wall and rushed over to greet Edgardo. Several priests bustled the boy into the convent. The Mortaras pushed their way in behind them.

"Now perhaps you will allow us to see our child," Signor Mortara said to the Rector who began to turn pale. Canon Sarra pushed Edgardo up the stairs.

"Cardinal Antonelli has decreed that we are to see our child!" shouted Signor Mortara.

They followed Edgardo up the stairs. He turned round. His mother ran up to him and embraced him, weeping and sobbing, and kissing him over and over again.

"Mama! You haven't forgotten me!"

"Of course I haven't forgotten you! I could never forget you

Edgardo."

She knelt on the floor in front of him.

"Look at you in your smock; they have dressed you up like a little priest," she said.

Edgardo smiled at her and then at his father. "Will you be taking me home, Papa?"

His father knelt down. "Edgardo, listen to me. I am hoping to obtain permission from the Pope himself to take you back to Bologna," he said as he took his hand.

"I don't mind sleeping in the carriage, even though it's a long way. It takes three days and three nights to get home. But they won't let me come unless you and Mama convert to Christianity, Papa."

"Edgardo, we are not Catholics! We are Jews."

"But if you don't stop being Jews they won't let me come home, Papa. You must pray to Jesus."

"Edgardo, we are Jews. You don't just stop being a Jew. You have not forgotten to say the Shema, have you?

Edgardo looked down to the ground. Signor Mortara took his hand.

"Say it with me now, Edgardo. *Shema Yisrael*. Hear, O Israel..."

Edgardo stood silent.

"Please, Edgardo. *Shema Yisrael*. Say it. Say it now. *Shema Yisrael*. Hear, O Israel. Say it, Edgardo." Signor Mortara started to shake him. "The Lord our God, *Adonai Eloheinu*... say it, Edgardo!"

"*Adonai Eloheinu*," Edgardo repeated.

"*Adonai echad*. The Lord is One!"

Edgardo looked up at the Rector and the priests, and then stopped.

Signor Mortara crouched down. "Why have you stopped, Edgardo?"

He looked into his father's eyes with a solemnness, which belied his six years. "But the Lord our God is the Father, the

91

Son and the Holy Ghost," he replied.

"The Lord is One, Edgardo!" Signor Mortara repeated. "Your God is a Jewish God."

The Rector grabbed hold of Edgardo, who began to cry as he was pulled up the stairs. "I think that is enough for today." He disappeared into a room with Edgardo, closing the door behind him. Several priests stayed outside to block off the entrance.

Closely followed by his wife, Signor Mortara rushed up the stairs, pushed his way through the priests, and angrily burst into the room. "We have been given permission by the Cardinal Secretary of State to see our son!"

"You have been told that you can see your son, Signor, only on condition that you do not attempt to disturb his growing convictions," the Rector pointed out. "Your son is a Catholic now. If any further meetings are to be allowed, I must ask that you do not indoctrinate him with any more Hebrew incantations."

"*Indoctrinate* him? My son is a Jew. He was born a Jew and he will die a Jew!"

"Our Lord Jesus Christ secured a place in Heaven by relinquishing his Jewish past, and I would urge you to allow your son to do the same," declared the Rector. "You and your wife might also think about conversion to secure your own places in Heaven."

Signor Mortara was incensed. "If your Lord Jesus Christ relinquished his Judaism, why was he celebrating the Passover the night before he was crucified? Why?"

Canon Sarra looked at him with disdain, a sardonic smirk moulded on to his lips. Signor Mortara continued with his attack. "Jews aren't allowed in Heaven? Is that it? Jews go to Hell and Christians go to Heaven. Is this the rubbish you are teaching my son?"

"Signor Mortara, I'm afraid that your attitude will render it impossible for me to allow any further meetings with your son," the Rector threatened, his lower lip twitching.

Madame Mortara broke down. "No, Sir, please. My husband does not mean what he is saying." She held Edgardo to her as she wept. "We will not talk of our Jewish heritage or our Jewish faith." She looked imploringly at her husband and then spoke with resignation. "We are not Jews in front of our son, Momolo."

The Rector then reluctantly agreed to a further meeting.

***

The next day around a dozen priests were present to watch every act and listen to every word that the Mortara's said. Instead of allowing them to converse with Edgardo, the Rector and the priests argued with them, prayed for their conversion and preached sermons at them. The Rector picked up his Bible and read from John, Chapter 19, verse 14 "...*and he saith unto the Jews. Behold your King. But they cried out. Away with him, away with him, crucify him. Pilate saith unto them, Shall I crucify your King?*"

Signor Mortara could stand it no longer. "We do not come to hear your preaching, but to see our child!" He grabbed hold of his son. "Edgardo, say after me: *Shema Yisrael!* Hear, O Israel! The Lord our God..."

The Rector and the priests threw themselves on to their knees and began reciting prayers to the Madonna. Edgardo stood frozen on the spot.

"Hail Mary," the Rector cried out.

"Hail Mary! Hail Mary!" chanted the priests. *"Ave Maria, gratis plena, Dominus Tecum..."*

"Holy Mary, Mother of God. Pray for us sinners, now and at the hour of our death. Amen."

In a moment of pure anger Signor Mortara started shouting over them.

"Hear O Israel... *Shema Yisrael, Adonai Eloheinu, Adonai*

echad!"

Signor Mortara saw that Edgardo was wearing the medal of the Virgin Mary around his neck, which was hanging over his smock. He took hold of it, a look of disgust on his face.

"You make him wear *this*?" he shouted at the Rector.

He snatched the medal from Edgardo's chest, pulled it roughly over his head and threw it violently on to the floor.

Edgardo began to cry. Several priests pulled him away from his father while others started to drag Signor Mortara and his wife down the stairs.

Signor Mortara shouted back to Edgardo. "You are a Jew my son, and it is your duty to remain one, always, until you die! You know the Ten Commandments, Edgardo. Tell these men the fourth commandment!"

Edgardo was too upset to speak.

"Honour thy father and thy mother, Edgardo!" Signor Mortara was becoming red-faced and breathless. "These priests here know that as well as I do, Edgardo. Christians as well as Jews are supposed to abide by the Old Testament, and the Ten Commandments clearly state that. How can you honour your father and your mother if we are not allowed to speak to you or educate you? How can we do that if we can't live with you and protect you?"

Madame Mortara was sobbing inconsolably. Edgardo broke away from the priests and ran into her arms. The Rector came running down the stairs.

"It is time for your parents to leave," he said. He watched Edgardo sobbing his heart out, the boy's mother doing the same, his father bent double in a fit of anger on the stairs, and realised these meetings were hopeless.

"Can't I go home with them?" Edgardo asked him, gulping through his tears.

The Rector shook his head.

"I bid you goodbye," Canon Sarra said to the Mortaras, and he left them and went back to his study.

Several priests took hold of Edgardo. He tried to pull himself away from them, but they dragged him, kicking and screaming, up the stairs.

Chapter 14

Bouhay, Liège, Belgium. 1939

Father Mortara stared at a young monk who was chopping wood with a large axe by one of the outhouses. He gripped the arm of the wooden bench, his arthritic knuckles making his hand look like a bird's foot.

"That was it," he said to Raoul as they sat in the gardens of Notre Dame de Lourdes. "The door slowly closed and my parents walked away. I was crying my eyes out, but as they looked back I still managed to wave through one of the windows. After that, the Rector obtained a formal order refusing admission to any Jew into the convent. No further meetings were allowed." Father Mortara sounded calm and philosophical. "I did not see my parents again for twelve years."

Raoul said nothing; he was stunned. He buried his head in his hands and sighed. He tried to make sense of a family being separated like this in the name of religion – in the name of God.

Brother Pius felt his shock. "It was God's will," he said.

'God's will?' Raoul could not help thinking that the whole thing was ridiculous, but he was too upset to speak.

They sat in silence until the Prior rang the bell for Vespers.

"It's getting chilly. We'd better get you inside," said Raoul. "I think it's going to snow."

They got up.

"Weren't you angry?" Raoul asked as they walked slowly across the gardens and then through the cloister. The evening service had started and the Canons could be heard singing inside the Priory church. "According to the fourth commandment you must obey your father and mother."

"There are three other commandments that refer to God,"

said Father Mortara. You must know that when the Pope removed me from my family, I truly believed that his actions were prompted by God's loving interest in me."

"Really?"

"Yes, I adopted the Christian faith of my own free will. I went to Rome willingly..."

"Willingly? But you were six years old!" shouted Raoul, annoyed that having shared all the traumas and tears of being separated from his parents, Father Mortara was now putting a positive slant on the events and seemingly believing what he said.

"I was, but even at the age of six I felt that my faith came to me before I was separated from my parents. Once I knew that I was a Catholic, I felt... how shall I say? An explosion of Christian sentiment," said the old man. "A strange impulse came over me and I felt I could not return to them, not even if I was allowed to. I had a great desire to receive a Catholic education and prayed that my parents would convert. I wrote to them, but they would not listen to my entreaties." He paused. "But in spite of that, I did love them."

Raoul sensed an aloofness and an emptiness in Father Mortara's words that overshadowed a denial of something deeper and he immediately felt pity for him. The Pope had taken him away from his parents and he had cut himself off emotionally from them. When Father Mortara spoke like this, the novice once again found him cold and detached, weak and self-serving, and he had no doubt that this was the result of a lifetime of suffering. He tried to imagine what the separation had done to him as a child, what a strange reality he must have been living in. When the young boy arrived at his convent and when he was told that a statue of the Madonna was weeping because the Jews would not convert, he had simply said to his captors, 'Then she must be weeping for my father and mother.' What kind of child would say that?

"You say you loved your parents, but you lost them," Raoul

said with great sadness. "You were deprived of a father and a mother."

The sun was going down across the hills to the west of Liège as they entered the Priory church. The choir was singing Vespers.

Father Mortara suddenly spoke in a soft voice. "But the Pope was my spiritual father and the Church was my mother... And when I saw how the Jews of Rome were living – I was glad of that…"

Chapter 15

Rome, The Papal States. 1858

The hot Roman sun glistened on the Fontana della Barcaccia, a half-sunken fountain in the shape of a ship with water overflowing its bows. Edgardo was led into the Piazza di Spagna by the Rector, Canon Sarra, and several priests.

A crowd had gathered on the Spanish Steps to watch a puppet show with two marionettes.

"If all the Jews are bad, why do the King of Sardinia and Prime Minister Cavour love them so much?" one of the marionettes demanded.

The Rector and the priests stopped, allowing Edgardo to watch.

"They don't love the Jews. Victor Emmanuel and Cavour will go to any lengths to drive Austria out of northern Italy," the other marionette said as he butted the first with his head.

"Ow! Why do they do that?"

"So they can pry Louis Napoleon loose from his alliance with the Pope and take over all the states and principalities of Italy," the other marionette shouted impatiently.

"What's that got to do with the Jews?"

The other marionette started hitting the first with a wooden stick. "You nincompoop! You dim-witted ninny!"

The crowd started to laugh.

"They will go to any lengths to weaken the leader of the opposition!"

"The opposition?"

"The Pope, you bird-brained dumbbell!"

"I don't understand," whimpered the first.

"You thick-skulled woodenhead! They will go to any lengths to prove to the heretical nations of Europe the desirability of stripping the Pope of his powers; they will use anything!"

"I still don't follow," cried the first marionette.

"Even the baptism of the Jew Boy! This is how they are using the Mortara case."

Edgardo looked up at the Rector with bemusement.

The second marionette grabbed hold of a jug of water. "I'm going to baptise you, for you must surely be an ignorant infidel," he cried.

He tried to pour water over his companion's head.

"Get away!" cried the first marionette as he pulled away.

"Come here!" the other one cried, and started to hit him hard again.

The crowd roared with laughter.

"You see, Edgardo, how lucky you are to be a convert!" the Rector said as they walked on.

They entered the dirty narrow streets of the ghetto at a sentry point by a large gate and passed crumbling, half-ruined buildings and people with haggard and woeful faces dressed in rags. Craftsmen were carving ivory and precious metals, embroidering lace, making watches and ornaments. Street vendors were selling Jewish foods from their carts: salted cod and twice-fried artichokes. Edgardo remembered eating them in Bologna. "You want to taste?" shouted one of the vendors, but the Rector pulled Edgardo away.

They turned a corner, arriving at an old Catholic church where Dominican monks were rounding up Jews and trying to make them take communion and listen to proselytising sermons.

A first-rate musician was playing his violin to several people in front of the church. At his feet sat a beautiful little girl of Edgardo's age, mending her rags. The Rector, the priests and Edgardo stopped walking.

"I wanted to bring you here, Edgardo, to show you how very lucky you are to be a Christian," said Canon Sarra loudly, a disdainful expression on his face. "Aren't you glad you are no longer a Jew? For as a Jew in Rome you would be forced to live in the ghetto."

Edgardo did not answer him.

"I understand, Edgardo, that it is your wish to convert the Jews," the Rector continued.

On hearing this, the musician stopped playing. "Why should you wish to convert the Jews?" he asked Edgardo.

The priests laughed.

"He is Edgardo Mortara, the Jew turned Christian, who is now happily on the road to Heaven," the Rector proclaimed triumphantly. "You've heard of him?"

"Yes, we have heard of him," replied the musician.

"He would be very happy to see you converted too – and your little girl, wouldn't you, Edgardo?"

Edgardo slowly nodded.

The Rector was now gloating. "And then you could swap your rags for riches, and we know how the Jews love riches, don't we?"

The musician spoke with an uncommon defiance to the little girl. "Rafaela, would you want to convert to Christianity if it meant you could wear beautiful shoes with buckles like this boy Edgardo Mortara here, and beautiful dresses, and if it meant you could have plenty of food to eat? Would you wish to turn Christian? Tell Papa. Tell me!"

The little girl looked into her father's eyes and shook her head. He lifted her up and kissed her.

Canon Sarra was about to lead Edgardo away when a Dominican monk accompanied by a Papal gendarme told the musician and his daughter to go into the church. The little girl held on to the *mezuzah* hanging around her neck and stared at Edgardo and his cross.

"Time for communion!" the Papal gendarme shouted.

"We are Jews!" she cried.

The gendarme laughed. "You should convert; I hear the Holy Office is giving eighty *scudi* to every Jew who converts!"

He pointed to an enormous crucifix on the wall, complete with a porcelain figure of Christ looking up to the Heavens. Underneath it there was an inscription. "What does it say there?" he asked.

The little girl refused to read it.

Canon Sarra peered at the inscription. "Tell her, Edgardo," he said, relishing the scene.

Edgardo read it. "All day long... I have stretched out my hands... to a... disobedient and..."

"... a disobedient and stubborn people," the Rector continued.

The gendarme laughed. The little girl spat on the floor in front of him as he herded her and her father into the church together with the other Jews.

Chapter 16

Liège, Belgium. 1940

The Meuse was a dark blue-black, in spite of a winter sun illuminating the Quai de la Batte. It was a peaceful scene, but Raoul felt unsettled as he walked along the river. Rumours of a possible Nazi invasion of Belgium in the spring had suddenly become rife after an incident where two German officers carrying plans for a Western offensive accidentally landed in Belgium somewhere near Limburg. So much for Belgian neutrality.

A young woman wearing a khaki trench coat, her long blonde hair dazzling in the sunlight, walked towards him, arm in arm with her boyfriend. It was Delphine and Jean-Louis. She let go of his hand, ran up to Raoul, and kissed him on the cheek.

"Raoul, have you met Jean-Louis?"

You know I have – how can you possibly ask me that? Raoul thought.

"Jean-Louis, this is Raoul." Delphine let go of his hand as she spoke.

"The monk!" said Jean-Louis, which made Raoul want to shout 'school-teacher' in his face. 'The monk'– it was said with a hint of scorn and the aloofness you might expect from someone who had grown up in Brussels, not in the village of Blegny in Walloon. Blegny, where everyone still had a grandparent who thought you could cure toothache by banging a nail into the bark on the north side of a sacred oak tree and then, with the moon ascending, take that nail and push it into the tooth until it bled. Jean-Louis's sharp check jacket and the slicked-back hair hid nothing.

"Yes," said Raoul. "I'm a novice monk. And you're a schoolteacher, I hear."

Jean-Louis shook his hand. "I'm sorry I can't stop and talk; I have a meeting to go to at the Havart House: a Rexist Meeting," he said. He grabbed hold of Delphine's neck and kissed her on her lips. Raoul looked across the river. The kiss lingered before turning into quiet mutterings about meeting her that night back in Bouhay.

"Nice to see you, Raoul," Jean-Louis said with a grin, before he crossed the quay and entered the old Havart house with its elegant facade of criss-cross wooden panels.

"Would you like to go for coffee, Raoul?" Delphine asked.

"I've a few errands to run, and I was going to pop in to the Librairie Pax in place Cockerill," said Raoul. He was angry. Jean-Louis had shown his true colours by kissing Delphine blatantly in front of him. And how could she have responded by kissing him back like that?

"We could climb the steps of the Montagne de Bueren and go to one of the cafés near the impasse des Ursulines," said Delphine. "Or have you got to get back to the Priory?"

"No, I've got the morning off," said Raoul, "but perhaps this is not such a great idea."

"Why?"

"I'm sure you can work that out for yourself," Raoul said very abruptly as he leaned against the quayside railings.

"Oh don't be silly, Raoul. You're my dear friend, and I don't ever want that to change. I know it hasn't been an easy time for you, and it's been hard for me, too. I don't want to see you being unhappy." She took his arm. They crossed the cobbled street and walked up the rue Saint-Jean-Baptiste, eventually arriving at the Féronstrée that was crowded with shoppers, the air pungent with the smell of brioche-like dough and caramelised sugar coming from the waffle-vendors' carts.

Raoul stopped walking and looked at her. "So your boyfriend is a member of the Rexist party."

"Is that so terrible?" said Delphine as she let go of his arm.

"No! Not if you support Adolf Hitler and the killing of Jews and innocent children."

A woman buying waffles, piled high with cream and strawberry syrup on top, turned round, surprised to see a man wearing a monk's robe shouting at an attractive blonde woman.

Delphine shouted back at him. "You're so angry, Raoul!" She walked on quickly, taking a turn into one of the medieval passageways that burrowed between the old town houses in the rue Hors-Château.

Raoul ran after her. "Well, isn't that worth getting angry about? The Rexists are fascists, Delphine. They're no better than the Nazis in Germany or the Blackshirts in Italy."

"They are not the same, Raoul. Rexism grew out of a Catholic protest movement – most Rexists are Catholics, for Christ's sake. Degrelle approves of King Leopold's policy of neutrality; they are not the same as fascists."

"Oh, aren't they? Is *that* what your boyfriend is telling you? So why does Leon Degrelle frequently slip across the frontier into Germany? You think the Rexist leader meets with Goebbels and Hitler every five minutes to discuss styles of lederhosen over bratwurst and Betzel beer?"

"You're being ridiculous, Raoul."

"Am I? Why is Hitler funding the Rexists to the tune of over a hundred thousand marks? Why are the Italian fascists throwing money at Degrelle?" Raoul shook his head. "I'm being ridiculous? We have Great Britain and France at war with Germany. Meanwhile here in Belgium, General van den Bergen, who favours cooperation with the Allies, has now been replaced as Chief of Staff by General Michiels. Your Rexist boyfriend must be very pleased."

Delphine turned round and shouted back at him. "Have you finished, Raoul?!"

"No! I haven't finished Delphine! The Rexists would have us sever all our ties with Great Britain and France and enter into a 'friendly understanding' with Germany under the guise of a neutrality agreement. They would love to see us break our ties with France, and some Walloons would embrace that because they think France uses Belgium as a catspaw. You know what? We might as well just open all our borders, bring about a downfall of the government, kick King Leopold off the throne and watch the SS take over Belgium for Adolf Hitler. Do you *want* Belgium to become a province of Nazi Germany, Delphine? Is that what your boyfriend wants?"

"If you feel so strongly about all this, why the hell didn't you join the army, Raoul, along with the other six hundred thousand Belgian men who have signed up, instead of joining a bloody monastery?" Delphine sounded just as angry as Raoul. She sat down on an old stone wall.

"Perhaps I should have done," said Raoul as he sat next to her.

For a long time neither of them said a word. They stared out over the disordered array of Liège's rooftops and walled orchards leading down to the River Meuse.

Eventually Raoul turned to Delphine. She looked away and lowered her eyes. She had long eyelashes that were light brown like her eyebrows, in contrast to her blonde hair. Usually she had a strong, expressive face that was punctuated every few sentences with warm smiles that would make her eyes open wide and draw you in, but now there were no smiles. Her countenance was still; there was no movement at all, just a delicate, vulnerable stillness, that made her face seem like a mask, albeit a beautiful mask, with its high cheekbones, straight nose and delicate mouth. Raoul desperately wanted to reach over and touch her lips and make them come back to life; he wanted to smell the subtle scent of violet water on her neck, which used to intoxicate him when he kissed her, but he felt paralysed. He had lost her.

He spoke quietly, but could not hide his fury. "Thank God most people in Liège don't see it like your boyfriend." He knew he had overstepped the mark with Delphine, but rather than shutting up he continued his tirade. "And for the record, Delphine, Rexist supporters might well be Catholic, but most of them are members of the Catholic bourgeoisie, taken in by simplistic and naive policies. Ask your uncles stoking coke all day in the steelworks around Liège what they think of Rexism. The unions fear for their workers' livelihoods, but then Degrelle, son of a wealthy brewer, isn't going to care if they are fired for no reason as they were in Germany, or if they can't find work and are forced to become beggars..." He noticed that Delphine was crying. "Now I've finished," he said, "do you want to go and have that coffee?"

Delphine said nothing. She stood up and walked down the steps leading to the rue Hors-Château. He shouted after her, "How often does your boyfriend go to those meetings?" which he immediately regretted.

The sound of her high heel shoes grew fainter. She was gone.

Raoul got up, walked along the impasse, and then began to climb the 374 steps to the top of the Montagne de Bueren and sat looking out over Liège. He tried to lose himself in the view to calm his agitated mind. Beneath him the Meuse snaked through the city, carrying the river boats on their journey to Antwerp and beyond. A few kilometres to the south-east, across the river, he could just make out the village of Bouhay and the church tower of Notre Dame de Lourdes in a sea of green fields.

'*Why the hell didn't you join the army?*' Delphine's words kept haunting him. Did she share Jean-Louis's Rexist principles? He was very upset that he hadn't managed to really talk to her. Perhaps he should have left politics out of the conversation. After all, he was going to be a monk; should monks comment on politics? It disturbed him that Degrelle incited hatred, yet he was a Catholic. And it was true that many of his followers were Catholics, but even as a monk he felt he had to condemn him for that. Surely a monk had the right to speak out against torture, the bombing of innocent people and the oppression of the poor? Left to his own devices, he would have been a socialist or a communist. Maybe it would have been better to join the army and fight for Belgium, and perhaps Delphine would have respected him more for doing that. However upset or disappointed he was, he still wanted to be with her. He still wanted to drown in her infectious laughter and her smiles, and her beautiful, wondrous eyes that would widen and marvel when hearing Billie Holiday singing 'I've Got My Love to Keep Me Warm' on the radio, or when picking dandelions and elderberries in the woods outside Bressoux.

He was overcome with sadness. For a moment he wondered if he could take his own life by throwing himself down the steep steps of the Montagne de Bueren. Then he stopped himself, put his hands together and prayed to God: for hope, for redemption and for guidance.

***

Raoul walked down the steps and back into the rue Hors-Château. He passed Silverstein the jeweller's, with its strange mantel clock in the window: a skull standing on a black plinth on which there was a gold plate with the sun and the moon and a Star of David at its centre. The jaws suddenly started to clack together. Someone leaned over Raoul's shoulder and said, "Eleven o'clock. They clack together on the hour. It's fantastic, isn't it?" Raoul turned round. It was Monsignor Kerkhofs. "My young novice friend, how are you?" the Bishop asked with a smile.

"I'm well, Your Eminence," Raoul replied.

The Bishop opened the shop door and asked Raoul to follow him inside.

A tall, middle-aged man with a white beard handed the Bishop a silver watch. "It's running like clockwork now, Louis," he said with a warm smile.

"Well it *is* clockwork," said the Bishop laughing. He turned to Raoul. "If you ever need a wristwatch fixing, Avram here is your man," he said. "He's a good friend of mine; I've known the Silverstein family for many years."

"We don't wear wristwatches at the Priory," said Raoul as he reached out and shook the jeweller's hand.

The Bishop laughed again. "Of course not! How much do I owe you, Avram?"

The jeweller shook his head and waved his hands at the same time. "I'm not charging you for that, Louis," he said.

"Well you know what I'm going to say, don't you Avram?"

The jeweller winked at Raoul. "He's going to tell me he'll give the money to the poor," he said with exaggerated hand gestures and head-nodding. "He wants us to believe that, anyway."

"Avram, will you join me for coffee?" the Bishop asked.

"I've got to mind the premises; another time," said the jeweller.

The Bishop hugged him, and he and Raoul left the shop. "Which way are you heading?" he asked Raoul.

"I'm going to the Librairie Pax in place Cockerill, to see if I can find the book you told me about," said Raoul.

"Good. That's on my way to the Cathedral. Come and have a quick coffee with me at Café Lequet," said the Bishop. "I want to continue the conversation we began at my house before Christmas."

They crossed the arcs of cobblestones on the Féronstrée, which prompted Raoul to tell the Bishop that his great-uncle Henri had worked in a forge on the street when he couldn't get work as a farm labourer in Bouhay, and how he'd smoked a Wingender clay pipe like some of the shopkeepers still did today.

"The pipe bowl was in the shape of King Albert the First's head, complete with a blue military cap," said Raoul.

"He could probably remember the time when dogs

manned the bellows and fans in the forges," said the Bishop. His face grew more serious as they walked down rue du Pont. "The man we met, Avram and his family the Silversteins, are quite well off, but most of the Jewish families in Liège have been severely hit by the economic depression. Lots of Jewish businesses have collapsed, and people don't realise how many of the Jews here are completely impoverished. As I told you at my house, I fear for them, especially with this terrible threat of Nazi invasion. It was just over a year ago that *Kristallnacht*, the 'Night of Broken Glass', occurred in Germany. Have you heard about that?"

Raoul nodded, "Yes. The Nazis attacked synagogues and Jewish shops, didn't they?"

"Indeed, and they vandalised Jewish homes and murdered some of the Jews," the Bishop added.

They entered the Café Lequet on the Quai sur Meuse, and were immediately hit by the rich aroma of Rombouts coffee diffusing oddly with lavender wood polish. They took their seats at a table under an old poster of the red cockerel of Wallonia on its bright yellow background and the Bishop ordered a pot of coffee.

Raoul leaned over to him and spoke quietly. "Monsignor, it bothers me that anti-Semitism in Belgium is being propagated by men such as Leon Degrelle who proclaim that they are staunch Catholics. Degrelle clearly has a lot of Catholic followers."

"He does, but just remember that not all Catholics are bad," said the Bishop. "As Christians it's not the words that matter so much as our actions, and on that subject I remember at my house you offered your help. I know the Rabbi of Liège and I know a lot of the Jews in this city. They are very worried, and we must support them."

"How?" asked Raoul as the waiter set down their pot of coffee and cups.

"I have already appealed to many priests and monks under

my jurisdiction. If the Jews need to be hidden, the Banneux monastery will afford shelter for many Jewish children and adults. I know that other monasteries and seminaries will follow suit; I have spoken with the Benedictine monks in Charneux and in Val Dieu, as well as in Liège. If any of the Jewish families want to convert to Christianity and be baptised, we can help them with that too. Many Jews in Antwerp converted last year, but we certainly don't want to force Christianity down their throats. Which reminds me, how is our mutual friend Father Mortara?"

"He is not too good and doesn't get out much at the moment," said Raoul. "I'd better get to the bookshop and then back to Notre Dame de Lourdes."

Raoul swigged back his coffee. Bishop Kerkhofs took his hand. "Will you help me, Brother Luc?"

"Of course I will, Father..."

The Bishop of Liège paid for the coffees and they left the café.

***

Raoul made his way to Place du Conservatoire and to Librairie Pax. A lanky young man was standing behind the till serving a couple of customers. Raoul waited to speak to him. He thought he looked familiar.

"Where is your English section?" he asked.

"Raoul!" It was Julien, a boy who had been in his class at school for several years. He peered at Raoul through thick, black-framed spectacles. "I heard you'd joined the monastery in Bouhay and were all set to become a monk, and now here you are in your monk's robe!"

"Yes," said Raoul. "What about you? You wear glasses now."

"I'm at the University of Liège, studying geography," said Julien, "but I work a few hours a week here in my spare time. Your friend Delphine comes in here sometimes. I always thought you two would end up together."

"So did I," muttered Raoul under his breath.

"I think she has a new boyfriend now: a teacher," said Julien. "He left these in here." Julien picked up a pile of pamphlets and handed one to Raoul.

'*Léon Degrelle – warrior of the Rexist Crusade,*' asserted the typeface around a photo of the young charismatic-looking Rexist leader.

"He's not my candidate," said Julien, and then plagued Raoul with questions about what time he got up, how many times a day he prayed and for how many hours, and whether he now felt more spiritual.

"I pray for about six hours a day," said Raoul. He picked up the pile of pamphlets. "Have you got any scissors, Julien?" he asked. The young bookseller handed him a pair and Raoul started cutting the pamphlets up, screwing the pieces into little balls and throwing them into the bin next to the counter. "I suppose I do feel more spiritual now," he said with a big grin.

When there were no more pamphlets left, Raoul handed the scissors back to Julien and asked him to direct him to the English section. It was at the rear of the shop. "Most of the English books are second-hand," said Julien. "There's a chair and table in there. Feel free to sit and read, if you like," he said, before rushing back to the till to serve a customer.

Raoul scoured the shelves. He saw a few English books on one of the top shelves: about seven of them. He read the titles: *Gulliver's Travels, A Guide to the Town of Colchester* that had no cover – and next to it, lying on its side, there it was: *The Diaries of Sir Moses and Lady Montefiore*. He looked at the sub-title: *Comprising their life and work 1812–1883*.

He took the book off the shelf and went to sit at the table. Inside the cover on the frontispiece was a drawing of a distinguished elderly gentleman of about eighty who had long white hair: Raoul flicked through the book, noting some of the chapter headings: 'Birth of Sir Moses Montefiore at Leghorn';

'Becomes a stockbroker'; 'First Journey to Jerusalem'; 'Visit of the Duchess of Kent and the Princess Victoria to Ramsgate'; 'Mr Montefiore elected Sheriff of London'; 'Liberation of the Jews of Damascus'; 'Russia– Interview with the Czar'; 'Sir Moses presented to the Queen on being made a Baronet'.

He wondered what the Bishop of Liège had been talking about. He was about to return the book to the shelf when he saw the chapter heading: 'The Case of the Abduction of Edgar Mortara...'

Chapter 17

Ramsgate, United Kingdom. 1858

A steamship escorted by a flock of seagulls made its way towards the Continent. Sir Moses Montefiore stopped to look out across the English Channel, holding on to his blue peaked cap in a bracing, late summer breeze. Lady Montefiore brushed the curls out of her eyes as she studied her husband. At nearly seventy-five and over six feet tall he was still a dashing figure of a man. They resumed their walk across the cliffs from Broadstairs to Ramsgate, eventually arriving at an iron gate that led into the gardens of their seaside home, East Cliff Lodge. The rapid song of a skylark greeted them. They watched as it swooped down to the base of a Scots pine. The skylark stood up straight on its twig-like legs, a bright green caterpillar hanging out of its beak and stared at them before flying off again.

Lady Judith smiled at her husband and took his hand. They crossed the lush south lawn. "Tell me about this Jewish boy in the Papal States, Mosey."

Sir Moses stopped in front of the Italianate domed greenhouse. "In spite of the protests of the father and the tears of the mother, the child has, according to the Press, been torn from them by Pope Pius and placed in a convent school: Saint Peter in Chains…"

Judith interrupted him, "Chains being the operative word no doubt!"

"Well, I'm sure it won't be a picnic," said Sir Moses as they sat down on a stone seat.

"It's abominable! Imagine if we'd had a child, taken away like that…"

"Awful," said Sir Moses, suddenly feeling his wife's sorrow

at never being able to have children. He took his wife's arm. They sat in silence for a while.

Eventually Sir Moses turned to his wife. "We've had a good life together, haven't we?"

Lady Judith leaned over and kissed him on the cheek. "We certainly have, Mosey." They got up and walked arm in arm towards the turreted mansion. As they approached a large back entrance, a butler came out to meet them. "The American gentleman, Gershom Kursheedt, has arrived and is waiting in the drawing room."

"Let's have tea on the terrace, Blacknell," said Lady Judith.

Mr Kursheedt, a man in his early forties, was brought out to meet Sir Moses and Lady Montefiore at a large wooden table on the terrace in front of the drawing room windows, where Earl Grey tea and scones were immediately served.

"You like perfume in your tea," Mr Kursheedt said, somewhat confused as he lifted a gilt-edged cup to his nose.

"It's bergamot. Earl Grey liked it in his tea and the nation followed," Lady Judith explained.

"Don't bore Gershom with the eccentricities of the English," Sir Moses chimed in with a wry smile. "We are here to talk about Edgardo Mortara."

Lady Montefiore offered Mr Kursheedt a scone. "I know, and what a revolting case it is. How are the Americans reacting to the kidnapping of the child?"

"The Jews in America are most indignant," Mr Kursheedt told her, his New Orleans twang causing his vowels to lengthen with every syllable. "What's the latest news over here?" he said as he spooned whipped cream on his uncut scone: an action that Lady Judith observed with fascination.

Sir Moses put down the silver tongs and a pink and white sugar cube he had been playing with. "The Jewish communities of France and Holland have taken up the case with their co-religionists in Sardinia and with the government there, and have requested them to appeal directly to the Court of Rome.

I myself have been approached by the Jewish congregations in Sardinia – over twenty of them. They have appealed to me in my role as president of the Board of Deputies of British Jews, asking if I would intervene on behalf of the unfortunate family. I shall certainly do all I can. I may request that the British Government take a stand in this case." Sir Moses screwed up his bushy eyebrows deep in thought before saying, "And I may do a little more besides."

Lady Judith turned to her husband. "What are you planning now, Mosey?"

Sir Moses smiled at her. "I intend to step into the breach and travel to Rome myself. I will go and speak to the Pope – this Pio Nono who only says 'No! No!' – and see what I can do. Perhaps we can rescue the boy."

Lady Judith sighed and said, "Oh Mosey!"

He took her hand and looked into her eyes. "Perhaps you would accompany me?"

She turned to Mr Kursheedt. "You'd think that at his age he would have had enough adventures; I certainly have! Russia, Syria, the Holy Land – always another 'trip'. Mr Kursheedt, let me help you with your scone. In England, etiquette has it that guests always cut and fill their own scones – jam first and then cream – but I shall do it for you."

"Thank you Lady Montefiore; it appears to be quite a business," said Mr Kursheedt.

"Which? The scone or the kidnapping of the boy Mortara?" Lady Montefiore asked drily as she spooned strawberry jam on to his plate.

"Both," replied Mr Kursheedt. He watched, mesmerised, as she performed the English ritual with the scone, jam and cream. "Perhaps I could accompany you on your mission to Rome, Sir Moses, as a representative of America?"

Sir Moses stood up, taking in the scent of the white jasmine flowers trailing down from a trellis and then doing the same with the crimson buds of a tall rose bush. "You would be most welcome, Mr Kursheedt."

"As indeed you were when you accompanied my husband to Jerusalem in his mission to establish almshouses in Palestine last year," said Lady Judith.

The American smiled and cast his eye over the cliff top gardens.

"Queen Victoria liked the gardens here at East Cliff very much," Lady Judith told him. Twenty-five years ago, when she was a young princess and holidaying in Ramsgate with her mother, the Duchess of Kent, Sir Moses not only offered her use of the gardens but also gave Victoria her own golden key to a specially made entrance."

Mr Kursheedt was impressed. "No darned way! That is something," he exclaimed in his unfamiliar tones.

Sir Moses nodded. "The Jewish people are fortunate to live in safe havens like England and America," he said. "I have heard that the boy Mortara is regularly paraded in the Rome Ghetto, arguably the worst place in Europe to be a member of our faith. The Jews, four thousand of them, live there in squalor by the banks of the Tiber in a climate of the fiercest anti-Semitism."

"Although I hear that Pio Nono doesn't mind the Jews bringing him money at the Apostolic Palace and I gather he does permit them to kiss his hands," said Lady Judith.

Sir Moses raised his eyebrows again before he and his wife escorted their American guest across the lawns and past the beds of lavender, rosemary and thyme, to show him Queen Victoria's private gate.

Chapter 18

The Vatican, The Papal States. 1858

Wearing a jewelled tiara, Pope Pius the Ninth sat on his throne in the Sale Ducale, a vast chamber of polychrome marble, watched over by stucco cherubs framing fresco landscapes. He stretched out his hand for the delegates of the Roman Hebrew Congregation to kiss as they filed past him in a line.

The last member of the group, the leader of the delegation, bowed and presented a large bouquet of flowers to the Pope. It was festooned with paper money.

"Again, we ask leave to stay one more year in the Holy City, Your Eminence," he said to the Pontiff as the garland was handed on. The Pope's Major-Domo took away the flowers and the money.

The Pope stared at the man coldly. "Why should I give you leave to stay?"

The leader of the Hebrew Congregation was shocked. "Because according to the relationship we have with the Vatican and because of the generosity of the Popes of the Holy See, this is what is done each year: it is now a tradition…"

"Normally the Jews of Rome are amenable and compliant, but now this is clearly not the case. You are stirring up trouble…"

"How are we stirring up trouble, Your Eminence? We are a loyal and law-abiding community who only wish to live in peace and harmony with our fellow citizens of Rome."

"You are making a European affair of the Mortara case!" the Pope shouted, revealing an anger he rarely displayed in public.

Cardinal Antonelli, standing at the Pontiff's side, waved a pile of documents at them. "All these memorials, petitions and addresses. The complaints of the Jewish community are becoming quite tiresome!" he bellowed.

Pius shouted out loudly to his Major-Domo. "Bring me Edgardo!"

The Major-Domo nodded. Two Swiss Guards opened the large doors of one of the chambers of the Sale Ducale, and Edgardo, dressed in his black cassock, was whisked in by Thomas and Laurent, the three of them laughing as they ran across the hall to Pius's throne.

"This is Edgardo Mortara, the boy who you are making an example of. How does he look to you?"

The leader of the Hebrew Congregation studied Edgardo and eventually shook his head.

"I can assure you he is very happy in my care," said the Pope. He nodded to Thomas and Laurent. "Alright, that's enough for now. Edgardo, you are joining me for lunch." The Swiss Guards chased Edgardo out of the hall.

Pius turned to the leader of the Hebrew Congregation. "Your complaints are very unhelpful..."

The man was shaking. He opened his arms and bowed his head. "Your Eminence, when you asked our community for help with the railways, we gave generously," he reminded him.

"And we gave you the freedom to practice your religion," snapped Cardinal Antonelli.

"For which we are most grateful, your Eminence, although I must point out that we are still dragged into churches to hear the sermons of the Dominican monks," the Jewish leader replied. He once again turned to the Pope. "Can we remind you of the liberal principles you displayed at the start of your reign when you ordered the gates of the ghetto to be opened? The Hebrew Congregation has always held you in the highest esteem for this. It was an act of generosity and courage for which..."

The Pope was clearly irritated. "Yesterday is not today!" he shouted.

The leader of the Hebrew Congregation continued with some trepidation, "With regard to the Mortara case, friends and enemies of the great Catholic Church alike eagerly look forward to the verdict of Pope Pius the Ninth. A declaration like that of your respected predecessor Gregory the First, God bless him, that you reject and prohibit secret baptism, would restore tranquillity to the despondent Jewish community, and would show the world the measure of your justice, your charity, your peace and humanity."

The Pope stared at him with contempt.

The man went as far as he dared: "The whole world awaits your Holiness's decision."

Pius looked at him. He knew that there was truth in what the Israelite had said, but he was in no mood to have his beliefs, his principles, or even his authority challenged by the man, and a Jew at that.

"Then I snap my fingers at the world!" Pius replied.

He called for his Major-Domo. "Bring me a basin! I wash my hands of this whole business," he shouted as he got up to leave.

***

"The contest raised over this boy could be one of the severest blows ever inflicted on Catholicism. Is there no way we can return him to his family?" Cardinal Antonelli asked as they walked through the long corridors of the Vatican that were lined with tapestries, statues, chandeliers, mirrors, velvet curtains and gold ceilings.

"Edgardo is in the house of his Father. How can he be returned to the Jews?" Pius replied as they reached the marble staircase leading to the Papal apartments.

Antonelli sighed. "Can we really not persuade the parents to convert?"

"That does not seem to be an option."

"Then I can only see trouble ahead," said Antonelli. "The Jews are indeed milking this case. They are whipping up incredible support in Sardinia and throughout the whole of Europe."

"The family of Jacob are a clever people," Pius reflected. "But they must be stopped. There are too many of them baying like dogs, howling in the streets and disturbing us everywhere we go."

"How can they be stopped? These dogs you talk about have had no problem in obtaining the support of the most powerful libertine journals of Germany, Belgium and France. The affair is causing no less than a sensation," said Antonelli.

"Most of those newspapers are owned by Jews," said Pius.

"But the support amongst Christians is also considerable," Antonelli pointed out. "The *Journal des Debats* is calling for the backing of the French Emperor in the name of this case. As you well know, an excuse for an outcry is valued in several quarters. There is talk of Protestants combining with the riff-raff of the revolutionary parties over this. Can you not see how the boy's case is being used against you?"

"Since the dawn of Christianity, there has not been one political passion which hasn't given way to anti-Catholic fanaticism," Pius declared. "Are you saying the Church should have regard for this clamour?" He did not wait for a reply. "I say woe to us if we allow passion or self-interest to affect the affairs of the Holy See, if we allow ourselves to be touched by the reproach of newspapers."

"But the reproach of governments is another matter," said Antonelli in frustration. "I don't have to tell you that people say the keys of the Vatican are held in Paris and Vienna... and now we have France planning to augment its garrison at Rome instead of quitting the capital! As to our own Papal Army, you must be aware that disillusionment is leading to desertion among the soldiers, in spite of the generous offers made to them to remain."

As they entered the Pope's imposing dining room, the Supreme Pontiff gave his Secretary of State a dismissive look of contempt. Antonelli waited for a further response, his eyes opening wide above his beak-like nose. The Pope studied his Cardinal Secretary of State. He had always found his arrogance very testing. There was something of the actor in him as well as something of the bully. He had a reputation for not wanting to assist in the ceremonies of Holy Week at which he was extremely disdainful and ill-mannered, and for never smiling at ambassadors or ministers whom he cajoled from morning till night. In fact he was hated by many sections of Rome society. His smiles were reserved only for members of the opposite sex. Antonelli, with his swarthy complexion and heavy jaw, was not short of admirers, who knew that behind the scarlet robe and cardinal's hat lay unlimited power and enormous wealth, and it annoyed Pius to know that he himself had created these privileges by propelling him into arguably the most influential position in the Papal States. For years he had tolerated his indiscretions: the parties and dinners that had seen him flattering and seducing the most beautiful women in Rome, some of whom had ended up being his mistresses. He had put up with Antonelli's infidelity, but he would not have the man manipulate him in matters of religion and doctrine.

They moved over to a large dining table where silver platters were already laid and piled high with fish, fruit, bread and cheeses.

Antonelli turned to the Pontiff, the furrows on his broad forehead deepening as he became more and more agitated. "Are we going to watch and wait until we see the temporal power of the Pope overthrown? Can we risk the future of the Papal States for the sake of this little neophyte?"

Pius stopped in his tracks. The Swiss Guards, Thomas and Laurent, entered, leading Edgardo in to lunch. The boy ran over to Pius and kissed him. The Pontiff sat down and placed his hand on Edgardo's head. "It is not in my power to part with this little one," he said. "I cannot in conscience replace a soul in the path of perdition that has, as if through a miracle, been won for Paradise. The great ones and the little ones of the earth may strive together to snatch this soul from my keeping: my answer to all and to each can only be the same. We cannot release him. We cannot! My conscience will not allow me to expose a Christian soul to peril."

Stony-faced, Antonelli continued to stare at the Pope.

Pius lowered his voice, but not his resolve. "Do you understand, Antonelli? We cannot! *Non possumus!*"

Chapter 19

Bouhay, Liège, Belgium. 1940

"*Non possumus*. It was not easy for Pope Pius," said Father Mortara at lunch one day. "Lots of people put pressure on him to return me to my parents, but it wasn't possible."

Raoul tried to make sense of Father Mortara's words as they sat at the end of a long table in the refectory. He passed the old priest a plate of sausage and *stoemp* – a mound of lumpy carrots and potatoes.

"You're saying Pope Pius wasn't prepared to give you back to your parents? He was determined to hold on to you whatever the cost?" questioned Raoul.

"There was no doubt in the Holy Father's mind that as I was a Christian he had to guide my soul to Heaven." Father Mortara's face screwed up into a frown and he pushed his plate away. He had only taken a couple of bites out of his sausage. He seemed to Raoul a little weaker and paler and his appetite clearly wasn't as good as it had been.

"You should eat something, we need to keep you strong," said Raoul, but Father Mortara just shook his head and said 'What for?' There was a world-weariness in his tone, which made Raoul suddenly aware that the old priest was ready to face death; ready to leave the world that had dealt him such an odd life, and it saddened the young man.

As the weeks passed by Father Mortara no longer got up for Matins. Raoul would leave him to sleep. He himself would get up at half past five, happy to enter the Priory church for early prayers, the psalms and the plainsong. He loved hearing the monks singing. He had a good baritone voice and quickly picked up the chants, which helped him to drift in and out of his memories or empty his mind.

In the Long Meditation, Raoul would sit in the cloister and try to make sense of his troubled thoughts. He imagined Father Mortara as a spirited young Jewish boy and tried to justify what had happened to him, but could not do so: Jesus had not taught his disciples to kidnap children. Surely Jesus would not have approved of a child being taken away from his parents, and yet the Holy Office had seen fit to do so, with no regard for his mother or father. He could not understand this and it made him angry; he found himself constantly putting his hands together in prayer, closing his eyes and asking God for help and guidance.

Raoul's thoughts would then turn to his own family: how would he as an only child have felt about being separated from his parents, simple people that they were? His father had never aspired to anything more than farm labouring, while his mother took in clothes to mend. Perhaps a life in Rome with the Pope would also have appealed to him at six years of age: a life of purple-plumed horses and gold carriages; discussing the scriptures with the most Holy man on earth; and meeting princes and monarchs from all over the world in the rose gardens of the Vatican...

But would he have been happy to leave his own family? His parents had done everything they could for him. He wanted to believe that they were proud of him: proud that he had received a decent education, even proud with the way he had turned out. But his resolve to take Holy Orders had left them cold; the Church had taken him away from them.

He thought of Delphine; in the Long Meditation his thoughts would always return to Delphine.

He had truly loved her, but he had failed to win her. He tortured himself over and over again for not having found a way to her heart. He blamed himself for that, and he blamed Delphine as well. In his worst moments he became angry and blamed God for not having given him the life he had craved. Sometimes he wept. He wondered how he could ever complete his novitiate with such feelings, and then he would put his hands together again and beg for God's help.

When the Prior rang the bell for Lauds he would go back to the church, and when the psalms and the prayers were over he would sing Mass with the monks, the Lay Brothers and the villagers who dropped in on their way to work.

After Lauds he would rouse Father Mortara, help wash and dress him, and take the old man down to breakfast. They would eat in silence before entering the church again for Terce, which they would chant on a tone for ten minutes or so.

With the Magnum Silencium over, they would talk again: in the gardens, the library, the common room, or the cloister. They continued to go for short walks and Father Mortara would tell more of his story. Raoul, perplexed at hearing how the old man's family were treated as Jews, would interrupt him. "Jesus of Nazareth was a Jew; his apostles were Jews. Surely any nation or any person that hates the Jews or persecutes them cannot possess the Spirit of Christ and cannot be His true disciple?"

Father Mortara always had an answer. "Yes, to obtain the spirit and grace of our Lord, we should all love each other, no matter what our faith may be. We should not bear enmity against our neighbour because he differs with us," the old man had replied one afternoon as they walked over the stone bridge crossing the stream.

"Yet look what is happening in Belgium – see how the Rexist party is aligning itself with the Nazis." Raoul replied angrily. "They distribute anti-Jewish propaganda and they persecute Jews. It is no different to how the Jews were treated in Rome, even by the Holy Office itself, even by the Pope."

Father Mortara turned to him. "The Pope?"

"Look how Pope Pius kept the Jews locked up in the ghetto," said Raoul. "I know at the beginning of his reign he ordered the gates of the ghetto to be opened - but he later decreed that they be locked! You saw it for yourself..."

The old priest took his time to reply. "Yes, as I told you I was taken there at the age of six..."

"Didn't it shock you to see how they were living: like prisoners? And didn't you mind being paraded in front of the Jews? After all, they were your own people."

Father Mortara looked over the wall of the bridge and for several minutes said nothing as he stared into the stream below. Eventually he spoke. "I was a Christian, Brother Luc, and I was hoping they would convert, just as I hoped my parents would convert."

Raoul's eyebrows raised at the coldness of the reply and the thought of such precociousness in a young child.

Then Father Mortara took his hand. "I am truly impressed by your principles. I have come to learn that you are a strong and fine young man, but you must know that in 1858 the Holy Office did not think as you do now."

"You mean the Pope did not think as I do!" shouted Raoul and immediately regretted it.

"You may not agree with everything the Pope did, but I must tell you that he was a good man and strong to have faced the world on my behalf. He became a father to me and held on to me not only for love but also a conviction that he should not go against the most fundamental teachings of the Catholic Church – in spite of the protests from people on the outside."

Father Mortara championed his adoptive father, the Pope, as though he had been a saint. Raoul closed his eyes in despair and couldn't help thinking about the boy's parents.

"The Pope felt that as my parents would not convert to Catholicism, I could not be returned to them," Father Mortara said as though reading his thoughts.

He spoke in an exaggerated, lilting sing-song Italian accent, albeit calmly and with a smile, which added to Raoul's frustration. How could he honestly have felt that the separation from his parents was acceptable? How could he say these things with such conviction? Was there no doubt in his mind, no uncertainty? Surely he must have suffered as a child? Raoul couldn't help wondering if the old man had been completely indoctrinated. Or had he just tried to please his new-found guardians at the Convent of Saint Peter in Chains and the Pope himself by telling them what they wanted to hear, that is, that he didn't want to go home and wanted to be raised as a Christian?

"Didn't you feel homesick?" said Raoul.

"Of course," said Father Mortara. "But the die had been cast. I had been baptised, and the validity of the baptism had been established. To return me to my non-Christian family would have been a transgression of canon law, and I therefore had to accept my situation."

"You couldn't go home and you accepted that? You must have been very unhappy."

"What choice did I have?" said Brother Pius. "In a way, I didn't want to go home, not if my parents wouldn't convert. There was, of course, a void in my life, but the Pope filled the void by becoming a father to me."

"But he was not your real father," said Raoul.

"I loved him as a father, although I admit I was torn between my love for the Pope and the love and duty I had for my parents." The old man looked down. It was clearly a painful matter for him.

The weather started to change. The sky became overcast and it began to rain. They crossed the bridge and walked back to the Priory. When they reached the cloister, Father Mortara began to speak again.

"The whole world was resounding with the words of Pio Nono, '*non possumus*' and like you, many people were outraged by my so-called abduction, but I was still unaware of this as a schoolboy at my lessons in the Convent of San Pietro in Vincoli, Saint Peter in Chains…"

Chapter 20

Rome, The Papal States. 1858

Edgardo sat at a small wooden desk staring into space. He thought of the people he had known in Bologna; he wondered what his father was doing; he imagined his mother blowing him a kiss; he saw Anna and Augusto laughing as they dipped their toes in the canal and pretended to smoke cigars. Noting his lack of attention, Brother Claudio, a young priest, stopped teaching, a frown taking shape on his brow. Edgardo turned, looked at him, and froze. Brother Claudio was about to pounce, but he suddenly noticed Fantoni, one of Edgardo's twelve classmates, chattering. As quick as a thunderbolt Brother Claudio darted over and grabbed him, pulling him out to the front of the class.

"The Ten Commandments please, Fantoni: one for each lashing." Brother Claudio's face turned red with anger as he pushed Fantoni over his desk and started to thrash him on the buttocks with a piece of leather attached to a wooden handle.

Fantoni burst into tears. "Thou shalt have no other God but me..."

"That is not the first Commandment, Fantoni," Brother Claudio shouted as he lashed him again. He jumped up in the air as he did so, to come down harder on the boy. Edgardo stealthily dug his *mezuzah* out of his pocket and looked at it sadly. The boy sitting next to him looked over at it. Brother Claudio noticed them and stopped beating Fantoni.

"What is that, Mortara?" he demanded.

Edgardo clutched his *mezuzah*. "Just a charm," he replied.

"Bring it here," Brother Claudio ordered.

Edgardo walked out to the front of the class.

"Show me!"

Edgardo stretched out his hand.

"Just a charm!" Brother Claudio mocked.

He smacked Edgardo's hand hard and the *mezuzah* fell on to the floor.

"Just a Jewish charm," Edgardo said quietly as he looked down on the floor.

"We will have no charms in here, let alone Jewish charms!" exclaimed Brother Claudio. "You are not a Jewboy now. Bend over next to Fantoni. Perhaps you would be so good as to finish the Commandments, as Fantoni does not seem to know them."

Edgardo took his place next to Fantoni.

"How hard do you want me to hit you, Mortara? This hard?"

Brother Claudio jumped up in the air and hit Fantoni on his legs with the whip. Fantoni screamed.

The schoolroom door opened and the Rector entered the room. He was carrying a large leather-bound book and a beautiful toy horse and carriage. "What are you doing, Brother Claudio?" the Rector inquired.

"I thought it was time to show Mortara some discipline."

"That will not be necessary. We will not hit Mortara and we will not shout at him, deride him, or do anything to him that will upset him in any way or undermine his... gratification and pleasure in his new-found convictions."

Brother Claudio started to protest.

The Rector spoke in a state of bemusement. "It has been ordained: from the Vatican Palace, no less."

He handed the beautiful Bible and toy horse and carriage to Edgardo.

"This Bible and this... toy... has been sent to you today by Pope Pius the Ninth. I trust that with true Christian compassion you will share these gifts with your fellow classmates," said the Rector.

Edgardo looked up at Brother Claudio defiantly, and

managed a wry smile at his classmates as he picked the *mezuzah* off the floor and put it in his pocket.

***

There was no shortage of gifts for Edgardo from the Supreme Pontiff. Every few days, toys, books, garlands of flowers and boxes of sweetmeats, would arrive beautifully gift-wrapped. The Rector, Canon Sarra, would hand them to Edgardo, always with a raised eyebrow. In his spartan dormitory, which he shared with six other boys, these presents were piled high around his bed. The Rector was unable to say anything. Mortara had been singled out, not only by an act of God, it seemed, but also by His Holiness himself. The other boys were at first wary of Edgardo; they knew his family were Jews, but as it became evident he had links with the Vatican and Pio Nono, the most important man in the world, they all befriended him and each in turn tried to make him his favourite.

Edgardo was frequently invited to visit the Pope. At the Vatican there were more surprises and treats waiting for him. He would throw his arms around his benefactor and thank him for his gifts. One Saturday, the week before All Saints' Day when Edgardo recited his catechism for the Supreme Father, Pius led him from the Papal apartments to an ornate panelled room. At the far end under a trio of gold-framed Russian triptychs was a large wooden rocking horse. Edgardo stopped in front of it.

"Have a go," Pius said, helping him up on to the horse.

The young boy began to rock to and fro.

"Would you like this horse, Edgardo?" the Pontiff asked him.

He shrieked with delight. Pius smiled.

"I am glad to see that you are happy, my son."

***

Several afternoons later when Edgardo was in the middle of his lessons, two open-topped black carriages arrived at the convent. Brother Claudio was chalking '*Jesus died for our sins!*' on the blackboard, and turned around in surprise. The Rector had a servile expression on his face as he led the Supreme Pontiff and his Major-Domo into the schoolroom. The pupils lowered their eyes, hands clasped together in amazement, some trying to steal a glance at the Pope. Edgardo alone remained relaxed. He smiled at his surrogate father, who walked over to him and placed his hands on the boy's head.

"Please continue with your lesson," the Pope said to Brother Claudio, but the young monk quickly became tongue-tied and obsequious. He found himself bowing and repeating the words 'Jesus died for our sins.'

"What does that mean exactly?" the Pope asked Brother Claudio, who bowed again before stuttering, "That is a very difficult question to answer, your Eminence."

"Edgardo, what do you say?" said the Pope as he massaged the boy's head.

"I say mankind was evil and God sacrificed his only son on the cross for that," said Edgardo.

"Exactly," said Pius with a big smile. He took a silver St Christopher coin out of his pocket and handed it to Edgardo before leaving the room.

The Pope's Major-Domo discretely addressed the Rector. "Canon Sarra, the Supreme Pontiff requests that he might have the company of young Mortara today. Can he be spared his lessons this afternoon?"

The Rector beckoned Edgardo. He ran joyfully out of the schoolroom, into the courtyard and through the gates to the Papal carriages. Thomas and Laurent in their red, gold and blue uniforms were in the second carriage. They leapt on to the pavement and gave Edgardo a big hug.

"He is to ride in my carriage with me," said Pius with a big smile.

Thomas and Laurent first helped Pius into the carriage and then, taking an arm each, hoisted Edgardo up to sit next to him.

Brother Claudio, Canon Sarra and Edgardo's classmates gathered around the schoolroom window, watching in amazement as the carriages pulled away.

Pio Nono and Edgardo drove through Rome in the open-topped carriage, passing the Coliseum, the Arch of Titus and the Capitoline Hill. People in the street recognised the Pope and greeted him with loud cheers, while he extended his arm as if to bless them. Eventually they arrived at the Quirinal Palace, a sparkling white building overlooking Rome.

"Today I am going to show you my other palace," said Pius to Edgardo who was nestled in his arms. "I am expecting the Queen of Naples this afternoon."

The carriages came to a halt. Edgardo jumped on to the pathway and then went over to smell the lavender growing by the side of the drive. Pio Nono joined him and rubbed the lavender flowers between his fingers, putting them to his nose. He held the boy's hand, his white soutane and majestic broad-brimmed purple hat contrasting with Edgardo's simple smock.

A magnificent cortège of carriages arrived in the driveway. They turned round to see a smart lady being lifted out of one of them. She walked towards them, followed by an array of equipages and domestics and a collection of her ten children ranging in age from two to twenty.

Pius whispered to Edgardo, "The Queen of Naples!"

In a moment the Queen was on her knees. Pius went over to meet her. A group of gardeners suddenly appeared from behind columns, fountains, naked statues and walkways, and they too knelt down on each side of the group calling out loudly, "Santo Padro, la benedizione."

Pope Pius smiled as he nodded and stretched out his arms to them, before laying his hands on first the Queen's and then on Edgardo's head. Edgardo looked up at him.

Holy Father, your benediction!

Everyone begged for the Pontiff's benediction, but to Edgardo he gave it freely. He gave his benediction and he gave him his love – unconditional love – which replaced the love he had lost from his parents. Edgardo wrote them many letters, but seldom received a reply.

***

That evening Canon Sarra called Edgardo into his study.

"There is someone joining us for supper this evening, Edgardo, someone who wishes to talk to you," he told him.

"My father?" asked Edgardo excitedly. "Is it my father?"

"No, not your father, " said the Rector. "The man is a journalist with the *Civilta Cattolica*, a Catholic newspaper. I would like you to speak to him so that the whole world can hear what you have to say. Pope Pius wishes this too. Don't look so sad. Why do you look so sad? You see how important you are."

"The monks have helped me write lots of letters to my father, asking him and my mother to convert, but they do not reply. I thought I would have heard from them by now," the boy confided in him. "Are you posting them?" Edgardo looked him in the eye.

"Yes, I am posting them, Edgardo."

"And you haven't had a reply? You swear – on the Bible?"

"Edgardo please do not be impertinent." At this moment the Rector looked away. He took some white envelopes from the top of his desk and quickly placed them in the top drawer.

"Edgardo, I do not wish to upset you, but perhaps your parents find it hard to communicate with you now that you are a Christian. Perhaps they will not convert," he said.

"Don't they love me?" Edgardo asked softly.

"I'm sure they do," the Rector reassured him, "but if they

will not convert, you have to question how much, indeed, you have to question whether they really want you back home with them."

At supper, as Edgardo sat at a long table with other pupils, he could only stare at his food. Canon Sarra and several priests entertained the journalist of the *Civilta Cattolica* across the refectory. He could hear the Rector talking in his loud voice. "They talk much of the rights of the father and of nature respecting the carrying away of the child, but divine rights surely override the rights of the father, of the family. A baptised child is surely our property."

After dinner Edgardo was brought into the library to meet the journalist. He shook hands with him. "I am very pleased and honoured to meet you, Edgardo," the journalist said to him. "How old are you?"

"Six," Edgardo answered.

"He is uncommonly advanced for his years," Canon Serra interjected.

The journalist turned to Edgardo. "I am sure you are aware that you are renowned in many countries all over the world. Readers of the *Civilta Cattolica* want to know what it is you really feel in your heart. How, for example, do you consider yourself? Are you a Jew or a Catholic?"

"A Catholic," Edgardo replied without hesitation.

"And what of your family?" he asked.

"I love my family; I would be happy to remain with them if they were Christians, and I pray to God that they may become so," Edgardo replied, a troubled expression on his face. "But while they are not Christians I pray not to be left to the..."

He looked over to the Rector who smiled at him.

"Left to what?" the journalist asked.

Edgardo looked down at the ground.

Canon Sarra continued for him. "We have talked about this. I think what he is trying to say is that he prays not to be left to any temptation his parents might have to prise him away from the Catholic Church."

"And what are your intentions now?" the journalist asked, turning to Edgardo.

The boy looked at him with a saddened expression.

"Tell the man what you told me today," Canon Sarra prompted. "Tell him."

Edgardo spoke slowly. "I shall devote myself to the conversion of the Jews…"

Chapter 21

London, United Kingdom. 1858

"Such zeal from a child of six-and-a-half years old!"

Sir Moses Montefiore peered over his spectacles as he addressed his wife and Gershom Kursheedt in the carriage. He tried to glean more as he shook open the foreign section of *The Times*, but the light was fading as they rounded Hyde Park Corner and the statue of the Duke of Wellington, a line of sparrows silhouetted against the red sunset as they perched on the back of the Duke's horse, Copenhagen. Each member of the trio was deep in thought as they drove along Piccadilly past the gaudy blue and red lamps of the chemist, the monster golden boot over the shoemaker's and the golden fleece over the hosier's. Not one shop, it seemed, was lacking a gold sign or a carved lion or unicorn proclaiming that these were the windows of the very best royal tradesmen.

Gershom Kursheedt declared that Piccadilly was more like a Parisian boulevard than a London street, but his opinion quickly changed as they crossed Piccadilly Circus and entered the Haymarket, bathed in a scented haze of roasted chestnuts, baked apples and burning charcoal. The shouts of Cockney street vendors echoed all around as if through some strange urban canyon of wall-to-wall supper houses and taverns, attracting rowdy crowds who queued for hot eels, pea soup and elderflower wine.

The carriage stopped outside the King's Theatre. Lady Judith stepped out on to the pavement assisted by Mr Kursheedt. Sir Moses jumped down, agile and spruce, with his silk-lined cape and top hat, and immediately opened his newspaper under a street lamp.

"Look at this rubbish! If we are to believe the Jesuit

newspapers as quoted here in *The Times*, Edgardo Mortara seems to have undergone a miraculous conversion and positively rejoices in his adoption into the Catholic faith!" They entered the foyer of the King's Theatre where crowds were gathering.

"On the other hand, behind this fervour, I believe there is a distraught and bewildered child caught in a tug of war between the two religions affecting his destiny," he said in front of a rather sombre poster announcing that Verdi's 'Nabucco' was 'now showing'.

"Now showing; the opera must have started – we must be late!" said the American, nodding at the poster with a smile.

His joke, however, was lost on Lady Montefiore, who turned to her husband, saying, "And what is the Pope doing about all this?"

"The Holy Father faces the storm with severe determination," answered Sir Moses. "It's more like severe obstinacy," said his wife, just as the Prince of Wales wandered into the foyer with a sizeable party. They all bowed to him.

"Put your newspaper away and stop your idle chatter, Montefiore, or you'll miss the Chorus of the Hebrew Slaves," said the Prince with boyish charm, a smile on his face.

They took their seats in the box next to the Prince. As the orchestra started playing, Sir Moses looked over to his wife. She looked troubled. "What are you thinking, my darling?" he whispered to her.

"His poor mother," was her reply.

Chapter 22

In the courtyard of her parents' house in Modena, Madame Mortara sat in a high-backed wooden chair under the shade of a fig tree. It was a tree that Edgardo had loved and had tried to climb as a toddler, the tree under which she had regaled him with stories about Daniel in the lion's den, Noah and his ark, and Joseph and his coat of many colours, as he had sat laughing and eating figs and bread dipped in green olive oil. She closed her eyes.

Augusto ran out into the courtyard. He said to her, "Will Edgardo ever be coming home?" He did not get a reply.

Her parents came out. As Madame Mortara turned away, they knew she did not want to talk, so they took Augusto back into the house.

For weeks she had sat in the garden in the same chair, every day dragging it out of the dining room as she told the children to leave her alone. She would sit there for hours, not saying a word.

She clutched the medal of the Blessed Virgin she had picked up from the floor of the convent after Momolo had wrenched it from Edgardo's neck. It was the last thing that had been in contact with Edgardo, a totem through which she could feel communion with him. Not an hour passed without her staring at it. She looked at the figure of Mary on the front: a halo around her head and the words around the medal's circumference: "O Mary, conceived without sin..." On the back of the medal was the letter 'M' surmounted by a cross and two hearts, one surrounded by a crown of thorns and the other pierced by a sword. Madame Mortara started to pray. "*Shema Yisrael* – Hear O Israel." When she had finished she looked again at the figure of the Blessed Virgin on the medal, and in a whisper begged her to return Edgardo to them.

Suddenly the wrought iron door swung open and Signor Mortara came running out. She immediately hid the medal in her fist. Her husband put his arms around her, but she did not respond to him. He stood back and took an envelope out of his pocket.

"It has come!" he said. "A letter from Rome." But she did not acknowledge his words.

"A letter from Edgardo!"

She turned to him. He handed the envelope to her. She took out the letter and began to read it.

Mama, Papa – I love you – more than I did before even, but I cannot give up being a Christian and therefore I cannot return home to you. If only you would convert, then I could come home and we could be a family again. The Pope says he will look after me, but Papa – you are my real father and Mama you are my real mother. If you convert we can all be together again and be a happy family. Tell Augusto that if he plays with my chess set he must put all the pieces back in the box, and tell him that he will break the box if he keeps forcing it closed like he does...

Signor Mortara watched his wife as she read the letter over and over again. Eventually she turned to him.

"We must convert," she said. "You once said we might do that for him."

Her husband looked at her with compassion. "No," he said firmly.

"Why can't we?" she pleaded. "Why?"

"Don't you see? Edgardo didn't write this himself," he replied. "It was the priests. We can't give in to this. We will never convert."

Marianna began to sob uncontrollably. "But then we could have him back and everything would be as it was before."

140

"I won't hear of it," said Signor Mortara. "We are Jews. Our children are Jews. I have sacrificed my business for this. All the time I have spent getting the Jewish communities of Italy to take up Edgardo's case; all the hours I have spent away from the business. Now there is no business."

"Yes, you have lost your business, and now we are ruined. We have had to leave Bologna over this – for what?" Red-eyed, his wife glared at him. "You are prepared to sacrifice Edgardo for this – sacrifice the whole family – for *what*?"

"Abraham was prepared to sacrifice Isaac – even to death..."

"You are no Abraham," she shouted, her voice rising to a high-pitched taunt. "You are such a good Jew, Momolo Mortara, such a good Jew! All the Jews of Bologna know you eat pork in the Piazza Maggiore."

Signor Mortara started to walk into the house. His wife shouted after him.

"You are no Jew and no father to Edgardo! Hypocrite! Now Edgardo can never come home. He will hate us forever. He doesn't even want to be a Jew."

Signor Mortara stopped and walked back to her. He hit her hard across her face and then walked back to the house. "Then let Edgardo be a Christian!" he shouted as he slammed the wrought iron door shut and went inside. He walked through to the parlour and sat down at a large, old wooden table. There lay some cards with which he used to play games and make houses with Edgardo. He got up restlessly and took some writing paper from an antique cabinet. He sat down again and started to write a letter.

"Our darling Edgardo..."

But he found he could not continue as tears welled up in his eyes. He picked up the cards and threw them across the table.

Chapter 23

The Vatican, The Papal States. 1858

"My trick! You are not concentrating today," Pius said to Edgardo as he took some cards from him. "You could have captured my Knave of Cups!"

Edgardo sat at the feet of the Pontiff on an embroidered footstool in the elegant Sala Clementina. He looked troubled.

"What is it?" Pius asked him.

Edgardo then spoke. "I have prayed and prayed, but my father is deaf to all my prayers. He will never convert. That means I can never go home, doesn't it?"

"As a Catholic you cannot," said Pius. He sat the boy on his knee. "I know it is difficult for you, but you must not be sad, Edgardo."

"But that means I can't see my mother and my father and my brothers and sisters ever again!"

The Pope said nothing.

"I might as well not have a family."

The Pope smiled at him. "You do have a family - you're not an orphan…"

"What's an orphan?"

"Someone who doesn't have a family."

"Well I might as well be an orphan," said Edgardo sadly.

The Pope suddenly became very serious. "There are people watching over you: Canon Sarra at the convent and all the teachers. I, too, will watch over you. I shall be your guardian and will give you a good education. Later on you will come to understand the greatness of the good fortune you have received."

Edgardo hugged the Holy Father.

As Pius got up, the Swiss Guards, Thomas and Laurent,

appeared at the doorway.

"Thomas, Laurent, how old are you?" the Pontiff asked them. Edgardo turned round to look at them.

"Nineteen, your Holiness," they both replied at the same time.

Pius turned to Edgardo. "Thomas and Laurent are young men, also parted from their families," he explained. "They are a long way from home."

"Where are your families?" Edgardo asked them.

"Mine are in the city of Geneva," said Thomas, taking off his helmet. He had cropped blond hair, "Laurent's are in Lausanne, also in Switzerland."

"Why did you leave your families?" Edgardo asked.

"We wanted to become Swiss Guards," Thomas said, "and serve the Pope!"

"More correctly, to serve the Holy See. That is why they left their families behind," Pius explained.

"And aren't you unhappy to be separated from them?" Edgardo asked.

"We miss them, of course, but we are proud and very happy to be here in service at the heart of the Christian world," Laurent answered. His face erupted into a warm smile. "And we get to wear these colourful uniforms. Here! Try on my hat." He took off the silver helmet with its red feathers he was wearing, which revealed his hair, a mass of black curls, and placed it on Edgardo's head.

Edgardo giggled.

Pius stood up. "I have state duties to attend to, though I would far rather sit here and play Scopa. Thomas, Laurent, will you play cards for a little while with young Edgardo here? He's very good and usually sweeps away all my cards." The Pope bent to kiss Edgardo on the forehead and left the room.

***

That night, as Edgardo got into bed in the convent of San Pietro in Vincoli, his sadness returned. He lay staring at the ceiling until Brother Claudio entered his dormitory.

"You are not asleep, Edgardo."

Edgardo half expected Brother Claudio to follow his comment with an angry eruption, even a smack, but Brother Claudio had stopped being mean to Edgardo. He still took his anger out on the other boys, and hit them too, but he found it astonishing that the Bishop of Rome had taken his pupil, Edgardo Mortara a Jewish boy, under his wing: that he – the Pope – sent a Pontifical employee to the convent every month to bring the sum of thirty scudos for his upkeep. Edgardo saw the Pope every other day, and Brother Claudio reckoned he had his own connection to the Pope through the boy. He was intrigued and fascinated, but most of all bemused.

Brother Claudio sat down on Edgardo's bed. "Are you alright?" he said quietly so as not to wake the other boys.

"I am still sad," Edgardo replied.

"How can you be sad? They say the Jews are the 'chosen people' and look at you: blessed, chosen by Pope Pius the Ninth above any other Christian child. Look at you: surrounded by toys, books and flowers sent by His Holiness the Pope, just to you, Edgardo Mortara. I have never known anything like it. Like most of the priests here, I was born in Rome, near where the Pope lives. As children, however, we could never have even dreamed of meeting him, let alone gaining the attention you receive: gifts, love and charity, from the holiest man in the world!"

"But you had parents," said Edgardo.

"No, I was an orphan. I had no parents. At least you know yours are alive. I would have been happy with that, even if I could never have seen them."

"It would have been easier if I had been an orphan too."

"No, it would not, Edgardo. You are truly blessed; you have the Pope as your father."

144

Brother Claudio leaned over and kissed him on the cheek and then ran his fingers very gently through his hair. "I think you'd better get some sleep," he said as he snuffed out the candles.

***

It took Edgardo a long time to get to sleep. When he did so he dreamed a disturbing dream. He saw himself walking through the hallways and corridors of the Vatican at twilight. He encountered the splendidly attired cardinals and priests; the councillors with their scarlet hats; and Thomas and Laurent and the other Swiss guards with their scarlet plumes – but their faces glared at him and became distorted. Two young priests pushed him through the Sistine Chapel, where choirs of eunuchs sang ugly, discordant melodies. The statues of Jesus and Mary, the paintings and the golden angels all dripped with blood. The two priests thrust him into the gardens, where tall palm trees, citron and orange trees dropped rotten fruit on to the lawns. The fountains in the Italianate gardens were all dried up; the wild flowers in the oak groves were all dead. He followed the pathway to the terrace in front of one of the huge towers of the Leonine Wall and there, on his ornate garden seat, Pope Pius looked across the Valle dell' Inferno.

Pius smiled at Edgardo as he walked over to him. They looked at the red roses together. Edgardo saw their thorns and stepped back. He turned to look at Pope Pius, but the Pontiff's face was now his father's. Signor Mortara looked very angry as he took Edgardo's hand and dragged him back through the gardens, through the Vatican Palace, through Saint Peter's Square; through the streets of Rome until they arrived at the ghetto. Among the people in rags he saw the musician, now playing a deathly dirge. He saw the musician's little daughter clutching her *mezuzah*, then saw his brothers and sisters, and in their midst, looking wretched and despondent, his mother.

He ran away from them, through the narrow passageways.

Suddenly in an alcove he saw a woman dressed like a statue of the Virgin Mary. It was Anna Morisi. He ran towards her. She embraced him and cradled him in her arms, just like the Madonna cradled Jesus. She led him down an alleyway. A wild yapping dog started to chase them. They ran through the alley to a road where the Pope's gold carriage, drawn by beautiful, black-plumed horses came to a standstill. Edgardo ran to the carriage. The Pope smiled at him before driving away at great speed, leaving him standing alone as a pack of yelping dogs ran towards him.

He screamed.

Chapter 24

"Aiuto! Aiuto!" Father Mortara was shouting in his sleep.

Raoul set his breakfast tray down on a small wooden table in the simple room and then sat down on a wooden chair next to the bed. He took the old man's arm and stroked it. Father Mortara opened his eyes as he mumbled, "I cani! The dogs!" Then he composed himself. "In my dream; it was the dogs!" he said. "You didn't wake me for Lauds."

Raoul smiled at him. "No, and I didn't wake you for Mass either. I thought you needed the rest, Father."

"It's true. I'm not sleeping well."

Raoul helped Father Mortara out of bed and took him to the window. He opened it. They looked out across the wheat fields to Bouhay where the sun was rising over the rooftops. For several minutes they did not speak.

Raoul broke the silence. "I'll never understand why you don't feel angry that the Church took you away from your family."

"The Church has also taken you away from your family. Does that make you angry?"

Raoul did not answer.

"You might have had a family of your own if you had not joined the Church. You have on more than one occasion mentioned a girl - Delphine… Didn't you want to marry her?"

Raoul turned away and looked out of the window. He could see the labourers in the distance, busy digging drainage ditches. Farmer Delacroix was ploughing his wheat fields with a pair of horses. He wondered where Delphine was, what she was doing at this moment.

"Didn't you love her?"

Raoul stared into the horizon. A large bird with a forked tail flew into the bare branches of a solitary field maple. "I think that was a red kite," he muttered.

"Did you love her?"

Father Mortara's persistence began to unsettle the novice. Raoul continued to gaze at the tree. The red kite took off and soared into the sky. "I loved her. Yes I loved her, Father, and, yes, I would have married her. She was... she is... the most beautiful... the most gentle and kindest of creatures."

Father Mortara said nothing. He waited for Raoul to continue.

"She did not have the same feelings for me. She left me for someone else."

Father Mortara turned and looked at him. "So you joined the Church?"

Raoul did not answer, instead staring at the wheat field, now a winter feeding ground of wild geese and wood pigeons, foraging for leftover stubble. He remembered the summers when the same field had been a great yellow sea of corn through which he had chased Delphine. He was overwhelmed by his feelings. He took a deep breath and reminded himself of why he was here, to serve and support the old man, and he resolved to put his feelings to one side.

"Come and have your breakfast, Father. My mother has sent over some delicious blackberry jam."

He went over to the table, poured Father Mortara a cup of tea, and buttered him two thick slices of white bread. Father Mortara continued to look out of the window, and then finally changed the subject.

"It is so quiet here. Rome was such a noisy city. Everywhere people were shouting, laughing, singing."

Raoul opened the jam jar and smelled the blackberries.

"I can almost hear them, Brother Luc," Father Mortara said after a long time.

"What, Father?" Raoul asked him. "What can you hear?"

"The Pifferari, the Pipers coming down from the mountains into Rome at Advent…"

Chapter 25

Rome, The Papal States. 1858

The air was filled with melodies that were getting louder and louder as the Rector and Brother Claudio led Edgardo and a group of boys through the gates of the convent on to the streets. They saw a noisy crowd dancing towards them, led by men who looked like brigands.

"Who are they?" Edgardo asked.

"The *Pifferari* – wandering musicians who have come down from the Abruzzi mountains and the hill villages to herald the approach of Christmas, which they've done for hundreds of years," Brother Claudio explained. "They play their bagpipes in front of all the shrines of the Virgin Mary. People think the *Pifferari*'s music will bring good luck."

A group of five of the musicians, wearing broad coats of brown cloth and pointed hats, smiled at Edgardo and the other boys, their wild eyes blazing, and with the music so loud that the boys had to cover their ears. They entered the courtyard of the convent, dancing as they continued to play their instruments, the music suddenly transforming into a solemn prayer-like chant in front of the statue of Our Lady of Tears. The boys followed them and listened as they played their bagpipes and oboe-like *pifferi*, their heads slightly inclined over their shoulders and their eyes filled with a pious love as they fixed their gaze on the statue of the Madonna.

Edgardo was spellbound as the bagpipes sounded the bass, playing a harmony of two or three notes over which a man with a medium-length *piffero* performed a melody. Then two boys of no more than aged twelve started playing the short *pifferi*, decorating the rustic melody with sweet-sounding trills.

The boys followed the *Pifferari* back on to the street where the music became more cheerful again, and some of them started singing in their strong voices to the delight of shopkeepers who were pouring on to the streets. The Rector and Brother Claudio led Edgardo and the convent boys all the way to Saint Peter's Square, crowded with pilgrims, tourists and war heroes who watched with enthusiasm as groups of the *Pifferari* converged, filling the square with the loudest cacophonous sound imaginable. People started to dance. Artists tried to capture the scene on their sketchpads: some of the *Pifferari* offered themselves as models. One artist asked if he could draw Edgardo, but the Rector pulled him away and he and Brother Claudio took the boys back to the convent.

For the whole of Advent the *Pifferari* filled the streets of the Eternal City with music, sometimes starting early and waking Edgardo and the boys in his dormitory at four o'clock in the morning.

On each of the Sundays in Advent Edgardo was invited by Pope Pius to attend Mass in the Sistine Chapel.

"Can we come to Advent Mass at the Vatican too?" a convent boy asked on one of the Sundays.

"No," said Canon Sarra sternly. "The Holy Father has invited only Edgardo."

"What is Advent?" said Edgardo.

Canon Sarra looked at him, his eyebrows rising, trying to curb his annoyance that a soul so ignorant of such a key Roman Catholic ceremony should be invited to it. "You surely know what Advent is, Edgardo?"

"I know it's the first season of the Church year, leading up to Christmas."

"And do you know what Christmas is?" asked Canon Sarra sarcastically, before telling Brother Claudio to deliver him to the Pope.

As the young monk took his hand and walked Edgardo to Saint Peter's, he explained how the *Gloria* of the Mass was omitted at Advent.

"The *Gloria* is like an angels' song," said Edgardo.

"Exactly, so when it returns at Christmas it is a glorious novelty," said Brother Pius. "You are so lucky that the Holy Father wishes you to be a part of all this."

"Am I?" said Edgardo.

"Oh my word yes. You will join the candlelit procession of the Holy Sacrament, which the Pope himself will lead, to the Pauline Chapel where it will then be carried in succession to all the churches and chapels in Rome," said Brother Claudio, his envy discernible. "Only the top priests, clerics and cardinals are invited to Advent Mass. I have heard that even the Patriarch of Antioch will be there."

"Who is he?" asked Edgardo.

"He comes from Antioch in Turkey, where lots of Jews lived at one time. It's where Christianity was first spread to Gentiles."

"So lots of Jews have converted to Christianity, haven't they?" said Edgardo.

"Oh dear me yes; you're not by any means the first Jewish convert, Edgardo."

On account of Edgardo's ties to the Pope, Brother Claudio had stopped being cruel and mean to him. When they arrived at the sentry point, where two Swiss Guards were keeping watch, he hoped and even tried to get through with Edgardo, but he was not allowed in. Only Edgardo was ushered in to the Apostolic Palace.

***

When Christmas Eve arrived, the friendly guards allowed Brother Claudio in too. Edgardo ran ahead through the eastern wing of the Vatican. He stopped to look out of a large window where the whole of Rome lay before him, and then continued to the grand staircase.

"You can leave me here," he shouted back to Brother Claudio.

"I'd better take you up," said Brother Claudio as he caught up with him. He was mesmerised by the frescoes and tapestries lining the corridors and eager to see as much of the Apostolic Palace as he could.

"It's alright, I know the way," said Edgardo.

A young Swiss Guard in his fancy blue, red, orange and yellow uniform came running down the stairs: it was Thomas.

"*Bonjour*, Edgardo," said Thomas. "It's alright. I will take him up." He signalled to another Swiss Guard to show Brother Claudio out.

"Shouldn't I wait here to take him back to San Pietro in Vincoli?" said Brother Claudio, desperate for some kind of involvement in the Papal Household.

"Oh no," said Thomas. "The Pope wants Edgardo to spend the whole of Christmas Eve here and tonight he wants to take him to the special Mass at the Basilica of Santa Maria Maggiore. We shall deliver him home from there."

"Why do we go to Mass there?" asked Edgardo as Brother Claudio was escorted out.

"Because the Pope likes to go out and pray with the people of Rome on Christmas Eve, and anyway in that church in a crystal container in the crypt are ancient fragments of wood. These are part of the manger used to hold Jesus when he was born in Bethlehem."

"How can that be true?" asked Edgardo.

"Because Pio Nono says it's true, and if he says it's true it must be true," said Thomas, laughing, as he chased Edgardo up the stairs, caught the boy, and started to tickle him. Edgardo shrieked with delight.

They entered the Pope's residential quarters on the third floor. A group of Pio Nono's private secretaries and servants greeted Edgardo with a smile and a '*Buon Giorno*'. They continued through the Sala Clementina where another young

153

Swiss Guard shouted, "Who goes there?" teasing Edgardo with a big smile on his face. It was Laurent.

"You know who I am," said Edgardo laughing, and they continued to a residential suite of rooms where a bright winter sun was pouring through the windows. Thomas and Laurent took Edgardo through to the Sala degli Arazzi, with its huge Gobelin tapestries adorning the walls, and there the Supreme Pontiff was seated on a magnificent throne-like seat. In front of him was a large pile of colourful boxes decorated with flowers and ribbons tied into bows.

Edgardo ran over and threw his arms around Pio Nono before jumping on his knee.

"What's in these boxes?" he asked.

"Presents," said Pius. "Presents for you, Edgardo, on your first Christmas – to celebrate the birth of our Saviour, Jesus."

Edgardo's face lit up, and then he suddenly screwed up his eyebrows. "But I haven't got a present for you, Father."

"That doesn't matter," said the Pope. "The Romans stopped giving Christmas presents many centuries ago."

"Why?" asked Edgardo.

"Because in ancient times the Pagans – non-Christians – used to give presents when they celebrated their winter festivals. So for a while it was thought to be un-Christian."

"But it's alright now?"

"Thanks to Queen Victoria and the English giving presents at Christmas, half of Europe gives them now," said the Pope.

"In my family we give each other money at Chanukah, which is like a Jewish Christmas," said Edgardo.

"Well there's no money in those boxes, only gifts. I hope when you open them, you will appreciate the books as well as the sweets and the toys."

Edgardo looked up at him. "I will, Father. I'll read all the books," the boy assured him.

Moretta the Vatican kitten suddenly appeared from behind one of the coloured boxes. She sat on the pile of presents and started washing her white bib with her tongue. Laurent picked her up and stroked her before handing her to Edgardo.

"What would you like to do today, before the Christmas Mass at Santa Maria Maggiore this evening?" Pius asked.

"Well we might play with Moretta and perhaps we could go and hear the choirs singing in the Sistine Chapel?" said Edgardo as he stroked the kitten. Moretta trembled a little as she purred.

The Pontiff smiled and nodded. Laurent took the kitten and placed her back amongst the boxes and Thomas led the way as they retraced their steps through the maze of rooms, Edgardo holding Pius' hand. Eventually they reached the Sistine Chapel where many candles were burning and a large choir was singing exquisite Christmas music. A group of *castrati* started to sing a solo Gloria section in their falsetto voices.

"How can those men sing such high notes like women do?" Edgardo whispered to Laurent.

"They are the eunuch singers; they have to see a doctor," said the Swiss Guard. "He does a special operation down there," he said as he grabbed Edgardo between his legs, making him giggle.

"Shh!" said Pius putting his finger over his mouth before leading them out into the courtyard.

"Edgardo you are not still sad, are you?" asked Pius as they entered the Apostolic Palace.

Edgardo mulled over the question and screwed up his eyebrows before he replied. "No, Father."

"Good," said the Pope. "Now you said you wanted to play with Moretta before the Mass?"

"Yes and may I open my Christmas presents?" asked Edgardo.

"Of course," said Pius. "You can also play with Thomas and Laurent in the gardens, or board games in the palace, and we can all have lunch together first. You can also feed

Moretta." He leant down and kissed his young protégé on his forehead. "You are very dear to me, Edgardo. I hope that after Christmas you will come and stay at Castel Gandolpho, my country home outside Rome."

"I should very much like that, Father," said Edgardo. "Can Thomas and Laurent come too?"

"I am sure that can be arranged."

Chapter 26

London, United Kingdom. 1859

Sir Moses Montefiore sat alone at the back of the Bevis Marks Synagogue in the City of London. He wore a *tallit*, a black and white tasselled prayer shawl, over his formal black frock coat, wing-collared shirt and emerald green cravat, with its diamond-encrusted pin. As he prayed he drifted in and out of his daydreams. The sun poured in through the large windows. He closed his eyes; his thoughts took him back to his modest beginnings in Kennington. He reflected on his life: his birth in Leghorn in Italy, a town famous for its straw bonnets; his appalling exam results at school; his apprenticeship at the grocer's and at the tea merchant's; his time at the London Royal Exchange as one of the City's twelve 'Jew Brokers'; his marriage to his beloved Judith, the daughter of one of the wealthiest Jewish families in London, whose sister had married into the Rothschilds; his knighthood from Queen Victoria; his trips to Syria, Russia and the Holy Land; and his beloved East Cliff on the cliff tops in Ramsgate. Life had treated him well. He was a foreigner and a Jew, but he knew he was truly blessed. Judith said this was because he was six foot three.

For a moment he smiled, but then he began to think about the boy Edgardo Mortara and the strange twist of fate now clouding the boy's life. Perhaps it was because he and Judith had never had children of their own that he wanted to help Edgardo and his parents: to put in place some kind of justice. The Pope had said the boy was 'blessed'. In some ways perhaps that was true. There was no worse place in the world to be a Jew than in the Rome Ghetto. At least he had been spared that fate.

Sir Moses pulled the *tallit* up to cover his head and prayed again, this time for the boy, rocking gently to and fro.

He got up and took off his *tallit*, which he had first worn at his wedding nearly fifty years ago and put it into its velvet bag that had a gold Star of David embroidered on the front. He wandered into the vestry, and took his seat among the assembled members of the Board of Deputies of British Jews who had gathered for their weekly meeting. One of the members, Mr Sebag, stood up.

"I believe I speak for all of you when I say that in the opinion of the Board it is desirable to petition the Pontifical Government on the subject of the Mortara case," he said.

Other members nodded as he went on.

"And I believe we are all agreed that Sir Moses Montefiore, Baronet, as President of the Board of Deputies of British Jews, be requested to present the same personally, if and when his engagements allow him to undertake the journey."

Sir Moses stood up.

"I will be honoured to proceed to Rome," he said.

"We are most grateful. No one can imagine the terrible suffering of that sad little boy," said Mr Sebag.

***

The large drawing room of the Montefiore's London residence resounded with the dissonant notes of the cello and the viola, finally resolving to a C major, as the musicians played Mozart's String Quartet Number Nineteen to a sizeable gathering.

"You have a wonderful view of Hyde Park from here, Sir Moses," Gershom Kursheedt observed as he looked out of large windows on to Park Lane.

Lady Montefiore came over with a distinguished looking gentleman. "Gershom, have you met the worthy and honourable baronet, Sir Culling Eardley?" she said as she introduced Mr Kursheedt to him. "Gershom is one of our co-religionists from New Orleans," she said with a big smile.

"I seem to recall, Mr Kursheedt, that you helped Sir Moses in the task of establishing almshouses in Palestine," said Sir Culling.

The American nodded. "Yes, and I'm now helping Sir Moses prepare for his appeal on behalf of the boy Mortara," the American replied.

"Maybe you can also help us, Culling," said Sir Moses. He turned to Mr Kursheedt. "Culling has met Garibaldi on more than one occasion. He passed several years on the continent, but here at home he co-founded the Evangelical Alliance."

"Sir Culling may preach for the Evangelical Alliance, but he is actually descended on his mother's side from the Jewish family of Gideon," Lady Montefiore chipped in.

"Although Judith tries to claim me for the Jewish people, to her chagrin I am a good Christian," said Culling Eardley.

"How do you feel about the Mortara case?" Kursheedt asked him.

Sir Culling was quick to reply. "I feel that the laws of nature and society have been violated. It seems to me Roman Catholicism is above all natural rights, and that these days parental affection is regarded as a Pagan prejudice! I must say, I feel for every Jew throughout the world, which is why the Protestant Association's appeal to the Foreign Secretary has my full backing. It's not only the Jews in this country who are angered, you know. Very many Christians are incensed by the news of this case."

Sir Moses nodded. "Yes, Roman Catholics are protesting too. Perhaps in this instance Pius and the Vatican have taken things too far. All the great Roman Catholic powers, even Austria, have now addressed appeals to the Pope for the release of the boy. And the French Ambassador, under instructions from Paris, has protested to the Cardinal Prime Minister, Antonelli, expressing the dissatisfaction of the Emperor with regard to the case. The French have taken the Mortara affair to their hearts: it is the talk of French Society."

"It's not only French Society; all over Europe, from St Petersburg to Edinburgh, the case is argued back and forth," Lady Judith chipped in. "All are united in their desire for the return of the poor child to his parents."

"But still Pio Nono says 'No, No!'" said Mr Kursheedt with obvious pleasure as he took a swig of port from the crystal goblet.

"If he keeps saying 'No', it could be political suicide for him," said Sir Moses.

"The wretched Pontiff will not care a bit," said Sir Culling. "All who do not agree with him are non-believers who want to drag a wretched young Jew boy of Bologna from Paradise, a miserable sinner whom he wishes to convert into an angel of goodness! Political suicide is one thing, Moses; religious suicide is another. If conversion of the Jews is the Sovereign Pontiff's aim, then popery itself must be the grand impediment to the conversion of the world."

Sir Moses smiled at him. "I am sure the Evangelical Alliance would rather convert the boy themselves – eh, Culling?" He went on to address the group. "Culling should really set up a society for promoting Christianity among the Jews." He turned to Gershom Kursheedt. "I secretly think Culling hopes that the Edgar Mortara incident might be a symptom of some coming change in Rome, and that the Jews, touched by the sympathy of Christ's disciples, shall come to know and love Christ."

"Exactly! Then at least Momolo Mortara and his family will not have suffered in vain," said Sir Culling defending himself. "On the other hand, they may not have suffered in vain because you are going to Rome to save the boy. Isn't that so, Sir Moses?"

Sir Moses smiled.

"Gershom here has agreed to come with us as a representative of the Americans," Lady Montefiore informed

160

Sir Culling.

"When will you go?" asked the baronet.

"Very soon, but Moses first has to perform a very pleasant duty of a political nature before leaving England," Lady Montefiore replied.

"What is that, Sir Moses?" Eardley asked him.

"I wish to assist in the election of Baron Meyer de Rothschild, as Liberal MP for Hythe."

"What a time this is for Jews in politics," Sir Culling remarked, "what with Lionel de Rothschild being allowed, as a Jew, to take his seat in Parliament last year."

Sir Culling raised his glass to Lionel de Rothschild who was standing across the room.

Sir Moses also raised his glass. "Exactly, and *he* never abandoned his faith," he said with a warm smile.

Lady Montefiore called Lionel de Rothschild over. "When are you going to put your weight behind the Mortara affair, Lionel?" she said as she smiled at him. "Now that you have a seat in the House, you surely have great influence with the Government. You must instigate a formal protest."

"The Foreign Office line is, as I'm sure you're aware Lady Judith, that the interference of a Protestant Government would be entirely of no avail after the earnest efforts of Catholic States have failed," Rothschild replied.

Lady Montefiore took his hand. "You should remind Pio Nono that your family lends money to the Papal Court," she said. "The Vatican, as we all know, relies as keenly as any other European territory on its Rothschild loans to keep itself out of debt, the more so at the present time when half of Europe is happy to watch the Papal States collapsing on its knees."

Rothschild laughed. "Montefiore, set your wife in front of Pope Pius and I'm sure it will only be a matter of days before the Mortara boy is back with his parents!"

Chapter 27

Castel Gandolfo, The Papal States. 1859

As quickly as autumn turned into winter, so winter turned into spring, and with the changing seasons the Pope took ever more responsibility for Edgardo. The boy had cost him dearly; Pius had paid a high price for his conversion, but Edgardo was still unaware of this when the Pontiff took him to stay at Castel Gandolfo, south of Rome: the summer residence and retreat of popes since the seventeenth century.

High in the Alban Hills, the early spring sun shimmered between two cypress trees in the garden of the upper terrace, throwing an incandescent reflection into the indigo waters of Lake Albano.

Pius looked out on to the lake from the balcony of the drawing room. He watched a bird in the distance soaring out of the pine forest on the far shore and lifted a three-drawer leather-clad field telescope to his eyes, a present from the King of Portugal. The bird, a large bird of prey, flew towards the palace. It was brown with a white underbelly and a broad black band at the end of its long tail: a Bonelli's eagle, he thought. It circled the lake before flying back to the forest.

Pius heard laughter. He lowered the telescope to the trees on the Galleria di Sotto, the avenue separating the Pontifical Palace from the ornate gardens. He saw a flash of red, a flash of blue and a flash of gold as two young Swiss Guards came into view. Thomas and Laurent ran through the trees, hand in hand with Edgardo. Every few paces they swung him into the air. Edgardo whooped with joy. He grabbed hold of Thomas' red-plumed helmet and put it on before running off across the lawns, richly decorated with their flower-beds, statues and fountains. Thomas and Laurent chased him along a row of

162

myrtle hedges and threw him to the ground, only managing to retrieve the helmet after a prolonged spell of frenzied tickling. Thomas pulled a face as he placed the helmet on top of his golden locks.

Pius called out loudly, "Edgardo! Edgardo!" He surprised himself, for this was a totally involuntary action. Edgardo looked up and waved, smiling at the Pontiff. Thomas and Laurent waved too; they were little more than boys themselves. They all got up and Edgardo did a funny little dance, turning round on the spot, waving his hands in the air and shaking his bottom. Thomas and Laurent copied his moves and they all waved again.

Pius smiled and thanked God that at least the boy was happy. He put the telescope down on a Sienna marble table with a grapevine motif and withdrew into the drawing room where Antonelli was lighting a cigar. Pius's Secretary of State picked up a newspaper and started to read from it.

I ask you – how is it that the ridiculous actions of a silly child could lead to consequences so serious as to agitate Jew and Gentile throughout Europe and America? How could these actions, rooted more in superstition than in religion, born out of treachery and dishonour – performed, if they were performed at all, surreptitiously by a child on an infant, ever be considered a Holy sacrament? No, it is an insult to the name of God to assert that these actions can meet with His blessing.

He paused, hoping for a reaction from the Pontiff, but Pius remained silent.

"The words of a Dr Raphall, a supposedly eminent Rabbi addressing a crowd of Christians and Jews in the Mozart Hall in New York," Antonelli explained.

Pius ignored him. He sat down on a carved, high-back gilt chair. Suddenly Antonelli started to chuckle. Pius's neck muscles began to twitch.

And supposing the child was baptised clandestinely by the servant girl – does that honestly make him a Catholic? Let us reverse the case and suppose a band of armed Jews were to penetrate the Vatican, to seize the Pope and with a razor or some other sharp instrument were to circumcise him – would that make the Pope a Jew, any more than the sprinkling of water made the child of a Jew a Christian?

Pius glared at him. "You think that is funny?"

Antonelli's tittering turned quickly into a scowl. He put down the newspaper, poised to change his tone and reason with the Pope, but Pius got up and left the room. He walked down the long gallery, not pausing as he usually did to look at the tapestries and brocades or the ornate panels painted by Carlo Dolci, Paolo Veronese, and Salvator Rosa. His mind was elsewhere. He quickly made his way to the glass doorway that opened on to the tiered gardens. He followed the pathways to the myrtle hedges

Suddenly Edgardo came running towards him. "Shh!" he said, "We're playing hide and seek."

On an impulse Pius lifted his white silk cassock.

"Quick, hide under here," he said.

Edgardo darted under the Pope's cassock just as Thomas and Laurent rounded the walkway.

"Where is Edgardo?" Pius asked them.

"We are looking for him," replied Laurent.

"Playing hide and seek," Thomas explained.

"We must stop now; it is lunchtime." Pius nudged Edgardo with his knee. Edgardo could hardly contain his laughter. "Please call him."

Thomas and Laurent called out, "Edgardo!"

They started to run around the gardens. Pius sat down on a country seat with Edgardo still under his cassock. After several minutes the young guards returned.

"We cannot find him."

"Oh? I did entrust him to your care." The Pope seemed very concerned. "I hope he didn't go down to the lake. You know he cannot swim."

Thomas and Laurent were mortified.

The Major-Domo of Castel Gandolfo walked over the lawn towards them.

"Have you seen Edgardo?" Pius asked him.

"No."

"He seems to have disappeared." The Pope stood up and suddenly Edgardo burst out laughing. Pius lifted his skirt and out skipped Edgardo.

They all laughed.

"Very naughty of us, I know," said Pius.

"Lunch is served," said the Major-Domo.

"Can we have a picnic?" Edgardo asked. His green eyes opened wide as he looked up at Pius.

The Major-Domo tried to reason with the Pope. "We have the food all ready to serve in the dining room, Your Holiness. Cardinal Antonelli is in there waiting for you. I don't think he likes to eat outside because of all the insects."

The Pope was indifferent to his words. "There aren't that many insects – it's not yet summer. It's such a lovely day – yes, let's have a picnic," he enthused. There was still a lot of the boy in Pius.

The Major-Domo's expression did not change. "In that case I will arrange a transfer of the food to one of the garden tables."

"Can we go down to the lake and have our picnic there and sit on the ground like the villagers do?" Edgardo asked.

"It's quite a long way and a steep climb down," said the Major-Domo, screwing up his eyebrows.

"But it's not that far," said Pius. "Yes, Edgardo, you and I shall picnic by the lake."

"Can Thomas and Laurent come to the picnic too?"

Edgardo looked into the Pontiff's eyes and gave him a big smile.

"We have not prepared lunch for Thomas and Laurent," said the Major-Domo.

Thomas broke an awkward silence. "Oh – we can have our lunch with the rest of the staff and then join you by the lake."

"No; you must be our guests for the picnic today," said Pius.

"Oh yes please! Thomas and Laurent said they will teach me how to swim; we could have a swim after lunch and go fishing!" Edgardo jumped up and down with glee.

The furrows in the Major-Domo's forehead started to crease one by one, and his eyes became slit-like. He knew that this change of plan would be littered with a hundred more requests and changes to his routine, and much as he loved his Pontiff he resented the orders for bathing towels and extra cutlery and fishing rods and 'play clothes' for two Swiss Guards who surely had not come to Rome from Switzerland to be nursemaids, for books and newspapers and rugs to be brought down to the lake where the common people of the village ate their bread and cheese. And all this for an errant Jew boy who seemed to have bewitched the Head of the Catholic Church.

"Is it not too cold for swimming?" But the Major-Domo pleaded in vain; nobody was listening to him.

As Thomas helped Pius down the steep path to the lakeside, Laurent and Edgardo ran ahead. Laurent suddenly disappeared into the foliage of a particularly large orange tree. Pius stopped to watch him as he jumped down again, clutching a couple of oranges. He shared one with Edgardo, dribbling juice over his stiff white ruff, oblivious of the fact that he was in his Swiss Guard uniform.

"Ugh – it's bitter," shouted Edgardo, spitting it out of his mouth.

Laurent threw the oranges into the undergrowth.

"Be careful of your clothes, Laurent: the Vatican has to pay your laundry bills," said Pius drily.

Chapter 28

Bouhay, Liège, Belgium. 1940

"That afternoon at Castel Gandolfo, platters of meat and cheeses and silver trays of fruit arrived by the lakeside for our picnic and wine... I had my first taste of wine by the shores of Lake Albano, laid out on a white lace tablecloth. We sat on rugs and velvet cushions, having our feast alfresco in the sunshine. Thomas and Laurent chased me round the lake before throwing off their clothes and diving in. They called me to join them and I waded into the cold water. They held me as I shivered and squealed, bobbing me up and down as we all called out to Pio Nono, who watched from a rough stone country seat..."

Father Mortara spoke slowly, smiling as he sat with Raoul on a wooden bench in the orchard overlooking the wheat fields.

"Over the next three days when the young Swiss Guards taught me to swim, I had no idea that Anna Morisi had now returned to the village of her birth in the commune of San Giovanni in Persiceto outside Bologna, or that my parents were struggling to survive in Modena. As we fished with rods in the waters of Lake Albano, we caught the largest carp you ever saw. I was unaware that the whole world was resonating with the sound of my name and that news of my abduction had reached its farthest corners. From London to San Francisco, Mortara meetings were being held, as my case was fiercely debated. As I drove through the streets of Castel Gandolfo in the Papal carriage, nestled against the Pontiff and bound once again for Rome and the Convent of San Pietro in Vincoli, little did I know that even in Sydney in Australia, speakers were campaigning for my release."

Father Mortara stopped and turned to Raoul, half-expecting that the young novice would be impressed, amazed, incredulous, but Raoul, saddened by what he had heard, barely reacted.

"You have lived an incredible life, Father," was all he said, but he couldn't help thinking what a sad life it was. Father Mortara had been to the Roman Ghetto and seen how the Jews lived in squalor, and probably could not believe how lucky he had been to be living in the lap of luxury under the watchful eye of the Pope, with Swiss Guards as playmates and food and gifts that he would never have had if he had gone back home to his parents. Maybe it was convenient for him that his parents hadn't converted; it had given him an excuse not to return to them. But what was it all for? Ultimately it had led to an empty, sad life, devoid of love and family. Suddenly he thought that this might be how his own life might end in seventy years time.

Raoul got up and took hold of the secateurs he had been using to prune the apple trees. He climbed the nearest tree, pulling his long monk's robe up between his legs. Father Mortara watched him as he quickly trimmed the outer branches into the shape of a wine glass.

"Should give a good crop next season," shouted Raoul as he jumped with no trepidation out of the tree. "Hopefully it will produce some beauties like these." He took a large apple wrapped in newspaper out of his pocket. "Fresh from the apple store - a Boskoop red," he said as he unwrapped it and offered it to the old man.

"I can't bite apples – nothing on my front teeth – it makes the dentures fall out of my mouth."

They both laughed and Raoul went back to pruning the apple trees. When he had finished he gathered up all the cut branches and took them to one of the woodpiles.

The bell rang for lunch. Raoul walked Brother Pius back to the Priory stopping to wash his hands at one of the outhouse taps.

**

"Where did these laws come from?" Raoul asked Father Mortara, over lunch in the refectory, vocalising his thoughts as he tried to cut into his fried liver.

"What laws? Good grief, my boot leather would taste better than this…" Father Mortara looked at him, shook his head, and laughed.

"The laws that say that the child of Jewish parents should be taken away from them. Do they come from the scriptures?" asked Raoul.

Some of the monks turned round to look at them both.

"No. It's not in the scriptures," Father Mortara said in a low voice.

"Then it does seem as if Pius the Ninth kidnapped you," Raoul said to him.

Father Mortara was weary. He had heard it all before: endless transcripts from meetings held all around the world, bandying words such as 'kidnapping' and 'abduction'. As a young man he had read them all: testimonies of cynics at the Great Mortara Meeting of 1858 in San Francisco; it was said to be the biggest meeting the city had ever held; speeches by the enlightened in a new age of progress in Sydney, who seemed to think that in the Papal States, where the Inquisition was still rife, the rack, the halter, burning and hanging were still in existence, and all overseen by a merciless Pope who stole children from their parents.

Father Mortara began to mumble in Italian, then in French. His conversations with Raoul were becoming more and more one-sided; he could not hear everything the novice said, and Raoul in turn could only decipher fragments of his speeches. As he cut Father Mortara's liver and potatoes into small pieces and put them on his fork for him, the old man mumbled something about England, where Jews in 1858 were allowed to take their seats in Parliament, and something about a meeting at the Mansion House in the City of London, led by Sir Culling Eardley of the Evangelical Alliance. Father Mortara's utterances were those of a learned man who had been familiar with even the most obscure organisations of the Christian world. The names went over Raoul's head, but he identified with a British aristocrat who addressed a large crowd of Christians proclaiming that Jews, in remaining true to their God, were no less loyal to their sovereign Victoria, contrasting this enlightenment with the sad state of affairs in Rome.

"Yes!" said Raoul, excitedly agreeing, but Father Mortara was only citing the meeting to illustrate yet another example of how his beloved Pius was once again ridiculed: how in Italy Pius the Ninth was mocked and called 'Pio Nono', who only said 'No No'.

"What they didn't realise was that my baptism had given me a vocation in Christianity," Father Mortara explained, "even at the tender age of six-and-a-half."

Raoul could hardly hold back. "How happy your father must have been with that!" he muttered, but Father Mortara did not hear him.

The old man stopped talking. One of the lay brothers started to serve them a very dry steamed pudding. Father Mortara pushed it away.

"Did Pius not appreciate a parent's rights? Didn't he see that enforcing his laws in defiance of the civilised world must have seemed very arrogant?" said Raoul.

"Pius was not arrogant; he was a good man, a saint even," said Father Mortara.

Raoul took the Boskoop apple out of his pocket and started to cut it into segments for him.

Chapter 29

Rome, The Papal States. 1859

In the light of an April midday sun, a line of carriages drew up in front of the grand hotels and apartment buildings in the Piazza del Popolo. Rome was filling up with wealthy foreigners and aristocrats escaping the colder weather of London and Paris. They disembarked with their luggage, the men sporting colourful neckties and the women wide-brimmed hats and blouses with pagoda sleeves.

Sir Moses stepped out of the carriage as the driver opened the doors for him. His wife followed with Gershom Kursheedt and their physician, Doctor Hodgkin, who Sir Moses had insisted on bringing over with them to oversee his wife's delicate health.

The journey from France had been exhausting. On their steam ship from Marseilles to Civita Vecchia, the main port of Rome, Sir Moses had found it hard to sleep. Being so tall he was not built for a cabin bed that was hardly five feet in length. He had spent most of the night going over the words of the prayer offered to him by the Rabbi at the Bevis Marks Synagogue. It had been awkwardly delivered, but he had been genuinely moved.

> *O Lord! Look down from Thy Holy abode and bless Sir Moses Montefiore and his illustrious consort.*

He had peered down to where Judith, still youthful in appearance, with a half smile on her face, had been sleeping in the berth below him.

> *Over the years they have cheerfully braved every danger,*

presenting themselves before mighty kings, in order to intervene on behalf of their people and now they venture to Rome in the just cause of a persecuted child.

The congregation had put all their faith in him and he had felt humbled by that. He had repeated the words but still could not sleep.

Give, O Lord, Thy angels charge over them. Direct their plans with Thy wisdom and cause them to return in safety to their beloved home.

As the ship had lurched through turbulent waves, he had recalled his meeting with the Foreign Secretary. Lord Malmesbury had been cordial, but not terribly encouraging. "You must bear in mind from a previous conversation we had about the boy Mortara that I can only entertain doubts as to the result of your mission," he had said. "But by God, I wish you well Montefiore!" He had slapped him hard on the back and given him all the letters of introduction he needed for the British Embassy in Italy.

At least Judith had managed to sleep, in spite of her stomach problem. He remembered her words on the deck as they had watched a magnificent red sun setting over the western Mediterranean. "It's not long since we returned from Palestine, Mosey! Is there no end to packet steamers, horses and litters, ships and mules?"

Sir Moses had put his arm around her. "It's a long journey and you're not well. Oh my darling Judith, perhaps it's wrong of me to bring you to Rome."

"At least we have Dr Hodgkin with us," she had replied, "and anyway I have never missed a trip with you before. Also, I know how important this is. Edgardo Mortara means a lot to you, doesn't he?"

"Yes. If we can only draw the world's attention to the

injustice of this kidnapping by Pope Pius, on account of a very questionable baptism, we have won a modest battle," Sir Moses had said as he looked out to sea.

He remembered how Judith had said sadly, "Yes we would have wanted to fight this battle for a son of ours."

***

Sir Moses took his wife's arm and helped her up the wide marble steps. A swarm of porters immediately appeared and started to shift a mountain of brown leather trunks, which the driver and his assistant had just unloaded on to the pavement.

Sir Moses recognised Colonel Bruce, the Prince of Wales' middle-aged aide, and nodded as the young prince himself bounded over to him.

"Montefiore, how are you? You know Colonel Bruce, my chaperone?" said the Prince with obvious resentment at having a minder travelling with him. The Prince took a long *figurado* cigar out of his mouth and smiled, revealing a set of teeth that were far yellower than those of most eighteen-year-olds. "And you, Lady Montefiore? What are you both doing here? It seems that most of London is in Rome for Easter Week, but I'm sure you're not here for that celebration."

"No, we haven't converted to Christianity," said Sir Moses. "We're in Rome to try to petition the Pope about the sad affair of the boy Edgardo Mortara. Do you know about the case?"

Colonel Bruce nodded gravely. "Yes. In fact we saw the boy today."

"You saw him?" Lady Montefiore was intrigued.

The Prince of Wales turned to the Colonel. "Are we talking about the sweet little boy who was with the Pope?"

"Yes," said Bruce as he turned to Lady Montefiore. "We had an audience with the Pope at Saint Peter's today. We arrived just as the Mortara boy was leaving."

"What was your impression of him?" Montefiore asked.

173

"The Pope: very congenial," said the Prince, "and the Vatican is exquisite."

Colonel Bruce interrupted him, raising an eyebrow by way of an apology. "I think Sir Moses means the boy Mortara. He didn't seem sad or unhappy at all."

"No," said the Prince. "He left the throne room playing 'blind man's buff' with two Swiss Guards. He can't be that unhappy, can he?"

Lady Montefiore, however, was unconvinced. "Children are very good at hiding their true emotions."

The Prince of Wales took off his frock coat and sat down on one of their trunks. "I think I heard the Pope say that he would arrange for the boy to go to the Roman Carnival tonight, but my Italian's not that good. I agree that he seemed to be in good spirits. He's probably having a better time than we are," he said as he blew smoke rings at Colonel Bruce.

"That remains to be seen," Sir Moses replied. "How long will your tour allow you to remain in Rome?"

"We are not sure, are we Brucey?" the Prince said, "We had hoped to be here for some weeks."

"We seem to have arrived at a particularly inopportune time," said the Colonel. "If the French troops withdraw from Rome, there may be great instability here."

The Prince of Wales took a box of Bryant and May's matches out of his trouser pocket and re-lit his cigar. "Will you be attending the Carnival this evening, Sir Moses? We noticed at Windsor that you are still a good dancer."

"I will stay with my wife. She has arrived in Rome somewhat indisposed with regard to health matters."

"Oh dear. Nothing serious, I hope?" said the Prince.

"A stomach upset," said Lady Montefiore.

"Well, I wish you better. We know the complaint well, don't we Brucey? The trouble with touring is that it can take a while to get used to the blasted food. It's the heavy use of olive oil and so much garlic. The Pope's Major-Domo today. Crikey!

174

One could smell him coming at thirty paces. Please do join us for dinner over the next few days. We are of course staying at the Hotel des Isles Britanniques. I'm travelling incognito as 'Baron Renfrew'. Brucey will let you know when our next soirée is, but for tonight I'm definitely going to indulge in a little revelry." The Prince smiled and showed his teeth again before disappearing in a cloud of Havana smoke, with Colonel Bruce following close behind.

"Baron Renfrew indeed," said Lady Judith to her husband. "Doesn't our Prince realise that everyone knows who he is? It's the worst kept secret in Christendom!"

***

In the gaslit Piazza del Popolo, excited crowds turned out to celebrate the Carnival in their motley gear. Musicians played wonderful soaring music. It seemed as though the whole of Rome was there, along with most of the French garrison. They danced, they sang and they embraced each other, sometimes removing their masks to steal a kiss.

Looking out of the tall windows of his apartment, Sir Moses watched the Roman revellers, none of whom appeared to have a single serious political thought. These were the privileged and happy children of their sovereign leader Pope Pius the Ninth, who led a bacchanalian life far removed from the wretched Jews of the Roman Ghetto and from the discontented activists calling for the 'Risorgimento', the resurgence and unification of the states of the Italian peninsula.

Dressed in their sombre black smocks and carrying lanterns, Edgardo and his classmates were enthralled by the crowds as they crossed the piazza with Canon Sarra and Brother Claudio. Peasants mixed with aristocrats and a host of foreign tourists: many were hidden behind their masks. Edgardo entered the amusements of the Carnival with youthful glee and started to do a lively jig with a group of market ladies, who grabbed hold of him. A French soldier joined Edgardo in the dancing. They both whooped and laughed loudly as the soldier hoisted him on to his shoulders and spun him round above his head. He put Edgardo down and then sidled over to one of the market girls, grabbing her to him and planting a big kiss on her cheek.

"Should we be subjecting the boys to all this so late at night?" said Brother Claudio to the Rector.

"The trip to the Carnival is 'ordained' by the Vatican; it's yet another decree from His Holiness," came the Rector's bemused reply.

A family ran into the square in front of them. The father picked up his young son. Edgardo stared at them as they laughed and played: he remembered how he and his brothers and sisters used to celebrate the festival of Purim in their fancy dress costumes, and how he would play with his spinning tops and bang on his drums and cymbals.

The following morning when Sir Moses looked out of his windows, the Carnival had subsided. The Piazza del Popolo was empty and silent; the gaslights were switched off; and rubbish blew across the square. A few early morning workers went about their business.

****

It was only a short walk from Sir Moses' apartment to the Hotel des Isles Britanniques. As he entered the thickly-carpeted lobby, he encountered a young man sitting at a rosewood table, half-hidden behind a fig tree that was perched in a large blue and white Wedgwood pot.

The young man shot up to shake Sir Moses by the hand, introducing himself as Odo Russell. "I remember having met you when I was with Lord Stratford de Redcliffe at Constantinople. May I say, Sir Moses, that the work you have done for both Christians and Jews in Syria is legendary."

"Thank you," Sir Moses said warmly. "I hear you are

currently the principal representative of Britain at the Vatican."

"Unofficially, yes. Please join me Sir Moses," said Odo Russell as he sat down, a fig leaf brushing against his face.

"You look as though you're hiding, Mr Russell," Sir Moses said to him.

Around them, dozens of English people seemed to have taken over all the settees and chairs, and a never-ending clinking of glasses of vermouth and cups of coffee permeated the snippets of conversation.

"I *am* hiding. Half of Belgravia is here 'doing Rome', Sir Moses, and our English compatriots have endless questions about what they see in the city and where they should or shouldn't go. I sometimes feel more like a tour guide than an attaché," said Mr Russell with a sigh. "I hear you are in Rome petitioning for the Mortara boy. Let's hope you can achieve great things."

"Well, perhaps you can help me to achieve them, Mr Russell."

"I certainly hope to obtain an interview with the Pope with regards to the affair," said the young man. "But you must know that both he and the Vatican Secretary of State, Cardinal Antonelli, are saying that it is a 'closed question'. I am just an attaché, and let me remind you that the French Ambassador with a whole army behind him has failed after every endeavour in the case of the boy. So we must not raise our hopes too much."

"No, we must not. I have not heard from anyone since I left London that there was the slightest chance of success for my mission."

The young man looked at his pocket watch. "Ah! I'm expected upstairs at Baron Renfrew's soirée. He has asked me to sing tonight!"

"Yes I'm invited too," said Sir Moses, "although I shan't be singing, I hope."

***

The Prince of Wales' apartment at the Hotel des Isles Britanniques was abuzz with a dozen or so English people who had done the 'circuit', spending the autumn in Florence, Christmas in Rome and the rest of the winter in Naples, before returning to Rome for Holy Week and Easter. Their frenzied chit-chat rang out over the strains of one of Beethoven's Razumovsky's Quartets, played by a very competent string ensemble. Sir Moses towered over a short, stocky gentleman, who said he thought the musicians' curly dark hair was somewhat long, before embroiling him and Odo Russell with arguments for staying at the Hotel de l'Angleterre, rather than the Hotel Brighton. At the same time Sir Moses managed to eavesdrop on an elderly dowager, who was giving a detailed account of where in the *Ghetto Inglese*, centred around the Pincian quarter, you could buy Crosse and Blackwell's pickles and Parkinson and Gott's stationary, to an over-excited young blonde woman with a very small waist who had just arrived in Rome. The Prince of Wales kissed her hand and then made his way over to Sir Moses, continuing to look at the woman who was wearing a tight bodice and a billowing, pale blue skirt.

"Her skirt is so swelled! How many petticoats do you think she is wearing?" the young Prince said with a glint in his eye.

"Probably one of the new cage crinolines with steel hoops," said Mr Russell.

"It's quite a feat of modern engineering," Sir Moses added.

The string quartet finished playing. The Prince of Wales applauded them enthusiastically and all the guests followed his lead.

The Prince's aide, Colonel Bruce, made a beeline for the group. "Would you like to sing for us now, Odo?" he asked and Mr Russell went to sit at a harpsichord decorated with ivory and mother of pearl. He announced that Mrs Chambers was going to join him for the musical entertainment and the clapping became feverish. The duo began a beautiful rendition of Purcell's 'Fairest Isle', Mr Russell playing the harpsichord and singing, while Mrs Chambers, a beauty of around thirty-five, harmonised with him.

"In spite of a shy modesty, I do believe Mr Russell as a tenor stands well above the rank of an amateur," the Prince said to Sir Moses in a loud voice. His conversation was very fluid for an eighteen year-old, in spite of his attention to the young woman in the billowing skirt, which was quickly diverting towards Mrs Chambers.

He took a puff on his cigar as he studied her. Even while performing, Mrs Chambers seemed to notice his attention, giving him a wide-eyed stare as she sang about 'despair that died for love'.

The Prince smiled at her. "How is Lady Montefiore?" he asked Sir Moses.

"In spite of her fragile health, she is keen to be part of this holy mission."

"And how is the mission going?" said the Prince. "What hopes are there for the little neophyte Mortara?"

Montefiore was about to reply when Mr Russell's musical turn came to an end. Again the applause was resounding. The Prince of Wales slapped Russell on the back, with a beaming 'Bravo', gave Mrs Chambers a lingering kiss on her hand, announced that he was starving, and then quickly led the guests into the dining room for supper.

"Is there the slightest possibility of Edgar Mortara being restored to his grieving family?" the Prince asked as Sir Moses took his seat opposite him.

Mrs Chambers answered for him. "I don't think anything will induce the Pope to give up the lamb that has thus been juggled into the Roman fold!" she exclaimed as she buttered a bread roll.

"I'm sure Pius would be as reluctant to abandon his jewelled tiara as he would be to relinquish the captured Jew!" added the

179

Duke of Arrans, a rather foppish gentleman who was wearing a multi-coloured waistcoat.

"I'm sure the situation is one which Pio Nono rather enjoys. It gives him the opportunity of displaying himself as a martyr, suffering for conscience sake," said the Prince as the first course of baked oysters with Parmesan was served by a trio of young Roman waiters, who were remarkably skilled at lifting the silver dome cloches in exact unison. "Sir Moses, I know you don't eat oysters on account of your religion, but there is a cream of celery soup to follow shortly."

Sir Moses nodded in gratitude as Mrs Chamber's shrill tones once again took over. "It's theft, stealing a child like that from its parents! It surely displays Pius at his most brazen-faced. I can't understand how his priestly cheeks don't redden with embarrassment on offering his imbecilic explanation for not returning the boy to his parents: '*Non possumus*'."

"Well, Odo, you must help Sir Moses to obtain an audience with the Pontiff," said the Prince to Mr Russell. "So that he can try and do something about all this."

"I fear that it's no easy undertaking," the attaché replied.

"They say even the humblest applicant may approach the Pope," said the Duke of Arrans as he scooped oysters from their shells.

"He recently gave audience to a Negro slave!" Mrs Chambers shouted so as to include the guests at the ends of the table.

"Well he granted me an audience!" said the Prince to rapturous laughter.

"I think you're all being a little ungracious to the Pope," Colonel Bruce remarked. "He was very generous in presenting your Royal Highness with an extremely beautiful mosaic table on the occasion of your visit to Saint Peter's."

"I should be careful taking anything as a gift from Pius the Ninth," said Sir Moses.

"Why is that Montefiore?" the Prince asked.

"Because you may be receiving stolen goods," joked Montefiore.

As the table again erupted into laughter, the Prince's chaplain, Reverend Tarver, tried to make himself heard. "Are you suggesting the Pope is a thief, Sir Moses?"

"I agree with Mrs Chambers that the abduction of the Mortara boy is a kind of theft," said Sir Moses.

Mrs Chambers was determined to reclaim the conversation. "It's scandalous that the child was torn away from his family! I'm surprised the Holy Office doesn't deprive the entire Jewish community of the authority they enjoy as parents and simply baptise all their children. Why wait until they are in danger of death? Put them all away in convent schools and proclaim that the Roman Catholic Church has a right to all their souls," she said as the celery soup was laid in front of them.

"Though there are times when children do have to be taken away from their parents," said Colonel Bruce. "Look how Lord Eldon as Chancellor deprived Shelley of the custody of his children on account of his being an atheist. Nobody then said he was a thief."

"Well if the Jewish boy's situation's not theft, I don't know what is," said Mrs Chambers. "Of course the Pope, having stolen his property, boldly announces his intention to keep it. On the same principle, he might just as well retain possession of communion vessels stolen from a goldsmith's shop, and argue that they had been consecrated by the Church's use of them."

"Behave yourself, Mrs Chambers!" the Prince shouted, chastising her with a good-natured smile and a raised eyebrow.

As courses of poached turbot, partridge in a suprême sauce, and mutton cutlets served with puréed chestnuts were consumed, Edgardo Mortara was the main topic of conversation, and Mrs Chambers showed that her behaviour was in no way going to be controlled by the Prince. After several fits of giggles and two desserts, including *glace à la*

Napolitaine and a *baba au rhum* drenched in lashings of liqueur, Sir Moses could hardly fail to notice that Mrs Chambers and the Prince were huddled together and almost sharing the same dining chair. When the Prince allowed her to take a puff on his cigar, providing him with the opportunity for his hand that had previously held it to dally over the buttons on top of her ample cleavage, Mrs Chambers suddenly caught the reaction of Colonel Bruce and the Reverend Tarver, who were looking at her with total disdain.

"I can't imagine why everyone is so gloomy after such a magnificent dinner," she announced as she raised a glass of pale Barolo wine. "I would like to toast 'Baron Renfrew' and thank him."

"Do call me Bertie," the Prince said with a grin.

Sir Moses smiled and clinked his glass with Mrs Chambers'. "Chin-chin."

"Dr Chambers, who you will meet later, and I are having a few friends and a little music upstairs. We would be very happy if you would do us the honour of joining us, Sir Moses." Although she had addressed Montefiore, she was fixing the Prince of Wales with a 'come hither' stare.

"In fact you're all very welcome, provided that you promise to enjoy yourselves."

***

The Chambers' party was a lively affair. Two drawing rooms were crowded with around 150 people. A singer belonging to the Royal Chapel at Rome, celebrated for his beautiful voice, performed with a string quartet. The Prince continued to stay in a group with Sir Moses, who felt this was not least on account of the presence of Mrs Chambers.

"What sort of man is this Pope?" asked the Prince of Wales, rolling his eyes over the contours of Mrs Chambers' upper body. "I mean he seemed very convivial when we met him this week."

A Roman nobleman, Prince Torlonia, stepped forward. "Although Pius comes from an old aristocratic family of Sinigaglia, long famous for nationalist sentiment down to their cats, as the saying goes, he is at heart inclined towards liberal ideas."

"So liberal that he allows Rome to maintain the last Jewish ghetto in Western Europe," said Sir Moses drily.

Prince Torlonia's response was a sardonic grimace that made his lip curl.

"Yes and so liberal that he can't rectify a few old canonical rules," said Mrs Chambers. "All his predecessors changed the rules when it suited them. Where is his spirit?"

"He seems to have lost it the older he gets," said the Duke of Arrans. "We are far from the time when Pio Nono indulged in foul language befitting a coal heaver, when according to my cousins, he couldn't beat the Princess Corsini even though he cheated the old trout at cards."

At this point the Reverend Tarver and Colonel Bruce left the group abruptly and Mrs Chambers' husband, who was more advanced in years than his wife, asked to be excused as late nights in Rome did not agree with his constitution.

"And what of the Pope's Foreign Minister in all this?" asked Mrs Chambers, sipping a large glass of amaretto. "Not a word is said against Cardinal Antonelli, who publicly lives in sin with the wife of an émigré."

"Antonelli is a crafty schemer who gets everything he wants," said the Duke of Arrans. "If the Pope were not the slave of Antonelli, I'm sure he would give up the poor little Jew boy, if only for the sake of peace and quiet."

Mrs Chambers took Sir Moses' arm, sensing he was a little taken aback by this exchange.

"The Duke and Mrs Chambers will have us all expelled from Rome with this gossip!" the Prince of Wales exclaimed.

Mrs Chambers turned to Sir Moses. "You know, I

remember how kind you were a couple of years ago, when you gave me a marvellous packet of very thin biscuits."

"Passover biscuits; we eat them at this time of year," Sir Moses replied. "I'll get you some more while I'm in Rome."

"Can I have some too?" asked the Prince cheekily, before whisking Mrs Chambers off to the privacy of her drawing room balcony.

Chapter 30

Rome, The Papal States. 1859

Edgardo squealed as he ran up the stairs of the large dome of St Peter's, closely chased by Thomas and Laurent, who emerged on to the balcony overlooking the main altar. Below them a group of around twenty cardinals in their red skull caps, and the Pope himself in white, were conducting a service. Edgardo laughed as Thomas grabbed hold of him. At least five of the cardinals looked up to see what the noise was. Laurent put his finger over his lips to silence him and then whispered, "It's the funeral service of a very important person from the Vatican." They watched as the cardinals in unison put on their pointed red galero hats and then filed out two by two.

Laurent and Thomas continued up the stairs with Edgardo, sometimes having to bend over sideways because of the curvature of the dome. "I hope you're not scared of heights," Laurent said as they climbed a further 320 steps to reach the top of the Cupola where the whole of Rome suddenly came into view. Edgardo nervously took the hands of the two Swiss Guards as they walked around the top of the Cupola and looked down at St Peter's Square, where people appeared to be the size of ants.

When they descended into the Basilica they found Pope Pius kneeling in prayer at the high altar under which lay Saint Peter's tomb. Edgardo ran over to him and knelt down at his side, and he too started to pray.

The Prince of Wales and his party entered the Basilica. Pope Pius and Edgardo finished their praying and stood up. Pius nodded at the Prince.

"Is that him, Edgardo Mortara, the Pope's son?" asked Mrs Chambers.

"Yes," said the Prince.

"I hope he's not abusing him in any way."

"What do you mean, Mrs C?"

"I just hope they are not up to no good! Everyone knows that half of the Swiss Guards are like that." She studied Thomas and Laurent as she spoke and noticed the familiarity with which Thomas leaned over to Laurent and straightened the white collar of his Swiss Guard's uniform.

"Like *what* Mrs Chambers?"

"You know perfectly well what I mean! Half the Swiss Guard and the eunuchs, as well as half the Vatican, are like that I should imagine."

"*Chacun à son goût,*" the Prince said drily as he gave the Swiss Guards a smile. "Clearly the boy brings out the paternal in our Sovereign Pontiff. I'm sure he considers him to be a surrogate son."

"He looks adorable," Mrs Chambers observed. "You don't think they will mutilate him and put him in with the eunuchs to sing in the Sistine Chapel, do you?"

"Good Lord, I hope not!" said the Prince.

"Can't we abduct the poor creature ourselves?"

"Behave yourself, Mrs C!" scolded the Prince as he took her hand. "Come, after I've spoken with Pio Nono, we'll go and see the Michelangelo frescoes in the Pauline Chapel."

"Quite the student of art, aren't you, Bertie," said the Duke of Arrans caustically.

"I think I'd rather climb the dome," said Mrs Chambers.

"Let's do both," said the Prince, and letting go of Mrs Chambers' hand he went over to talk to Pope Pius and Edgardo.

***

When the Prince and his group exited into the bright sunshine they encountered Sir Moses entering Saint Peter's square, together with Gershom Kursheedt.

"Sir Moses, if you'd come to the Basilica with us, you could have seen the Pope's son and spoken with the Pontiff yourself," said Mrs Chambers. "Sadly they've now left."

"I'm optimistic that I will get a chance to meet them both," said Sir Moses.

A group of French soldiers ran through the square, followed by a couple of gendarmes, a priest and a group of civilians, who were all shouting 'Viva Pio Nono!' as they chased a couple of poorly dressed youths who had broken away from a larger group.

"What's all that about?" asked the Prince.

"Priests, soldiers, officers, spies – they run about in a state of utter confusion, shouting 'Long Live the Pope!' Pius is so incompetent a tyrant that his people are only kept down by foreign bayonets," said the Duke of Arrans scathingly. "Gendarmes are now insufficient to arrest the criminals. As a result, everywhere in Rome there is agitation and terror bubbling under the surface. There is fear of everything: of words, of the press, of meetings. This is what civilised life in Rome is like now. The French and the Austrians have misruled the country long enough, and the situation is getting worse every day."

"It's probably time for us to head back to London," said the Prince of Wales. "Why can't the French and the Austrians just leave?"

"Louis Napoleon is not yet prepared to withdraw his troops from Rome and break with the Pope, which is a shame," said the Duke of Arrans. "He has such power over the Pope."

"If only he would exercise that power in the name of the boy Mortara," said Sir Moses. "One word from the Emperor would rescue the child from the clutches of his kidnappers."

"I'm hoping we won't have to return to Britain till after Easter," said Mrs Chambers. "Are you planning to participate in the Easter festivities at St Peter's, Sir Moses?"

"I'm not sure that my religion will allow it," said Sir Moses.

"You should come along just for the spectacle."

The Duke of Arrans laughed. "She speaks as if it were a masquerade!"

"Well, in truth it is!" said Mrs Chambers. "The tickets can be bought at the lowest quarters and even at the doors of the churches, like tickets for the theatre. The communicants often come fresh from riot and debauchery, and in a state of complete inebriation. It *is* a masquerade."

"Really?" said Sir Moses.

"Yes! And the Pope doesn't take communion fasting like other Catholics. When he celebrates Mass he has refreshments provided for him in a tent in the middle of the church…"

***

Pope Pius the Ninth emerged from a tent in the middle of St Peter's Basilica wearing a triple crown. He was carried in state through the body of the church and then seated on a high throne opposite the altar. Two cardinals took the consecrated bread and the cup, and carried it towards the throne. Pius rose as they approached. The cardinals bowed and gave the Pope the wafer. He drank from the cup by means of an ornate golden tube.

"I wouldn't mind taking communion like that m'self," the Prince of Wales whispered mischievously to Mrs Chambers, from where he was sitting at the centre of the English group. His hand had found a resting place on her leg.

Edgardo was led down a side aisle by the Pope's Major-Domo and the two young Swiss Guards, Thomas and Laurent. Sir Moses watched with fascination as Edgardo and the Supreme Pontiff managed to exchange glances.

"The prelates are of two kinds: *mantellone* and *mantellata* on account of the robes they wear," Odo Russell explained to Sir Moses. "The former wear the long purple mantellone cloaks, with wing-like sleeves over their cassocks. The prelates of the mantellata are the highest class and their outer mantellata robes reach only to their knees." He pointed to them as he spoke. "The prelates di mantellone are often married…"

"Unlike the eunuchs in the Sistine Chapel!" interrupted Mrs Chambers in a loud voice while eating from a tin of sweet biscuits.

"Oh not the bloody eunuchs again, Mrs C!" said the Prince of Wales, chuckling as he put his finger over her mouth. "We're all going to get thrown out of here."

Odo Russell tried to bring a tone of sobriety to the group. "I hate to say this, but I hear from Cardinal Antonelli that the Pope finds the conduct of English and American visitors in Rome during Easter week both noisy and vulgar."

"Well quite!" said the Prince of Wales. "One must put an end to this disgusting habit of talking, whispering and even eating biscuits," he said, fixing Mrs Chambers with his stare and grabbing the tin of biscuits as he felt the robes of a procession of venerable churchmen brush past him. The procession of six cardinal bishops, fifty cardinal priests and fourteen cardinal deacons was a striking picture of religious pomp as it made its way to the Sistine Chapel. In the ceremony of the adoration that followed, all knelt before the Pope. While the cardinals embraced his knees, the other prelates embraced his feet.

Edgardo stared at the English group. He watched as Mrs Chambers grabbed the tin of biscuits back from the Prince of Wales.

A warden marched towards her and hissed. "Madame, if you do not stop this, I must ask a Swiss Guard to come and remove you,"

Mrs Chambers took a pink iced rose biscuit out of her mouth. "May I choose which Swiss Guard is to remove me?" she said flippantly. "They're all so engagingly handsome!" She gave the warden a stern look that seemed to unsettle him.

"Perhaps we should give the biscuits to the Pope's son,"

she said to the Prince of Wales as she watched Edgardo, and in perfect Italian she told the warden to give the biscuits to the boy.

Chapter 31

Pius was not arrogant – he was a good man, a saint even... Father Mortara's words were still ringing in Raoul's ears as he walked along the lane, taking the shortcut behind the old granary. The sun was low in the sky over the Priory church. He sat down on an old stile, took the Montefiore Diaries out of his satchel, and resumed his reading. Father Mortara had been famous; in 1859 it seemed that people all around the world had heard of him: lords, priests and princes, all battling over the boy. Who would have thought that Edgardo would have ended up in a monastery in a tiny corner of Walloon, where the smell of manure was carried in the breeze over the cornfields?

Delphine's invitation, which Raoul was using as a bookmark, fell on to the ground. He picked it up and read it. He stopped at the line "I know you are angry with me, but please come – you have never missed any of my birthdays..."

How could he go to Delphine's party? He was still overwhelmed by the feelings he had for her and the tricks his mind was playing. In the past she had been flawless and perfect, but now in his thoughts he constantly found himself trying to discover her imperfections: she had betrayed him; she had cold-heartedly traded him in for someone else; she was fickle; she was cruel. How could he celebrate her birthday as a joyous occasion? But it was true: he had never missed her birthdays and she had never missed his. He could almost remember as far back as his own third birthday, when, on a hot summer's day, they had taken off all their clothes and dived into an old metal bathtub at the back of the alehouse. They had then proceeded to walk down the main road of Bouhay stark naked except for their hats: his, a brown urchin's cap and hers, a golden tiara, which her father had made out of cardboard. It had little coloured stickers on it for jewels. The neighbours had complained bitterly. Raoul had often wondered why they were upset about three-year-olds having no clothes on. The incident had been turned into legend in Bouhay, and the villagers would often try to embarrass Raoul or Delphine with references to his brown cap and her golden tiara as though they were euphemisms for depravity.

Raoul wanted to go back to the Priory; he would have been happy spending the evening reading the Montefiore diaries. He got up and started to walk back. In the distance he saw some of the monks making their way to the Priory church for Vespers. He could make out Martin up a ladder trying to clear the gutters of one of the outhouses. The novice hurriedly climbed down and ran across the gardens to make the service on time. Martin was a boy of few words, who would answer Raoul's questions with an annoying and repeated nodding action, which reminded Raoul of the little wooden cow's head on a coiled spring he used to have as a child. He found himself contemplating a lifetime with this rather simple soul at Notre Dame de Lourdes and shuddered. He wondered how many of Martin's nods he would have experienced by the time he was ninety, and whether Augustinian monks ever went mad.

Raoul sat down on an old stone wall. Why had the Prior encouraged him to go to Delphine's birthday? Was it because he sensed his doubts: his confusion? Perhaps it was a test of the Prior's: a way of allowing him to say goodbye to a normal life outside the Priory before living there for the rest of his life. How many of these secular events would there be, when he would don an old pair of trousers with leather braces and a fraying shirt: the odd birthday, a wedding – or a funeral?

He looked at his tattered shirt-sleeves, knowing that he shouldn't care if they were darned. They were a reminder that he had sacrificed a life of prospects for a life of poverty. As an engineer he might have been quite wealthy; he used to walk past the coloured town houses in the rue Hors-Château in Liège and imagine which one he and Delphine would end up living in; a far cry from living in a cell at the Priory. The words of his friend Guy popped up in his mind: *I don't see you as a monk, Raoul. Are you sure you're making the right decision and not just running away?* Raoul was determined to prove them all wrong. Let them all judge him; he would trust his instincts and make all the necessary sacrifices – and he would serve God.

Raoul stood up, and with a new-found resolve decided that after all he would go to Delphine's party. He looked at her invitation and put it to his nose to see if there was any trace of her fragrance on it. He imagined he could smell the faint scent of the violet water she wore.

He got up and crossed the fields and the road to Liège with its avenue of larch trees, and reached the main street of Bouhay. He passed the tiny general store and made his way to the far end of the street where a crowd had gathered outside Delphine's small village house with its adjoining barn. At the front door he saw her mother and her younger brother Jacques with his mass of curls. There with them, speaking in a much louder-than-necessary voice, was a young man in a brown tweed jacket. It was Delphine's cousin, Félix, another of her entourage who was rumoured to have joined the Rexist Party and apparently couldn't wait to welcome the Nazis into Belgium. The door opened and out came Delphine, a vision of smiles and long, blonde hair falling over her pale blue cotton dress.

Raoul's heart sank. There with Delphine was her beau, Jean-Louis, tall and bearded and wearing a pressed linen shirt. He was laughing as he drank his beer.

Raoul was about to turn back, but Jacques had spotted him. "Raoul, Raoul! *Bon soir*," yelled the twelve-year-old.

Delphine turned round; Jean-Louis turned round; and Delphine's mother ran across the road to welcome him. She pulled him vigorously to her and hugged him.

"You're not wearing your monk's habit!" she said.

Raoul smiled at her.

"Do you still drink beer?" she asked, leading him across the road as if he were a child.

"I would love a beer," he said.

Delphine took Raoul's hand and prised him away from her mother, leading him through the large wooden doors that led from the street into the barn where two trestle tables were laid with plates of sausages and bread and her father was setting out bottles of beer and lemonade.

"A beer for Raoul, Papa," she said. Monsieur Fabron handed Raoul a bottle of Dubbel. "It's from a Trappist monastery, so it should fit a young priest," he said with a hint of resentment, which Raoul immediately picked up on. He knew that in the grand scheme of things, Delphine's parents, like his own, had wanted him to woo their daughter and make a family with her.

"How's life in the Church?" Monsieur Fabron asked, but he never got a reply as Delphine's mother came into the barn and promptly dragged her husband out into the street, telling him to leave the youngsters to themselves. Raoul opened his satchel and took out her birthday card.

"Happy Birthday," he said as he handed Delphine the card and a painting of a jar of wildflowers on a wooden table.

"I love delphiniums!" she said with a grin as she looked at the pink, blue and purple bluebell-like stems in the picture.

"That's because you're named after them," said Raoul as he looked away.

"You're such a good artist, Raoul. You're wasted in the Church," said Delphine, still looking at the painting.

She put the card down and leaned the artwork against a crate of beer. She kissed Raoul on the cheek, but he pulled back, nearly knocking an accordion off an old bentwood chair.

"Jean-Louis plays the accordion; you must stay and dance. You were always a good dancer, Raoul."

God! Jean-Louis would play the accordion, Raoul thought.

"I can't stay very long; we get up at the crack of dawn," he said, relieved that he had an escape plan. He stood silently looking at the floor.

"Dear Raoul. I know how angry you are with me, but I so wanted you to come to my birthday party."

Raoul then looked up at her. "Why?" he asked. "You must know I wouldn't enjoy being here."

She took his hand and laughed. "Raoul! You are such a baby."

He pulled his hand away from her.

Jean-Louis came into the barn to pick up his accordion. He smiled at them both.

"I'm taking requests," he said.

"Play something for us first," Delphine said as she turned to Raoul. "He can play Django Reinhardt – jazz!"

Raoul wanted to tell her that Jean-Louis' beloved Hitler hated jazz and banned it in Germany, associating it with Negroes and Jews – but said nothing.

"Later, your mother wants to hear 'In the Mood'!" said Jean-Louis.

He turned to Raoul and barraged him with a load of quick fire questions. "When do you receive your Holy Orders?" "What time do you get up?" "What's the food like?" "Do you have to work in the fields?"

Raoul felt bitter. It was as though Jean-Louis was subtly trying to humiliate him with his small talk in front of Delphine.

For Heaven's Sake, you're a teacher! Can't you come up with better conversation than this? he thought. But Jean-Louis did not wait around for answers; he dashed out on to the street with his accordion.

Delphine took Raoul's hand again. He tried to pull away, but she wouldn't let go. "You are my friend and you will always be my friend, and I won't hear anything to the contrary," she said. "And I think God wouldn't want it any other way!"

Raoul felt that she was taunting him, bringing God into it. He was about to get angry with her, but she knew exactly how to pacify him. "Do you remember how we used to run round my grandfather's garden, along his precious edging tiles, and how enraged he was when we loosened them all? How he came running after us shaking his fist. We ran away terrified and hid on the river bank till eleven o'clock at night, and we were all of five years of age! Raoul, you have been such a big part of my life. I never want to lose you; I always want you to be in my life."

Raoul said nothing. He wondered if she was a little drunk.

Delphine turned and picked up the card off the table and opened it to find brightly coloured calligraphy inside: 'Happy Birthday D. Love R.x The 'D' and the 'R' were hand-painted like an illustration from a Book of Hours.

"Very monastic!" said Delphine as she smiled at him. "Thank you. It must have taken you hours."

He did not answer, partly because he was embarrassed that he had spent so long on its creation. He knew it looked like a desperate attempt to win her back. He got up and went out into the street. Delphine followed him. "Come and say hello to my cousin Félix," she said.

Félix was holding court with half the villagers, including Raoul's good friend Guy. He had the same flaxen hair as his cousins.

"How are you, Raoul? I hear you've joined the Church."

"Yes and I hear you've joined the Rexist party."

Félix smiled. "You should be pleased, Raoul. Rexism calls for the moral renewal of Belgian society in conformity with the teachings of the Church."

Raoul could feel himself getting red in the face.

"No, Félix. Alignment with Nazi Germany and Nazi-style anti-Semitism doesn't please me," he said. "Nor does it conform to the Church that I want to belong to."

And with that he once more wished Delphine happy

196

birthday and set off down the village street, determined not to turn round. He heard someone running after him and felt a hand on his shoulder. He turned round – it was Guy. Delphine was close behind.

"Don't let that fascist twat upset you, Raoul," said Guy as he gave his friend a big hug.

"Do you mean Félix or Jean-Louis?" said Raoul pointedly directing his words to Delphine. He turned again to Guy. "How's your history course?"

"It's going well," said Guy as he took a drag on his cigarette.

"I hear the University of Liège has a good library," said Raoul. "Could you look something up for me there?"

"What is it you want to know?" said Guy.

"I told you a little about Father Mortara, the priest I'm looking after. I'd like to know something about the Risorgimento – he lived through all that and he knew Pope Pius the Ninth and Cardinal Antonelli – anything you can find as long as it doesn't interfere with your studies."

"I'm sure I can do that for you," said Guy. "Can I come and visit you at the Priory?"

"I'm sure that'll be fine," said Raoul. He hugged Guy again, nodded at Delphine and then walked quickly to the fields, crossing the little bridge over the brook.

Delphine came running after him. "Please don't think badly of me," she said.

She took his hands and smiled, the setting sun making her squint a little. He turned away, immediately regretting it. He did not want her to think badly of him, nor did he want her to think he was being childish. On an impulse he turned round and kissed her warmly on her soft lips – quickly, but not too quickly, pulling back so that she would not take this as some kind of desperate flirtation. He smiled back at her, not saying a word, overcome by how beautiful she looked. His lips were tingling from the kiss and his heart was beating quickly. In that moment he wanted her to know how much he had loved her. He wanted her to know what might have been. He wanted her to know that this was a moment that would stay with them all their lives; a moment that would define their love and never be forgotten; a moment that would override running over edging tiles and cardboard crowns. He stopped smiling, and, looking deeply into her eyes, he suddenly pulled her head to his and kissed her again, lost in the moment as the sun set beyond the forests to the west.

When he drew away, he found it impossible to speak. He turned and walked across the fields. He sensed her watching him, but he did not turn round. As he walked back to Notre Dame de Lourdes he was overcome with a sense of loss and overwhelming isolation.

Chapter 32

The Vatican, The Papal States. 1859

"Your Eminence, may I present Sir Moses Montefiore?" said Odo Russell to Cardinal Antonelli.

The Cardinal Secretary of State stood up and shook Sir Moses' hand cordially. "Come and sit 'ere," he said, pointing next to him on the silk brocade settee in his salon, his pronunciation of English thick with Italian vowel sounds.

Mr Russell sat in a chair opposite them.

"Montefiore, that is not an English name," the Cardinal pointed out.

"No: my family once lived here in Italy," said Sir Moses. "It is believed that, as with many Italians, they took the name of their home town – in their case the Apennine hill-town of Montefiore."

"You are a true Italian, then?" said Antonelli.

"I was born here, but England is well and truly my home now," Sir Moses declared, his English upper class accent not revealing the slightest indication of his Italian origin.

"And what are your impressions of the country you abandoned?" the Cardinal asked him with a forced smile.

"As a foreigner, one can hardly fail to detect the feeling of civil unrest which is so evident here in the Italian Peninsula," Sir Moses volunteered, "and, as a Jew, I must tell you how extremely disturbing it is to hear that my co-religionists live in abject misery in the Roman Ghetto."

Antonelli was not prepared for Sir Moses' reproach. "Signor Montefiore…" he began.

Mr Russell corrected him. "Your Eminence, it is 'Sir Moses'. Queen Victoria honoured her worthy friend with a knighthood many years ago."

Cardinal Antonelli was clearly irritated by being corrected. "Have you visited the ghetto?"

Sir Moses nodded his head, "No, I haven't yet had that pleasure…"

Antonelli was quick to respond. "Well, I can assure you that the ghetto is welcomed by some members of the small Jewish community who think that its walls protect them from possible attacks by Christian mobs, and from the exodus which might follow from assimilation. At the same time it enables Jewish religious customs to be observed without interference."

Sir Moses replied calmly. "I see. How terrible if the Jews of Rome should assimilate with the rest of the citizens, as is the case in most other European cities. Clearly I will have to be careful here that the authorities don't lock me up in the ghetto, which it seems they have a perfect right to do." He turned to Mr Russell and chuckled. "I'm surprised that I'm allowed to live in well-furnished lodgings off the Piazza del Popolo in the via Baburino."

Cardinal Antonelli was not amused, but he smiled. "Sir Moses, these are difficult times for everyone in Rome, a fact that you yourself have alluded to. I only hope your impressions will not prejudice your trip to the Papal States."

"The impressions of which I speak are not my only disappointments," said Sir Moses. "I am dismayed at not being able to obtain an audience of the Pope to present him with the memorial of the Board of Deputies of British Jews regarding the matter of the Mortara boy. Every endeavour I have made has failed. I must therefore request that Your Eminence presents the appeal to the Sovereign Pontiff on behalf of my people. I shall be remaining at least a week in Rome and would hope for a response by then." Sir Moses opened his ox-leather Gladstone bag, took out some papers, and handed one of them to Antonelli.

The Cardinal Secretary of State put the memorial down on a table next to the settee. "I must tell you that the abduction of

Edgardo Mortara is a closed question," he said. "A child once baptised is a Christian. It is impossible to do anything about this particular case, but I assure you every precaution shall be taken to prevent so unfortunate an occurrence for the future."

"Are you saying the child can never return home?" said Sir Moses.

"It will be given up at seventeen or eighteen, when it will be free to follow its own inclinations."

"Seventeen or eighteen!" Sir Moses shook his head in disbelief.

"As far as we can say; who knows? Political changes may yet influence the fate of young Mortara. If he had lived in a country in which conscription was in force the State would have taken him away a little later, and perhaps he would never have been returned. In any event you need not fear; the child is very happy and wants for nothing. The Pope pays for his education out of his own private purse. The Church will turn him into a good Christian."

"I have no doubt about that," said Sir Moses grimly.

Antonelli went on. "You must understand that although the law of the Church prevents the child being given back to the parents, in the meantime the parents shall have free access to the child."

Sir Moses protested. "I hear that this is currently not the case."

The Secretary of State ignored his remark. "I have to say that this affair demonstrates the importance of the law that Jews should not have Catholic servants. After all, any dedicated maid on seeing a child dangerously ill and close to death might well baptise it. However..." The Cardinal started to slide his gold signet ring up and down his finger. "... I am glad to tell you that the Roman court will now be enforcing laws concerning the Jews with a view to preventing secret baptism. We are giving new orders that all Christian domestics serving in Jewish families should immediately be separated from their Jewish masters."

"As we are all the children of one God, it is deeply to be lamented that we cannot dwell together in peace," Sir Moses replied.

"The laws of the Roman Catholic Church have to be respected and upheld, just as you, I am sure, would expect Jewish laws to be upheld," said Cardinal Antonelli, still speaking with a smile. "Your adopted country of England broke with the laws of the Roman Church, and we know the turmoil that created."

"To what do you refer?" Mr Russell inquired.

"One has only to look at Henry the Eighth, who had no regard for Catholic doctrine and ended up with eight wives and chopping their heads off."

Mr Russell corrected him. "Six wives, and I think we've come a long way since then, Your Eminence. May I reiterate Sir Moses' request to present his address to the Pope?"

"As I have already said, this is a closed question. I would not wish to raise your hopes in the expectation of any answer. Gentlemen, it has been my pleasure." The Cardinal shook hands with both men and quickly showed them to the tall ornate doors of the salon where attendants were waiting to escort them out. Then he made his way through the apartment to his bedroom, picking up Sir Moses' memorial on his way. He looked out of the window. In the gardens, two storeys down, Pope Pius was playing ball in the sun with the young Mortara. Antonelli folded the memorial into a paper dart. He knocked on the window and opened it. The Pope and his protégé looked up.

Antonelli threw the paper dart out of the window. It soared into the gardens. Edgardo caught it and handed it to Pope Pius. The Pontiff looked over it and put it down on a garden table.

Antonelli then retreated back into his bedroom.

"Are you going to give me any attention at all today?"

202

clamoured his mistress from the bed.

The Cardinal laughed as he took off his robe.

Outside it clouded over and started to rain. Pope Pius rushed inside with Edgardo, leaving the memorial from the British Jews on the table where it became soaked in the storm.

Chapter 33

Rome, The Papal States. 1859

Following the storms of the previous night, Rome awoke to a scorching sun. Sir Moses and Lady Montefiore, accompanied by Gershom Kursheedt, travelled by carriage through the Piazza del Popolo, stopping as they saw the Prince of Wales leaving the Hotel des Isles Britanniques with Mrs Chambers, Colonel Bruce and Odo Russell.

"War! War! War!" shouted the Prince to Sir Moses and his party. "Now the English are in a frenzy about taking their departure from Rome."

"I hear hostilities have commenced between Piedmont and Austria," Sir Moses shouted. "They've deployed fourteen thousand Tuscan troops to the Piedmont."

"Yes. Time to go home. Damned hard to get a berth on the Vesuvius from Civita Vecchia, however. We will leave on Monday. You should think about leaving too, Montefiore. It's only brave men like Odo here, who stay in Rome."

"Such a shame you never got your meeting with the Pope," said Mrs Chambers. "I only hope Edgar Mortara is the last Jewish child His Holiness decides to kidnap..." She took the Prince's hand to the dismay of Colonel Bruce.

As the Montefiore's carriage pulled away, the English group all shouted 'Adieu'.

***

The Montefiores and Gershom Kursheedt arrived at the Piazza Giudia, where they left their carriage. They entered the walled Jewish Ghetto by means of a small gate.

"What's your business here?" a sentry asked them in Italian.

"We are going to look at the synagogues," Sir Moses told him.

The sentry raised an eyebrow. "Are you from Rome?"

"London," said Sir Moses.

"You are from England?" said the sentry suddenly switching to heavily accented English.

"And America," Gershom Kursheedt replied.

"You are a Yankee?" The sentry was dazzled. "Where from?"

"From New Orleans."

"Yankee Doodle," the sentry said, and then kept on repeating the words, much to his own amusement. Gershom Kursheedt, however, did not find this even remotely amusing.

"You don't want to go in there," the sentry said reverting to Italian.

"We do want to go in there," said Sir Moses. "Is there a problem?"

"There might be," said the sentry. "There was a lot of flooding last night."

"Well I am sure we can deal with that," said Sir Moses very firmly and marched in, closely followed by his wife and Mr Kursheedt.

They were immediately greeted with rank squalor. The narrow streets were crowded. Dark alleyways branched off in all directions. Dirty rags hung on lines in front of crumbling old buildings and the smells of fish, damp, decay and sewage seeped out of every crevice. Beneath their feet the waters of the Tiber covered the slippery cobblestones and the soles of their shoes. The buildings were oppressively tall, blocking all traces of sunlight; the only way for expansion was vertically.

Scores of urchin children played and ran in rings through archways and porticos. A small boy and girl chased a little wooden top as it span down a flight of stone steps and came to rest in a deep pool at Lady Judith's feet. They looked up, staring with big eyes at the Montefiores and Mr Kursheedt.

Their faces were pale and dirty. The boy's trousers were torn to shreds and the girl's dress stained up to her waist with mud and green slime.

"How do they live here?" Mr Kursheedt asked, shocked by what he was seeing. "Is it always flooded like this?"

"So I believe. This particular bend in the Tiber is by all account the worst flood zone of Rome; not the best place to be incarcerated," Sir Moses informed him.

"It must be a serious health risk," said Lady Judith as she picked up the top and handed it back to the little girl with a warm smile.

The girl smiled back and then started to splash the boy with her bare feet. They giggled. The Montefiores stepped back, but a passing gendarme, realising that the girl was soaking his dark blue uniform, span round. "*Puzzolente porcellino!*" he shouted and then continued to scream a mouthful of expletives at her.

Mr Kursheedt asked Sir Moses what the gendarme was saying.

"I think an accurate translation might be 'godless heathens', 'filthy stinking piglets', and 'offspring of unrespectable Jewish whores'," he told him with a world-weary edge to his voice.

The gendarme started to kick water from a large pool all over the girl before grabbing the whip and top out of her hands. Still shouting, he placed the whip against a step and stamped on it with such force that it snapped in half, and then stormed off. The little girl sat down on the step next to the boy, her hair and ragged dress drenched. She looked at the broken whip before bursting into tears. The boy put his arm around her.

Sir Moses went to her and spoke in his native Italian. "How old are you?" he asked.

The girl did not answer.

"Don't cry," he said, taking some *scudi* out of his pocket.

The boy first looked at the coins and then at Sir Moses' polished shoes and Lady Judith's fine clothes.

"She's five," the boy said, smiling at Sir Moses. "And I'm four."

Sir Moses gave them the coins. "Take these and buy yourselves new whips and tops," he said.

"*Grazie mille*," said the boy. The girl stopped crying.

The Montefiores and Mr Kursheedt proceeded through the narrow crowded streets. The ghetto was not large, just seven acres, but it was here where all the Jews of Rome were forced to live.

"How can they bear to be confined like this? How?" Mr Kursheedt kept repeating in his southern twang.

"It's all they know," Sir Moses said. "For three hundred years they've lived here in poverty like this."

"More to the point, how can Pius allow these inhumane conditions to continue?" said Lady Montefiore. "In all my days I have never witnessed anything like it, not even in Syria. Damascus was overcrowded but not like this; and at least it was dry."

Some of the alleyways opened into tiny squares. They passed lines of wooden barrows with large wheels; animated stallholders tried to sell them fish, fried artichokes, old watches and tarnished candlesticks, all shouting in accents peppered with Romanised Hebrew words.

"Buy the lady a necklace: real mother of pearl," shouted a young man as he shoved a tray of tarnished jewellery in front of Sir Moses' nose. "Show that you love her!"

Sir Moses stepped back. He took some change out of his pocket, taking his time to examine the portrait of Pius the Ninth on a five *scudi* coin before smiling at Lady Judith. "I think my wife knows that I love her very dearly," he replied. He told the young man he would not buy anything, but flipped a few coins to him and to the other stallholders, none of whom was wearing shoes. He asked a toothless old lady the way to the synagogues. "There, there!" she shrieked, pointing through a small archway.

As they entered a small square, Sir Moses read the street sign on the corner. "The Piazza of the Five Schools; yes, the five synagogues are here, all grouped together," he said, and they saw that a crowd was gathering outside a tall building.

They followed men in skullcaps into a large hallway. The main synagogue was on the ground floor. A choir of young men with beautiful tenor voices assisted the Cantor in chanting the hundredth psalm. Round candelabra stacked with burning candles hung down from the ornate wooden ceiling, illuminating the faces of the congregation. Here people seemed happier, even rather noble, in comparison to those outside on the streets of the ghetto, where they had seemed depressed, anxious and humiliated.

Sir Moses and Mr Kursheedt took seats at the back of the hall and Lady Judith made her way up a narrow wooden staircase to the gallery where the women were sitting. The two men gazed up as Lady Judith took a seat next to the ghetto women, who were looking down through wrought iron grilles at their menfolk. The married women wore headdresses that hid their locks, but the younger ones had long hair that flowed down over their shoulders and framed their coquettish grins.

"These young Jewish women are extremely attractive, aren't they?" Sir Moses whispered to his companion. "And yet they have a genuine look of innocence and self-esteem, which I believe stems from a strict morality." He spoke with a sense of pride as though he were personally responsible for their virtuous behaviour. He automatically fell into reciting the words of the Cantor in Hebrew. *"Know ye that the Lord he is God: it is he that hath made us and not we ourselves; we are his people and the sheep of his pasture."*

As they left the Synagogue, Sir Moses was still repeating the words of Psalm one hundred, verse three. *"...it is he that hath made us and not we ourselves..."*

They came upon a violinist and his young daughter who was dancing to the rousing capriccio he played in front of a crowd. For a while they stood and listened. It was a moving piece, possibly by Paganini, thought Sir Moses. He wondered by what means a young man in the ghetto would have come across this music as he threw several *scudi* into the man's hat.

Just then a passer-by approached them. "Take care, or the Jews will murder your children and use the blood to make Passover cakes!" he shouted, his eyes staring wildly at them.

Sir Moses and Lady Judith exchanged anxious glances. The man started shouting at the musician. "Don't think we don't know what you do with our Christian children!"

The violinist stopped playing, but Sir Moses appealed to him to ignore the man and continue. The musician reluctantly started to play again, just as a young boy, wearing a priest's cassock, was being led into the alley by a group of churchmen.

"That's the Mortara boy," said Sir Moses to his wife and Mr Kursheedt. They all watched him.

The Rector, Canon Sarra, stepped in front of the crowd. "Don't forget: it's never too late to convert, as our young protégé, Edgardo Mortara knows," the Rector shouted as the boy was paraded in front of them all.

The crazed man approached Edgardo and leered at him. "Careful, or the Jews will sacrifice you and drink your blood."

Edgardo stared at him. The Jews recoiled in horror as the man started pelting them with stones.

A group of French soldiers ran forward and grabbed hold of the man. Two of them hit him and led him away. Another exchanged greetings with the musician and his little girl. "Now you can get on and celebrate the Passover. Will you take in French soldiers for a Passover dinner tonight?" one of them asked cheekily in broken Italian. He had a big grin on his face.

"You are welcome in my home," the musician replied.

"And mine!" another Jewish man shouted.

Fear gradually disappeared from the faces of the Jews.

Sir Moses smiled. "Can you believe this? In a country where Christians are not supposed to have anything to do with the Jews?" he said to his wife and Mr Kursheedt.

One of the Jewish men heard them talking. "We like to see the French soldiers here in Rome. Our only hope is with them. The good will of the French keeps us going," he told them. "But forgive me now for we have to go to church."

"Church?"

"Yes every Sabbath – even at Passover. First the synagogue and then the church."

"*Baruch Hashem*," Sir Moses said to him.

"Blessed be God," the Jewish man replied with a quizzical look, surprised that Sir Moses, dressed in his fine clothes, could speak Hebrew.

The Rector led Edgardo away in a flurry of priestly robes.

"Let's follow them," said Gershom Kursheedt.

Lady Judith hitched up her skirts to avoid the floodwaters that were drenching them, and she and her husband followed Mr Kursheedt who tried to keep pace with Edgardo and the priests. They quickly made their way through the dark alleyways that had become a string of elongated ponds as the waters of the Tiber ebbed and flowed through them.

"The water levels are dramatic, aren't they?" said Lady Judith staunchly as she pulled her wet hem up over her boots.

"Yes, they're worse after the severe storms that hit Rome yesterday. I should never have brought you here," Sir Moses said to his wife, but she insisted that her health was much improved and Dr Hodgkin had raised no objections. She tripped along over the rough cobblestones, dodging the deeper pools as she spoke.

"You move like a dancer, Lady Judith," Mr Kursheedt observed.

"She has always moved beautifully," Sir Moses agreed, "and she has always been very stubborn."

At the end of one of the alleys they rounded a sharp corner and found themselves caught up in a frenzied crowd who were being herded through a tiny gate by gendarmes and

Dominican monks. In their midst was Edgardo Mortara and the Rector, who was leading the boy towards the small Church of San Gregorio at the Bridge of the Four Heads on the banks of the Tiber.

They made their way to the square in front of the church and watched as priests delivered speeches to the crowd of Jews, the general theme being repentance for not having converted to Christianity. Some of the monks were shouting to the Jews to get into the church to take Communion.

"Does it always have to be on the Holy Sabbath, even at Passover!?" one of the elderly Jews cried out, but a gendarme immediately ushered him into the church.

Canon Sarra stood up on a wooden box in front of the crowd. "Make way for the young boy Edgardo Mortara, the Jew turned Christian, who is now happily on the road to Heaven and wishes to convert the Jews," he announced as if he were presenting a freak show at a travelling fair. You have heard of him?"

"Of course we have heard of him; you ask us the same question every week. You are humiliating that child almost every hour of his life," yelled a middle-aged Jewish man as he pushed to the front. A gendarme threw him back into the crowd. The priests laughed as they helped to herd the Jews into the church.

"Let's go in and help them with the Communion," said the Rector to Edgardo as he took his hand. The square emptied.

"I think we should hear how Catholics try and convert the Jews," said Gershom Kursheedt.

The Montefiores followed him into the church and stood at the back of the nave.

A priest marched up and down alongside the altar, fervently imploring the Jewish congregants to look to Jesus for their salvation, just as Saint Paul had done when he converted from Judaism to Christianity on the way to Damascus. "How come Paul knew the true divinity of Jesus as God's son on earth, but you don't?" he shouted. "How come Paul knew that the true God was a Trinity: the Father, the Son and The Holy Ghost?"

Sir Moses looked around the church as the bearded Jews shook their heads. One elderly man started shouting. "God is one deity not three." Another shouted out, "Jesus was a Jew just like us, until the day he died."

The priest retaliated in frustration. "Yes till he was crucified. And who put Jesus on the Cross?"

"The Romans!" the man cried out as he looked to his friends for support.

Some of them echoed his cry. "Yes, the Romans!"

The priest started stamping his feet. "It was his own people who put Jesus on the Cross. It was the Jews who killed Jesus."

Lady Montefiore turned to her husband. "I knew it would not be long before we would hear the Jews being cast as Christ-killers." She looked over to where Edgardo was standing with the Rector. He was staring sadly at the ground.

The priest was now striding back and forth in front of the altar. "It was the Jews who killed the Son of God!" He turned to the congregation, his face reddening. "And now you refuse to repent for your sins!"

At this point the Jewish congregation hardly reacted to him; they had heard his speeches every week.

The priest called out for the sacramental bread. "Right. I think it's time for Communion."

Some of the Dominican monks stepped forward to help line the Jews up.

Lady Montefiore took her husband's arm. "Don't they understand that this is not the way they are going to get people to convert?" She led him out of the church.

For a while they stood in silence outside. Lady Judith squeezed her husband's hand. "Penny for your thoughts," she said.

"Can you believe that for hundreds of years this little church has been packed every Saturday, the Jewish Sabbath, with Jews forced by decree to listen to Christian sermons and take Communion?"

An inscription on the wall under a large Crucifix caught Lady Montefiore's eye.

"What does that say?" she asked her husband as she looked over to the church.

Sir Moses read the Italian words out loud and then translated. "It is a message from Jesus to the Jewish people here." he said, "'All day long I have stretched out my hands to a disobedient and faithless people that have lost their way.' Actually, it's from Isaiah, but the quote is twisted to give it an anti-Jewish slant."

"It's outrageous!" his wife said, just as Edgardo and the Rector and their entourage emerged from the church.

Sir Moses called out to them. "May I speak with Edgardo?" he asked the Rector.

"I am sure Edgardo would be very happy to speak with you, but he is due to take part with other boys from his convent in the Mass at the Basilica of San Pietro in Vincoli. We must not make him late." In an instant the group had disappeared amongst the fish-sellers on the Via di Pescaria.

The Montefiores retraced their steps through the ghetto. In one of the streets they encountered a large group of gendarmes. Several of them started to enter the buildings.

"What are you doing?" Sir Moses enquired of one of them.

"We are searching the homes of the Jews while they are in church," a gendarme replied.

"Searching for what?" asked Sir Moses.

"Christians. Just making sure they are not keeping Christians as servants. It's against the law now."

"Isn't that a ridiculous law? How can the Jews living their wretched lives in the ghetto afford servants?" said Sir Moses.

"Well we are instructed to check. By order of the Holy Office," said the gendarme.

"It would seem that everything in this city is done by order of the Holy Office," said Sir Moses drily.

The gendarme stepped forward. "Yes, that's true, Sir. If I may say so, you don't belong here. This part of the city is only for the bloody Jews."

Sir Moses translated the words for his wife and Gershom Kursheedt.

Lady Montefiore glared at him. "We *are* 'bloody Jews!'" she shouted.

Sir Moses took her arm. "Let's get you home," he said.

They left the coldness of the ghetto and entered the Piazza Giudia that was baking hot, with the red tiles on the rooftops almost iridescent. They were relieved to see sunlight again, although it took a while for their eyes to adjust to the brightness. Sir Moses helped Lady Judith into their waiting carriage.

"Gershom, will you take my wife home?" he said. He took his wife's hand. "There is one more place I wish to go to."

He set off on foot and asked a passing priest how to get to the Church of San Pietro in Vincoli.

***

Sir Moses headed north to the Capitoline Hill, with its ruined temples overlooking the Roman Forum. For a while his thoughts of Edgardo were usurped by tales of Romulus and Remus running around with their goats. The sun was hot. He wiped his brow and wondered how Romulus had founded the city of Rome on such a small hill. He turned east towards the Arch of Septimius Severus, through which triumphal processions had made their way home from the Empire. The crowds and legions were long gone, their cheers replaced by stillness and emptiness and the Imperial route now a row of fallen columns. He reached the Coliseum and imagined he could see the gladiators through the arches in its crumbling circular walls. He also imagined the lions, tigers and elephants, and the spectators in their thousands watching sea battles with real ships and real water. Now, though, it was quiet: just a scattering of polite European tourists with their parasols, stepping around the stones that hadn't been stolen to build Saint Peter's Basilica. He wondered how they used to flood the Coliseum. He suddenly wished he had had a son with whom he could have discussed this, a son with whom he could have shared the sights of Rome. He felt sad that he and Judith were childless, knowing he would have been a good father. For all his wealth and success there was a great void where a family should have been. He circled the Coliseum with a heavy heart, his thoughts now returning to Edgardo Mortara.

He thought he saw Mrs Chambers holding court with a group of gentlemen under the Arch of Constantine across the road. Usually he would have made a point of being polite and saying hello, but today he did not want to be distracted. He knew that the Basilica of San Pietro in Vincoli was nearby, a few streets to the north he had been told, and he headed that way up the Esquiline Hill until he reached a long flight of stairs under the Borgia Arch.

Arriving at the square in front of the church he spotted a stone seat on the opposite side and rested there in the shade of a pine tree. On the outside, the Basilica of San Pietro in Vincoli looked quite plain. The Rector and several priests emerged from the church and then some of the boys, including Edgardo, with a younger priest. The Rector bid them farewell and hurried off. A group of boys, all older than Edgardo and all dressed in white, started to throw a ball around in the cloister in front of the church. Sir Moses crossed the square and entered the cloister discretely. Edgardo, dressed in a black cassock, sat under the shade of a fig tree on the decorated wall of an old well. He seemed to be deep in thought.

Sir Moses approached a priest at the other side of the cloister. "The Mass is over?" he asked, speaking in English.

"Yes, you have missed it," Brother Claudio told him. "The

boys here appear once a week as choristers. You are English? Are you touring Rome?"

Sir Moses nodded.

"The Coliseum is just a few streets away," Brother Claudio told him abruptly, as if he was trying to dismiss him as a tourist.

"I saw it on the way here," Sir Moses said to him. "It looks like a giant plant pot with all the foliage growing out of its top tier."

Brother Claudio remained stony-faced.

"Can you tell me something about this church?" Sir Moses sat down on the bench next to him. He looked over at Edgardo as Brother Claudio talked to him in very good English.

"San Pietro in Vincoli was an old monastery, probably three hundred years old or more before it became a church, dedicated to Saint Peter. *In vincoli* means 'in chains'. Inside the church you can see the actual chains that shackled Saint Peter in Jerusalem for preaching about Jesus. And you can see Michelangelo's statue 'Moses'. It was meant to be part of the tomb of Pope Julius II, but it was never finished. You should go inside and look at it." Brother Claudio then became conscious of Sir Moses gazing at Edgardo as he spoke.

"The decorated well over there is charming, eh?"

Sir Moses nodded. "The boy sitting on the well does not play with his companions. He looks rather sad."

Brother Claudio agreed. "You have probably heard of that boy; it's the Jew boy Mortara, baptised at Bologna."

"Indeed!" Sir Moses replied.

Brother Claudio called Edgardo over. The boy rose slowly, took off his cap and stood before the two men with his eyes on the ground.

"Is he in good health?" enquired Sir Moses.

"Excellent health," replied Brother Claudio. "Isn't that so, Edgardo?"

"Yes Sir," the boy replied as he looked up.

"Are you a good scholar?" Sir Moses asked him.

"Tell the Englishman, Edgardo," Brother Claudio said.

"I think so."

"He is very intelligent; he likes all his subjects, especially Latin, for which he seems to have a marked inclination." Brother Claudio turned to Edgardo. "You're doing well at school, aren't you?"

Edgardo nodded awkwardly and then returned to the well. Sir Moses looked at him while he continued talking to Brother Claudio. "And his parents, do they come to see him? I hear they have permission to do so," said Sir Moses.

"No," Brother Claudio replied. "They came last year. The father tried to enter a church. We were warned to keep ourselves on guard, because he wanted to carry the boy away."

"He will surely be able to leave the convent at some point?" said Sir Moses.

"At the age of seventeen; but we believe he has an ecclesiastical calling."

"Does he often speak of his father and mother?"

"No. He has written to them, imploring them to convert, but the parents don't reply to his letters. The mother, they tell me, is a good woman, who would willingly convert, but the father is a hardened sinner. It was he who was the cause of the fuss that was made on account of the child being carried away. Henceforth the child belongs to God."

"It must be very hard for him," said Sir Moses.

"Not at all. The Pope is like a father to him. He spends a lot of time with him at the Vatican and pays for everything. If you ask me, he spoils him. Some people call him 'the Pope's son'."

The bells of San Pietro in Vincoli began to ring.

"Boys, we have fifteen more minutes, and then we must go back to the convent," shouted Brother Claudio. He called Edgardo over to them again. "Edgardo, show this English gentleman the statue of Moses inside the church."

The boy led him into the church, which was beautifully decorated with ornate altars, statues and paintings. They walked to the main altar where a large candelabrum lit a bronze and glass cabinet, holding a rope of grey chains.

"Those are the chains of Saint Peter," Edgardo told him. "The angel broke them to free him from captivity."

"Fascinating," said Sir Moses, not wishing to dampen the enthusiasm of the child. The chains struck Sir Moses as being in extremely good condition, the sort you could still buy in any ironmongery shop and certainly not particularly ancient looking. Sir Moses studied them and found it hard to believe that they were the real chains, but then he thought that about most religious relics. "How do they know?" Sir Moses found himself saying out loud.

"Pope Pius knows," said Edgardo. "Saint Peter was the first Pope of Rome, and Pius knows about all the Popes."

The boy took his hand and directed him to the side of the main altar. There was the tomb of Pope Julius II, a magnificent tableau of sculpted marble standing like an enormous wall, its recesses filled with large statues. At its centre opposite them was Michelangelo's Moses.

"That's Moses," Edgardo said. He pointed to the right. "If you stand over there he looks like he's staring at you."

"He's quite spectacular, isn't he?" said Sir Moses. "My name is Moses too."

Edgardo chuckled. "Really?" he said.

"Yes. Moses Montefiore."

"That Moses has horns," Edgardo said pointing at the statue.

"Why do you think that is?" Sir Moses asked him.

"Canon Sarra says it's meant to be rays of light coming out of his head, but I think they look more like horns. Some people think the Jews used to have horns."

Sir Moses shook his head. He couldn't help thinking it was rather unfortunate that Michelangelo's rays of light did indeed look more like horns, linking the image of Moses with the medieval notion of Jews colluding with the Devil. "The

218

Jews never had horns," said Sir Moses.

"Then they must be rays of light," said Edgardo.

Sir Moses smiled at him.

"I saw you in the ghetto," Edgardo suddenly said to him. "You are a friend of the English Prince, aren't you?"

"The Prince of Wales, yes. But I'm more a friend of Queen Victoria, his mother." Sir Moses said in a matter of fact manner. "How did you know that?"

"I also saw you in St Peter's with him and the Pope at the Easter celebrations. Are you an Englishman?"

"Yes, but I was born in Italy. My family was Italian like yours, and Jewish."

"Do you live in a ghetto in England?"

"There are no ghettos in England," said Sir Moses. "I live in the centre of London and I have a house by the sea."

Edgardo's eyes opened wide. "Are Jews allowed houses by the sea in England?"

"Yes," said Sir Moses.

"I was born Jewish," said Edgardo. "But now I am a Christian." He took the cross around his neck and showed it to Sir Moses. And then he reached into his pocket and drew out a little enamelled multi-coloured object. He handed it to Sir Moses. "It's my *mezuzah*. I still carry it with me," he said.

"*Baruch ata Adonai…*" Moses Montefiore began to say.

"*…Eloheinu melech ha'olam…*" Edgardo continued, as he smiled at Sir Moses. Then he abruptly changed the subject. "Where is Wales?"

"Next door to England. Don't you want to go back home to your parents?"

Edgardo looked at him. "My parents will not convert to Christianity," he said with the conviction of a boy twice his age. "That means I can't go home. Don't you think that if they really loved me, they would convert?"

"I'm sure they love you very much," Sir Moses said to him, a little taken aback, "but they are Jewish."

"Jesus was Jewish too," said Edgardo, "and Saint Paul was Jewish, but he converted to Christianity like I did."

Sir Moses remembered the words of the man in the ghetto church and wanted to remind Edgardo that Jesus had remained a Jew for the whole of his life, right up to his crucifixion, but he did not want to upset the seven-year-old boy, for whom he felt a great sadness.

Sir Moses saw that Brother Claudio was standing at the entrance of the church. He looked into the boy's eyes. "If you want to go home I am sure we could help you. There are many people in England, indeed in the whole of Europe, who are demanding that you should be allowed to go home. I am one of those people. We might be able to get you back to your mother and father."

Edgardo took a while to reply. "Thank you, but I do not want to go home. The Pope is now my father."

Sir Moses was taken aback by the boy's words. He noticed that Brother Claudio was walking over to them and quickly handed the *mezuzah* back to Edgardo. "*Shalom*," he said. "If you ever have the good fortune to find yourself in England, please contact me."

"How will I find you?" said Edgardo.

"Oh, I'm sure you will," said Sir Moses as he took hold of the boy's hands. "Is there anything I can do for you? Are you sure you are alright?"

Edgardo looked hard into the old man's eyes.

"Tell me," Sir Moses urged him softly.

Edgardo nodded, just as Brother Claudio reached them. He explained to Sir Moses that they had to return to the Convent. "We must go back for lunch and then Edgardo has schoolwork to do."

The doors of the church opened, letting in rays of sunlight, and two young Swiss Guards bounded across the nave.

"Edgardo! Edgardo!" they shouted in unison. It was Thomas and Laurent in their multi-coloured outfits. They ran over to Edgardo. Laurent lifted him on to his shoulders.

"We are in a church!" said Brother Claudio reproving them.

"Yes, and it is a lovely church," said Thomas. "And we have found Edgardo," he added with a big smile, making little sense to the people around him as was often the case when he got excited.

"The Holy Father wishes Edgardo to join him in the Vatican Gardens this afternoon, and he wants him to help with the pruning of the rose bushes," said Laurent. "And he wants him to have a picnic with him and maybe have a swim in the Galleon Fountain." Laurent winked at Edgardo. "We have the carriage outside."

Without engaging in any more discussion, the Swiss Guards carried Edgardo off to the door. Brother Claudio followed, clearly humiliated.

Sir Moses took a seat in front of the statue of Moses. "Perhaps it is time to join the other English travellers leaving Rome, and take out births on the Vesuvius at the Civita Vecchia," he said to his marble namesake.

Chapter 34

Edgardo jumped into the ice-cold water from the edge of the mountain of rocks surrounding the Fountain of the Eagle. The large bird with its unfurled wings stood on the summit surveying the Vatican Gardens, and beneath it the winged dragons were spitting water from their rocky grottoes and crevices. Thomas and Laurent jumped in after him, grabbing him and tickling him, causing him to gurgle as much as the bubbling water cascading into the fountain.

"Today, Edgardo, it's the breast stroke," said Thomas as he supported him in the water and Laurent showed him how to move his legs.

After Edgardo had spent half an hour swimming from one Swiss Guard to the other, they all climbed out on to the rocks. Laurent threw a towel round Edgardo and quickly dried him off. He did the same for Thomas who reciprocated.

They gathered their towels and clothes and ran naked through the woods of the English garden, shrieking with laughter as they chased each other round its numerous oak trees: holm, downy and durmast oaks. Eventually they arrived at the terrace in front of one of the towers of the Leonine Wall to find Pope Pius sitting in the shade. In front of him a table was laid with lemonade, iced lemon cakes and chestnut tartlets. A servant was waving his arms to keep a colony of screeching seagulls off the cakes. He stopped to serve Edgardo a big slice of cake and a tartlet.

"Why are there seagulls here?" said Edgardo.

Pius laughed. "They fly from the coast and follow the course of the River Tiber all the way to Rome," he explained.

Edgardo jumped on to the Pope's knee.

"Tell me what you have done today, my son," said Pius.

"I went to the ghetto, which I don't like. I want to convert the Jews, but I don't like being paraded around in there." Edgardo screwed up his nose. "I also swam in the fountains today and learned the breast stroke with Thomas and Laurent."

"Thomas, Laurent! Come and help yourselves to cakes and lemonade," the Pontiff shouted.

Cardinal Antonelli came striding across the lawn.

"What are you doing here?" Pius asked him.

"I might ask the same of you," Antonelli said as he looked over to Thomas and Laurent. "It seems that everyone is half naked."

Thomas and Laurent clutched their towels to themselves, moved over to a cedar tree and started to change into their undergarments, but before they had time to put on their coloured pantaloons the Pope shouted out to them. "Put those on later; we're all going to have a game of La Scopa with Edgardo!"

Pius lowered the boy from his knee, handing him his towel. "Put your underclothes on, Edgardo, and we'll start the game." He gestured to the servant, who got out a deck of cards.

"I think La Scopa will have to wait," said Antonelli as he handed Pius a large scrolled document. "We have another memorial from the British Isles."

Pius put it down on the table. "No, the memorial will have to wait. As I have said, we are about to play a game of La Scopa."

Antonelli took a seat at the table and begrudgingly helped himself to a chestnut tartlet, which he cut into quarters. He ate one of the pieces and then started to tap his fingers on the table in frustration.

"Edgardo, sit opposite me: you'll be my partner. Thomas and Laurent, you are the other team." Pius glared at the Cardinal Secretary of State, as his tapping got louder. "Antonelli, you'll have to move. We have to sit opposite each other in pairs."

The Cardinal got up. There were no spare chairs, and he was adamant that he was not going to sit on the rug. He stood back from the table and folded his arms.

"Take your tartlet with you, Antonelli," said the Pope.

The Secretary of State did not move. The servant handed him the dissected chestnut tartlet, which was obscuring an illustration of 'Cupid' climbing a tree on a blue ceramic plate.

Pius began shuffling the deck of Neapolitan cards and then dealt each player three of them face down. He dealt four more face up in the middle of the table.

"Three Kings; that means we have to throw our cards back and have a new deal," said Edgardo.

Antonelli rolled his eyes up to the heavens. He found it extremely insulting and humiliating that the Pope should consider a game of La Scopa, played with two half-naked Swiss Guards and a half-naked boy, more important than matters of state.

Pius sensed his anger. "Please don't sulk, Antonelli. I'm sure I don't have to remind you of how many times we've had to wait for you on account of your extra-curricular activities." The Pope reshuffled the cards. "And be careful with that plate: it's sixteenth-century Casa Pirotta."

Antonelli tried to stem his anger as he sat through numerous 'turns', in which they all laughed loudly on capturing each other's cards, on seeing the Pope take the elusive Seven of Coins, and with he and Edgardo sweeping the table clean and winning the game.

Antonelli then stepped forward. "Perhaps now..."

"I think it only fair to our opponents, Thomas and Laurent, to allow them to have the opportunity of winning a game to equalise," said the Pope with a big grin.

Antonelli stepped back again, banging his knuckles together in frustration as the second game, won by Thomas and Laurent, gave way to a deciding game, which seemed to take forever, with endless Coins, Cups, Clubs and Swords being captured by both teams. It was only after Edgardo and the Pope took all the Cup cards as well as capturing all the 'sevens' that they managed to exceed the fifteen points necessary to take the match.

Pius gave Edgardo a big hug and a kiss and then Thomas and Laurent swung him over their heads before running back to the cedar tree to put on their pantaloons and shirts.

The servant helped Edgardo to get dressed.

Pius picked up the memorial and looked at it with disdain, before reading through it.

"Do you know what this is?" he said to Edgardo.

"No," said the boy.

"A petition for your freedom. First we had memorials from the Sardinians, then the French, and now we have a memorial from the British Isles."

"It's signed by two thousand prominent British Christians," Antonelli informed him with great irritation as he picked it up. "Two thousand! Including the Archbishops of Canterbury, Dublin and York... and Lords – the Duke of Wellington's name is here – magistrates, judges..."

"This is how important you are, Edgardo," said the Pontiff quietly.

"What does it say?" said Edgardo.

Pius handed the document to Antonelli. "Tell him," he said.

"It talks of the usual matters relating to the case, of the boy Mortara being secretly baptised and seized..." Antonelli was visibly angry.

"Read it to him!" the Pope snapped.

"Perhaps we should read this in private," said Antonelli. "Not in front of your attendants."

The Pope made an audible and exaggerated sigh. "Very well. Thomas, Laurent, please help Marco take the picnic things inside."

"And perhaps they could take Edgardo inside as well,"

Antonelli suggested.

"Edgardo will stay here with us," said Pius firmly as the servant cleared the picnic and he and the Swiss Guards started walking back towards the Apostolic Palace with towels over their shoulders. "Leave the cards here, Marco." He then flicked his fingers at Cardinal Antonelli, saying, "Read it then!"

Antonelli could hardly contain himself. *"...and whereas the Government of France has in vain urged the Court of Rome to restore the said child to his parents... and whereas Sir Moses Montefiore Baronet, at the request of the Deputies of the British Jews went to Rome in their name to present a memorial to the Pope..."*

"That was the man who told me to visit him in London," Edgardo informed them.

"When was that?" Pius asked him.

"It was not very long ago. He came to San Pietro in Vincoli and we looked at the statue of Moses together. The day we had the last picnic and I learnt the front crawl."

"Well at least I am providing you with friends from around the world," said the Pope.

Antonelli angrily continued with his reading of the memorial. *"...and whereas the Pope refused even to see Sir Moses Montefiore, Baronet..."*

Pius interrupted him, his cheeks reddening. "I cannot see every person who visits Rome," he shouted.

Antonelli ignored him. *"...and whereas it is a dishonour to Christianity in the eyes of the Jews among all nations that the seizure and detention of the said child Edgar Mortara, should be supposed to be consistent with the principles of the Christian religion... Now we the undersigned British Christians, do hereby protest and declare that the proceedings of the Pope of Rome, in taking away the Jewish child Edgar Mortara, from his parents and educating him, contrary to his parents will, in the Roman Catholic faith are repulsive to the instincts of humanity, and in violation of parental rights and authority, as recognised in the laws of all civilised nations, and, above all in direct opposition to the spirit and precepts of the Christian religion..."*

Antonelli threw the memorial down on to the table. "I do not have to repeat that it is now not only the Jews who are protesting," he shouted, his voice becoming almost high-pitched. "And I hope you do my common sense the honour to believe that I judge the Mortara affair an unmistakable blunder."

"What does he mean?" Edgardo asked Pius.

"He means that he thinks it was a mistake to fight for religious principle in the case of your baptism and that he is prepared to bend to public opinion," Pius said to him calmly.

Antonelli was furious. "What I actually mean is that I feel I am no longer able to stem the torrent: I have been borne down and carried away. It has stimulated a wave of hostility, which the Church can ill afford at a time when it is fighting for its physical existence. Here we are in the strife-torn Italian peninsula; our public appeal in countries like France and England at its lowest ebb; and with relations between the French and Papal Governments strained, to say the least. The Mortara case has undoubtedly strengthened the forces of Italian unification. The people of Romagna no longer submit to your temporal government and desire annexation to Sardinia under the sceptre of Victor Emmanuel. You are being driven behind the walls of the Vatican. Are we to sit by and watch as the deterioration of the Roman Catholic Church in Europe is accelerated? Now for the first time in history, Protestants, Jews and non-believers are joined in a united front against you, and even European Catholics are weakened in their loyalty to the Church. This British memorial is the first public admission by a Christian nation that the Jews have been wronged in the name of Christianity!"

Pius glared at his Cardinal Secretary of State. "I have made it clear to the world that returning the boy would be impossible. *Non possumus!* Let anything happen, rather than tear from Christ a soul he bought with his blood."

Pius turned to Edgardo. "How say you, my son? Can I return you to your parents? Tell Cardinal Antonelli."

"*Non possumus*," said Edgardo.

Chapter 35

Bouhay, Liège, Belgium. 1940

"*Non possumus*," Father Mortara repeated as he sat in the gardens of the Priory. "It was not possible for Pope Pius to give me back to my parents.

He gazed across the lush lawns that were edged by a border of low box hedging surrounded by tall chestnut trees. In the distance Brother Martin and some of the other monks were digging up the vegetable beds and spreading cow manure.

"Sir Moses Montefiore failed in his attempt to liberate you," said Raoul.

Father Mortara continued to watch the monks. "They're getting the soil ready for planting the potato tubers," he said.

Raoul wondered if the old man had heard his comment, but after a long silence it eventually became clear that he had.

"Yes, Brother Luc, he failed," said Father Mortara with a hint of irritation as he turned to him. "They all failed; the good men, the bad men, memorials, meetings, protests – all of them! They threatened the Pope; they said that if he didn't return me they could not be responsible for the security of the Papal States.

"Who said that?" said Raoul.

"Francis Joseph of Austria, Napoleon the Third of France, Cavour, Victor Emmanuel – all of them. But Pius remained firm and constant." Father Mortara shrugged his shoulders and his words tailed off to silence.

"How did you feel about that?" said Raoul purposefully as he squinted at the sun.

"I was a child. I knew I was a Christian and happy to be so," said the old man. I had been baptised and my father was the Pope. And I loved him for that – no son's love was ever greater."

"What about your real father – didn't you miss him?"

Brother Pius's voice faltered. "I'm not saying it wasn't difficult. It was hard being separated from him – and my mother..."

The old priest closed his eyes. Raoul thought he heard him say 'God bless my father' before he continued. "My father didn't give up and then Victor Emmanuel II, the King of Sardinia, captured Bologna from the Papal Army that year and declared Bologna to be independent. There was great excitement in the streets of the city; the citizens were no longer forced to submit to the temporal government of the Pope, and annexation to Piedmont was adopted unanimously. The Bolognese were confident that Victor Emmanuel would be declared King of Italy. My father immediately re-established the family in the city."

"Your father must have felt there was a real chance of getting you back home at that time," said Raoul.

"Yes, he received a letter from Cavour, no less, assuring him that Victor Emmanuel's government would do all in its power so that 'the child, in whom the public opinion of Europe is so strongly interested might be restored to his family'. There was much speculation that I would now be 'liberated'. Especially when Victor Emanuel dealt a blow to the Holy See by putting Feletti, the Head of the Bolognese Inquisition, on trial. It was he, you may remember, to whom Anna Morisi confessed. It was an unprecedented move. Feletti was brought to trial in October 1859 for the crime of my kidnapping."

"But Feletti did not issue the orders for your removal; surely those had come from the Inquisition in Rome?" said Raoul."

"Yes, that was what the defence lawyer argued: that the orders for my 'supposed' abduction had come from the Holy Tribunal and Pope Pius himself."

Raoul did not fail to notice that Father Mortara referred to the Holy Tribunal rather than the Inquisition with its connotation of medieval bigotry, and that he qualified the abduction with the word 'supposed' in a weary manner, suggesting that in his mind there was no question of any wrong-doing or illegality.

A bell rang from inside the Priory. Brother Martin put down his spade and came running over the lawn. "Lunch," he said with an awkward grin. He disappeared into the cloisters.

Raoul turned to Father Mortara. "What happened to Feletti, Father?"

"Oh he was acquitted, pleading as he did that the orders were from his superiors, I don't know what other verdict could have been given. He was a pawn in my story – they all were – the servants, the priests, the police… I don't blame any of them," said Father Mortara. "At the trial, the chief of police, who had overseen my removal, called it a crime, an atrocious crime that had saddened the noble city of Bologna, and said that he would never undertake such a task again. But I don't blame him either."

"No! The order for your abduction was issued from the Holy See," said Raoul angrily.

The old man looked at him quizzically. "You know that it was not Pope Pius who issued the order for my removal."

"No, but he did approve the deed, Father. Surely some of the blame lies there?"

"The blame does not lie anywhere, Brother Luc," said Father Mortara firmly. "All these people played their part in bringing me to God."

Raoul said nothing more. As he helped Father Mortara on to his feet and took him into the Priory for lunch, he couldn't help thinking what a shame it was that Victor Emmanuel had not captured Bologna a year earlier; if that had happened the abduction would probably not have taken place.

***

231

That afternoon Raoul received a visit from his old friend Guy. One of the monks showed him into the Priory common room where Raoul and Father Mortara were sitting alone, listening to the news on a large wooden Phillips radio shaped like an upside-down shield.

"Belgium has just signed a new trade agreement with Great Britain and France that will halt re-exports to Germany," said Raoul as he gave his friend a warm hug.

The boyish smile lighting up Guy's face quickly disappeared. "So much for King Leopold's proclamation of neutrality; *that'll* help keep Belgium out of the war, won't it?"

Raoul introduced him to Father Mortara who stood up and shook his hand.

"My friend Guy," said Raoul. "He's studying history at the University of Liège."

"I'm honoured. I've heard a lot about you and the very interesting life you led as a child," said Guy. "I would love to talk to you about growing up in Rome. You lived there in the days of the Risorgimento, didn't you Father?"

"I did. That was a long time ago," Brother Pius said as he smiled.

"Father Mortara also lived in New York," Raoul told his friend.

"For a short while at the turn of the century. I went to help establish missions for the Italians of the city," said Father Mortara.

"Now I know why you want to be a priest, Raoul," said Guy. "It'll get you out of Bouhay and allow you to travel around the world."

"That is not the reason for wanting to become a priest, as Brother Luc well knows," said Brother Pius.

"Father, would you like to take a short walk around the cloister with us?" said Raoul.

"No, I'm a little tired. I'll stay here and listen to the news. I must confess, it all sounds rather bleak. We must pray for peace, for Belgium and the rest of the world," said Father Mortara as he sighed and sat down in an old armchair. "You go with your friend, Brother Luc; it's a lovely sunny day out there."

Raoul covered Father Mortara's knees with a woollen rug and the two young men left him, Raoul in his floor-length habit and Guy in a checked shirt, bow tie, trousers and sleeveless pullover.

As they walked across the fields, they were glad to catch up with one another.

"Have you seen Delphine?" said Raoul.

"I'd like to say no, but I see her all the time," said Guy. "Liège is a small place. She always pops up somewhere: the rue Hors-Château or in Féronstrée with that new boyfriend of hers; he's such a twat." Guy then immediately apologised for what he'd just said. "I'm sorry, I shouldn't be using profanities in front of a priest."

"Don't worry; I'm not ordained yet," said Raoul.

"You know it should have been you and Delphine – not an idiot like him." Guy lit a cigarette and offered one to Raoul. "Here you go, Brother Luc. Is that what I should call you, or is it still Raoul with old friends?"

"I don't mind; as long as you don't call me a twa..." Raoul stopped himself and they both laughed. "I don't smoke now."

"No, monks don't smoke do they? Why is that? I suppose it's because they don't need to look suave and self-possessed. You still drink beer, though?"

"Yes, I still drown my sorrows," said Raoul as they made their way to the brook. They sat down by the water's edge and watched the stream bubbling over the rocks and through the ferns.

"Do you remember when we caught a massive trout here?" said Guy.

"We! I caught the trout!" said Raoul.

"Well I did most of the work, and it was my cane pole

and my line which I put together to make a terrific fishing rod. And I collected the worms! You always made me do all the hard work," said Guy with a wry smile. "Things haven't changed, have they? Now you've asked me to find out about the Risorgimento, about Pope Pius and Cardinal Antonelli. I've done quite a bit of research for you in the university library, you know."

"Thanks," said Raoul. "I hope it wasn't too much trouble. I've done a bit of reading as well, in the Librairie Pax."

"Why do you want to know about all this, anyway?" asked Guy.

"I want to understand Father Mortara more, before he leaves this world. And I want to familiarise myself with the background to his case. In 1859 the whole world knew about his abduction; it was considered to be a scandal at the time."

"It's certainly an interesting case," said Guy. "Doesn't the old boy talk about all this himself?"

"He does; he tells me his story," said Raoul. "But it's almost as if he censors what he says to throw a positive slant on everything. For instance, take the young servant girl who baptised him in Bologna: he constantly blesses her. He'll never say a word against her. In some of the literature, and certainly in the diaries I'm reading, she is more or less described as a prostitute: a fourteen-year-old country girl who slept around with Austrian officers. And she'd been dismissed by at least one family for theft."

"She probably couldn't believe her luck; coming to Bologna to work for a wealthy Jewish family – who worked in what?"

"Lace," said Raoul. "Actually, I don't think Father Mortara's family were that well off."

"Lace! Well they were wealthy in comparison to hers. Her family were probably incredibly poor; most likely they all lived in one room in a home made of mud or stone if they were lucky, lived on a diet of cornmeal mush and cabbage and her parents couldn't afford to send their kids to school. She had little hope of rising above her station in life. At that time children were required to work and provide income to help support the family; she'd probably been sent out to work at five or six."

"You don't know this for certain," said Raoul.

"No, but that was what life was like for most Italian peasants in the nineteenth century. It was a bit like life here in Bouhay now." Guy grinned. "My cousins still wash in a big metal tub in their yard once a week, with the least dirty going first!" He lit another cigarette. "So here she was in the middle of Bologna eating scrumptious Jewish food and fornicating with Austrian officers, but in spite of that she was probably, in her own mind, religious in the extreme, worshipping countless patron saints and celebrating all their feast days with a superstitious fervour. That I'm afraid is the questionable girl whose path crossed Father Mortara's when he was a baby."

"She wasn't the only morally suspect character in the case," said Raoul. "There was Feletti, the Head of the Bolognese Inquisition, and, of course, Cardinal Antonelli who was happy to throw aside his scarlet robe so that he could enjoy the sweet pleasures of life. Why would Pope Pius the Ninth, acknowledged as a virtual saint in his lifetime, keep such a libertine in his service? Didn't he know what his secretary of state was like?"

Guy took a long drag on his cigarette. "The Pope was well aware of the stories which circulated about his minister, not least because a series of anonymous letters that were sent to the Pontiff, recounting the Cardinal's alleged escapades, lurid sex life, and disloyalty, and calling for Antonelli's removal. Pius, as you can imagine, was distressed by these letters and discounted them. In response to the members of the College of Cardinals who urged the Pope to dismiss Antonelli, Pius inevitably asked, 'Do you believe that you could replace him?' They always had to admit they could not. Why? Because Pius knew that he was energetic and hardworking, and frankly far more talented than anyone else in his entourage. Furthermore, Pius never forgot Antonelli's heroic loyalty during the 1848 revolution, when he was one of the few who remained by his side. At that time Pius had gone from being the most popular man on the Italian peninsula to having to flee Rome in disguise as a regular priest to the Kingdom of the Two Sicilies, leaving Rome to the radicals and the mob."

"That's very interesting; you've done your research very well," said Raoul. "I hope you can put some of this work into your history degree."

"Don't worry; I'm sure I'll weave it in somewhere," said Guy. "I'm definitely going to do a module on the Italian Unification."

"So it seems that Antonelli got away with doing anything he wanted," said Raoul.

Guy nodded. "He was incredibly shrewd. When he died the Vatican finances were found to be in a state of total disorder with a deficit of 45,000,000 Lire, and yet he himself had amassed an immense personal fortune and was one of the wealthiest men in Rome. Not bad for a boy born in a village in the mountains, eh?"

"How could a man of the Church make a fortune like that?" said Raoul.

"He was no more religious than you or I – or maybe I should just say me," said Guy with a short laugh. "He was a layman. The Vatican later stopped laymen becoming cardinals. He was one of the last before it was decreed that all cardinals had to be ordained priests."

"What happened to his wealth?" asked Raoul.

"I think most of it went to his family; he didn't leave a sou to the Holy See. There were rumours of many illegitimate children, including a young countess who made claim to his fortune."

They got up and headed back across the fields to the Priory. A black and white woodpecker with a red cap announced its presence with a drumming display as it clung to the trunk of a pine tree.

"It sounds like it's trying to bang its brains out," said Guy.

"Yes," said Raoul impatiently. "Do you think the abduction of Edgardo Mortara contributed to the downfall of the Papal States?"

"I do," said Guy. "Francis Joseph of Austria and Napoleon III of France both advised the Pope to yield and give Edgardo back to his parents rather than incur the wrath of his enemies, and they, of course, were many at the time of the Risorgimento. I would go so far as to say that the case undoubtedly strengthened the forces of Italian unification, which later were to drive the Pope behind the walls of the Vatican."

When they arrived at the Priory they found Father Mortara wrapped up in his robe, scapular and cowl, sitting on a bench in the cloisters outside the Priory church. The voices of the monks singing plainsong seeped into the gardens. The old priest beckoned to the two men to join him.

They sat down with him and the conversation quickly turned to the Italian Unification.

"The Risorgimento grew out of secret societies like the Carbonari (which means charcoal burners) plotting against the Austrians, didn't it, Father?" said Guy. Brother Pius nodded. "And they were named after the charcoal burners' huts they used for meeting places…"

"Only you of all people, Guy, would pick up something as obtuse as this," said Raoul with an endearing smile.

"Your friend is right," said Father Mortara. "They hated foreign rule and in the 1820s and 1830s there were various revolts – but they were crushed by the Austrian troops."

Raoul was pleased to see how quickly Father Mortara engaged with Guy. He was always much more relaxed when the conversation was not so personal.

"Things of course changed in the 1850s when I was a boy,"

said the old priest and then he went on to explain how Cavour had cleverly won an alliance with Napoleon III of France; how Austria was goaded into declaring war; and how France and Sardinia-Piedmont defeated Austria at Magenta and won Lombardy for a united Italy.

Guy relished the twists and turns in the conversation. He questioned how Cavour had arranged plebiscites in the small states that were dotted throughout northern Italy and how Garibaldi and his red-shirted volunteers had managed to win Sicily and Naples. Each step towards a united Italy seemed to fascinate him.

"There remained only the Papal States and Venetia to be joined to the newly-made Italian nation when Victor Emmanuel II was proclaimed King of Italy in 1861," said Father Mortara. "In Rome, French troops still guarded the Pope's sovereignty, and Victor Emmanuel knew that attacking the French could undo all that had been accomplished. Venetia was gained in 1866, after Austria had been defeated by Prussia…"

Raoul suddenly interrupted them. "And even with the country's boundaries and rulers changing so drastically over what – seven years – you were still not returned to your family?"

"No," said Father Mortara. "*Non possumus.*"

The old priest began to tap his stick on the ground.

"Even with rulers fighting your corner and Italy united against the Pope?" said Raoul.

"Nearly united." said Father Mortara. "The Papal States alone were outside the Kingdom of Italy when I decided I wanted to take my vows at the age of fifteen."

Chapter 36

The Vatican, The Papal States. 1867

I'll never forgive you! You're dead to me!

Signor Mortara's words kept repeating in Edgardo's mind as he crossed Saint Peter's Square. The bells rang loudly – there were always bells at the Vatican – but today he hardly heard them.

Did you have no thought or feeling for your mother and I? Did you never miss us?

At six-and-a-half they indoctrinated you, and for years we read a load of idiotic rubbish about you wanting to convert the Jews.

At thirteen, in Jewish law, you became a man. You could have come home then, but no. You decided less than a year later to become a novice, with the name Brother Pius Maria in honour of your new father; to sacrifice the rest of your life, your religion. For what?

There is no more valuable treasure for a man, no possession holier, than the religion into which he was born. In that religion, all his feelings, his thoughts and his actions, will mature and grow. The religion of our childhood, the religion of our forefathers, fills our hearts with the sights and sounds and smells that inspire us for the whole of our life. Your religion was the most powerful inheritance we could give you. Now you are fifteen and you have thrown that inheritance away. Now I know you will never be my son.

In choosing to become a priest you are excluding yourself from the most tender, the most blessed of human relationships and will know nothing of the joys and responsibilities of fatherhood in which a man aligns himself most closely with his Maker, the Father of us all.

Your mother has been driven to the edge of insanity. I hope you

239

appreciate what you did to her, in the name of the Virgin Mother...

I hope it was all worth it for you.

You are no longer part of this family.

I will never forgive you. You're dead to me.

Edgardo fought back the tears. He didn't want to weep again; he had spent half the night weeping, but as soon as he found the Sovereign Pontiff in his library, sipping a glass of Médoc wine, he ran over to him, hugged him, and broke down.

Pius sat Edgardo down beside him on a Bergère settee, nestling his head under his arm as he had so often done over the last eight years. "Oh my dear Fra Pio, what is wrong?" he asked as he put down his glass of wine.

Edgardo took the letter out of his shoulder bag and handed it to him.

Pius read it and after a long silence eventually spoke. "That is harsh for you, but in some ways your father is right."

"I have no father except you, Papa," said Edgardo as he sat up.

"You know that's not true. Your birth father has made a fair point. The religion you are born into is a holy possession."

"People often change their religion," said Edgardo as the Pope gave him a handkerchief.

"True," said Pius. "People do change religions. Our first Pope, Simon Peter, was born a Jew, but he converted to Christianity, as did Saint Paul. They certainly had no dilemma in being born Jewish and converting."

"There is no dilemma for me, father, only sadness that in leaving my religion I have caused a rift between myself and my family."

"Do you miss the sights and sounds of the synagogue?" Pius asked.

"No," said Edgardo. He laughed as he dried his eyes. "But I do miss some of the Jewish food, especially the fried artichokes."

The Pope laughed too, but quickly became serious. "Do you miss your family?"

"It may seem strange, Father, but in many ways I do not miss my parents."

Edgardo's full eyebrows were screwed up in thought. Sometimes after supper, or Compline on warm evenings when he wandered the streets around Saint Peter in Chains, he would wonder what his mother was doing. He longed to see Anna and hear the laughter that punctuated her sentences; and he wished he could race Augusto round the arches of the Coliseum.

After the villegiatura in Alatri and the last meetings with his parents all those years ago in Rome, he hadn't heard anything more about them, although he had written to them several times with letters about his life and his religion, trying to convince them of the truth of the Catholic faith. They seemed to have ignored his letters. He had never received any replies until recently, when a letter arrived at the convent assuring Edgardo of his family's undying affection. They said that they had not responded to his letters before because they believed it was the monks, not he who had written them. They now hoped, however, that he would be able to correspond with them 'without controls'.

His mother had begged him to return home. He had replied, telling her that he was a Christian, and that if she and his father would convert he would return to them. The next letter had arrived with a change of mood. "You are a Jew and you will die a Jew!" In his heart Edgardo had responded with the words; "*I am a Christian and it is as a Christian I want to die.*"

When Madame Mortara had replied that his father demanded he return home, he had responded with '*Mama, the Pope is also my father...*'

Clearly that had angered Signor Mortara and caused him

to write the cruel letter, which Pius handed back to Edgardo.

He turned to the Pope. "I know my parents tried every means to get me back, but I have no desire to return to them, a fact that I do not understand myself. You are my family now and God has blessed me. I must belong to Him."

The Pope took his hand. "You know, when you were first put in the convent, they told me that you had cried for your brothers and sisters and begged to be returned to your parents."

"That was a long time ago," said Edgardo. "I soon realised that as I was a Christian you couldn't return me to my family. At first maybe I had mixed feelings, but I believe I entered the Church of my own free will."

"I am glad to hear that," said Pius, "I often wondered if all this was too much for you to bear, but you adjusted to your new surroundings very quickly. It made me think that your conversion was almost miraculous. You know I have always believed that you were singled out for the special love of God, and that the separation from your family was prompted by God's loving interest in you." Pius took another sip of his wine. "But I know that your beliefs did not come without suffering."

"The most religious people in the world have always suffered," said Edgardo. "St Sebastian, St Agnes, Jesus... I have not suffered as they did. And at least I have always had a father in you as well as a father in God... And I have always had your love."

"That you shall always have, Fra Pio."

Edgardo leaned over and fleetingly kissed the Pope's hand. However troubled his past had been, he knew how privileged he was. He still blessed the day when the Pontiff had taken him to his heart. He had lost his family, but he had gained a new adoptive father in Pius. He was a father who took care of his education and secured his future; who supported him spiritually and financially. Pius gave him a regular allowance and he wanted for nothing; he supervised his spiritual journey and had helped him to the priesthood.

After some time the Pope spoke again. "And so my dear Edgardo, today you take your vows at St Agnes Outside the Walls."

"Do you approve of my decision?" said Edgardo. "You don't think I am too young?"

"I know you have always wanted to join the Canons Regular of the Lateran. Of course I approve, just as I approved of you becoming a novice at the age of thirteen. I was very pleased then that you had decided to become a monk, and even happier that you took my name: Pius Maria," said the Pontiff. "At fifteen you are very young, but I also recall that according to Jewish law the thirteenth birthday marks a youth's majority in religious matters, and makes him a Son of the Covenant..."

"Yes, a Bar Mitzvah. I would have become a man at thirteen," said Edgardo.

The Pope nodded and smiled. "As we celebrate the festival of St Agnes, it is worth remembering how that noble girl became a martyr at thirteen. Do you know how?"

"She refused to marry the son of a high-ranking Roman official. She said she was already married to Jesus," said Edgardo.

"And of course she was sentenced to death for that." Pius paused to reflect. "You will be a good monk and one day a good priest; I have no doubt about that, Fra Pio." "It's all thanks to you," said Edgardo.

"No, you have achieved this yourself," Pius replied. "You have always been a good student; I remember even when you were six years old how well you translated passages from Italian into Latin. I wanted you to be educated by the Jesuits in a school for the nobility, but Antonelli was worried it would give the Press an excuse for controversy. As if we didn't escape controversy! In some ways I regret that I didn't follow my instincts."

"I've been happy at St Peter in Chains," said Edgardo.

The Pope's Major-Domo entered the room, closely

243

followed by Moretta. Edgardo crouched down to stroke her as she stretched out on the floor.

"Your Holiness, the carriage is ready for your departure to the Basilica of St Agnes Outside the Walls," the Major-Domo announced.

The Pope stood up. He reached for a silver-gilt statuette perched on a mahogany table next to the settee and handed it to Edgardo as he stood up. "For you, my dear Fra Pio, to commemorate this landmark day: a statue of St Agnes."

Edgardo looked at the cloaked figure; her gaze directed to the heavens in ecstasy. A lamb, a symbol of her innocence, was crouched at her feet. He made the sign of the cross and kissed the Pope's hand again. "Thank you Father," he said.

As they left the Papal apartments, the Pope whispered to his Major-Domo, "Tell the chef we want fried artichokes for dinner tonight, cooked in the Jewish style."

***

Following in the tradition of ancient Popes, but unlike his immediate predecessors, Pius the Ninth liked to celebrate ceremonies with much pomp. He wanted to resurrect the splendour of the Church. That afternoon, therefore, on the firing of a cannon, a small but magnificent cortège left St Peter's Square. At its head were dragoon guards with bearskin hats and white and yellow plumes, four Swiss Guards, including Thomas and Laurent in their armour, and a couple of secular chamberlains in their sixteenth-century costumes, all on richly adorned horses, their heads also ornamented with plumes. The forefront of the cortège was followed by the equipage of a number of prelates and bishops in their violet vestments, with the Pope's ceremonial carriage at the rear as a splendid finale.

The procession crossed the River Tiber at the Castel Sant' Angelo and weaved its way past the Quirinal Hill. Along the route people greeted the Holy Father with loud cheers as he constantly blessed them with a raised hand. His other hand rested on the back of the hand of the boy by his side; a lad between the age of boy and youth: Edgardo, handsome, excited, but also nervous about taking his vows.

The bells of the church were ringing as the Pope and Edgardo arrived at the Basilica of St Agnes Outside the Walls. They were helped out of the carriage by Thomas and Laurent, who squeezed Edgardo's shoulders and gave him friendly grins, while the canons of the church gathered around the Pontiff and kissed his hand. They led them to a makeshift throne that had been erected in front of the altar. A large congregation was bolstered by many of the young pupils from Saint Peter in Chains, and also by the monks and Canon Sarra and the other teachers. Edgardo stood by the Pope's side and a gold tiara was handed to him to place on the Pontiff's head. He bent forward and kissed the Pope's outstretched hand.

The service that followed was like some strange dream for Edgardo. When in due course he took his vows of chastity, poverty, and obedience, Padre Strozzi, the Abbot General of the Canons Regular of the Lateran, aptly preached on the verse of Isaiah 65:1; '*I was found by those that did not seek me: I appeared to them that asked not after me.*'

Edgardo then addressed Pius before the congregation. "Your Holiness, you have been more than a father to me. I thank you for all that you have done for me. You intervened and directed my person towards God, my soul towards Heaven." He spoke with considerable eloquence and with a maturity not often met with in boys of his age. "I am grateful for the education you gave me, for your love and your guidance. I am eternally your son." Tears welled in Edgardo's eyes. He knelt before the Pope and again kissed his hand.

Pius helped him to his feet, smiling as he said, "Today I am at your service, Edgardo." He kept his gaze fixed forward. He seemed modest and detached and yet he dominated the large congregation. He was a striking figure. His blue eyes and his angelic smile enhanced an aura of purity and profound calmness, but this gradually evaporated as he began to speak.

"My son, you are very dear to me, because I acquired you for Jesus Christ at a very great price. You cost me a heavy ransom and I have suffered significantly for that. If you only knew how much you have cost me!"

Pius turned to the congregation. "The great and small wanted to take this child from me, accusing me of being barbaric and merciless. A universal raging burst out against me and against the Apostolic See; governments and journalists, who these days seem to control public opinion, declared war against me. Some kings placed themselves at the head of this campaign and caused their ministers to write diplomatic notes and stir up trouble."

The Sovereign Pontiff again turned to Edgardo, his anger increasing with every sentence. "All that was on your account. I pass those kings by in silence. I do not wish to remember the outrages, the lies, and the curses pronounced by so many ignorant people who appeared indignant that God had conferred the gift of his true faith on you in liberating you from the darkness in which your family is still plunged."

Edgardo found the speech awkward and embarrassing.

Pius paused for a while as he took in the congregation. Edgardo looked across at him. One of his eyes always looked somewhat askance when he was angry or upset.

"They lament for his parents and do not think that I, too, am a father," Pius continued. "They do not pity me, the father of all the faithful. I had the right and duty to do what I did for this boy, and if it were necessary I would do it all again." Pius then started to shout. "Not even all the bayonets in the world would have forced me to return him. You should suffer anything rather than commit a grave sin, and it would have been a mortal sin to abandon this soul."

There was rapturous applause from the congregated

prelates, bishops and monks.

***

On the return journey to the Vatican, Pius put his arm around Edgardo and smiled at him, but the mood was sombre and little was said.

'If you only knew how much you have cost me!'

What had he cost him?

Edgardo knew that for years the media in Europe had created a great uproar over his abduction; he had heard that in cities all over the world no one had talked about anything else. He knew that a tragedy had been staged in Paris, entitled 'Le petit Mortara'; that the Jewish communities of the Piedmont region had appealed to all the synagogues of the world and had organised a campaign against the Pope and the Roman Church; that political powers had been asked to intervene. Edgardo knew that there were people who had said his abduction had indirectly led to the invasion of the Papal States in 1860. Was all that his fault? Was that why the people of Rome favoured the House of Savoy and Victor Emmanuel, or why the Papal Army had suffered a crushing defeat at Castelfidardo that year?

When the war for Italian Unification had broken out, Pius had started to lose all his Papal territories, one by one. Only the presence of French troops protected Rome, and yet Pius was ungrateful and unflattering about them. Edgardo had often heard him launching into a tirade about the miseries the French had brought with them upon this unhappy land, transforming it into 'a country exhausted and bleeding under the swords of its enemies, robbing it of its prosperity and of its spirit'.

When the liberal Kingdom of Italy was established, Pius remained from the start its bitterest enemy. Edgardo had seen the Holy Father mad with rage against Victor Emmanuel, so

247

much so that he had once banged his snuff-box so hard on his precious walnut writing desk that it broke in half.

Was all that what he had cost him?

As they arrived at the Vatican, Pius turned to Edgardo and asked him how he felt about having taken his vows and being on a journey to becoming a priest.

"I feel very happy and very humble," said Edgardo. "But I am sorry for all the suffering I have caused you."

"And as a good son you have brought me joy," said Pius as Thomas and Laurent helped them down from the carriage.

"Thomas, Laurent, as dear friends of Edgardo, I want you to join us for dinner tonight," the Pope said. "We must all celebrate Fra Pio pronouncing his vows."

That evening in the Pope's dining room, over a feast starting with fried artichokes prepared in the Jewish style, Pius the Ninth insisted that Edgardo should try a glass of Médoc wine. The Major-Domo filled their glasses and they raised them for a toast.

"My son Edgardo, God bless you on the long road to becoming a priest."

Chapter 37

Rome, Kingdom of Italy. 1870

As soon as Signor Mortara heard that Victor Emmanuel had taken Rome, he hastened to the city in the hope of seeing Edgardo.

Hour after hour, day after day, Signor Mortara would linger outside the Convent of St Peter in Chains where he knew his son was still living. Sometimes he would bang on the wooden door with the brass knocker and ask to see Edgardo, but the monks, ever furtive, dismissive and non-committal would make up endless excuses as to why he was not available: he had services or seminars to attend; he was with the Pope, either at the Vatican or the Quirinal Palace; he was visiting the sick or the poor; he was helping the young orphans or visiting the Jewish Ghetto. He was never at home at St Peter in Chains. Signor Mortara could not bear to hear the name of that church; it triggered off an uncontrollable anger in him and he would rail against the monks. Then the door would be slammed in his face.

At other times Signor Mortara would wait in Saint Peter's Square, his sad gaze now honed with a new instinct in detecting each and every group of young monks and priests as they walked by, always in the hope of seeing Edgardo. His head would dart round. This one, that one, surely that must be him? Sometimes he wondered if his mind was going. Would he know him if he saw him? Would Edgardo even want to acknowledge him? Signor Mortara felt ever more wretched, for much as he was angry with the Church, with Antonelli and the Pope, with the whole world, indeed, even with God, in truth it was Edgardo's rejection of his family that gave him little reason to live.

As he walked back to the modest lodging house where he was staying with his son Augusto, he found himself at the Spanish Steps and sat down for a while by the fountains. A young girl selling lemons from Amalfi took his arm, showing him that his jacket sleeve was getting drenched. He had not even noticed.

He got up and headed off down the Via Gregoriana: it was only a few streets back to the lodging house.

"The monks of St Peter in Chains will not let me see your brother!" Signor Mortara told Augusto as he entered their dingy room. "After a week of shouting and begging, my request to see him has been denied again!"

"Why am I not surprised to hear that, Papa?"

"The whole of Rome has changed; this is a liberal city now. Don't they know that? The kingship of Pio Nono has been terminated and Victor Emmanuel is the new king, but still the monks of St Peter in Chains hide your brother away in there."

"The liberals and the unification of the Italian states have cost the Church its temporal power. You think they suddenly want to talk to you?" Augusto was studying a book on Italian law and making notes as he spoke. "They don't wish to be encumbered with a filthy Jew from Modena who wants his son back after eleven years." Augusto laughed.

"We are not filthy Jews!" Signor Mortara protested.

"No, but in their eyes…"

"They need to move with the times. Look at Isaac Artom, Cavour's private secretary and now Secretary of State for Foreign Affairs of the United Italy – he's a Jew!"

"Under-secretary, Papa…"

"Giacomo Dina, a Jew, is the editor of *Opinione*, but still the monks of St Peter in Chains say 'No No No' to the Jews, dutifully allying themselves with their beloved Pio Nono."

Augusto looked up from his notebook, a stern expression in his steely eyes. "Edgardo also says 'No', Papa."

Signor Mortara sat down on a wooden chair that rocked

on an unsteady leg. "We don't know that, Augusto. Not for certain."

"Well he's not exactly racing over here to see us, is he Papa? How many times have we heard from the new liberal authorities themselves that Edgardo has been offered every opportunity to return home to us and resume his former life, but has resolutely declined to do so?"

"Obviously my messages and letters aren't getting through to him," said Signor Mortara, raising his eyebrows. "It's been the same story ever since he was taken away from us."

"For the last ten years you have been saying the same thing, Papa. It's highly unlikely that he hasn't received any of your messages."

"I know for a fact that when Edgardo was a child our letters never got through to him. Augusto, are you listening to me?"

"I am listening Papa, but I'm also trying to study. Remember that in two weeks' time I have to hand in my thesis to the university." Augusto put his book down again. "I seem to remember, Papa, that a few years ago when Edgardo did write letters about the Catholic religion and his utmost conviction in his faith, you replied to him then. As we both know, some of your letters definitely got through. If I remember rightly, when he said he wanted to become a priest, you wrote back and said *You are no longer part of this family. I will never forgive you! You're dead to me!* And you wonder why he doesn't want to see you?!" Augusto, bristling with honesty and reason, knew just how to annoy his father.

"Yes I was angry when I wrote that letter; who wouldn't be? A Jewish boy telling his father he wants to become a priest! I was fucking annoyed!" Signor Mortara shouted loudly.

Augusto felt his father's pain but said nothing. Eleven hard years, some of them spent on the bottle, had coarsened his father's behaviour.

"He was indoctrinated and manipulated from the moment he was taken away from us. And just for the record, some of

251

those letters he supposedly wrote at the age of six and seven couldn't possibly have been written by a child. Those bastard monks clearly interfered with his letters. The only things in them that were authentic were his name and signature." Signor Mortara shouted again. "You would have us stand by and be manipulated in this way, Augusto? *Dio Cane!*"

"Keep the fucking noise down!" a woman in the next room shouted as she started banging on the paper-thin walls.

"Me keep the noise down!?" Signor Mortara shouted back. "The bed in there never stops rattling. I can't imagine how it stands up to your screwing every hour of the day!"

"*Vaffanculo!*" the woman shouted.

"It's not only the bed; it remains to be seen if these walls will stand up to her fists," said Augusto, with a dry smile.

Signor Mortara sat down on the bed. "You know what, Augusto. I'm sick of being the outcast. Over the last few years we've written to him, saying we would always love him and that we wanted him to correspond with us."

"Was that before or after you told him he was 'dead to you' Papa?" said Augusto as he blotted his paperwork.

"The truth is he never wrote back; he wanted to cut himself off from us."

"Perhaps it would have been easier for you if you had converted, Papa."

Signor Mortara stood up, took off his overcoat and threw it down on his bed. "Whose side are you on, Augusto? I knew I shouldn't have asked you to come with me, to Rome."

"If I am to become a good lawyer, maybe even a great lawyer... and, dare I say it, join those illustrious Jews in the government of a united Italy, which I have to point out is something you are frequently telling me I'm more than capable of doing, then I have to be able to look at both sides of the coin."

"Yes, you are more than capable. You have a good legal mind, Augusto. And perhaps one day, God willing…" Signor

Mortara rolled his eyes up to the low ceiling in their room before fixing his son with a serious gaze. "However you should always put your family first." He sat down on the bed. "If we could only have seen Edgardo for just one meeting; he was so fond of you. Good God, Augusto, you used to make him laugh so. I wish he could see how you've turned out, how well you are doing, and what a persuasive tongue you have."

"I'm sorry I couldn't have helped more, Papa. It just wasn't meant to be."

"There must surely be a legal case here. Even the head of the police is saying Edgardo should be forced to return to his family."

"Perhaps that's why the monks of St Peter in Chains want to keep him indoors: imprisoned like their founding Saint. But nobody is going to force Edgardo to return home. How old is he now?"

"Nineteen."

"I'm afraid, Papa, that at nineteen in this new liberal country of ours, Edgardo is free to do whatever he would like to do."

"Well if you can't find any legal loopholes around this, nobody can. It's pointless for you to stay in Rome. We'd better get you back to Bologna and make a lawyer out of you yet, Augusto."

"Oh Papa, I almost forgot; this letter arrived here this afternoon." Augusto picked up an envelope with black handwriting on it. It said *Signor Mortara – By Hand.*

Signor Mortara looked at it. "This is from Edgardo! Don't you know your own brother's handwriting?"

"No," said Augusto. "Why should I? He's never ever written to me!"

Signor Mortara ripped open the letter, saying "Read it to me, Augusto…"

Augusto put down his law book, took the letter, and opened it.

"Convent of St Peter in Chains."

"Yes, we know where he lives…"

"Over the years I have written to you often. My greatest wish was that you would become Christians so that I could return home, but I am now so firmly attached to the Catholic religion that I can no longer identify myself with you. Henceforth I can acknowledge neither father nor mother, nor any earthly tie. God has given me such great graces; I must belong entirely to him…"

Augusto put the letter down, got up from the small wooden table, and placed his hands on his father's shoulders.

"See what they have done to him, Augusto…" Signor Mortara was holding back his tears.

Augusto said nothing; he squeezed his father's shoulders and after a long silence spoke out. "Edgardo seems very clear in his letter. What, honestly, is there to be done? He's a committed Christian and is clearly disappointed that his family did not convert to Christianity. From what he says I would say that he is resentful you didn't convert so that he could come home."

Signor Mortara's sobs were loud; he almost seemed to be choking. "So in spite of everything I've told you, you are taking his side in this? Against your mother and I?"

"I am not taking sides, Papa. I'm stating no more than what is obvious Edgardo has stated his case. If it were a legal case, I would say that you had lost it."

"What!? That we should not fight on for this?" Signor Mortara had raised his voice and the woman in the next room started to bang on the wall again.

"You must do what you feel you have to do," Augusto replied quietly, "but perhaps we should rejoice in the fact that Edgardo seems to have found happiness with his God."

Signor Mortara found his son's whispering even more annoying. "You'd better go straight back to Bologna!" he shouted. "Maybe you should let us know when you are planning to convert yourself!"

"You know that I have no plans to convert, Papa; not that I'm a Jew in anything but name. I've never pretended to be a good Jew. Remember that we both enjoyed those non-kosher sausages this morning…"

Signor Mortara's face was becoming visibly crimson. He picked up an old Bible on the bedside table and threw it at his son. It hit him on the cheek, drawing blood.

"You are right in saying I should go straight back to Bologna, Papa," Augusto said, calmly as though nothing had happened. He wiped his face with his handkerchief. "Maybe you should come with me. There's a train first thing in the morning."

"You think I am going to leave Rome now, Augusto?"

"Well, clearly Edgardo doesn't want to see you," Augusto said as he put the Bible back on the bedside table.

***

The next morning, after Signor Mortara had seen Augusto off at the Stazione Centrale, he made his way once again to the Convent of St Peter in Chains. For some minutes he sat on the wall opposite the main door, remembering how he had waited in the same spot with his wife all those years ago. He was once again about to go and bang on the brass knocker when a woman in her apron came out on to the street with a sack of rubbish. He thought she might be the same one who had told him that Edgardo had gone to Alatri for villegiatura. If it was her she was now wizened and half-stooped and her protruding eyes made her look crazed.

Signor Mortara went over to her.

"Where is Edgardo?" he shouted.

"Edgardo? I don't know anyone of that name here."

"I cannot believe you don't know Edgardo Mortara," said Signor Mortara. He helped her put her sack down.

"Of course; we know him here as Brother Pius; he's a convert, you know. He's really a Jew!"

"Yes I know that; he's my son!"

"Your son? Really? You know what they call him, don't you? The Pope's Son!" She laughed. "That's why he took the Pope's name: Pius Maria. The Pope's been round here lots of times, you know, and Edgardo goes to his house. He has tea with him, and spends Christmas at the Quirinal Palace. He also goes to Castel Gandolfo; only special people go there." She laughed again as she went into the convent to get another sack of rubbish.

"Where is he?" Signor Mortara shouted as she disappeared.

When the old woman came out again, Signor Mortara helped her put the second pile of rubbish next to the first one. In a much quieter voice he said, "I would like to see him."

"All the monks are at Saint Peter's today," said the woman. "He's a nice boy, your son. I've known him since he was tiny. He might be a Jew, but he's a nice boy. I knew this woman once; she said that if she had her way, she'd chop all the Jews into little pieces."

As she mimed a chopping action with her hands, Signor Mortara was off. He quickly made his way to the Vatican and walked into Saint Peter's Square, looking around him. There were lots of priests in the square and many tourists and vendors selling Holy artefacts: rings, medallions and engraved Bibles.

A group of four young priests crossed in front of Signor Mortara. From behind he fancied that one of them might be Edgardo. He called out to him. He studied the hair, the build, the way he walked: it must be him! The priest turned round; it was not him. He had a round face and a broad nose; it was nothing like Edgardo at all. Signor Mortara's heart sank.

"Are you alright?" the priest asked with a smile.

Signor Mortara sat down on the pavement next to the Egyptian obelisk in the centre of the square. He stared up at the balconies of the Basilica, dazzled by the blinding sun, through which the rooftop statues almost seemed to move against the drifting clouds. The obelisk, pointing to the heavens like a gigantic sundial, cast a long black shadow.

A couple of Swiss Guards in colourful costumes guarded the entrance to the Basilica. Near them were the statues of Saint Peter and Saint Paul: Peter holding the keys given to him by Christ and Paul holding the Book of the Epistles and a sword. Signor Mortara's gaze travelled round the Bernini Colonnade. A procession of young priests and monks was entering the square. His heart leapt. In the midst of the procession was a handsome young priest with straight black hair and a serious expression imprinted around a delicate mouth. He had no doubts: it was Edgardo!

He staggered to his feet and ran across the square. For a moment he lingered in the hope of speaking to him. He followed the priests around the square, his shadow darting in and out of the procession. Edgardo turned and in a flash recognised his father. He stopped dead in his tracks. Slowly he dropped out of the procession and as if in a trance walked over to Signor Mortara.

"Edgardo, is it really you?" said Signor Mortara as he looked up and down at his son, who was dressed in his monk's habit. "How could you have done this to us? How?" The words were delivered in a harsh tone heralding an imminent angry tirade.

Edgardo said nothing. He just stared at his father.

Signor Mortara was overwhelmed but he managed to stop himself. He realised it was pointless to go on. He repeated his son's name. "Edgardo..."

"Yes, Papa."

"How you have grown..." Signor Mortara was screwing up his eyes in the bright light. "Are you happy?"

"Yes, Papa..." Edgardo looked away, trying to conceal his pain.

"I'm glad. I can't say it's what we wanted... but I can't turn the clock back. Perhaps it was God's will."

"Yes Papa."

"Let me see you. You were always a very special boy. I wish I could have known you as a son."

Signor Mortara hugged Edgardo taking hold of his hands.

Edgardo recoiled. He was uncomfortable and did not smile. "Papa, I can't stop and talk with you now; we are in the middle of a ceremonial." He looked back at the procession to find that the other monks were staring at him. He broke away from his father and quickly said goodbye.

Signor Mortara turned away and walked across the square.

Having rejoined the procession Edgardo stumbled, collapsed on to the steps of the Bernini Colonnade, and from the depths of his being let out a loud groan as he sobbed and begged God to forgive him.

Chapter 38

Rome, Kingdom of Italy. 1870

Edgardo was sure he was being followed. He ran down the Spanish Steps into the Piazza di Spagna, turned round and looked up at the Trinità dei Monti Church. At the top of the grand staircase he saw two policemen in their blue peaked caps and silver buttoned uniforms watching him. He quickened his pace and took the small streets leading down to the River Tiber.

Walking in any part of Rome was not particularly easy as the streets were paved with small lava stones, which made them very slippery especially after the rain. There were no pavements, and as the carriages tore along their wheels brushed against Edgardo's habit. He crossed the river at the Ponte Sant' Angelo and made his way to Saint Peter's Square, scanning the Bernini Colonnade to see if any policemen or members of his family were hiding behind the large columns. At the sentry post he recognised the two Swiss Guards on duty: both courteous and friendly, but lacking the fun and laughter of Thomas and Laurent who had long since returned to Switzerland. One of them ushered him through to the Apostolic Palace.

When Edgardo reached the Papal apartments, he found Pio Nono sitting alone at his desk in the library drinking a cup of hot chocolate; in his lap Moretta appeared extremely self-satisfied. On seeing Edgardo, Pius's face lit up. His venerable hand stopped stroking the adored black-faced Vatican cat, and he shouted out, "*Caro figlio!* My own Fra Pio! How good to see you!" Edgardo ran over and hugged him. Moretta mewed loudly and showed her lack of pleasure at the interruption to her pampering by dragging her sharp claws along the Pontiff's thighs, which were fortunately protected by his white soutane.

Pius patted the seat next to him and told Edgardo to sit down. He began to stroke Moretta again and she soon began to purr. "At least someone around here is happy," he said with a smile. "Do you remember when Moretta was just a kitten? Now her own offspring are littered around lots of convents and palaces in Europe." Edgardo stroked the cat under her chin with his fingers. Pius turned to him. "You look troubled. What is it?"

"Things are becoming intolerable," said Edgardo. "Last week the chief of police, Signor Berti, came to St Peter in Chains. He kept saying 'So you're the Pope's son'. He became quite angry and harangued me for over an hour. He told me off and said that the public were sick of priests ruling in the name of God and would not be happy until I returned home to my family. He then ordered me 'for my own good' to return to them."

"Berti's a trumped up little upstart who cannot bear the fact that priests in Rome have governed for so long," said Pius as he tapped the desktop with his snuff box. "It's a symptom of this new Italian Government. They've robbed me of my temporal power and now, with the three-coloured flag fluttering impudently over the city, they think they can overrule anything to do with the religious life of the nation as well." Pius sighed. "To people like Berti you are a cause célèbre; a symbol of the Italian unification. He won't be happy until you are back with your family."

The Pope stroked Moretta under her chin and then handed her to Edgardo. He watched as his adopted son took over the coddling.

"Do you want to go back to your family?"

"No, I wouldn't do that. The truth is that my family will never be happy about my conversion and my new life; but I will never give up my faith now, and certainly not on Berti's orders. His attitude shocked me," said Edgardo as he stroked

Moretta. The cat stretched out on his lap and rubbed herself against him as she purred with pleasure. "I don't want to be told how I should live my life by a man like that. It's bad enough that the police follow me around Rome. They wait outside the convent of St Peter to make sure I don't escape. It's been getting so bad lately that I felt I had to speak to the Governor-General of Rome: La Marmora."

"Really? That was enterprising of you."

"I would have seen King Victor Emmanuel as well if that had been possible," said Edgardo.

"Did La Marmora help you?" Pius asked him. "You mustn't forget that he is part of the anti-clerical regime, in spite of what he says to the contrary."

"I know. Perhaps that's why he immediately granted me an audience."

"I'm sure. How was he?"

"He was civil and decent. I told him that the police were all but forcing me to return to my parents."

"And what did he say?"

"He asked me how old I was. I told him I was nineteen. He said that I was free to do whatever I liked. I replied, saying that although I might have freedom of choice I was constantly being threatened by the police. He then said I should go to him and that he would protect me."

"Well maybe he will," said Pius.

"In spite of La Marmora's words, I think that would become intolerable. I'd be spending half my life hiding away. It's no way to live."

"So what will you do?" asked Pius.

"Father, I think it's time…" said Edgardo, and then trailed off.

"Time?" Pius looked at him with bewilderment.

"Time to leave Rome and Italy…"

Pius got up, closed his eyes and walked to the window. Edgardo put Moretta down and joined him. A seagull flew off a balustrade and into the crowds in Saint Peter's Square. Edgardo watched it as it landed at the stockinged feet of a Swiss Guard.

For several minutes neither of them spoke.

There were tears in Pius's eyes. He took Edgardo's arm.

"It's the right time," mumbled Edgardo, struggling with his words. "The political events of 1870 have brought about great changes here in Rome. I heard about another Jewish convert, a boy name Coen; by all accounts a mob abducted him and tore him from the school of the Piarists."

"I know all about Coen," said the Pope as he continued to look down into the square.

"Maybe I'm next." Edgardo laughed nervously. "If I stay, they might somehow try to take revenge on me. It will save further trouble if I leave."

Pius went back to his seat and sat down. He sighed and started tapping the table again with his snuff box. "Cardinal Antonelli doesn't think it necessary for you to leave Italy. You could stay here with me."

Edgardo said nothing.

Eventually the Pope spoke. "If you really feel you must leave Italy, I can arrange for you to be accommodated in virtually any monastery in Europe. There is one in the Austrian Tyrol where you could go immediately and complete your theological studies," he said as he tried to smile. "I'll give you a letter and you can leave tomorrow - I know the Abbot there very well and I know he'll take you. Perhaps it's good that you leave quickly. At least we're not prolonging the agony that way. I've dreaded this day, but if you have to go, spread your wings with my blessing, Edgardo. Go and see the world. You know I will help you financially. I suppose it's better than being holed up. Look at me: I'm now virtually a prisoner in the Vatican. I'm a very different man from the one you knew as a child."

"You will always be the same person to me," said Edgardo as he took the Pontiff's hand.

"I'm sure you'll find happiness outside Italy, Fra Pio. I am so proud of the way you coped with the unusual childhood that God laid out for you; it must have been very difficult. God works in strange ways." Pio Nono spoke slowly; he was clearly very upset.

"When I was a boy in Sinigaglia in the Marche, I was destined to be a Count you know. My family were all aristocrats: the Mastai-Ferrettis. You might say I was very privileged, although I had a strict Jesuit upbringing. I was keen to join the army and live a life in the barracks. I was tough: good at ball games like *la palla*." Pio Nono laughed. "I was a fierce player and had a reputation as a bit of a brute, but I also had a sensitive side. I spent hours playing the flute and the cello. I also wrote romantic poetry and around that time fell in love with my foster-sister." Again the Pope laughed. "I was good at maths and science, but there was a problem because I had epilepsy. I had seizures while studying, which caused me to have blackouts. I begged God to cure me, but nothing changed. A friend of the family wrote to me, saying, 'Caro Giovane, you are suffering from two diseases: epilepsy and love. Be advised by me, enter the Church and you will be cured of both.' That's what I did and indeed I was eventually cured – of both. Or at least I grew out of them."

Edgardo smiled. He had heard much of this previously, but nevertheless loved listening to the Pope reminiscing about his early life. "Will you play me something on the cello before I leave, like you did when I was little?" he said.

"Only if you agree to spend the rest of the day with me; it may be a long time before we meet again," said Pius. "Bring me the cello."

Edgardo walked across the library and took the Pope's cello and its bow from the wooden cradle they were standing in. He passed the instrument to the Pope who handled it as if it were some holy artefact, placing it delicately between his legs and launching straight into the Prelude from Bach's Cello

Suite No.1, the music with its arpeggiated chords resonating throughout the Papal apartments.

A group of Swiss Guards in their harlequin costumes looked though the doorway and were quickly joined by a couple of chamberlains, wearing their ancient costumes of breeches, buckled shoes, blue doublets, black cloaks and black caps ornamented with a black feather. A short while later the Pope's Major-Domo and the cleaners, young laymen with their non-clerical beards and moustaches who had been working in the drawing room, came to see what was happening. They watched and listened in awe as their beloved Pio Nono filled the library with the deeply sonorous music. When he finished playing, they all clapped and some of them shouted 'Bravo'.

Pius waved his arms in the air for them to stop, muttering something about the piece needing more work, especially with regard to the articulation and dynamics. He got up, told the Major-Domo that Fra Pio would be joining him for lunch, and led Edgardo through to the dining room, which was situated between the library and the drawing room. Moretta followed them and jumped on to Pio Nono's lap as soon as he sat down.

A simple lunch of minestrone soup, roast meat and potatoes mashed with butter was conveyed from the kitchens by the chamberlains and served by two waiters, who also poured Castelli Romani wine into glasses.

"How did you become involved with the Church, Father?" asked Edgardo as he watched Moretta eating directly off Pio Nono's plate. In fact Moretta seemed to be eating most of it.

"Every morning after Mass in our family chapel my mother arranged for me to study the liturgy with one of the old Canons from the cathedral."

"You had your own chapel?"

"We did; my family was wealthy. I didn't take to learning my prayers so easily, but my mother was insistent that I worked at them: the Pater and Ave, acts of faith, hope and charity, and the Creed – I even found that hard. I swear our parrot could have learnt it better than me. My uncles also taught me. Uncle Paulo, a Canon of Saint Peter's, would come down to Sinigaglia with Uncle Andrea, who was the Bishop of Pesaro. I spent hours on my knees praying in the chapel with them, and eventually at the age of around twenty Uncle Paulo took me to Rome, and I lived with him in the Quirinal Palace – at first as a Papal Noble Guard to Pope Pius VII."

"So you did eventually get to live a life in the barracks?" said Edgardo.

"I did, but I was soon dismissed after having an epileptic seizure. One day I threw myself at the feet of Pius the Seventh and begged him to help me. He was a wonderful man; he promised that he would support me in my theological studies."

"Like you did with me," said Edgardo.

"Yes," said Pius. "My father was not happy about me joining the Church. Like your father, he wouldn't accept it at all. When I received the tonsure and they chopped off my curly locks, he was really disgusted.

Pio Nono sighed and then stood up. "Please join me for my afternoon walk, Edgardo."

"Were you happy with your new life?"

"Yes, I quickly became one of the Pope's family. I knew all the cardinals – one or two of them are still here with me in Rome today – and they became as familiar to me as my own uncles. I loved my new life in the Quirinal; it was a happy place, even under the French occupation."

They descended a staircase and walked along a corridor that led to the vast galleries of the Vatican, closely followed by Moretta. Eventually they entered the gardens by the gate, leading from the statue gallery to one of the sheltered terraces that was brimful with fragrant orange trees. The terrace overlooked a flower garden across from which was an imposing view of the dome of St Peter's. At the end of the terrace walk they stopped for a few minutes in front of the iron gates of the aviary that contained a noisy collection of birds, including pigeons, ducks and fowl.

"They were never particularly exotic, but as a young child you used to love watching these birds. Do you remember?' said Pius.

"Yes," said Edgardo, "and you would always go and sit with the cardinals on that bench over there." He turned round and pointed to one of the rough iron garden seats that were positioned in a semi-circle under a large tree.

"You're right, it was always that one: it still is," said Pius as he took Edgardo's arm and they went to sit on it.

"What will you do now, Father?" said Edgardo.

"The Italian Government is trying to sweet talk me by offering me a pension and freedom as a religious leader if I toe the line. I shall, of course, refuse such overtures." Pius shook his head and sighed. "Having been stripped of my temporal powers, I shall probably go down as the last Pope to rule over Rome. In truth, Italian nationalists would like nothing better than to see me leave this city. They speculate as to where the future seat of the Papacy might be best located. I hear that Jerusalem would not be viewed with displeasure by Victor Emmanuel." Pius suddenly started to shout. "Let me tell you, Edgardo, I will not be going to Jerusalem! I will not leave Rome! I shall always refuse to recognise the new Italian state, and frankly anyone who calls themselves a true Catholic should do the same!"

Eventually Edgardo spoke. "I know how awful this is for you."

"We have lived through a lot, you and I, Edgardo; the invasion of our provinces in 1860 and now the loss of our beautiful city, Rome. The political attacks; the endless setbacks. Most of them were nothing less than direct attacks on the Catholic Church. Some of them were even attacks in your name." Pius placed his hand on Edgardo's. "So it is. I do not conceal the regret and the sadness that I felt when I first learned of the circumstances surrounding your conversion."

Edgardo listened as tears welled in his eyes.

"But I was determined at whatever cost to remain firm. I paid dearly for your baptism, but I was powerless to invalidate a religious principle that the Church has for all time considered as belonging exclusively to the spiritual kingdom and which could not therefore depend on my personal will…"

"What was your personal will, Father?" said Edgardo softly.

The Pope paused. "God's will, Edgardo. As you were baptised in Jesus Christ and by that regenerated, it was my duty to protect you. *Quicumque enim in Christo baptizati ester Christum induisti.*"

Edgardo recognised the quote. "Ad Galatis, 3: 27."

"You have been a most worthy scholar and a good Christian, my beloved Fra Pio."

They returned to the Pope's apartment and had a light supper together with a glass of Bordeaux wine. They said very little. When dinner was over Edgardo read to him from the newspapers as he often did. Pius quickly fell asleep in his chair, with Moretta asleep and gently snoring on his lap. Edgardo stroked her for one last time leaning over to kiss her on her forehead. He then kissed the Pope on his broad brow. "Goodbye," he whispered.

Pio Nono opened his deep blue eyes. His final words were: "God bless you, Edgardo."

Chapter 39

Bouhay, Liège, Belgium. 1940

Father Mortara sat with Raoul at the back of the Priory church where the canons were chanting the 'Te Deum', their voices undulating in unison as they followed the square notes of the plainsong on the four line staves they used. Raoul joined in, but Father Mortara rocked gently to and fro in silence. The chanting always made Raoul feel intensely spiritual and washed away his doubts; it cleansed his heart and soul and made him glad to be a Catholic; it lifted his spirits and, like some strange primordial elixir, was always guaranteed to prepare him for the day. How strange and wonderful, he thought, that this sacred music had survived for fifteen hundred years and God had travelled through the centuries with it. His Latin was adequate enough to recognise *'Jesus you are the way the truth and the life...'* As the hypnotic music faded into silence he slowly came out of a trance-like state.

The canons filed out of the Priory church. Raoul and Father Mortara stayed where they were.

Raoul prayed for peace, for members of his family and for guidance. He opened his eyes and stared at the old stone buttresses of the church and then at the windows where the setting sun caused the multi-coloured stained glass to sparkle.

Eventually Father Mortara opened his eyes and began to speak. "'God bless you'; that's what Pio Nono said to me."

Raoul turned to him and took hold of his arm.

The old priest continued with his story, speaking slowly and breaking his sentences up with long silences.

"Pope Pius's blessings always gave me strength and courage. As I returned to Saint Peter in Chains that evening, as usual I found a group of policemen surveying the entrance. I hurried in, bidding them a good night. 'That's him; that's the Pope's Son,' I heard one of them say...

"The next morning after saying my 'goodbyes' to the Rector and Brother Claudio, and all the monks and the boys and the staff, I left the convent with an older priest, both of us in civilian clothes... We were smuggled out through the back door and the gardens, and once on the streets we made our way to the central station. I prayed as I walked that I would not see anyone I knew, especially my family and I prayed for a safe escape from Italy.

"As we boarded the train I heard some youths in front of us talking about how they'd heard from the police that Edgardo Mortara had just escaped from Rome. From the red bands they were wearing it was obvious that they were followers of Garibaldi and they blamed the Jesuits with their Papal fanaticism..."

"That must have been very scary for you," said Raoul.

"I was shaking, and extremely concerned that news of my escape had travelled so quickly. My companion, however, remained calm and chatted away with them, cleverly managing to change the subject and steer the conversation to local folklore in Tuscany – about which he knew nothing!" Brother Pius laughed. "They forgot about the 'fugitive' and we travelled without further incident via Bologna... I would've loved to have looked around my native city, but we stayed on the train and eventually, after many changes, arrived at Bressanone in the Austrian Tyrol where I joined the brothers of the parish of Nova Cella and completed my theological studies...

"I later heard that when Pope Pius was informed I had arrived there safely, he said 'We thank the Lord that Mortara has escaped'."

For several minutes they said nothing. Raoul helped Father Mortara up to his feet and they walked out into the cloister. The red sun was disappearing over the Priory roof, heralding the cloak of darkness that was night. There was a golden glow in the sky and for a moment the dark green leaves in the garden turned crimson; then they quickly turned ink black: it was night in Bouhay. Raoul looked across the valley towards Liège. He wondered what Delphine was doing – probably dining with Jean-Louis in the Féronstrée – drinking, laughing... He couldn't bear to think about it. He turned to Father Mortara. "Do you want to go in and eat, Brother Pius?"

"Sit with me here for a while," said the old priest. "The gardens are so peaceful at night."

They sat down on one of the wooden benches.

"So General La Marmora had offered you protection, but you chose to escape from Italy?" said Raoul.

"Yes, for me it would have been no way to live. Spending half your life hiding away from the world…"

Raoul interrupted him. "Isn't that what we do as monks in joining monasteries?"

"Perhaps, but we usually have a free choice in the matter," said Father Mortara.

They watched the yellow crescent moon, framed by the branches of a beech tree.

Raoul couldn't help wondering what free choice Father Mortara had had in the matter of his life following his baptism. He said nothing but it preyed on his mind. After all Father Mortara as a child – Edgardo – had not had any free choice in joining the Church. Once the Holy Water had been sprinkled over his head as a baby, his whole life had been mapped out. In effect his life had been taken from him. Until he was eighteen there was absolutely no question of him being allowed to return home unless his parents converted to Christianity.

"You must have really hoped that your parents would convert," Raoul said suddenly, breaking the silence.

Father Mortara replied with an intense sadness. "Yes. Perhaps it was naïve and childish of me – selfish maybe – but I believed and hoped they would. It was the only possible way I could have returned home. I admit I was disappointed that they didn't convert."

Raoul turned to Brother Pius. "Surely when you were eighteen after the Italian Unification and with King Victor Emmanuel on the throne, you could still have returned to your family whether or not they converted?"

"No, it was too late," said the old priest. I was fully ensconced in my life as a Catholic monk and by that time completely estranged from my family. He sighed deeply and loudly. "I couldn't go home. I was not the same person at eighteen as I was at six when I lived in Bologna. At that age I was Jewish by birth, by my religious inheritance and by my very nature. I did not know then that I had been baptised and chosen by God, by the special love of God, to be nurtured by the Catholic Church and by the Pope…" Father Mortara closed his eyes.

The old man's words deeply troubled Raoul and his passivity irritated him. What purpose was there in having been chosen for the special love of God if he had never really fulfilled his potential and done something with that love? What had he done? Humanitarian work? No. He hadn't helped the Jews in the ghettos; in fact he hadn't helped anyone. The Church might have nurtured him, but what for? For a life of suffering and separation from his family? No wonder he was disappointed that in all those years his parents hadn't converted; not that Raoul thought they should have done. But if they had done so, at least he would have been returned to them and that might have been the key to his freedom; the freedom which the Church had taken from him.

Also, what had the Pope's crusade led to? Nothing! Just years of disappointment. Was that why on leaving Italy, Father Mortara had chosen to hide away in monasteries all his life? Then Raoul's thoughts turned to his own life: his own disappointments and his own suffering. Was this why he himself was also choosing to hide away as a monk in monasteries?

For half an hour they sat in the darkness, the silence only

broken by a barn owl communicating with its mate. Raoul stood up and helped Father Mortara on to his feet. He took the old priest into the refectory for dinner.

Chapter 40

Poitiers, France. 1872

"It gives me great satisfaction to know that my adoptive son, now aged twenty-one, is currently residing in your diocese..."

The Bishop of Poitiers, Monsignor Pie, read the words slowly and emphatically before putting the letter down on a dark oak table. "It seems that Pope Pius is keeping an eye out for you," he said as he turned to Edgardo. "You are very blessed, Brother Pius. He really is a father to you, and you've taken his name."

"Yes, he is my true father." Edgardo replied in fluent French.

"He clearly cares a lot about you, which is why he wanted me to find you a home here in Poitiers. And I hope you will allow me to be part of your extended family, because as Roman Catholics, that is what we all are: a family."

Edgardo felt awkward. Not only was there no regard for his real father or family in the conversation, but also the Bishop, a robust man in his fifties, was gazing at him as though he were a specimen. He'd already had two years of such scrutiny and still felt insecure and uncomfortable with it. When he'd left Italy at eighteen and found shelter with the Canons Regular in the Austrian Tyrol, eyes were always on him. In the refectory, in the convent church, in the library, and in the gardens: eyes always followed him. He had lived incognito under an assumed name, but he was well aware that through the thin veil of rumour, everyone knew who Brother Pius Maria was: Pope Pius's Jewish son. And they stared at him, fascinated by his notoriety and his closeness to the Supreme Pontiff, always trying to determine what the relationship might hold for them: a passage to the Vatican maybe? A personal insight into the Pope? Maybe a meeting with the Pope? Most of the monks tried to get close to him. They were drawn to him, not only by his celebrity but also by his good looks, which seemed to improve as he moved into his twenties. He was dark, with a slim, angular face and sleek black hair, which softened his forehead and framed his gently smiling eyes. He looked more Italian than Jewish. His nose was more straight-edged than aquiline or Roman and his lips were full and pale. His demeanour was reserved but still displayed warmth and a good nature. He was handsome, intelligent and charmingly boyish, with a slightly haughty air that had evolved after fifteen years of being attractive to men who lived in a single-sex community. He had never sought attention but had always received it: from novices, priests, monks, clerics, Swiss Guards, bishops, cardinals and even the Pope himself. They were all drawn to him and circled him, like planets orbit the sun. They wanted to talk with him and hear what he had to say; they wanted to sit next to him at mealtimes and in church. There was an endless queue of men offering him help with liturgical studies, singing lessons, language studies, bread-making, seconds at mealtimes and help with making his bed.

When he was younger he had thrived on this constant attention, but recently had felt irritated by it. In the Austrian Tyrol it had seemed to be increasing and he had looked for ways to deflect it. He would study hard and try to keep his head in his books. He kept his conversations with the monks superficial, often conversing with them in their native tongues. He had an appetite for languages and a good ear for German, French, English and Spanish. He could stutter through the odd sentence in more obscure languages such as Romansh and Basque. He found this to be a good defence mechanism as it enabled him to evade questions about his life in Rome or about the Pope and instead dwell on the pronunciation of 'Pass me the jar of marmalade', in Polish or Portuguese. He found ways to deflect attention, but this left him feeling isolated, and in that isolation he had started to panic. He was a young man facing a life of predictable devotion, and, in the faces of old monks who were not many years away from dying, he saw his older self: the aged Brother Pius Maria. His life was all mapped out for him.

He couldn't recall all the details of the family life he had left as a six-year-old, but he did remember warmth, boisterous laughter, fun, and loud conversation and delight. The distorted recollection of his early life would hit him like a heady infusion, and when he was feeling sad, which was often, he would invoke this as an antidote to the quietness, sombreness and discipline of his life in the Church. He had found little warmth in the Church, little joy and hardly any human connection. Lots of attention yes, but an isolation and loneliness that was remarkable, considering he had been living in a community of dozens of monks. Pio Nono, however, had always been generous, giving and warm, even at a distance, and he was grateful for that.

He would often feel guilty that he thought too much about his life. He wanted to be hopeful and optimistic. He truly believed God had chosen him for a strange and unusual life: something 'special', and he had always felt he had no choice in the matter; he had to do God's work.

But he struggled: there were constant nightmares and lack of sleep. He spent long days in a state of submissive exhaustion, constantly questioning himself as to why he had indeed chosen the Church over his family, Austria over Italy, celibacy over intimacy.

In the solitude of his room he would think about his olive-skinned body with its mysterious manhood and outcrops of black hair, aware that deep within it lay the seeds that might have fathered a whole tribe of descendants. And he felt guilt for the fact that they would always be redundant.

One day, while digging turnips out of the ground, he had snapped, burst into tears, thrown down his spade and run into the library to write a very honest letter to his beloved Pius, to tell him that his nerves were jangling and that he must leave the Austrian Tyrol and come home.

The outcome was not totally satisfactory. Pius wrote back, agreeing that a change of scenery was necessary, but felt it was not the right time to come back to Italy if only for his own safety.

Edgardo wondered if Pius wanted to keep him away from his family, perhaps worried that his parents might try to convert him back to Judaism, but he accepted the Pope's love and concern and his pleas for him to remain strong, and agreed to move to France.

"Why did you want to leave the Austrian Tyrol, Brother Pius?" the Bishop of Poitiers asked him.

Edgardo was uncomfortable, but glad that the Bishop did not seem to know the reason for this. He was quick on his feet. "I'm happy to travel around Europe, maybe even the world, and do the best I can. And I'm happy to study and converse in new languages."

"Very good," said the Bishop as he continued to stare at him. "Pope Pius tells me that you wish to become a priest. At twenty-one you are young for that, but I will help you all I can in that mission. The road to the priesthood is certainly not for the faint of heart. As a practising Catholic you need to involve yourself in the work of the diocese of Poitiers. At some point soon I shall be sending you with a group of monks of the Canons Lateran from your current monastery to the new Sanctuary of Notre Dame de Beauchêne in the Bocage Vendéen, about eighty kilometers from here. It won't be for a few months yet, as the renovation works are dragging on terribly."

The Bishop of Poitiers draped his arm over Edgardo's shoulder and told him he must come and dine with him and that he would be able to help him, perhaps, with his French. "Although I have to say your French is almost perfect," the Bishop added. "It's certainly good enough to take Mass."

Edgardo sensed that the arm rested just a little too long on his shoulder and that the moving fingers were about to caress his neck.

Edgardo pulled away and looked directly at Monsignor Pie with his haughty look. The chin rose, the neck elongated and his smiling eyes turned steely and cold as he spoke. "I think I'm expected back for Vespers and supper. The Abbot wishes to introduce me to some of the other monks."

"Ah yes. Well I hope you will take up my invitation another time," the Bishop replied.

"I shall tell Pope Pius that we've met," Edgardo said by way of a warning, a reminder that his protection came from Rome.

Monsignor Pie was clearly taken aback. "Yes, send him my greetings. I hope you'll be very happy here in France, and do let me know if you need anything. There may be... I don't know... material goods or books that you need to buy." The Bishop continued to stare. "I know, Fra Pio, that as a monk, there isn't the money for some things..."

Edgardo nodded. He would have liked to have told the Bishop that he didn't need his money; that the Pope looked after him financially; that he had given him a very ample lifetime trust fund. Instead he took his leave and adeptly managed to turn a farewell hug into a firm hand-clasp. He was transported from the centre of Poitiers back to the monastery in one of the Bishop's horse-drawn buggies. He felt restless in his new environment, anxious even, but thankful that he had a spiritual father in the Supreme Pontiff who he could conjure up in times of need. "Thank God, I have Pius in my life," he said out loud as he entered the monastery church.

The Abbot greeted him. "You have missed Vespers. Come with me to the refectory." He took him round two sides of an arched cloister that framed a pretty garden of wild flowers and into an old stone hall, where he sat him down with some of the monks who proceeded to study him.

There were brothers with the names of Pierre, Jean and

Antoine who were all middle-aged. A younger monk, Brother Lambert, fetched him a bowl of lamb tripe stew and half a baguette.

"I'd like you all to make Brother Pius very welcome here," said the Abbot. Brother Lambert gave him a warm smile. It was a quick supper, followed by Compline in the monastery church, and then bed. Brother Lambert showed him to his bedroom, which was on the first floor and overlooked the garden in the centre of the cloister. Edgardo peered out of the window. The flowers were colourful: purple bellflowers and yellow pansies dotted amongst the bay bushes, together with ivy trailing over the walls. The room was still warm from the hours of hot July sun that had blazed through the leaded windows and was infused with the smell of musty old linen.

"It's one of our larger rooms," Brother Lambert told him, breaking the no speech rule of the Magnum Silencium. "Did you have a bag?"

"I left it downstairs outside the Abbot's room." Edgardo told him. "I'd better get it."

"I'll get it for you. Settle yourself in." Brother Lambert swept his blond hair behind his ears and rushed out of the door.

There were two small beds in the room, an upright oak cupboard with a chest next to it, a wooden chair and a small dresser, on which were placed a large, glazed bowl, a pitcher of water and a block of green olive oil soap in a dish. Edgardo opened the window. It was a clear night. He looked up at the stars and fancied he could see Jupiter, a brilliant beacon, low in the western sky. Across the quadrangle, clusters of flickering candles lit the shadowy rooms, where monks were retiring for bed.

Edgardo wondered if he would be sharing this room with Brother Lambert; he had forgotten to ask. He sat down wearily on one of the beds. He wondered how long the province of Poitou would be his home. Two years? Ten years? A lifetime?

Would he find happiness and fulfilment here? Within minutes he had dozed off.

He felt his woollen cassock being pulled up over his body. He opened his eyes and sat up with a start. Brother Lambert then pulled the garment over his head and hung it up in the cupboard for him.

"I'm sorry to wake you. You will sleep better without this heavy robe on." He smiled at Edgardo, who crossed his arms over his legs in an attempt to hide the knee-length cotton drawers he was wearing.

"We shouldn't really be talking, should we?"

"No, but we need to get you settled in. I think God will forgive us." Brother Lambert again swept his fingers through his hair as he spoke, which struck Edgardo as rather an odd habit for a monk. "You must be exhausted, from all your travelling. There's fresh water on the dresser if you want to wash and a cotton towel and a flannel there by the window. Oh, and there's a chamber pot under the dresser if you need to pee in the night."

"Thank you," said Edgardo, as he pulled back the cotton sheet on the bed.

Brother Lambert sat on the other bed and watched him, his steel-grey eyes glistening in the candlelight.

"I presume I am to share this room with you?" said Edgardo.

"No, with Brother François; the bed you're in is usually his bed," said Brother Lambert.

"I'm sorry; I didn't realise." Edgardo got up and straightened the sheet.

"You can have it if you like," said Brother Lambert, his face breaking into a smile, "or you can sleep in the bed by the window – whichever you prefer. Brother François is on leave for a week or so to see his parents in Burgundy: his father is very ill."

"I'm sorry," said Edgardo.

"The Abbot has asked me to sleep in this room with you

279

until Brother François returns while you're settling in. I can help you to find your way around the monastery, get you to the church for Matins, and so on." Brother Lambert laughed. "At the crack of dawn."

Edgardo got up and went over to his leather bag. He took out a pig bristle toothbrush, wet it with water from the pitcher, and quickly cleaned his teeth over the bowl on the dresser. He gave his face a quick wash and splashed water under his arms and round the back of his neck.

"Actually, the Abbot said that after your travelling you are more than welcome to sleep in tomorrow morning," said Brother Lambert.

"I'm sure I'll be fine," Edgardo replied, in spite of being exhausted.

"Sit down on the bed," Brother Lambert said to him, "Let me wash your feet for you; they're very dusty."

"It's all right; I can wash them myself," said Edgardo. He felt uncomfortable, even though washing feet was commonplace in the Catholic Church. He had washed Pope Pius's feet for him on Maundy Thursday, and once or twice the Pope had washed his feet for him.

"Come and sit down," said Brother Lambert as he helped Edgardo take his sandals off before lifting the bowl of water from the dresser and placing it under the young monk's feet. He took the olive soap, rubbing it between his hands to make a lather, and gently washed Edgardo's feet, splashing water over them and smearing the soap between his toes. Brother Lambert's hands were soft.

Edgardo laughed. "How do you say...?" He searched for a word that meant ticklish. He laughed again and tried to pull his feet away. Brother Lambert tickled him; he looked up at him and also laughed. "Ça chatouille," he said as he rubbed Edgardo's toes and dried his feet with a towel, before leaving the room with the bowl of dirty water and the flannel.

Edgardo got into bed. He suddenly felt self-conscious and

uncomfortable; he had not shared a room with anyone since he was much younger.

Brother Lambert returned with the bowl. He filled it with water from the pitcher and proceeded to take off his robes and then his underclothes. Edgardo pretended to be asleep but watched him surreptitiously; he reckoned the man must have been in his late twenties. He was tall with long limbs. Once again he smoothed back his blond hair and splashed his face in the water. His moustache was almost white but the hair on his short beard was a commingling of gold and chestnut brown. He took the flannel and washed himself: his shoulders, arms, torso and then his thighs and genitals, where the hair on his body was darker, and down to his feet. The candlelight made flickering shadows across his body. He had a grace as he moved, almost as if he were dancing. He suddenly turned round and caught Edgardo watching him. Brother Lambert's steel-grey eyes were wide open. "I'm sorry," he said gently, his warm smile erupting, "I must be keeping you awake." He took the towel and dried himself, before blowing out the candle and getting into bed. "Good night, Brother Pius," he whispered.

"Good night," said Edgardo.

For several hours, Edgardo lay deep in thought, feeling apprehensive about his future. He was tired, but could not sleep until three or four in the morning, and when he did doze off it seemed as though hardly another hour had passed until the cocks started crowing. He woke again, feeling as anxious as he had in his last weeks in the Austrian Tyrol. The lack of sleep added to his worry; he knew that this would lead to ill health. At least the Abbot had said he could lie in. He tried to sleep, but was restless. He tried to picture Anna Morisi kissing his cheek; he tried to remember the names of all his brothers and sisters: the older ones, Riccardo, Ernesta, Erminia, Augusto and Arnoldo: the younger ones, Ercole, Aristide who had died, Imelda and the second Aristide. He wondered how they all were. As he started to fall into a light snooze, he heard Brother Lambert starting to snore. Someone rang a bell, knocked on the door and shouted 'Benedicamus Domino'–'Let us praise the Lord'–as a wake-up call. Edgardo replied half-asleep, 'Deo gratias'–'thanks be to God'. He half heard the door close as Brother Lambert left the room. He lay staring at the ceiling, drifting in and out of a light sleep as the morning rays of sunlight drenched the room in a golden glow. He looked over to the window. The other bed was empty. He rolled over. Just as he was about to doze off again, Brother Lambert entered the room. "Good morning, Brother Pius." he said with a wide smile.

"Have I missed Matins?" Edgardo asked.

"Yes, and Lauds and breakfast, but don't worry; I've brought you something to eat." He put down a glass of milk on the dresser and opened a napkin with bread and an apple inside it.

"Thank you," said Edgardo as he got out of bed. "I'm not very hungry." He washed his face and under his arms and reached into his bag for his hairbrush, shaving brush and razor; all had matching carved ivory handles with a rococo foliage design.

"Very smart," said Brother Lambert, his eyebrows rising as he picked up the hairbrush to have a look.

Edgardo suddenly felt self-conscious. They were gifts from Pope Pius, not a monk's usual grooming kit, but then Pius had always showered expensive gifts on him. Edgardo liked having them around him; it made him feel that his Holy Father was with him wherever he was.

"Don't worry about shaving," said Brother Lambert, "we have a barber here, Brother Antoine, or I could shave you later myself. Come on, we can probably make Mass."

He got Edgardo's robes out of the cupboard, helped him to dress and then took him to the monastery church where they had been the night before. It was a small, dark church, with old wooden benches and narrow windows that cut out most of the sunlight: the rays that did get through were diffused by airborne dust particles, creating a smoke-like aureole above the twenty or so black-robed monks who were chanting the morning prayers.

Edgardo was relieved when Mass was over, happy to go outside and get some fresh air. Brother Lambert showed him round the gardens: a maze of contrasting sections. A stone path led to a walled herb garden bordered by fragrant lavender bushes; steep steps led to a rose garden with a pergola at its centre; and a wrought iron gate led to an orchard looking on to sloping wildflower meadows, at the bottom of which was a babbling stream. They walked back to the monastery buildings by way of the vegetable patches, past the toilet block with jasmine growing along one wall, and then on to a pathway lined by damson trees, eventually arriving at the cloister. They went inside the monastery, where Brother Lambert showed him the library, the refectory, the common room, the laundry room and various other utility rooms before returning to the cloister where they sat down on a bench.

The Abbot came out and joined them. "Brother Lambert, I thought you might show Brother Pius Maria around the neighbourhood this afternoon so that he might get a sense of the local terrain. It's certainly a beautiful day. Perhaps you could walk along the River Clain into Poitiers. I'm sure you will be back in time for Vespers." The Abbot turned to Edgardo. "You can start your monastic life properly tomorrow. This is a lovely part of the world, Brother Pius, and I do hope that you will be very happy here." He smiled and went back inside.

Brother Lambert went to the kitchens to get some food to take with them and then he and Edgardo set off along a lane bordered by ancient hedgerows and tall trees with overhanging branches above their heads and gnarled roots beneath their feet. They followed the lane to the River Clain and then on to a high stone-walled pathway that led into Poitiers.

Edgardo said little as Brother Lambert took him to the medieval Church of Notre Dame la Grande, which, in spite of its name, was rather small; although Brother Lambert described it as impressive, it certainly did not match the grand churches he had been used to in Rome.

They stopped in front of the sculpture of the 'Burial of Jesus', painted in various shades of red, brown and ochre. "It's beautiful, isn't it?" said Brother Lambert as he put his arm around Edgardo's shoulder, a gesture Edgardo took to be an attempt to bring them together to appreciate the work, but the sculpture's hatted figures struck Edgardo as belonging more to sixteenth-century France than biblical Palestine. He was starting to like Brother Lambert.

"It's interesting," Edgardo answered.

"Are you tired, Brother Pius?"

Edgardo sat down on one of the pews and Brother Lambert joined him, his arm still around Edgardo's shoulder. Brother Lambert then started telling him about a legend relating to the keys of the city. "At the beginning of the thirteenth century, when the British army besieged Poitiers, the mayor, having taken a bribe, wanted to open the doors of the city, but the keys were nowhere to be found..."

Edgardo tried to keep his eyes open. Brother Lambert's warm, rich voice was hypnotic, and it was only when he laughed and became more animated and the arm squeezed him tighter that Edgardo managed to stay awake. There followed something about the Virgin Mary appearing to the British enemy who were then so frightened that they started fighting among themselves before running away, and something about the keys of the city being found hanging from the hands of the statue of the Virgin Mary.

"And look: there she is holding the keys of the town," said Brother Lambert turning round to the statue of 'Our Lady of the Keys' in the middle of the church. "It's a copy of the original statue that was destroyed by the Huguenots in the sixteenth century."

"Incredible," said Edgardo, searching for something to

say. He was actually more awestruck by Brother Lambert's confidence and demeanour than by the legend. "You know an awful lot about the history of the region."

"Well I was born near Poitiers," Brother Lambert replied. "Actually, the legend is a load of nonsense from a historical point of view. The idea that the British ran away when the doors of the city were opened is ridiculous: in 1202 when all this supposedly occurred, Poitou actually formed part of the English duchy of Aquitaine under the reign of Henry II's widow, Eleanor of Aquitaine!"

As they left the church, Edgardo tried to reconcile Brother Lambert's scorn with a legend involving the Virgin Mary.

"So you were born near Poitiers?" said Edgardo as they walked along the narrow streets that led to the Cathedral of Saint Peter's.

"In Saint Benoit, further down the river," Brother Lambert explained. He did not walk in a humble monk-like way, but rather in an extravagant, meandering manner as though he were holding court. "And I believe you were born in Rome?"

"Bologna," said Edgardo as they arrived at the cathedral.

"It's built in the early Gothic style," said Brother Lambert. "There's a marvellous stained-glass window called the 'Rose Window' that I must show you."

"I saw it yesterday," said Edgardo, "when I met the Bishop, Monsignor Pie."

He suddenly realised how aloof he must have sounded, but Brother Lambert just laughed heartily, tossing his hair back and saying, "You're very well connected, my Italian friend. Not only do you know the Bishop of Poitiers, but you also know the Pope, personally!" He spoke in such a loud and flamboyant manner that several visitors entering the cathedral turned and looked at them as though they were both mad.

Edgardo was embarrassed. He knew that the monks must know about his relationship with the Pope, but it shocked him to have it announced like that. "I don't need to see the cathedral today," he said and started to walk across the square.

Brother Lambert ran after him. "I'm sorry. Have I upset you?"

Edgardo did not reply.

Brother Lambert clasped him in his arms and gave him a big hug. "It must be hard for you," he said softly. You are young and alone in a strange place."

"I'm used to that," said Edgardo in a detached manner. "Do you mind if we make our way back?"

They walked along the banks of the Clain. It was a hot afternoon. At a bend in the river they sat down to eat lunch in the shade of a willow tree, the branches of which were hanging over the water. Brother Lambert took some bread and goat's cheese out of a cloth bag that he carried on his shoulder and offered it to Edgardo, cutting a wedge of each with a wooden-handled pocket-knife.

"A little less for me," said Edgardo.

"You need to keep your strength up. The Abbot will be expecting you to start work tomorrow," Brother Lambert said as he laughed.

Edgardo took the bread and cheese, and for a while they both eat in silence as they looked across the river that was flooded with sunlight. A mother merganser with a long black crest swam along the riverbank, followed by eight little ducklings. They immediately made Edgardo think of his own mother and his brothers and sisters. It saddened him. Brother Lambert saw him watching them. "It's nice to see a happy family," he said. Edgardo thought it was uncanny the way his companion seemed to have tuned into his thoughts. "I understand you were separated from your family and were once Jewish?"

Edgardo turned to him. Although Brother Lambert's face was half-hidden behind a drooping willow branch, the steel-grey eyes were penetrating. "Yes," said Edgardo in a guarded manner. He wasn't used to talking about his past.

"Perhaps, when you are ready, you will tell me your story – how you ended up here," Brother Lambert said as he shuffled forward to sit nearer to him. He took a green glass bottle out of his bag and loosened the wire bail around its neck to open it, explaining that it was a local wine diluted with water.

"What about you?" Edgardo asked him. "Why did you join the monastery?"

"Oh, now there's a question," Brother Lambert cried out. He offered the bottle to Edgardo and then started to stroke his moustache with his thumb and forefinger as he thought about it. Eventually he spoke: "I started to question things a lot when I was sixteen years old. My mother, God bless her, died in childbirth around that time. I was a good student at school, but my father wasn't happy with me because I didn't want to stay and work on his farm as my two brothers had chosen to do. I thought I might be better off choosing a life with the Church."

Brother Lambert suddenly stood up. He took a large swig from the bottle before taking off his robe. "I'm going in for a swim," he said as he unbuttoned his drawers and peeled them from his legs. Edgardo looked away. It was the second time in two days he had seen Brother Lambert naked. The monk stood almost defiantly proud before diving into the river with a big splash, and then he surfaced through the foam he had made and swam back to the bank. He stood up, the water up to his waist; the droplets on his torso glistening like diamonds in the sun. "Come on in," he shouted to Edgardo, "the water is so cold; it's wonderful."

Tentatively, Edgardo took off his robe. He walked to the riverbank, his hands crossed in front of his drawers.

"There's no one around; don't be shy," shouted Brother Lambert.

Edgardo pulled down his drawers and threw them on to his robe.

"You are circumcised," said Brother Lambert watching him

with fascination. Edgardo suddenly remembered the bullies in Bologna who had kicked him and spat on him and ripped open his breeches and wondered if having no foreskin meant the older monk would think he wasn't a proper Christian.

"It's wonderful. It means you are like Jesus," said Brother Lambert with a smile.

"Like Jesus?"

"According to the Gospel of Luke, Jesus was circumcised eight days after his birth. He was Jewish after all. When were you circumcised?"

"I don't remember," said Edgardo as he sat down on the bank and dipped his foot into the water. "It's so cold," he called out.

"Jump in," shouted Brother Lambert. "Can you swim?"

"I haven't swum since I was a boy," said Edgardo.

Brother Lambert waded to the bank and, taking hold of Edgardo under his shoulders, lifted him into the icy river, just as Thomas and Laurent had done in Lake Albano when he was seven years old. Edgardo let out a loud squeal. Brother Lambert laughed loudly as he held him in his arms before setting him down on his feet. "There's a bit of a current," he said. "Swim along the bank with me." The older monk swept aside some of the willow branches as they bobbed along through the water. "You're a good swimmer," Brother Lambert said to him.

"I was taught by two Swiss Guards," Edgardo told him, checking himself and deciding not to add 'at Castel Gandolfo, the Pope's summer home, with the Pope looking on'.

Even so, Brother Lambert was impressed. "Swiss Guards! Oh my word!" he shouted. "You really have led an incredible life, Brother Pius."

Were it not so cold in the water, Edgardo's face would have reddened more. He started to shiver.

Brother Lambert noticed. "Let's go and sit on those rocks," he said, pointing to an outcrop of large boulders nearby. "We can warm up in the sun." They waded over to the boulders a few metres away from the bank.

Brother Lambert pulled himself out of the river, the water streaming down his back, and then turned round and hauled Edgardo up after him. "The rocks are hot; you could fry an egg on them," he said as he sprawled out, lying on his back with one of his knees bent upwards. His body was muscular and athletic, the whole of it bronzed; a body that had spent a lot of time in the sun, and Edgardo could not help thinking he was a fine figure of manhood.

"Do you see your family at all?" Edgardo asked as he sat upright hugging his knees.

"No. As I said, my father was unhappy with me," said Brother Lambert. "When things got bad, he would beat me... and bruise me... and try and break my will... So I left home and took refuge in the Church. I joined the monastery when I was nineteen years old. The Abbot and the monks are my family now...The Church is my whole life, and in truth I'm happy to be a monk."

Edgardo wondered how anyone could be happy with a sad story like that behind him. Brother Lambert straightened his leg and lay down flat on the rock, closing his eyes as the sunshine beat down on his chest and abdomen, with his pubic hairs glowing in the glare.

Edgardo couldn't stop staring at him, until something diving into the water diverted his attention.

Brother Lambert sat up. "What was that?"

"I'm not sure," said Edgardo.

The older monk pointed to the bend in the river. "It's an otter swimming downstream, see?" He put his arm round Edgardo's shoulder as they watched it for a while. He lifted his other arm and swept his wet hair behind his ears. He then did the same for Edgardo, running his fingers through the length of his hair. "Yours is so black and silky," he said softly, "so different to mine."

"Do you miss the company of women?" Edgardo asked him suddenly.

Brother Lambert took his time to answer. "No. I miss my mother, but I like the company of men. It suits me; the monastery provides me with a good way of life." He brushed a leaf from his thigh as he continued to speak. "I don't think I was ever meant to be mated with a woman."

It was the first time that Edgardo had seen the monk looking sad. He slid off the rock and into the river, catching his breath as the icy water covered his legs.

Brother Lambert joined him. "Let me look at you," he said facing him. "You know, you've the body of an Adonis."

Edgardo was taken aback. He suddenly felt embarrassed and vulnerable. The words sounded trite, but he wanted to know what was behind them. Was Brother Lambert becoming intimate with him under the guise of teaching him French and improving his vocabulary? The language barrier was insignificant; Brother Lambert had had to repeat the odd word or sentence for him during the day, but Edgardo's French was good and he understood most of the conversation.

Edgardo was silent as he stood still.

"Your chest hairs are black too," Brother Lambert said as he touched them with his long fingers. His palms began to rub Edgardo's hard chest. It felt good. Something stirred within him. Edgardo felt himself getting aroused. He raised his chin and looked away before submerging himself in the water.

They half swam and half waded back to the riverbank and climbed out. Brother Lambert squeezed the water out of his hair and shook his arms and legs like a dog. "It helps you to dry quicker," he explained, laughing loudly. Again he stood naked in front of Edgardo; he seemed to celebrate his physicality in a reckless way and noticed that the young monk was no longer looking away. He took a swig of wine from the bottle and offered it to Edgardo. They lay down on their robes under the willow tree, the sun shimmering through its branches. Edgardo felt Brother Lambert's leg pressing against his and suddenly felt aroused again. He rolled over on to his stomach. A ladybird was basking on a blade of grass in front of him. He tried to count how many spots it had in an attempt to calm his mind. The sun and the wine were making him sleepy; he put his head down, and slowly dozed off.

He woke up a couple of hours later to lilting music. He turned round, to find Brother Lambert sitting cross-legged under the tree playing a small tabor pipe. He stopped playing. "Good morning," he said.

"Morning?" Edgardo was confused. He peered through the willow branches where the hot afternoon sun was still shining.

"Just joking," said Brother Lambert as he reached over and started tickling Edgardo under his arms.

"No," cried Edgardo as he giggled.

"*Ça chatouille?*"

He stopped and put his arm around Edgardo's waist.

Edgardo pulled away, grabbing his drawers and putting them on. "Keep playing," he said as he put on his robe.

Brother Lambert finished the song. "It's a local folk tune about harvest-time," he said, his face breaking into a big smile. He uncrossed his legs, stood up and got dressed.

They arrived back at the monastery in time for Vespers. They sang with the other monks in Latin, facing each other in the choir stalls, Edgardo aware even in the darkness that Brother Lambert was constantly looking at him and smiling.

At dinner in the refectory they faced each other again: two handsome men, the centrepiece in the middle of a long wooden table of black-robed monks who ate together with a low drone of conversation. Edgardo thought he heard Brother Jean say something about how the pair of them brightened up the dinner table. He was reluctant to lift his head from his plate of bean stew, knowing that Brother Lambert would be staring at him. After the meal he followed the other monks into the monastery church for Compline. Brother Lambert pushed his way past Brother Antoine and Brother Jean to sit next to him; he kept turning to Edgardo, to smile, to stare, and to study him.

Edgardo could not concentrate on the service at all. The Latin, with which he was usually so familiar, seemed to be a jumble of disconnected words, and he could not tell whether or not Brother Lambert's knee was deliberately touching his. He felt relieved when the service was over but also anxious about Brother Lambert's attentions and where they were leading.

On the way back to the bedroom, when the older monk said he was going to the toilet block, Edgardo was determined to undress and wash quickly, get into bed and put his uneasy feelings behind him, but when Brother Lambert came into the room he was still washing himself at the dresser, wearing only his cotton drawers.

The ritual began again: Brother Lambert sat down on the bed and watched him in the candlelight, then he came over to him and asked if he could help him.

"No, I'm all right," Edgardo replied.

Brother Lambert ignored him, and standing behind him rubbed his back gently with a wet flannel before drying him with a rough cotton towel. Edgardo was not quite sure if at one point Lambert touched his neck with his lips, so fleeting was the kiss – if indeed it were a kiss.

Edgardo got into bed and lay rigid as Brother Lambert left the room to empty the ceramic bowl and fill the pitcher. When he returned, he got undressed and washed himself. Edgardo watched him. Brother Lambert walked over to Edgardo, not wearing a stitch, and sat down on the bed. He leaned over and kissed Edgardo softly on the temple. "Good night my young friend," he said.

***

The following day, after another sleepless night, Edgardo found himself washing sheets in the river with Brother Antoine and laying them out on the grass, an activity which gave him some respite from Brother Lambert's attentions, but as the morning went on he realised that he missed being with the older monk and felt a little lost not spending all his time with him.

At Sext Brother Lambert once again sat next to Edgardo. He leaned over to him and whispered, "I've missed you."

"It's only been two hours," Edgardo whispered back.

"I wish we could spend the afternoon swimming again," said Brother Lambert, "but at least we can study together after lunch."

Later at lunch in the refectory he said, "Maybe I can arrange for you to come and milk the cows with me tomorrow," not hiding his words from the assembled monks.

"Would you like to work with Brother Lambert?" the Abbot asked him.

"I don't mind where I work," said Edgardo.

"In that case you might as well help Brother Lambert," said the Abbot.

Brother Lambert gave Edgardo a wink.

"It's another lovely day; you can do your bible study in the gardens if you wish, Brother Pius," the Abbot said as he left the table.

Brother Lambert took Edgardo to the pergola in the rose gardens and they sat together on a wooden bench, reading the Book of Matthew in French. Brother Lambert was very tactile, and as he read would stroke Edgardo's hand or would clasp his hand in his, which made Edgardo flinch.

Occasionally he would stop and ask if Edgardo understood, but the young monk's mind was elsewhere. The attention was flattering and thrilling even, but also disturbing and confusing to him. Brother Lambert put the book down and started stroking the hairs on Edgardo's arm, just as Brother Pierre entered the garden.

"There is just time to prune a few roses before Nones," he said to them.

Brother Lambert turned to Edgardo. "In medieval times they used to say of mid-afternoon prayers: as the sun sinks on the horizon at the hour of Nones, man's spirit tends to lower itself also; he is more open to temptation..."

Edgardo got up and moved around the garden. Brother Lambert followed him.

"Do you want me to take you back to the room and shave you?" he asked him. "Or maybe you'd like to grow a beard like me?"

"I can shave myself," said Edgardo, "but in any case, Brother Antoine has agreed to give me a shave. Perhaps I'll go and find him now."

Brother Antoine was helping with dinner duty in the kitchens so Edgardo went back to the bedroom. The door opened as he was taking an ornate silver-backed mirror out of his bag. It was Brother Lambert. "I'm wondering if you've got the Papal tiara in there as well," he said, opening his eyes wide.

Edgardo disregarded the remark; his chin rose in disdain as he set the mirror on the dresser. Brother Lambert sat on the bed and watched him as he took the shaving brush and made a lather out of the green olive soap.

Brother Lambert stood up. "Let me help you." he said. "You'll get soap and water all over your habit." He pulled Edgardo's scapular and robe up over his head. Edgardo sat down on the chair, while the older monk reworked the soap into a lather. He crouched down in front of Edgardo and brushed the foam on to his face, all the while looking into his eyes, before taking Edgardo's razor from the dresser. "May I?" he said with a big smile as he felt the blade on his thumb.

Edgardo nodded awkwardly as Brother Lambert crouched down at his side, put his arm around his bare shoulder and with his free hand started to shave his cheek. His face was only centimetres away from his and his breath felt warm as he spoke quietly to him. "In some orders moustaches are forbidden, because hair on the upper lip impedes the drinking of the chalice at Mass. I ask you... Do you think this would stop me being able to drink from the chalice?" He put the razor down and took Edgardo's fingers; he placed them first on his lips and then on his moustache. "Feel," he said.

Edgardo ran his fingers quickly around the monk's soft lips, the neat moustache and the trimmed beard, and then pulled away. He knew that Brother Lambert was teasing him, but he could also feel himself becoming attracted to him. He looked away. Brother Lambert picked up the razor and finished shaving him; he flannelled his face and then ran his fingers over his cheeks. "There, as smooth as silk," he said.

***

The rest of the day passed very slowly. There were three more services to get through and supper and private study. By the time he was back in the bedroom Edgardo was once again exhausted, but he knew he was too confused and disorientated to sleep.

Brother Lambert brought fresh water into the room, lit the candles and sat on his bed while Edgardo started to wash himself. "I've still got some wine left from the other day," he said as he got up and took a bottle from his bag in the cupboard. He flicked open the wire bail. "Have some, Brother Pius," he said.

Edgardo stopped washing. "No thanks," he said.

"It's mainly water," said Brother Lambert.

Edgardo drank some of the wine and handed it back to Brother Lambert who took a large swig, his Adam's apple moving up and down as the liquid ran down his throat. He put the bottle on the dresser and helped Edgardo wash his feet and flannelled down his body for him. "If you take your drawers off, I can wash you down there," Brother Lambert said.

Edgardo unbuttoned his underwear, lowered it to the floor and let Brother Lambert slowly soap and wash him from his chest to his ankles, before drying him on the cotton towel. He felt himself getting aroused. For a few moments he stood looking at Brother Lambert, wanting to surrender to him, but he reached into the cupboard, rummaged for some clean drawers, and quickly got into bed.

Brother Lambert did not change the water that night. "I am happy to bathe in your water, Brother Pius," he said. As he undressed and soaped himself, he knew Edgardo was watching him. He turned to him and smiled. Edgardo turned away and faced the wall. "Good night," he said.

"Good night," Brother Lambert replied, planting a kiss on his temple.

Edgardo had hardly slept a wink when he was awakened by the sound of water. He sat up and realised Brother Lambert was peeing in the chamber pot.

"I'm sorry," he said, "tonight it's me who is not sleeping well."

"Why?" asked Edgardo.

For a long while there was no reply. Then Brother Lambert sat down on his bed.

"I'm unable to stop thinking about you… my feelings…. I can't help it."

Edgardo said nothing. He felt the covers lift as the monk got into bed with him.

Brother Lambert lay down on the pillow, his head next to Edgardo's. He rubbed Edgardo's back and then stroked his arms, his neck and his face; he kissed his lips and gently prised his mouth open with his tongue: he stroked his chest and his stomach; he unbuttoned his drawers and gently pulled them open. He so aroused Edgardo that before the cocks crowed at dawn the young monk had ejaculated and saturated the bedclothes.

***

In spite of his lack of sleep, Edgardo got up and went down to Matins. He was angry about what had taken place in the night and could not concentrate on the psalms being chanted. Brother Lambert once again faced him in the choir stalls, but Edgardo chose to ignore his smiles and barely looked at him, instead trying to harness the thoughts that were rapidly racing through his mind and causing him to go into a tailspin.

Edgardo believed that having been baptised by Anna Morisi he had been truly blessed by God, and that a journey into the realms of male love was not preordained for him or what he wanted for himself.

Like every other monk, he had, of course, come across men who were attracted to members of their own sex. He remembered seeing Thomas and Laurent kissing. In many ways they were like Brother Lambert: open, physical and expressive, and he had liked them – in fact, he would go so far as to say that as a seven-year-old he had loved them. Looking back, he felt they had truly been in love – but they were Swiss Guards and had not pledged themselves to God.

When he was growing up at the convent of Saint Peter in Chains, there were rumours that Brother Claudio had regularly bedded a young monk named Rafaello, and he knew that at least ten of the monks in the Austrian Tyrol, including the Prior, had been gratifying themselves with each other. He also knew that some of them were the most pastorally able and devoted monks in the monastery and he had a lot of respect for them. In spite of this, however, he felt this was not meant to be his own path.

At breakfast Edgardo walked past Brother Lambert, who quickly stood up and said to him, "You are ignoring me." He went to sit on his own, but was soon joined by Brothers Pierre and Antoine who asked him how he was settling in.

"It still feels quite strange for me," said Edgardo.

"I'm sure it will take time," said Brother Pierre as he spread butter on his bread.

"Your French is excellent," said Brother Antoine. "Where did you learn to speak the language so well?"

"Thank you," Edgardo said with a smile. "It was at my convent."

The Abbot came to join them.

"We had Austrian and French garrisons in Rome when I was growing up, so there were lots of French influences," Edgardo added.

Brother Lambert kept looking towards them and trying to hear what they were saying.

Edgardo asked the Abbot if he could come and speak with him after breakfast.

"What is it you wish to talk about?" asked the Abbot in the privacy of his study.

"I'm not sleeping well here," said Edgardo, "and I'm afraid my nerves are a little on edge."

"That is to be expected in a new environment," said the Abbot. "I have no doubt that after a few days of fresh air here you'll be fine. You're going to milk the cows with Brother Lambert this morning, I believe?"

"I'd like your dispensation to rest and spend some time in silence," said Edgardo.

The Abbot frowned. He did not reply.

"This morning I want to write to Pope Pius to let him know of my current situation," said Edgardo. "As I'm sure you're aware, he's always been like a father to me."

The Abbot nodded, "Yes you are privileged. Very well, for the next few days, you must take things at your own pace and only join in the liturgy if you're feeling well enough."

As Edgardo was leaving the Abbot's study, he turned round. "The Bishop of Poitiers mentioned that I would soon be sent to the new Sanctuary of Notre Dame de Beauchêne – when will that be?"

"It could be several months; it could be next year. The building work's been delayed. I can't say at this stage," said the Abbot.

"Will anyone else from here be going there with me?" asked Edgardo.

"That I can't tell you either – most likely Brother François and Brother Lambert."

Edgardo's heart sank as he heard Lambert's name. The Abbot walked over to him. "Is it the thought of going to Beauchêne that's bothering you. I know it's a remote region in the Bocage Vendéen, but I'm sure we could change that and have you stay here if you would prefer it."

"No, it's not that," said Edgardo.

"Well if you need to talk to me about anything, please come and see me immediately," said the Abbot, somewhat confused.

Edgardo thanked him and went back to his room. He closed the blind and lay in the darkness on his bed, going over every detail of the last two days he had spent with Brother Lambert. He lay there ridden with guilt. He could almost hear his father shouting at him: *This is what you left the Jewish religion for... this is what you left your mother, your father, your family for – for pederasty and sodomy!*

The words kept on repeating in his mind over and over again. At one point he felt as if his father had transformed into the God of Abraham who was shouting the same words: an inner Jewish voice taunting him constantly. In the end Edgardo wept. For hours he wept until there was a knock on the door.

Brother Lambert came into the room with some bread and cheese and found Edgardo sobbing uncontrollably. He sat him up and held him in his arms. For half an hour he just held him and let him cry. Not a word was said. Eventually Edgardo stopped.

"Would you like me to stay with you?" Brother Lambert asked him. Edgardo shook his head.

"I'm so sorry," Brother Lambert said as he left the room.

The Abbot came to see him in the afternoon. Edgardo was weeping again.

"I heard that you were very upset. Is there anything I can do?" The Abbot was visibly shocked. "Do you need to confess anything?"

"I need to be alone," Edgardo said.

When the Abbot left him, Edgardo again lay down on his bed.

In the evening Brothers Antoine and Pierre brought some supper for him.

"Hot vegetable soup and bread," Brother Antoine said as he put a bowl and a plate down on the dresser.

He saw that the lunchtime bread and cheese was untouched. They took it away.

Later that night, Brother Lambert returned to the room. He sat down on Edgardo's bed for a while and put his arm around him. He kissed him on the temple, got up and started to remove his robe.

"I know the Abbot asked you to sleep in with me, but I don't think that is necessary now," said Edgardo.

"You don't want to sleep with me any more?" Brother Lambert asked.

Edgardo did not reply.

"In that case I will go back to my own room," said Brother Lambert, and he left.

Edgardo opened the blind. There was a bright moon and stars in the night sky. Once again he wept. The thought of going down to the river and drowning himself occurred to him. For a long time he dwelt on the idea, but when he stopped weeping he decided that there was only one thing to do. He would surrender himself to Christ and place himself in his hands. He knelt by his bed, put his hands together and prayed for the whole night.

The next day the Abbot came to see him again. "It's not

good for you to stay in your room," he said. "We are all very worried about you. Have you written your letter to Pope Pius?"

"No," said Edgardo.

"Perhaps that is just as well. You should leave that until you are better," said the Abbot. "Clearly something has been very unsettling for you and your nerves have taken a big strain. You do still want to be a monk, maybe a priest?"

"Yes," said Edgardo.

"Well, we clearly don't understand the turmoil you are in, but in my experience the fact that you are struggling may be an indication that this is the right vocation for you. I'm sure the Pope himself would agree," said the Abbot. "We have arranged for a doctor to come and visit you this afternoon, just to be on the safe side." The Abbot then left the room.

That afternoon the Bishop of Poitiers, Monsignor Pie, arrived at the monastery with a doctor from the town. They entered Edgardo's room with the Abbot.

"You were well, Brother Pius, when we met less than a week ago," the Bishop said with some concern. "We will leave you alone with the good Doctor Durand who will examine you." He left the room with the Abbot, muttering, "What have you been doing to the Pope's son here?"

The doctor spent over an hour examining and talking to Edgardo. When the group recongregated around Edgardo's bed, the doctor proclaimed that Brother Pius was in the throes of neurasthenia, on account of depression, anxiety, and disorientation, all exacerbated by sleep deprivation.

"Is it serious?" the Bishop asked.

"It could be, but I think the patient will come out of this all right," the doctor said as he smiled at Edgardo.

"What treatment does he need?" the Bishop asked, "The cost is immaterial."

"He needs lots of fresh air and rest, good food, plenty of sleep and some good company," the doctor said.

"Brother Pius must visit me regularly," the Bishop

announced. "I will get my cook to make you some healthy stews," he added as he turned to Edgardo. "I'll send my buggy round for you."

The Bishop left with the doctor.

The Abbot took hold of Edgardo's hand. "Would you like to go and swim in the river with Brother Lambert?"

Edgardo's face screwed up a little; he tried to smile as he shook his head.

"We won't have Brother Lambert here for very long, now. He has just announced that he wants to join a monastery of the Canons Regular in Spain, which he's been talking about for years. It'll be a good move for him," the Abbot said as he left the room.

***

The next day, Edgardo decided that he had to write a letter to Brother Lambert; right now he felt it was more important than a letter to the Pope. In the evening he went downstairs for the first time since his illness and wandered through the cloister. The flowers were fragrant, having just been watered. He made his way to the wildflower meadow and heard Brother Lambert playing his tabar pipe down by the stream. Lambert put the pipe down when he saw him coming.

Edgardo sat on the bank next to him.

For a long time they were silent. Brother Lambert swept back his hair and then spoke. "You gave me such searching looks that I hoped you felt the same way as I did," he said looking across the stream.

"How did you feel?" Edgardo asked.

"Sometimes I may have looked indifferent, but my heart was consumed by you," said Brother Lambert.

"You never looked indifferent," said Edgardo.

Brother Lambert continued to look across the stream where the sun was sinking in the sky. "I've never felt this way about anyone," he said gently.

"And yet you've known me for such a short time," said Edgardo.

"Yes. In some ways I wish I had never known you at all: never looked into your eyes," said Brother Lambert. "I now know you did not feel the same way for me."

"I will never forget you, Lambert," said Edgardo. "I have a letter for you." He stood up and reached into his pocket. "Here, take it with you or burn it, but don't leave it here."

He bent over and kissed Brother Lambert on his temple, turned, and then climbed the hill to the monastery. At the orchard he looked round. Brother Lambert was reading the letter.

Dear Lambert,

I have never been attracted to another man before, not in that way, and it scared me. I clearly have desires, perhaps all men do, but I feel that for me to express them is a sin in the eyes of God. I did express them, and for that I feel wretched and overwhelmed with guilt. Clearly, dear Lambert, you are a different animal. You seem to want to celebrate and inhabit the world of your desires, and in some ways I envy you for that. Perhaps I could have loved a man like you; perhaps we could have hidden away and I might have had you to myself. Failing that I think we could have had a deep friendship, but I fear we overstepped the mark where that would have been possible.

I cannot even begin to imagine how your love would have changed my life.

But God sees everything.

He will know how I felt when you held me and embraced me. He will always know what you stirred within me.

In spite of my intense feelings, I cannot reject my faith.

It would have been enough for me just to have lived with you here in the monastery or in the new Sanctuary of Notre Dame de Beauchêne; to have been close to you. It would have been a joy to

*have a loving friend like you: a soulmate. But that was not meant
to be.*

I wish you well with your new life in Spain.
God Bless You.
Your affectionate Brother, Pius Maria Mortara

***

The next morning Brother Lambert left. When he was gone
Edgardo felt very miserable and wondered what his life in the
province of Poitou would be like now. He could only see a
melancholic and joyless future ahead of him with a load of
older monks. Who could have imagined that his journey
would have ended up here? It was such a contrast to his happy
childhood in Bologna, but he continued to surrender to Christ
and prayed for redemption and His blessing.

Two days after Brother Lambert had left, Brother François
returned to the monastery and learnt that he was sharing a
room with Edgardo. His father had died.

"I'm sorry," said Edgardo.

"Don't be. He had a good and a long life: he reached the
age of fifty-three. That's not bad for a farm labourer."

Brother François was a jovial, good-natured young monk,
also aged twenty-one. He was handsome, too, which made
Edgardo a little apprehensive. As the days progressed, he and
Edgardo quickly became good friends. They became intimate,
but not sexually. They swam in the river, naked, but Brother
François' smiles were never laden with flirtatious innuendo
and Edgardo thanked God for that.

"You're a good-looking lad; did Brother Lambert ever try
to seduce you?" Brother François asked him one day as they
lay in the sun.

Edgardo was taken aback but said nothing.

"Your silence tells me everything," said Brother François.
"He tried it on with me as well. I told him that if he continued

304

with his advances I'd smash his head in half with a church candlestick."

Edgardo laughed.

"I don't know about you, I said, but I've taken a vow of celibacy," continued Brother François. "Agh; he wasn't a bad chap. He had a lot of problems growing up. If he spent less time playing with his hair and his pipe, he'd make quite a good monk. He'll do all right in Spain."

Brother François didn't stop talking until the Bishop of Poitiers' buggy arrived for Edgardo to come and dine with him.

***

That night over a *Ragout de quenelles de volaille aux petits pois*, served out of a silver tureen, and a vintage Pinot Noir wine, Monsignor Pie asked Edgardo about his future plans. "I gather you wish to become a priest," he said. "Do you think you will find happiness as a priest?"

Edgardo found the question hard to answer. In truth he did not really know if he would ever find happiness. God had chosen him and singled him out for a special kind of love, but that had come at a price: being unreconciled with his family and the religion of his birth. "I am not looking for happiness," he said, pausing as he took a sip of his wine. "And yet I hope I can make others happy. I feel that in this world of suffering, it is my calling to become a priest and to spread the word of Jesus Christ. My father Pope Pius has prepared me well for that."

The Bishop raised his glass of wine and moved his chair in close to Edgardo's. "That's very good," he said as he took Edgardo's hand and squeezed it.

Edgardo discreetly slid back in his chair.

"Tonight we must celebrate," said the Bishop, his face flushed from the wine as it veered towards Edgardo's.

"Celebrate?" said Edgardo as he stood up.

"I received a dispatch from Pope Pius today. I have some good news for you, news that I hope will lift your spirits - although I must say you seem to be in a much better mood than when we last met at the monastery," said the Bishop. "I trust that your nerves are better now," he added as he topped up Edgardo's glass.

"What is the news?" asked Edgardo impatiently.

"Clearly your father, the Pope, has great things in mind for you. Although you are technically too young at twenty-one to become a priest, Pio Nono is giving you a special dispensation to become one before the year is out. It would seem that you'll be going to the Sanctuary of Beauchêne as a fully-fledged priest."

Chapter 41

Bouhay, Liège, Belgium. 1940

"Did you find happiness as a priest, Father?" asked Raoul.

Father Mortara took his time to answer. "I'm not sure I really did. You know, sad as it may sound, Man can live without happiness, but Man cannot live without love. People's lives are meaningless if they don't encounter love. And I've had so much love, not least from Pope Pius the Ninth, from Anna Morisi and from God." Father Mortara laughed. "There were happy times. When the Bishop of Poitiers told me that I was to become a priest at the ridiculously young age of twenty-one, I couldn't stop smiling for a week. I was so excited and yes – happy."

From the top of one of the hills in the distance, a farm labourer and his wife were making their way to the Priory church. They were accompanied by a young woman, with long blonde hair.

Raoul recognised them as they got nearer. "That's my parents coming to church," he said.

He got up and ran over to them. He hugged and greeted them before taking them back with him to Father Mortara.

"My parents, Brother Pius," Raoul said as he introduced them. Delphine stood behind them clutching a little bunch of yellow primroses tied up with string and had a big smile on her face. He had not seen her since they had kissed on her birthday.

The old priest stood up and in turn shook their hands. His gestures were very gracious, if a little exaggerated, some of them having been learnt directly from Pius the Ninth. He continued to hold one hand of each of Raoul's parents, gently shaking them up and down, which Raoul could not help noticing caused his father great unease. He wanted to shout out that on many occasions Brother Pius's hands had held those of the great Pope Pius the Ninth himself.

Father Mortara looked into Raoul's parents' eyes, trying to soak up who they were. Eventually he let the hands go as he spoke, "I have seen you over the years in the Priory church. Your son is a very good young man." The accent still contained hints of a Bolognese dialect. "He looks after me very well."

Monsieur Dubois raised his eyebrow, which Raoul took to mean, *So you look after an old foreigner like this instead of doing an engineering degree?*

Father Mortara then turned to Delphine. "And I'm sure I've seen you before, haven't I? You are…"

Delphine was the only member of the group who was at ease with herself. "Yes. I've seen you many times in the church here. My name is Delphine. I was born and bred in the village of Bouhay."

Raoul's mother spoke for her. "Delphine and Raoul have known each other since they were babies. She's a lovely girl, Father, and very clever."

Delphine smiled, but Raoul could hardly bear the pain of looking at her and avoided any eye contact.

The bell rang for Mass.

"We always go to Mass on my wife's birthday," Monsieur Dubois said quietly to Father Mortara.

"Happy Birthday," Brother Pius said, taking her hands again.

"Oh Maman, I forgot!" Raoul screwed up his face. "Bon Anniversaire." He ran over to her and gave her a kiss on the cheek.

"You are a priest now, Raoul. You don't need to celebrate my birthdays, and frankly I'd rather forget about birthdays at my age."

"I'm not a priest yet and I shouldn't have forgotten your birthday, Maman."

The bell rang again for Mass. Delphine handed Madame Dubois the flowers.

"Primroses - very pretty - you can eat them, you know." Father Mortara spoke softly as he touched the petals of the yellow flowers. "When I lived in France I knew people who put them on their salads or crystallised them and put them on top of cakes."

Delphine laughed out loud. "I'm sure Madame Dubois won't need to eat them. She'll have waffles for her birthday tea!"

"Delphine made them for me. Perhaps you could join us later," Madame Dubois said to Raoul.

"I don't think I can. I have my duties here," said Raoul, relieved to have an opt-out.

His parents walked away with Delphine towards the Priory church.

Father Mortara smiled as he nodded to them. He turned to Raoul. "I am sure you could have tea with your mother on her birthday. I can look after myself for an hour or two this afternoon."

"You are not well, Father."

"She is beautiful – the girl."

"That's Delphine," said Raoul.

"Yes, so she said." Father Mortara studied Raoul's expression. "I see. I think you still have feelings for her." He made this statement rather bluntly.

Raoul cast his gaze across the gardens. "I don't know, Father," he said and then turned round and watched Delphine entering the Priory church with his parents.

"You should go in and join your family for Mass. I'm happy to stay out here."

"Don't you want to go to Mass, Brother Pius?"

"I'm not feeling too good. I'll sit here and then go back to my room and have a lie down."

"In that case I will sit out here with you, Father," said Raoul.

They looked out across the fields.

"If you need to talk to me about anything, please feel free to do so," said Brother Pius. "If there's something on your mind, it's no good keeping it to yourself."

"Thank you, Father."

"We all have struggles in our lives. As I told you, I had a nervous breakdown in France, but it wasn't called a nervous breakdown in those days."

"Why do you think this happened, Father?" said Raoul.

"When I moved to Poitiers I was young and confused – like you. Maybe it was the years of intense study; maybe it was because of the attention I'd always received: the pressure the government had put on me to go home: my parents' upset and disappointment in me. To a degree it was having to accept a lifetime in a community of men, without the love that goes with familial relationships... It all became too much for me." Father Mortara looked very sad but suddenly he laughed. "I think having been born Jewish I never got rid of my guilt! Guilt is a Jewish affliction, you know."

"But you still continued in Holy Orders?" said Raoul.

"Yes. I didn't think there was anything else to do or anywhere else I could go."

"Couldn't you have gone back to Italy?" said Raoul.

"I don't think I could. No."

"And in spite of all this you became a priest in Poitiers, Father, even though you were in theory too young?"

"Yes, Pope Pius gave me a special dispensation to be ordained to the priesthood."

"But you recovered from your breakdown?" said Raoul.

"I don't think the after effects of this illness ever completely disappear..."

"You must have felt very isolated without your family," said Raoul.

"I felt isolated without my adoptive father Pio Nono," said Brother Pius.

310

"Did you ever see him again?"

"No," said Father Mortara. "He often wrote to me in Austria, and when I moved to Poitiers in France he wrote to me there too. But I never saw him before he died. That was in 1878.

When eventually I visited the Eternal City many years later, I went to the Basilica of Saint Lawrence outside the Walls. I was heartbroken that I never managed to see Pope Pius again. I broke down in tears and prostrated myself in front of his tomb. Here was my venerable father and protector, the saintly Pontiff to whom I am eternally so grateful. In his epitaph the faithful are invited to pray for him: '*Orate pro eo*'."

Father Mortara closed his eyes and put his hands together in prayer.

When he eventually opened them, Raoul turned to him. "And what about your real father?"

"My real father?"

"Did you ever see him again?" said Raoul.

"No, he died when I was in France a year or two after he saw me in the procession of monks and priests in Saint Peter's Square in Rome." Father Mortara closed his eyes.

The more the old man said, the more Raoul felt that he had no real connection with his family: no connection at all. He felt sad about that.

"What about your mother? Did you see her again, Father?" "After twenty years I was allowed to return to my native Italy. Not having performed my military duties I had to obtain special permission from the King to re-enter the country. I preached Lenten Sermons in Bologna and Modena where my mother was now living…"

Chapter 42

Modena, Kingdom of Italy. 1891

The smell of frankincense filled the interior of San Carlo Church. Rows of candles burned in the ornate iron candelabra in the aisle along the west wall, creating a light smoke that seemed to blend with the high notes of the choir's Kyrie from Palestrina's Missae Papae Marcelli, before rising to the angels of red, green and orange on the stained glass windows. Father Mortara stared at the baptismal font and wondered if it was like the one in the San Salvator Church where he had been baptised. He closed his eyes and thought of Anna Morisi. He tried to invoke her presence; her smile and her words; her songs about soldiers going off to war and returning as heroes as she danced the Salterello. For a moment he imagined he was in her arms again. He felt her love; her unconditional love. It was she who had saved him. He thanked her now as he had thanked her thousands of times. He heard his name, felt his neighbour gently nudging him, and realised that the Archbishop of Modena was introducing him to the congregation.

"We are very honoured to have Father Pius Maria Mortara with us today. He joins us fresh from preaching Lenten sermons last weekend in Bologna. Some of you may know that Bologna is where he spent a fortunate childhood, before his calling to the Church was sealed by his baptism at the age of six. And, as many of you are also aware, he had the blessing of having as his mentor none other than the late Pope, Pius the Ninth. Since then he has travelled all over Europe. And now, in his fortieth year, we are blessed to have this good man with us today."

Some of the congregation started to clap. Father Mortara got up and smiled at the Archbishop as he walked slowly over to the pulpit, stopping at the baptismal font and caressing the cold marble with the tips of his fingers. He climbed the wooden steps of the pulpit and opened a large, leather-bound Bible, pausing as an elderly lady with a black veil was being shown into the church by a young priest who found her a seat at the back of the nave.

Father Mortara addressed the congregation. "Before I speak to you, I should like to read from the First Letter to the Corinthians, Chapter Thirteen." He looked around the church, the nave a sea of faces, most of them smiling at him with recognition and warmth in their eyes. He continued. "Love never faileth. But where there be prophecies, they shall fail; where there be tongues, they shall cease; where there be knowledge it will pass away. For we know in part and we prophesy in part, but when perfection comes, the imperfect disappears. When I was a child, I spoke like a child, I thought like a child..."

Father Mortara stopped. He found the incense overpowering. For a moment, he closed his eyes. He looked around the congregation. A young lady with extremely red lips smiled at him. He smiled back before scanning the pews row by row. Sometimes he wondered, even hoped, that he would see Anna Morisi in one of these congregations. At one time he'd heard rumours that she'd entered a nunnery. She would be in her fifties now. But she wasn't there.

He continued, "And I reasoned like a child..."

Then, at the back of the church, he noticed the little old lady dressed all in black, weeping behind the mask of her veil, her hands over her eyes, her lace cuffs hanging down over her sleeves. She was small and her silk necktie was disproportionately large. He recognised the way her head hung over her body. He felt blood rushing to his head.

"...I reasoned like a child..." He heard himself repeating the line – two, maybe three, times. He stared at the woman, knowing it was his mother. She lifted the veil to dry her eyes with a handkerchief; his voice faltered; he stopped reading as she stared back at him. Some of the congregation turned round to see who he was looking at. Father Mortara wished he could bolt out of the door and run away. He continued awkwardly but automatically. He knew most of the phrases by heart.

"I reasoned like a child, but when I became a man, I put away these childish things. For now we see through a glass darkly; but then face to face: now I know in part, but then I shall know even as I am known. And now these three remain: faith, hope and love..."

He lifted his head again and looked over to his mother.

"But the greatest of these is love..."

***

Father Mortara quickly told the congregation about his life in Europe and in France where he now lived, and how he preached to congregations including Jews. He spoke about the blessed servant girl Anna Morisi and heard his mother shrieking audibly at the sound of her name. He thanked the congregation for their interest in his life and their support, and then, taking a deep breath, he went over to join his mother at the back of the nave. He was closely followed by the Archbishop of Modena and the Vicar of San Carlo Church. He mustered a brave smile. He did not want to show that he was deeply troubled by the presence of his mother, or by her weeping which he took to be a question mark for his existence and his life as a Catholic priest.

He introduced the people who followed him to his mother and wondered if they took her weeping as a mark of pride in him. The Archbishop took her hand and kissed it. The Vicar of San Carlo followed suit and Father Mortara took the seat next to his mother, lifted her hands, and kissed them before wrapping his arms around her and locking her in a long embrace.

Most of the congregation had made their way over to watch them. He heard one old lady say that they looked like Jesus and the Madonna. Another whispered that it was good he was Jewish – like Jesus.

For several minutes they watched him embracing his weeping mother.

When he pulled back, making the sign of the cross, several young people, an old man and a child stepped forward forming a makeshift queue and asked him to bless them.

The Vicar of San Carlo Church then intervened and asked if he would like to speak to his mother in private in the Vestry.

Father Mortara quickly laid hands on several members of the congregation, and then helped his mother to the Vestry where her sobbing stopped. The Vicar quickly hung up his green robes.

"Will you be joining the Archbishop and myself for lunch?" the Vicar asked him.

"I will take my mother home; she lives here in Modena," replied Father Mortara.

"The Archbishop was hoping to hear about your life story in a little more detail," the Vicar said. "Perhaps your mother would like to join us too? Kidneys with anchovies and lemon. My housekeeper is a decent cook."

Father Mortara awkwardly looked over at his mother. She was shaking her head.

"Perhaps next time I visit Modena," he replied.

The Vicar bade him farewell and left them alone. Shortly after, the Archbishop popped his head into the Vestry.

"I am sorry we cannot hear more about your life, but I know you need some time alone with your mother. Until next time." Before leaving he turned to Madame Mortara, "You must be very proud of your son."

Madame Mortara did not reply.

Nor did she reply when her son looked into her eyes and

told her how happy he was to be with her again, and she did not reply when he told her how much he loved her.

"I don't understand what you have done with your life, Edgardo, and I never will," was all she said to him in the Vestry. For once, Father Mortara, usually eloquent, chatty and quite frequently good-humoured, sat with a glazed expression on his still handsome face, in stony silence.

***

Father Mortara took his mother's arm as they crossed the Via Emilia and she led him through a tiny alley that opened on to the Piazza Mazzini. She sat down on a bench in front of the synagogue and spoke slowly. He remembered how she used to speak quickly, with her fiery, wide-open eyes and throw her arms around as if she was on a stage. Her hands still moved elegantly as she pointed with her index finger and rolled the palms upwards. She took off her black lace gloves as if to free her hands and allow them more expression. Her voice was shrill and slightly more croaky than he remembered it, with words that were laced with sadness.

"We used to play in this square when I was a girl; it was the centre of the Jewish Ghetto. They used to come and lock the gates at night. Lock us in like animals in a cage. There was no synagogue then. They built it about twenty years ago. Do you want to go and look inside?"

"Perhaps later," said Father Mortara as he took hold of his mother's hand and placed it between his.

"You could have gone for lunch with the Archbishop of Modena and the priests. You can still go; I don't mind."

"I'm happy to have lunch with you."

She freed her hand from his.

"Let me look at you, Edgardo. Stand up."

He got up, walked back a few paces and opened his arms, awkwardly conjuring up a playful smile.

"When you were six and we met you at the convent in Rome, I told you they had made a priest out of you. They dressed you in a little black smock and a crucifix and look: you are still wearing it!"

She laughed. Her joke was bitter. He lowered his head.

"Are you eating properly, Edgardo? You look thin to me," she said. "Do they give you proper food?"

He nodded. He sat down again and asked about his brothers and sisters, and their husbands and wives and children. For a while, his mother's eyes lit up as she spoke about his nephews and nieces: their schooling, which one was good at mathematics and who was good at literature, their musical prowess and how handsome they all were.

"Your brother Augusto writes books about law now," she told him.

When there was no more to tell she stood up.

He looked into her dark brown eyes.

"I am sorry you are so unhappy with me," he said simply.

They walked to his mother's home in silence. She only spoke to point out the street off the square where her parents had lived.

Do you remember going there? she asked him.

He didn't remember.

As they reached her ground floor apartment a few streets away, in an old townhouse with ochre walls, he continued to feel his mother's sadness and her disappointment with him. Belonging to the Church had made him feel worthy, but with his mother he felt worthless.

He did not know what to say to her. He commented on the pot of basil on the kitchen table. He told her he liked the tinted herb bottles on her shelves and her olive oil decanter. He asked if the silhouette framed by lace and stained wood was of Augusto. She nodded, but did not speak. During a long silence he sat down on an old beechwood chair at the kitchen table and watched her stirring lunch with a long copper spoon.

He closed his eyes, put his hands together and prayed in silence. He summoned the courage to say what he had always wanted to say, and then blurted it out.

"Mama, it would mean so much to me if you would put your pride away and follow God through the example of his Son."

Still Madame Mortara did not speak; reacting only by stirring lunch with renewed vigour. The smell of garlic and rosemary from meatballs and dumplings almost intoxicated him, bringing with it a new wave of memories. He remembered sitting at the kitchen table in Bologna thirty-three years previously when she made the same food. Father Mortara felt the carved wooden leg of the table and immediately recognised the ornate grooved spheres midway down. He remembered hiding under the table when he played hide and seek with Anna Morisi; he ran his hands over the soft velvet of the rust-coloured table cloth, which in several places had lost its nap; he played with the frayed tassels hanging over the side as he looked around the room. Two blackened pans hung over the small range, remnants of the large kitchen in Bologna, where, under a canopy of iron pots and kitchen utensils, dramas of family life had been played out. But this kitchen was bare and quiet; there was none of the chattering and laughter of his brothers and sisters that he had known in the old days; none of the fun; the endless shouting; the card tricks and games; the fights. Only the sound of his mother stirring the food and the bubbling of boiling water broke the silence. He watched her standing at the range, steam condensing on her face, her long black lace dress at odds with the old worn apron she had thrown over it.

He fancied he recognised the little silver menorah and the copper candle-snuffer on the small dresser in front of the kitchen window.

"Is it the same tablecloth we had in Bologna?" he asked, trying to sound like a son rather than a stranger.

His mother turned to look at him. She did not smile or respond, the muscles of her face almost paralysed by three decades of grief. She poured a glass of red wine and placed it in front of him with a hint of childlike petulance.

He smiled at her in an attempt to lighten the atmosphere. He thought he could detect a twinkle in her eye but then she looked down, ignoring his comments as she began to serve up the food in a couple of old, cracked majolica bowls, the blue peacocks embedded in a maze of yellow leaves quickly disappearing under a sea of tomato sauce.

"Mama, it would be pure joy for me if you would consider becoming a Christian. I could help you; show you the paths of eternal blessing and happiness," he went on.

Madame Mortara sprinkled rock salt over the food. "I don't know about the table cloth, Edgardo, but you might remember the bowls," she said, in a whisper. "They were given to us by your uncles, the Padovanis, in 1851, the year you were born. You used to like the blue peacocks. You refused to leave food in them so you could see them. It was a good way of making you eat."

She stared into the bowls, suddenly raising her voice, the whisper turning into a shout, the Romagnol vowel sounds becoming harsher.

"I will never convert for you, Edgardo. I would have done once. When they took you away from us I begged your father to convert. I would have done anything to get you back. But your father wouldn't hear of it. Now it's too late. I would never convert – not even if you were to become a cardinal or a Jewish pope!" She brought the bowls over to the table. "The meatballs are kosher. I hope that is all right for you. Will you eat kosher food, or have you lost your appetite for it? You used to love my dumplings with meatballs."

"I would like to eat kosher food with you, Mama."

"You were not the only victim, Edgardo. Your father had to give up his business – a good lace business. For years he moved from land to land like 'The Wandering Jew'. Why? Because of you! He appealed to everyone – kings and emperors even – to get you back. And when your poor father, God rest his soul, begged the Inquisitor, Cardinal Antonelli and the Pope himself to restore you to us, they made him writhe like a worm. These were the men of your newfound God. Eternal blessing and happiness they may have had, I don't know, but I do know they burdened your family with misery and despair. Now you are a man, Edgardo, you must know this. When your Pope took you away from me, he took my life as well. And now, to add insult to injury, he has also taken your name."

"He did not take my name, Mama."

"No; you took the Pope's name as if he was your father. Everything your father and I ever gave you, you abandoned and rejected. Your family, your religion, even your name, your beautiful name, Edgardo! Your father so wanted you to be named Edgardo!"

"Did he, Mama?" Father Mortara lowered his head, and with one of his fingers tried to curb a tear of anguish falling on to the velvet tassel he was holding. "Why?"

"Your father was a cultured man. He wanted to give you a special name. He came across Edgardo … I don't know where … in an opera by Donizetti, I think."

"Lucia di Lammermoor," Edgardo said as he fought back the tears. "The opera was based on a novel by Sir Walter Scott. The character was called Edgar Ravenswood."

Madam Mortara closed her eyes. "Your father, God bless his soul, used to sing arias from all the operas. Do you remember?"

"Yes," said Father Mortara sadly.

"If your father were alive he could have told you all about it, but he never had a chance to do so." She sat down next to him. "Do you think Jews in Via Lame in Bologna had names like Edgardo? Not one. Your father never dreamed that you would change your name to – what? Pius – after the man who stole you from us and Maria after the woman who got pregnant

320

with Jesus, even though she never lay with her husband and was a virgin."

"The Blessed Virgin," said Father Mortara softly.

Madame Mortara looked at him. "The Blessed Virgin! I prayed to your Blessed Virgin every day." She got up and went over to the dresser; she opened a drawer, took out a medal on a chain, and showed it to him. "The medal of the Blessed Virgin. I picked it up off the floor after your father ripped it off you at the convent. I begged her to send you home to us, but did she answer my prayers?" Madame Mortara grated Parmesan cheese over the meatballs, repeating the words 'Pius Maria'.

Father Mortara wrapped strings of the tablecloth tassels around his little finger.

"When your father returned home all he had was debts; an honourable man had been reduced to a pauper. He had to go cap in hand to the Jews of Bologna to help him get a roof over his head." Madame Mortara passed a bowl of meatballs over to her son and poured him a glass of water from a jug. "And then the taunting began. Your father was constantly taunted by priests from the Holy Office, who pressed him to turn Catholic to get you back. The whole civilised world was on your father's side – everyone except your beloved Pio Nono and the Catholic Church. They had no respect for your father; they only seemed intent on humiliating him."

Father Mortara stared into his bowl, pushing a dumpling around with his fork.

"It seems you don't like my food any more. Perhaps I should have made you tortellini with pork salami."

"I'm not hungry," said Father Mortara, stifling his tears.

"I don't know if you knew, but the winter before your father died they arrested him and tried him in Florence on the charge of having murdered a servant girl by throwing her out of a window. The testimony rested upon two priests living in the same house who swore they saw him do the deed. The girl had actually committed suicide. It was your father's reputation as a peaceful and kind man that convinced the judges of his innocence. He was defended free of charge by Mancini, one of the top advocates in Florence, and honourably acquitted – much to the annoyance of his enemies in the Catholic Church."

"Why would the Catholic Church be annoyed?" Father Mortara lifted his head.

"His conviction would have justified your baptism, because all Europe would then have blessed the hand that had removed a child from an immoral family. Public opinion was not to be deceived, however. The jury was unanimous in acquitting him. Honest people greeted the verdict with joy, which was at least some compensation for your father, because his health, God rest his soul, after seven months of confinement in prison, was shattered. Several months later he died, scarcely fifty-three years old, a broken man." Madame Mortara took off her apron and sighed loudly. "I was reduced to begging. Our family was reduced to nothing. You say the Catholic Church allowed you to follow the path of eternal blessing and happiness, but you must know that it inflicted unutterable woe on your family."

"I am sorry you see it in this way, Mama."

"I cannot see it in any other way. For me it will always be a crime that has never been avenged. In the history of our people, loving parents would have massacred their offspring and hurled them into rivers and wells rather than see them snatched from their arms and defiled in this way. Your father and I were brought up with a religion that we clung to with every fibre of our heart and spirit. When you had a chance to return to us after Unification, you still rejected us: your family; your religion. You never came home, even though you were free to do so. Like Esau you denied the historical birthright of your religion. Your father never said it, Edgardo, but I cannot even begin to tell you how unhappy this made him. What child would leave a father who embraced it in his arms? What child would forsake a mother who nursed it with her kisses?

You left your family lonely, helpless and forsaken."

Madame Mortara stood up and took off her apron. She left the room before he could reply.

In the late afternoon shadows of her kitchen Father Mortara sat alone for a long time.

Chapter 43

Bouhay, Liège, Belgium. 1940

"I fear Brother Pius's health is declining rapidly," the Prior said to Raoul as they walked into the gardens of Notre Dame de Lourdes. Father Mortara was sitting alone on a bench, looking sad and forlorn. "He will soon be facing his Maker. But you must not be sad, Brother Luc. You have looked after him well. As your novice master I am very pleased with you." The Prior then quickly changed the topic of conversation. "Have you been thinking about your ordination? You must be excited about taking your vows next month."

Raoul chose not to reply. He looked over the old stone wall where two Brothers in an adjacent field were checking frames in a long line of wooden beehives, their white veils hanging down on to their habits from their wide-brimmed hats.

The Prior put his arm around Raoul's shoulders. "I know you must be feeling nervous about it. I remember my own ordination as if it were yesterday: forty-five years ago in Ghent! I, too, was afraid, but full of anticipation and joy – and excitement! I remember choosing the vestments, the chalice and the liturgy. You must invite your family. Mine were all there – my grandparents and all my little cousins running amok..." The Prior laughed wildly at the thought of them. Over the months, Raoul had become immune to his high-pitched histrionics. "My brother was the cross-bearer that day. It is a day for you to celebrate your coming to God. You can also help the music master choose the music!"

Raoul smiled at the Prior as he pulled away. He looked over to Father Mortara.

"Shouldn't he be in bed?" he asked.

"He wanted to sit out in the sun," the Prior replied. "One

must remember he is Italian!"

'But one must remember it is still March and it's not exactly hot,' thought Raoul.

They walked slowly towards the old man.

"Do you know Father Mortara's story?" Raoul asked him.

"Of course. Most of the Catholic world knows his story. He is highly renowned; one of the most distinguished ecclesiastics of Rome. He was adopted by Pope Pius the Ninth and educated for the priesthood in Rome under his immediate supervision. You know he speaks twenty-two languages?" He laughed as though what he had said had been intensely humorous.

Raoul jumped in. "Yes, I know all that, but I'm talking about how he arrived in Rome; about his secret baptism; how he was wrenched from his family. He was abducted – you know that?"

"I know we all come to God in strange and mysterious ways, Brother Luc and I know Brother Pius has led an extraordinary life. He has lived and worked in France, Spain, most of Europe, even the United States, as a worthy and devout Christian, and he has preached all over the world. In the 1880s his eloquent sermons so moved the Queen of Spain and her courtiers that they assisted him with funds for the convent chapel he built at Onate in the Basque Highlands, and I believe that in Marseilles he once enjoyed the great privilege of a visit from Don Bosco who had recently been canonised. Can you imagine that, Brother Luc? Meeting a living saint! What other monks here can say they have done that? We are really very privileged to have had him here in Bouhay with us. Yes, his life has been quite incredible."

Raoul cut the Prior short.

"His life has also been very unhappy," he said. "He told me that when he lived in France he suffered a nervous breakdown, the after effects of which never completely disappeared. His separation from his family must have been devastating, both for him and for them."

"I am sure his family managed all right." The Prior was

indignant. "We, too, as members of a Holy Order are separated from our families. His brother, Augusto Mortara did very well. Even as a Jew he was appointed Inspector-General of the Treasury in the Italian Government at the turn of the century. Do not fret for his family or indeed for Brother Pius himself.

"His siblings may have achieved great things, but tell me, Father, what good did Brother Pius's kidnapping do for him?"

The Prior was clearly vexed. "He wasn't kidnapped," he replied, his discomfort punctuated with a high-pitched chuckle. "Yes, he was taken to Rome…"

Raoul could not contain himself. "He was abducted – he was taken away from his parents at the age of six!"

"He was brought up as the Pope's son and given opportunities that you and I can only dream about," said the Prior shaking his head.

"I'm sure he led a charmed life as a child with Pio Nono, but once he was out of the Pope's orbit all that came to an end very quickly. After the age of nineteen, when Edgardo left Italy for Austria, apart from a few letters, the Pope had nothing more to do with him, and as far as I can see it all led to Father Mortara having a very sad and empty life."

"You think so?" said the Prior shaking his head.

"Yes – was it all worth it? What did he really achieve? It's wonderful that he spoke twenty-two languages, that he travelled extensively, that he met some famous people including royalty who put money into the church, but what happened also led to him having a nervous breakdown and in spite of an extraordinary childhood with so much promise, he is ending his life in obscurity!"

"Consider, Brother Luc, that Brother Pius experienced enough fame and notoriety as a child to last a lifetime. More importantly he found God! For some people, serving God is good enough. And he made a good priest – as I believe you will, too!"

Raoul closed his eyes for a while before speaking out.

"I fear not, Father. In fact I question my very allegiance to the Catholic Church."

"What do you mean?" the Prior asked him.

"Father Mortara's story has affected me profoundly." Raoul paused for a while and looked over at the old priest. "I cannot condone the way the Catholic Church took him away from his family. If I had been the local priest whom the servant girl Anna Morisi had confessed to, I would have ignored the law and rebuked her for her actions. After all, she did not have the consent of the baby's parents. And I certainly would not have reported the affair to the so-called Holy Office. If I had been the Archbishop of Bologna I would not have sent the police to kidnap the child, and if I had been the Pope himself, I would not have separated the child from his parents. I can't see it as anything but a travesty that caused so much pain and suffering to Father Mortara and his parents."

Raoul caught himself shouting and shaking with anger. He wanted to add that the Church had used Father Mortara as a religious example and had then spewed him out and forgotten about him; that the Church had robbed him of his identity and ruined his life in the process, but he stopped himself. Two of the canons who were pruning rose bushes were staring at him.

He lowered his voice. "Father, when Jewish parents brought their children to Jesus that he might lay his hands on them, He gave them back to their Jewish parents. But Pius the Ninth kept this child. It was as though the disciple was above his master."

The Prior failed to reply and neither did he interrupt Raoul; he could see that he was deeply troubled.

"What sort of man was this Pope?"

"A man of conscience, who was merely adhering to the edicts laid down by previous popes," the Prior replied.

"What have edicts from ancient popes got to do with a one-year-old child?" Raoul argued. "Was Pius the Ninth so powerless that he was unable to change a single facet of canonical law?" He became agitated and red in the face. "I am not like these men, Father. My first regard would not have been for the Church, but for the child and for the most natural earthly ties there could be: those of the family. I cannot help thinking about his bereaved parents: about the agony his mother went through. How can devout Catholics overlook the outrage done to her in the name of the Virgin Mother? Perhaps my future does not lie with the Church."

The Prior looked at him with all the compassion he could muster. He took his hand.

"I am sure there is not one man of the cloth who has not had his doubts about devoting his life to God and the Church," he said reassuringly. "You will make a fine priest, Brother Luc, I have no doubt about that."

Raoul gazed over to Father Mortara who looked as though he was about to fall off the end of the bench.

"Perhaps I should put Father Mortara to bed," he said.

He started to walk over to the old priest. He turned round and smiled.

"Thank you, Father."

"Remember: all the events which you speak about happened nearly ninety years ago. Things have changed," said the Prior.

But Raoul could no longer be appeased. "Have they, Father?"

Chapter 44

Bouhay, Liège, Belgium. 1940

Raoul had already been up for hours by the time Monsignor Kerkhofs arrived at the Priory of Notre Dame de Lourdes in a large chauffeur-driven Minerva.

The Prior offered him breakfast, somewhat bewildered by the fact that the Bishop of Liège would want to show a novice monk around parishes in his diocese, an invitation that had never been extended to him. Little did he know that Monsignor Kerkhofs had actually asked Raoul to join him on a visit to the monasteries at Val Dieu and Banneux, where he hoped the Jews of Liège might take refuge should their lives become endangered.

The Bishop declined the offer of breakfast, but asked to visit Father Mortara. He and Raoul popped in to see him, but the old priest was asleep.

"I am, as you know, very concerned for the Jews of Belgium," the Bishop told Raoul as they drove north-east through the fields and forests of the province. "I have heard that the Nazis want to remove the Jewish people from the whole of Europe and resettle them in other parts of the world."

"Don't these people realise that Jesus was a Jew?" Raoul said in frustration.

The Bishop raised an eyebrow. "That's true. Jesus was born a Jew and died a Jew." He sighed. "The 'Jewish Question' is an odd thing; Jews are blamed for the crucifixion of Jesus, yet the apostles never saw Jesus as anything other than Jewish."

They passed through the municipality of Blegny. Raoul looked through the back windows of the car, half expecting to see Jean-Louis, but the only people on the streets were a group of coal-miners returning from their night shift.

"We can only pray that the Jews of Belgium will not be persecuted as they are in Germany," said the Bishop. "In treating the Jews as an inferior race and blaming them for everything from Germany's economic depression to their defeat in the First World War, the Nazis are putting themselves above God. Their hate-mongering has completely stripped them of their citizenship and all their human rights."

"I've heard that Jews now can't go to German schools," said Raoul.

"They can't go anywhere!" said the Bishop. "They are banned from going to the theatre, the cinema and holiday resorts, and in some neighbourhoods they aren't even allowed to walk anywhere. The Nazis are also forcing them to close their businesses or sell them at bargain prices. God forbid that they should be humiliated and degraded here in Belgium like that, or forced to wear a yellow Star of David on their clothes."

The car drew up outside the main entrance of the magnificent Abbey of Val Dieu, an ecclesiastical island with nothing but gardens and fields surrounding it for miles around. The chauffeur, a middle-aged man with spectacles and greying hair, opened the doors for them and they were immediately hit by the aroma of boiled hops that swept over the building.

"That's why we must be prepared to hide the Jews in places like this if we need to," said the Bishop in a low voice as they entered the abbey.

Raoul was introduced to the monks and the Bishop spoke quietly with the Abbot for half an hour. They were each given a large glass of beer from the abbey's brewery and an hour later they got back into the car. The excursion continued with a half-hour drive to the south-west. When they arrived at the Banneux monastery introductions to the monks and Abbot were repeated and once again large glasses of beer were dispensed.

On the way back, Raoul asked to be dropped off just beyond Chaudfontaine, as he wanted to walk back along the river to Bouhay.

The Bishop got out of the car with Raoul and spoke quietly to him. "It is good to know that you are here and keen to help us if necessary with the Jews of the province. I will introduce you to the Rabbi of Liège and he can tell you about some of the Jewish families who live in the city, but of course all this must be kept hush hush."

Raoul nodded.

"And please send my best wishes to Father Mortara," the Bishop said. "I know he has not been well and his days are numbered, but I've heard you are a great support to him."

Raul suddenly looked troubled. "Monsignor, why did the Catholic hierarchy not help Father Mortara more when he was a child?"

The Bishop took his time to reply. "At that time I understand it was Pope Pius's belief that as a Christian he had to guide the boy's soul to Heaven. In his eyes it would have been a mortal sin to abandon this soul. Edgardo himself was an extraordinary boy: a committed Christian, even at the age of six. Also, the laws were different in Rome in the 1850s: a Jewish child who was baptised had to be separated from his parents."

"That can't be right," said Raoul.

"It was the ecclesiastical law. I don't think anything like that would happen now; I hope not, anyway. On the positive side, he has had a good and interesting life and I believe he has fulfilled his mission as a monk here in Belgium."

"You do?" said Raoul quietly.

The Bishop hugged him, got back into the car, tapped his chauffeur on the shoulder and they drove off.

Raoul headed for the river and walked back through the woods and villages that led to Bouhay. He continued through several fields towards the village. The midday sun was unusually warm for early spring. He crossed a wheat field and sat down in the shade of the solitary apple tree, the one where he'd left his notes for Delphine – their apple tree. A gentle wind rustled through the leaves. He couldn't help thinking again about their row, but immediately tried to blank Delphine out of his mind. He wondered if he should pop in and see his parents for lunch, but fearing an argument with his father, he decided to remain where he was. He leaned against the tree and pulled his legs up to him; an early Brimstone butterfly with sulphur yellow wings landed on his knee: its upper-side pale, like a piece of cabbage – probably a male he thought. He wanted to stroke it. He remembered coming to this field as a child with his butterfly net and catching red Vulcains and marbled Whites with Guy and Mathieu. He heard a bird singing in the tree – a short, loud trill ending with a flourish; he looked up to see a chaffinch perched on the branch above his head. He smiled to himself, recalling how as children they would come and trap birds here in wicker baskets and try to sell them for their birdsong or for the delicacy of their flesh. If they couldn't sell them they would have 'finching' contests and line their captured birds up in the street. The bird that sang its song the most times in an hour was the winner. Sometimes they had played pirates under the very tree he was now sitting under, or down by the brook, and occasionally the boys would let Delphine be the Pirate Queen...

In the distance he heard the Priory bells ringing. The Brimstone butterfly fluttered away and did an airborne dance down the hill, before searching the hedgerows by the brook for females awakening from hibernation. The sun was high in the sky. Raoul undid the neck buttons of his robe and vest, stretched out, and lay down. Two large beers before noon had made him a little drowsy. He started to doze off.

After a while he suddenly felt hands over his eyes. "Well! And who is this handsome young man sleeping under the apple tree?" It was Delphine, and she had laughter in her voice that never failed to make him smile. "I saw you when I was getting off the bus," she said as she took her hands away, leaned over him and kissed his forehead.

"You have incredibly good eyesight," Raoul said as he sat up. "I was just thinking about you and how we used to play pirates here and catch butterflies and birds in this field."

"I only played pirates," said Delphine. "I drew the line at wounding innocent little creatures like you boys did. Honestly! You were quite barbaric and cruel." Then she laughed. "Have you the time to have lunch with me? It's warm enough to have a picnic." She got up, not waiting for an answer. "I'll be back in ten minutes," she said.

Raoul watched her, mesmerised, as she took off her shoes, pulled her floral skirt up and held it in her hands, then ran barefoot through the cornfield, her long legs and flowing blonde hair giving her the appearance of a luminous goddess.

His heart sank as he sat alone in the field. It had been several weeks since he'd kissed Delphine on her birthday. He had relived that kiss so many times: it was the definitive kiss of his life, when he had totally lost himself in her, when the world had stood still and his life as a monk had stopped. She had looked up at him with the bluest of eyes, her hands pulling down on his shoulders, while his fingers had traced a path up her spine to the back of her neck, his straight nose pushing against hers before it nuzzled against the translucent skin of her delicate pink cheeks; her lips soft, quivering and moist had gently parted with no resistance at all and her tongue had sought out his in strange, sweet surrender, the tenderness of it all wrapped up in a haze of violet water and longing... He would take that kiss to the grave with him.

But the kiss was cruel: she had a lover and he was a novice monk.

He knew that his feelings for Delphine would never change. He felt that a kiss like that was not possible without love, but even with love there was no future for him and Delphine: there was no alternative but to let her go.

That evening he had returned to the Priory across this same

cornfield with tears in his eyes; he had resolved to surrender himself to God and a life of monastic devotion. From that moment onwards, things became easier. When he got up for Matins, before the sun had risen, he felt at peace. He had always loved the solitude of the early morning hours; they felt like stolen hours and were the best part of the day. When he popped his head in to Father Mortara's room, to see if the old man was alright and still breathing, he said a prayer for him and asked the Almighty to cherish him in the final chapter of his life. As he chanted the morning psalms in the darkness of the Priory church with the other monks he felt grateful that he was starting his day with God. As he prayed and breathed in the incense he felt His intense presence; it gave him strength for the rest of the day. When he sat in the cloisters in meditation, watching the magnificence of the breaking dawn, the sunlight scattering over the clouds in reds and yellows and oranges, filling the world with light, he accepted God into his heart and resolved to have greater faith in Him.

In the Mass his relationship with God intensified and in the Eucharist, when he received the bread and the wine – the body and blood of Christ – it was at its climax. He appreciated the rare gift he was receiving. Now he was ready to face the day; now he felt enlightened, euphoric almost, and he knew that with six or seven hours of daily prayer still to encounter, he was ready for anything and certainly ready to help the two remarkable men whom God had brought into his life: the Bishop of Liège and Father Mortara. He would serve them and he would serve God.

His thoughts returned to Father Mortara and his dramatic life in Rome, and how strange it was that the Pope's son would end his days here in the quietness of Bouhay. In spite of all the conversations he'd had – with the Prior, with Monsignor Kerkhofs, and with Father Mortara himself – he could not quite curtail his anger at the young boy being separated from his parents and family, and he still could not understand how the Catholic Church had behaved towards him in the way that it had. What had happened still shocked him, but, as he stuck a blade of grass between his teeth, he knew he would have to reconcile his conflicting thoughts or else jeopardise his relationship with God. The Bishop had said he didn't think anything like that could happen now; he hoped it couldn't. With the Nazi threat hanging like a dark storm-cloud over a mainly Catholic Europe, Raoul wondered what the new Pope – Pius the Twelfth and the present Catholic hierarchy – was going to do about it.

He saw Delphine returning. She climbed over a stile and ran to him. "Why are you so serious? I was thinking how serene you looked before and how being a monk suited you; now I'm not so sure."

Raoul didn't say anything. He gazed at her as she put down a checked woollen blanket and a wicker basket under the tree.

"What do your parents think about you becoming a monk?" she asked him as she laid out a large napkin on the grass.

"They're thrilled," he said sarcastically. "Haven't they told you that themselves?"

"No, they haven't. They don't talk about it, but they'll be proud of you when you become a monk or a priest. They'd never say anything bad about you." Delphine arranged a crusty round loaf, a brick of Herve cheese, a couple of apples and two bottles of beer on the napkin.

"Lunch," she said as she started to cut the apples into segments. She popped one in Raoul's mouth. He would have been happy to watch her all day as she cut the bread with a serrated knife and then the brown cheese with its pale yellow interior. She put a piece of the Herve cheese on a slice of bread and gave it to him. He guzzled it down with wide-eyed abandon.

"Don't they feed you at the Priory?" She laughed as she flicked open the wire bail on one of the beer bottles and handed it to him.

"My third beer today," he said with a smile, and immediately took a swig.

"Good Lord!" she said. "I thought you were preparing for your religious vows. They don't feed you, but they let you go out boozing all morning? What on earth have you been doing today?"

He was about to say that he had been to the monasteries of Val Dieu and Banneux with the Bishop of Liège in his chauffeur-driven Minerva, but immediately stopped himself. He couldn't risk talk of helping the Jews and Monsignor Kerkhofs getting back to the Rexist Jean-Louis. He changed the subject. "How is Jean-Louis?" he asked, trying to eradicate any contempt or bitterness from his voice.

"He's away at a conference."

"A teachers' conference?"

Delphine looked down. "No, a Rexist conference, in Antwerp." She half-expected him to condemn her and start an ugly argument as he had on the Montagne de Bueren, but Raoul said nothing. He just took a swig of beer and watched her.

"He wanted me to go with him," she said as she cut him another slice of cheese.

Raoul lay down on the rug. Delphine lay down next to him. Small clouds above them drifted over the branches of the apple tree.

Raoul turned to her. "Didn't you want to go to the conference with him?"

"No," said Delphine, still looking at the sky.

For a long time, neither of them said a word.

"Do you remember how you used to make the clouds disappear? I thought it was magic; you used to scare me," said Delphine, the laughter returning to her voice.

Raoul smiled. "I can still make them disappear," he said.

"See that one – like an elephant's head with a trunk – make that one disappear," said Delphine.

Raoul raised his hands towards the cloud and pointed his fingers. He made them undulate as if he were playing a strange musical instrument in the sky. "Time for the elephant to disappear," he said over and over again in a strange deep voice. Delphine giggled. Eventually the elephant trunk disappeared and the head evaporated, leaving two cloud halves. He sat up and waved his arms at the cloud, still calling for it to disappear.

"Go!" he shouted, and after ten minutes the cloud was gone.

"It still scares me," she said as she put her hands around his shoulders from behind.

"If you wait long enough any cloud will disappear," said Raoul as he looked across the cornfield, intoxicated by her closeness, the violet water, the soft arms draped around his neck, her head resting against his back.

The sun appeared from behind the remaining clouds.

Delphine stroked his neck. The top of his robe was open and her fingers brushed against the hairs on his chest.

"It's warm for March," he said.

"Why don't you take off your robe?" she said.

"I don't think so! We can be seen from the road," said Raoul.

"I'll race you to the brook," said Delphine suddenly.

He didn't have time to react. She gathered up the remains of the picnic and put it into the basket with the beer bottles and the rug, picked up her shoes, and started to run down the hill to the brook.

He got up and chased after her, catching up with her as she reached the boulders at the water's edge. He threw his arms around her as she stepped on to one of them: it was wet and slippery.

"I'm going to fall in the water," she screamed.

Raoul laughed and steadied her as he joined her on the rock. For a moment he held her tight, his arms around her waist, her pale green wool cardigan soft against his chest. She turned round and smiled at him. "My pirate king, you saved me!" she cried. For an evanescent moment he looked like he did as a nine-year-old child and she smiled and kissed him on his cheek.

He looked down at the water and then back into her deep blue eyes, and feeling a rush of complete intoxication he pulled her to him, held her tightly and kissed her, parting her lips with his tongue. She pulled away and ran over the rocks to the meadow on the other side of the brook. Raoul chased after her through the long grass. He was a good runner, even in a monk's habit, but she was more than a match for him. She raced him to an ancient oak tree; he grabbed hold of her and they tumbled to the ground, completely out of breath. They lay for while, their arms around each other, their bodies entangled. She nestled her head against his chest, her arm around his waist, savouring the feel of his strong body. They lay in the stillness of the meadow for a long time, the silence only broken by the murmuring of the distant brook.

Delphine sat up and took off her cardigan. She ran her fingers through her blonde hair: it was long, reaching to meet the grass. "The bottom of your habit's all wet," she said, "hang it on the tree and let it dry." Raoul did not move; he sat looking at her, serious with longing. She moved over to him and unbuttoned his robe and lifted it over his head. "There, I've de-robed you," she said as she laughed.

Raoul smiled at her, feeling somewhat exposed in his knitted cream-coloured vest, with its buttons half open and his knee-length undershorts.

Delphine laughed again. "You don't need to be coy," she said. "Remember, I've seen you completely naked – on more than one occasion." She hung his robe on one of the branches of the oak tree and then started to gather snowdrops. There were hundreds of them around the tree.

She sat down next to Raoul and threaded a cluster of the white flowers in his tousled hair and embedded another bunch between the top of his vest and his chest hair. "Very becoming," she said with a chuckle.

Raoul tried to stop her. He grabbed hold of her by the arms and pulled her down on to the grass, rolling round in abandonment with her and causing her to shriek with pleasure. They stopped in a grassy dip next to the gnarled roots of the oak tree.

She gently stroked his chest. "Your hair here is much softer and darker than the hair on your head," she said. Raoul felt himself becoming aroused. Holding her hands, he laid her down under the tree, pushed her arms out over her head, and gently pinned her with his body to the ground. He devoured her with his eyes. Their smiles evaporated; his on realising the enormity of his love for her and hers on feeling his arousal as he pushed hard against her. He leaned over and kissed her.

She pulled away. "This is not fair of me," she said. "You've been drinking; we need to make a good monk or a priest out of you."

Raoul ignored her. The rush of feelings for her was overwhelming him. He rolled over on to his back and pulled her on top of him. She straddled him, sitting on his muscular thighs. At that moment he was no longer a young monk with snowdrops in his hair, comical and whimsical and awkwardly erect in his course woollen vest and underpants; no longer the novice whom she had laughed at moments before; no longer the childhood friend she had grown up with and known since he was a baby. In a fleeting moment Raoul had woken up to the reality of his masculinity and had suddenly metamorphosed into a man. Delphine ran her hands along his square jaw line, feeling the stubble on his chin.

He sat up and kissed her, pressing his lips and body firmly against her, telling her how beautiful she was and how he had always loved her. Even at that moment he felt the presence of God. He felt he had been put on earth by God to love Delphine. Their attraction was unquestionable. It was like a divine magnetic force with no self-determination, and he wanted to accept it without question. He was impatient now. He had to know God's plan for him: was it the Church or Delphine? He felt no sense of sin: this was no issue for a priest or a prior or a bishop or cardinal or even a Pope to decide, nor was it for them to tell him what was right or wrong.

He needed to know now, here, under this oak tree, where they had played as children, if their union was to be complete. He wanted no question marks punctuating this dialogue. It was Delphine or the Church. Pure and simple. God must show him and spare him any more pain or ambiguity.

The floral dress came off; she stood up and threw it over the tree. Her slip and her bra came off, revealing her firm young breasts. He stood and joined her; the woollen vest and underpants joining her undergarments on the tree. Only the white snowdrops in his hair remained. She looked at him in wonder, taking in every inch of his body: his broad shoulders and his strong muscular arms, then lowering her eyes to his phallus, suddenly jerking in its frame of coarse hair. She thought he was much too handsome to be a priest. "You've changed a lot since you were three," she said gently with a smile.

"So have you," he said in a hoarse whisper. He kept repeating her name. 'Delphine!' He said it first with earnestness, then with seriousness, and finally with longing. He continued saying it as he leaned forward and cupped her tender breasts in his broad hands, only stopping to plant kisses on her nipples.

He took the rug from the basket and threw it on to the grass, lowering her gently on to it and then lying down next to her, he pulled his monk's robe over the top of them. He kissed her all the while - on her neck, on her lips, and on her chest, as he ran his fingers down the small of her back and into the moistness between her thighs. She grabbed him to her as he explored the mysterious curves and folds and the softness of her body. She yielded to him as he stroked her smooth pale skin, felt her heartbeat and the quickening of her breath.

Her mouth opened. She threw back her head and grasped his hair in her hands as he climbed over her and took her with the force of his manhood, her body convulsing with each thrust of his hips.

By the time the Priory bells chimed three o'clock their union was complete.

She didn't want to let go of him. They lay locked in each other's arms, basking in the afternoon sun half-covered by his monk's habit, the musky smells of fresh sweat dispersed by the light breeze.

Raoul sat up and lifted her to him; her soft breasts pressed against his hard chest.

He smiled as he looked into her eyes.

"Why so serious?" he asked.

"Can you still take your vows?"

"I'm not sure about chastity! Maybe just poverty and obedience." He laughed, but Delphine was not amused.

"Can you still be a monk now?" she asked

He stood up and leaned against the tree,

"Come here," he said, still smiling.

She moved to him and he held her naked in his arms, kissing her greedily, running his fingers through her hair, down her back and then round her hips where he rubbed the hairs on her mound of Venus with the flat of his hand. She felt him stirring against her again.

She pulled away from him and slipped into her clothes.

He grabbed his undershorts and vest and got dressed in front of her. He put on his habit and his sandals. They walked across the meadow to the brook. He helped her across the stones and in the cornfield they said their goodbyes.

"Can you? Can you still be a monk?" she whispered as she took the last of the snowdrops out of his hair.

He smiled and gave her one last kiss, a deep, warm kiss. "I don't know," he said, and without another word he set off for the Priory.

Chapter 45

Bouhay, Liège, Belgium. 1940

"It's so beautiful out there," Raoul said as he watched the sunrise out of the window in Father Mortara's room. "It's strange isn't it? To know that beyond these hills and valleys around this little village of Bouhay there is a world of so much misery and suffering."

Father Mortara did not react. He lay, still breathing, in a semi-conscious state.

"Look what is happening in Germany," Raoul continued, "and even here in Belgium: the Rexist party, all poised to welcome the Nazis into Belgium with outstretched arms and 'Heil Hitler' salutes. It's only a matter of time before the Nazis invade Belgium. Maybe weeks or even days – and then what of our freedom? It will be violated by the Nazis, just as your freedom was violated by the Catholic Church!"

Raoul thought he noticed a reaction from Father Mortara – a small movement around the eyes. He continued to speak, slowly and now urgently, "Monsignor Kerkhofs has wonderful plans to help some of the Jewish families here in Walloon. I wanted you to know that before you..."

Raoul moved over to the bed and sat beside Brother Pius. He lowered his voice.

"He is preparing the monasteries at Val Dieu and Banneux to take in Jewish children, in case they need to be hidden there." Raoul did not know whether Father Mortara could understand anything he was saying, but he nevertheless kept on talking, his words and whispers delicate and poignant. "I drove there with the Bishop last week. It was a lot faster than walking. I once walked to Banneux through the forests... with Delphine... It took us about four hours. It's so beautiful there...

342

"And the Jewish parents – Monsignor Kerkhofs plans to hide them too – as domestic servants with wealthy families. They will change their names: the 'Miriams' will become 'Marias' and the 'Jacobs' 'Johns', and they will be instructed not to speak Yiddish."

Raoul took Father Mortara's hand; the old man was clutching something. Raoul gently unfurled Father Mortara's cold fingers to have a look. It was a little silver tube with a bronze-coloured Star of David on the front. "This is your *mezuzah* – the Jewish charm you took with you from Bologna to Rome. You kept it with you all that time!"

Raoul closed Father Mortara's hand around the charm. "Father Mortara, can you hear me?" he said, "I must tell you: I am going to join the Resistance. I will do everything I can to fight the Nazis."

He paused and stood up, putting his hands together as if he were about to pray. He felt shaky and found it hard to swallow, but he spoke with clarity and determination.

"I will not be taking Holy Orders."

Raoul's words echoed around the whitewashed room, but there was no response.

He went over to the window again. "I so wanted you to know before you died because I felt you would understand," he said as he watched the sun rise above the black trees and distant rooftops of Bouhay.

"And I do love Delphine, Father. The thought of her stirs within me a passion and a feeling... which the plainsong and choirs and polyphony of Palestrina and all the finest psalms, the finest sections of the liturgy and simplicity of the Compline, however moving, cannot even begin to compare."

He looked across the cornfields towards the village. He could just make out the silhouettes of a couple of labourers crossing a stile, and above them the magnificent stratified layers of a gold, crimson and purple sky. More villagers followed – he tried to make out who they were – but tears

343

were welling in his eyes. He wiped them on the rough cotton curtain before turning round.

"I wanted you to know that, too, Father. I love her with all my heart. And I pray that God will look upon me favourably and give me the strength to win her and love her… for the rest of my life…"

Father Mortara's *mezuzah* fell to the floor by the bed. Raoul turned round as it dropped. He moved over to it, picked it up and handed it back to Father Mortara.

"Did you hear what I said, Father? I will not be taking Holy Orders."

Father Mortara managed to place the *mezuzah* in Raoul's hands, slowly closing his fingers around it as he just managed to speak.

"I am happy for you. Make something of your life. You are fortunate… to have a choice. I never did…" Father Mortara took Raoul's face into his hands and kissed him. His head fell back and his green eyes, now ghostlike and remote, closed.

Raoul fell to the side of the bed, sobbing uncontrollably.

Conclusion

Bouhay, Liège, Belgium. 1940

It wasn't a knock but a loud banging that accompanied the bell outside the large wooden door at the entrance to the Priory.

The banging continued relentlessly.

Someone started shouting on the outside. It was a German voice.

"Open up!"

The banging continued.

"Open up! Where is the Jew?"

"Open up, by order of the Third Reich!"

Raoul put his canvas bag down and walked over to the door.

He pushed it open to find two Nazi officers standing outside. One of them spoke while checking a list he had in his hands. "You live here?"

Raoul nodded.

"Where is Father Mortara?"

Raoul looked at them incredulously. They were young officers, hardly much older than he was, decked out in grey military uniforms, polished knee-length boots, peaked caps and red and white swastika bands round their arms. Their heads rose arrogantly from a sea of belts, braiding and badges adorning their jackets that enhanced their air of superiority. This was the enemy on the brink of taking over the world he thought: self-righteous and deluded. At first he felt compassion for them, but his feelings very quickly turned to pity and then scorn.

"Why do you want to know?" he asked them.

"We have reason to believe he is a Jew!" the officer shouted.

Raoul did not react, which prompted the other German to

thrust his right arm straight out from his neck, while shouting '*Sieg Heil!*'

Raoul tried to conceal his contempt. "Father Mortara is no longer a Jew. For almost ninety years he has not been a Jew!" he said.

"Where is he?" the Nazi bellowed.

"He is not here. He is dead. He is now neither Christian nor Jew."

Raoul fixed the officers with his stare, saying, "And I thank God for that!"

The Prior and some of the monks came running down the corridor and joined Raoul at the entrance of the Priory.

"Father Mortara is dead?" shouted one of the Nazis.

The Prior spoke nervously. "Let me get you the death certificate."

He went running back inside.

The Nazis looked at Raoul.

"And you; you live here? Why?" one of them asked.

Raoul shrugged as the Prior came back with Father Mortara's death certificate and showed it to them.

One of the soldiers studied it and eventually said, "Father Mortara is dead," almost as though he had discovered the fact for himself. Raoul thought that the Prior might burst into a high-pitched laugh. The officer handed it back to the Prior.

"Do you want me to show you round?" the Prior asked them.

"We'll be back, I'm sure," one of the Nazis replied.

The two men left, walked down the drive, and got into a large black car which immediately drove off.

Raoul hugged the Prior and Brother André, Brother Paul and the novice Martin.

"The Lord works in mysterious ways," said the Prior with a chuckle. He suddenly became serious. "Raoul, I think that spending all these months looking after Father Mortara and hearing all about his unusual life has given you purpose, strength and determination."

Raoul nodded. "Yes, that's true, Father."

"God bless you. Go out into the world and do some good, my son."

Raoul picked up his bag and left the Priory on foot.

He stopped at Father Mortara's newly made grave, put down the bag, reached into his pocket and took out Father Mortara's childhood *mezuzah*. He looked at it for a while, smiled and then put it back in his pocket before continuing along the road that wound through the cornfields and across the railway track into the village of Bouhay.

The End

Notes

I first discovered this story in the 1980s in an original *Jewish Chronicle* article, in a book of anecdotal stories in Swiss Cottage Library, London. There was a small article about the 'baptism', and in the same book an article relating to the meeting of Signor Mortara and his son, the novice priest in Saint Peter's Square in Rome, about twelve years later. These two articles inspired me to write *The Pope's Son*.

Approximately 90 per cent of Edgardo/Father Mortara's life and events as written in *The Pope's Son* are based on fact.

Almost the whole of the nineteenth century section of the novel is fact, including the account of Edgardo being taken from his parents. Pope Pius the Ninth refused to give the child back to his parents, despite protestations from very many countries, including the United States and the United Kingdom.

Most of the story as related to the 'Italian' characters is factual. Extensive research was carried out in the British Library and the British Newspaper Library, reading through newspapers of the 1850s and 1860s. Many of the locations in the story were visited: Bologna, Rome, Alatri, Castel Gandolfo, Liège, Bouhay to further the research and provide authenticity for the novel.

Edgardo Mortara, his parents, his brothers and sisters were all real characters. So too were their relations the Padovanis, the maidservant Anna Morisi (who secretly baptised him), Lepori the apothecary, Feletti the Inquisitor in Bologna, the agent of the Holy Office who took him to Rome and the neighbour Regina Bussolari. The acts and actions attributed to the them, as relating to the baptism and abduction are true to history; peripheral events such as Anna Morisi's flirtation with Austrian officers and Edgardo being attacked as a child for being Jewish are however fiction.

With regard to Anna Morisi's character, when the case was made against her, documents signed by a previous employer, a Helena Bignati, referred to her dismissal for theft and for being of questionable character.

What came out of my research was occasional conflicting information as reported factually. For example, did Anna Morisi actually baptise Edgardo in the San Salvator church or not? I have read one report where it was stated that she did. Other reports suggest that it might have been done surreptitiously at home.

In Rome, Edgardo was taken to the Convent of Saint Peter in Chains. Canon Sarra was based on an actual character; the other characters at the convent are fictional.

Meetings with Cardinal Antonelli are factual and my research led me to various sources (including newspapers of the time) suggesting that it was common knowledge that Antonelli kept a mistress.

The section of the story where Edgardo spends a time in the countryside village of Alatri is all true, and his parents did visit him there and the church door was slammed in his father's face.

It is a fact that the Mortara parents were allowed to visit Edgardo (aged seven) a few times at the convent, but fearing that they were trying to indoctrinate their son, further meetings were not allowed.

The first meeting after that was not until Signor Mortara saw his son in a procession of young priests and monks in Saint Peter's Square over ten years later.

Edgardo was in fact paraded in the Roman Ghetto and the Jews were forced to attend proselytising services at the Church of San Gregorio at the Bridge of the Four Heads on the banks of the Tiber.

Once a year, the Roman Hebrew Congregation were made to kiss Pope Pius as they filed past him in a line at the Vatican and were expected to bring the Pope money in a bouquet of flowers in order to be allowed to remain in the city for another year.

The controversial quotes by both Pope Pius and Cardinal Antonelli are all documented. For example, in answer to '*the whole world awaits your Holiness's decision*', the Pope did say, '*then I snap my fingers at the world!*' Pope Pius was also recorded in one newspaper of the time as '*having the language of a coal heavier and cheating the Countess Corsini at cards.*'

Interviews with Edgardo as a young boy in the Catholic press of the time are all factual. He said he would devote himself to the conversion of the Jews, but in reality never fulfilled this wish.

In my mind there is no doubt that Edgardo as a child was a precocious and rather odd little boy, but that is understandable considering how he was wrenched away from his family. The following is attributed to him in the newspapers of the time on his arrival at the convent in Rome (and on noticing a statue of the Madonna over the gate). "*Why does she weep?*" "*Our Lady of Tears? She weeps because the Jews do not become converted and are not willing to acknowledge her Divine Son!*" "*Then she must be weeping for my father and mother.*" In a number of other interviews, as a child, his responses in the Catholic press also present him as being rather detached and cold.

Lots of the fine details are factual, for example the scene where the Queen of Naples asks for the Pope's benediction (albeit happening in a different location) and the gifts lavished on Edgardo are all based on fact. Pope Pius did have a cat called Moretta and was indeed fond of hot chocolate. Many other details such as the English behaving badly at the Vatican during Easter week are all documented in the newspapers of the day.

The only fictional event of note in the 'Italian' section is Edgardo visiting Castel Gandolfo.

Sir Moses Montefiore and his interest in the boy are

all factual and chronicled very carefully in his diaries. His connections with Queen Victoria and the Prince of Wales are entirely factual and accurate: he did in fact dine with the Prince of Wales in Rome at the time he went to try and petition for the Edgardo's release. Gershom Kursheedt from New Orleans did in fact travel to Rome with him and his wife Lady Judith. The entire English contingent, including Colonel Bruce, Odo Russell, and all the Italian aristocracy named are real characters. Most of the acts attributed to them in this story are factual.

Pope Pius the Ninth was determined to hold on to Edgardo in spite of it causing him political problems and defied Cardinal Antonelli many times in the process. Antonelli was so angry on occasion that he is quoted as saying: '*I feel I am no longer able to stem the torrent: I have been borne down and carried away.*' He actually wrote this in a letter, but I have included the quote in the novel as dialogue.

The Supreme Pontiff, in declaring '*non possumus,* felt that he had to '*guide Edgardo's soul to heaven*'. From his interview in the *New York Times* in the late nineteenth century it seems that Father Mortara accepted this.

Edgardo very sincerely thought that his parents should convert to Catholicism, and certainly between the ages of six and a half and fifteen hoped they would do so.

Until he was eighteen there was absolutely no question of him being allowed to return home unless his parents converted. Meetings with them were banned. In letters, he asked his parents to convert, but (as stated in the novel) there is uncertainty as to whether these letters got through to them.

In 1870 when he escaped from Italy as a young man, he was fully ensconced in his life as a Catholic monk and by that time was estranged from his family.

The locations in the novel are all factual. After Father Mortara left the Pope, he moved to Austria, France (where he had a nervous breakdown), the USA and Belgium.

With regard to Edgardo's nervous breakdown as a young monk in France, I have speculated in *The Pope's Son* that apart from the obvious traumatic separation from his family, aggravating factors might have related to the fact that he was torn between the love of the Pope he had and the love and duty that he felt for his parents.

Once Edgardo left the Pope at the age of nineteen he never saw the Supreme Pontiff again. They corresponded with each other but that was all.

Father Mortara did return to Italy as a middle-aged priest and met his mother again there.

In an interview with the *New York Times* in the 1890s, Edgardo (at that time a middle-aged Father Mortara) said: *"I felt an explosion of Christian sentiment. A strange impulse came over me and I felt I could not return to them [my parents], not even if I was allowed to. I had a great desire to receive a Catholic education and prayed that my parents would convert. I wrote to them, but they would not listen to my entreaties. But in spite of that, I did love them."*

Later in his life it is well documented that he felt that in being *'baptised'* by the servant girl Anna Morisi, *'he had been 'chosen for the special love of God'* and that he could not go back to his parents.

In spite of a childhood wish to convert the Jews to Christianity there is no evidence of any real humanitarian work; certainly not with regard to the Jews.

Edgardo/Father Mortara's brother, Augusto, who remained a Jew, was appointed Inspector-General of the Treasury in the Italian Government at the turn of the century.

All the Belgian characters are fictional except the Bishop of Liège, Monsignor Kerkhofs. When I went to Liège to research this part of the story, I discovered that Kerkhofs – unlike some senior Catholics in Belgium and Walloon at the time (who were anti Semitic) – hid Jews in monasteries during the Second World War that are named in the novel

– Banneux, Charneux and Val Dieu – and was later declared Righteous Among the Nations at Yad Vashem in Israel for this. As my fictional character Raoul ends up joining the Belgian Resistance, I thought it would be interesting to include Kerkhofs as a character in his narrative and align Raoul to a true character who found the Nazi threat sinister (and also serve to show the good in the Catholic Church at the time).

All the events described in Belgium relating to the imminent Nazi invasion are completely factual.

Father Mortara died a few weeks before the Nazi invasion of Belgium in 1940.

In spite of a remarkable and notorious childhood with Pope Pius as a guardian, his adult life was relatively unremarkable. Although he supposedly spoke 22 languages and travelled extensively, none of Father Mortara's achievements were particularly great. When he died in Belgium he was almost unknown.

Acknowledgements

I would like to thank my agent, Sonia Land; my editor, Loulou Brown; Esther Freud and all the people at Faber Academy who helped me get the novel off the ground; Barry Adamson; and Simon Gough.

Above all I would like to thank my wife Alix for putting up with all my absences whilst researching for many years at the British Library and the British Newspaper Library, as well as interminable trips to Liège, Rome and the Vatican.

About the Author

Rick Friend was born and grew up in Yorkshire. After studying at London University he qualified as a dentist. He has since combined dentistry with writing, singing, song writing and acting.

The Pope's Son is Friend's first novel and *Non Possumus*, his screenplay of the book, won Best Epic/Historical Screenplay at the Angel Film Awards at the Monaco International Film Festival. He wrote many plays: his first play including *Stuck*, which received Time Out critic's choice for Best Plays in London, and *Victory?*, a musical dealing with the Arab-Israeli conflict.

In the 1980s Friend was signed as a recording artist by Trident Records in Soho, London, was a songwriter for the Metropolis label and was contracted for three years with Warner Brothers Music. As a singer Friend has performed in venues such as Stringfellows, the Barbican Centre and the Royal Academy of Music, both as a solo artist and with various bands.

Friend was also prolific in various theatrical and television roles. His current film projects include *Stuck*, an adaptation of his own play, which won Best Comedy Drama Screenplay at the Angel Film Awards.

Friend enjoys open-air swimming, hiking and yoga and lives in north London with his wife and son.

Made in the USA
Middletown, DE
21 August 2021

46579700R00215